To Die for a Night

To Die for a Night

Published by The Conrad Press in the United Kingdom 2019

Tel: +44(0)1227 472 874
www.theconradpress.com
info@theconradpress.com

ISBN 978-1-911546-89-4

Copyright © Abraham Lewis, 2019

The moral right of Abraham Lewis to be identified as author of this work has been asserted in accordance with the Copyright, Designs and Patents Act 1988.

All rights reserved.

Typesetting and Cover Design by: Charlotte Mouncey, www.bookstyle.co.uk

The Conrad Press logo was designed by Maria Priestley.

Printed and bound in Great Britain by Clays Ltd, Elcograf S.p.A.

To Die for a Night

Abraham Lewis

Author's note

This story is based on the experiences and written works of the soldier and journalist P. Alistair C.

It is a novel, though based substantially on fact, about covert warfare, persecution and restitution in South Africa during and after the counter-insurgency Border War lasting from 1966 to 1989. It explains the burden of the soldier who works diligently to protect his friends, family and citizenry, while commanding officers, politicians and men of money often conspire in secret for their own continued advantage.

We are only as good as we actually did, not as good as we say we did ...

Abraham Lewis November 2019

For Jackie, May, the Admiral and Harold who
took care of me
For I, H and P for their sacrifice
For all those war buddies who 'came back for me ...'

Oh God said to Abraham, 'Kill me a son.'
Abe says, 'Man, you must be puttin' me on.'
God say, 'No.'
Abe say, 'What?'
God say, 'You can do what you want Abe, but the next time you see me comin' you better run'
'Well', Abe says, 'Where do you want this killin' done?'
God says, 'Out on Highway 61'

Bob Dylan - *Highway 61 Revisited.*

Alistair's Prologue

My good friend Jackie has always been someone really worth listening to.

I am always amazed at how quickly she can gauge any situation or problem and come up with a well-ordered analysis that makes perfect sense, while the underlying truth she imparts with admirable humility is always memorable.

I suppose it has something to do with the fact that she is not only bright and a prolific reader of a wide variety of literature, sometimes to Sam's complete surprise and even slightly bemused exasperation. He may enthusiastically be pointing at a far-off horizon or mountain or some other aspect of interest while presenting all the facts pertaining to this vista, only to turn around and find that Jackie has already found some shade and a suitable tree trunk to sit on and is already completely lost in the book she is never without.

She is beautiful in all aspects and remarkably strong, brave, bright and loved most by everyone.

Years ago she shared a poem with Sam and me quoted by Terry Waite in his book *Footfalls in Memory: Reflections from Solitude*. I was immediately interested and I wrote it down and kept it safe and then, after I wrote the manuscript, I included the quotation in this prologue. By some strange coincidence, it describes day and night in a way that is immediately in harmony with what I have written about Sam after our initial chance meeting in Dover during 2006.

When the light goes, men shut behind blinds their life to die for a night
And yet through glass and bars
Some dream a wild sunset waiting the stars
Call these few, at least the singers, in whom hope's voice is yeast.

When the light goes by Ezra Weston Loomis Pound - from a poem written by an Italian poet and translated by E.W.L. Pound.

Darkness comes with every night. It is almost always unexpectedly sudden and somewhat unwelcome. It creeps ever closer during the day but remains hidden behind the hustle and bustle of our daily work.

When darkness arrives, we deal with it in a quiet sort of way. We dutifully switch the lights on and close the doors and windows and draw the blinds and curtains to keep its sticky fingers outside. Nevertheless, it descends upon us with its known inevitability and then envelopes us in its impenetrable folds, which sometimes resemble temporary dying, especially when one is alone.

Luckily, gazing through our man-made barriers we know that beyond the sunset at least we have the stars while we busy ourselves with evening tasks and rest until we sense the light behind our protective screens again. We break free from our nightly captivity and walk out into the early daylight to work and play, and then suddenly hope dawns.

This is our natural path from day to day while hours pass into days and days into weeks and weeks into months and months into years and years into the length of our lives. It has a certain comforting predictability that makes it a sure thing that covers and protects us momentarily from an often uncomfortable and uncertain world.

In some people's lives darkness arrives in slightly different form and with unexpected ferocity. Its essence and speed of approach is so frighteningly fast that there is hardly time to close doors and windows and draw blinds and curtains. Awareness of one's own vulnerability and ultimate mortality becomes deeply ingrained and soon so utterly unbearable that even a trained sense of direction and proportion slowly but surely gives way to confusion, disorientation and a sense of being slowly strangled and ultimately smothered to death.

Any man who has ever been declared an enemy of the state (true or false) will have a deep and chilling understanding of this darkness and the fact that a continuing furtive groping for light and even the smallest space to breathe is often the only option available.

Enemy of the state. What is that? Is it always real or is it more often than not the fabrication of some political apparatchik publicly clothed in the finest apparel and manipulated by money driven spin doctors for the benefit of the populace? I often wonder about the substance of such claims when I read about state persecution and especially the underlying dirty secrets.

Years spent gaining hard-earned experience and knowledge in the intelligence world has taught me two important lessons. No political target has ever been successfully met without some filth being swept under the carpet and no war has ever been won without soldiers bleeding and dying needlessly and ultimately without recognition as if further insult is required. My God, even survivors spend their remaining lives huddled in corners and talking softly out of doors at parties, nursing their mutual memories and old wounds out of earshot of the more refined amongst us, who cringe at the mere sight of a blade or a gun or the scarred appearance of those who stand on the walls at night.

So, what was the cruel essence of the darkness that nearly killed my friend Sam and took Jackie's youth and sheer exuberance away from her? What made them so vulnerable and confused and what caught them in such a disoriented and slow stranglehold, smothering them to near death?

Alarmingly, it was the truth and an attempt by the state to cover it in darkness. The truth about the killing of a president, the blatant treason committed by comrades in arms, the sale of a country, the demise of a people, the spreading of chemical biological poison into the Middle East leading to a bloody conflict that cost so many lives, the killing of Sam's friend and an attempt on his own life that crippled him for the rest of his days.

Despite all this, Sam and Jackie fought this darkness and kept on reaching for dawn's light and hope. I believe that this capacity to reach for the light is probably the one heroic act we all have in our souls. After all is said and done, how else will we ultimately have a good death?

When it comes time to die, be not like those whose hearts are filled with the fear of death, so when their time comes they weep and pray for a little more time to live their lives over again in a different way. Sing your death song, and die like a hero going home.

The Mohican Chief Aupumut – 1725

That is really all I can say about that. I can only hope that my own life will not have been spent in vain and that I will also have a good death.

P. Alistair C. Santiago, Chile 15 December 2009

Chapter 1

Sector 20

It was the year 1980. South Africa was engaged in an internal low intensity counter-insurgency war against growing internal freedom movements - the ANC (African National Congress) and the PAC (Pan Africanist Congress)- while also fighting a long drawn out counter-insurgency war against SWAPO (South West Africa People's Organisation) in South West Africa and on the Northern border with Angola.

Both SWAPO and the South African ANC and PAC freedom movements' military arms underwent operational training in Angola under the auspices of the Angolan MPLA's (Popular Movement for the Liberation of Angola) military wing FAPLA (Armed Forces for the Liberation of Angola) and with the help of foreign instructors.

This strategy would ensure a gradual increase in military and political pressure through the cross-border uniting of South Africa's enemies. In Angola's southeastern Cuando Cubango province, South Africa befriended the UNITA movement (National Union for the Total Independence of Angola) because they were the MPLA's main opposition. There were however other forces on the loose.

My friend Sam went into this war with an honest belief in

the cause for the survival of the Afrikaner people. He would however soon be drawn into a game with much higher stakes in which he would ultimately have to choose between loyalty and betrayal.

I first met Sam on a blistering hot military airstrip in Sector 20 in the northern part of South West Africa in December 1980, where I was serving a tour of duty as an intelligence analyst for the Military Intelligence Corps during the Border War.

I was his designated accompanying lieutenant with only a concise brief 'to assist him' sent to me two weeks earlier from CS1 - lieutenant General Pedro 1. This man identified him and appointed him and was apparently his military mentor. It was said at the time that Sam would walk through fire for him.

He was standing alone amidst the incredible noise of aircraft engines in the swirling white dust having just walked down the tail ramp of a C130 Hercules transport aircraft.

The tall man's navy commander shoulder straps, black beret with golden cap badge showing a lion supported by a silver anchor, and black combat boots appeared awkwardly out of place against the stark nutria brown of his infantry fatigues. He looked across to where I was standing, swung his tightly packed light brown navy kitbag onto his left shoulder and started walking towards me.

His measured gait strangely reminded me of a tiger I once followed, watched and photographed while working as a journalist on a tiger conservation project. I also remembered that that same tiger was shot and wounded by poachers but had escaped with a limp the next time I visited to do a follow-up camera shoot.

He put his hand out and greeted me with a hint of a smile and inquired in a soft voice where he could find a glass of cold juice. I noticed the neatly placed 9mm semi-auto in a non-military issue light green closed canvas holster and an accompanying black Tekna fighting blade in a resin clip sheath on his right hip. Everything about him appeared 'well organised, but subtle'.

Then he said, 'Very different to Scotland, is it not? I often dream about that place. In a way it seems so clean.'

That's when I first found out how that far flung wind and snow swept place inspired him.

I had the distinct albeit strange feeling that this was the beginning of a story that could be written. On that day a friendship of eight years began that would last through a war and the early signs of a political defeat despite the military successes and then ended abruptly at the end of 1987 when he literally 'fell off the face of the earth'.

The next time I met Sam was eighteen years later, in a coffee shop at the Dover White Cliffs lookout point during late 2006. I walked in to rest and eat during the closing days of a short final research visit for a new series of articles for my newspaper on what was the topic of the day - global warming - that would appear within days.

It was winter and bitterly cold with the English Channel wind raging around the building. I noticed a man in a thick black sailor's pea coat and a well-worn Breton cap fashioned to the back sitting in the corner of the room with his back to the wall, gazing out over the English Channel. I walked over to him and recognised my friend who had disappeared for nineteen years.

'Sam', I said, as I moved closer to him.

He greeted me with his familiar smile although clearly surprised and - as was his way - offered me a cup of tea. I distinctly remembered his adage that if you first offer the man next to you water you would always have some to drink. I sat down and I noticed for the first time his mangled right hand holding a folded chair walking stick and the swirling darkness in his eyes. I immediately felt uncomfortable and unsure of what to say. He noticed my unease and smiled.

'Oh, my hand, it's really nothing.'

'What the hell happened to you?' I asked.

He looked at me and smiled again, 'I ventured onto Highway 61.'

He looked at me with some sadness in his eyes and said with a smile, 'Haven't lost your Spook 's touch, eh, Alistair?'

On that day in Dover began chapter two of our friendship that would result in a story so unreal in its essence and so violent in it's ending that it would prove hard to explain to others.

It would be underscored by the brutal reality of life, death, loyalty, betrayal, mercy and cruelty that were all so different and yet so strangely alike. It would certainly change my life permanently. I gazed across the channel and smiled at the coincidence of us being there where some sixty years before another bloody life and death battle played itself out on D-Day. I could almost hear the pounding of heavy artillery fire and the rattle of heavy machine guns.

'What really happened on Highway 61, Sam?'

He looked at me with eyes that remained dark and said,

'How much time do you have, Alistair? I have made some notes for a story, but progress is painfully slow. Maybe you could help me?'

A middle-aged woman with short silver hair in a natural style, metal rimmed glasses and dressed in a white T-shirt, brightly coloured scarf and loose fitting black wollen jacket, black trousers and boots with two cameras slung over her right shoulder, fought her way out of the howling wind through the door and walked over to where we were sitting.

I recognised Jackie as she offered both her hands. Her kind eyes were the same, but they showed a certain sad strain.

'My dearest Alistair, how are you? Have you eaten, Sam? You know you have to eat regularly. I have done my shoot, are you ready to go?'

Sam nodded and held her hand while winking at me over his shoulder with a slight smile. I understood immediately, he always loved her. No detail required, no nonsense and direct to the last point, I thought to myself. This was still the same unassuming straight up and down person I met a few years ago during a few military social events. I was honestly amazed at her enduring resilience after all this time. We said our goodbyes and agreed a date to meet at their home hidden away in rural England for a visit.

Sam stood up and shook out the walking stick with several sharp cracks as the sections snapped into place. As he turned and walked away I noticed his distinct limp and slightly bent shoulders with some alarm. There remained only a hint of the measured, catlike gait I could recognise so well a mile away. He paused at the door and called to me,

'You will like Alejo, my fox. He's a reminder of better, less complicated times.'

I noticed that despite everything that had happened they still held hands.

The dusty army and air force base in South West Africa lay in Sector 20 near the small town of Rundu in Kavango. Sector 20 with its dense vegetation was black ops paradise. Walking away from the din on the aircraft apron towards the watering hole Sam and I tried to shield our eyes from the fine white dust sucked up and thrown high into the air by the C130 cargo plane's four huge turboprop power packs.

Across from where we stood dust devils were dancing wildly on the landing strip to the steady rhythmic sounds of Ringo Starr's *You're sixteen, you're beautiful and you're mine* rhythmically thumping from a parked Casspir IFV (Infantry Fighting Vehicle) on the edge of the runway.

A 'Koevoet' police counter-insurgency operator in camo sat on the turret with his legs hooked around the twin LMG 7.62 mm machine gun barrels, cigarette drooping from the corner of his mouth, shaking a monkey wrench in tune.

Dust-covered military vehicles were racing in all directions, smaller Perspex canopied ageing French Alouette 111 K-Car gunship choppers with clearly visible door mounted single barrel 20 mm cannons and their specially developed heat shields around the screaming turbines, spewing exhaust gases up into the rotor blades to cheat the SAMs, were preparing for take off at the far end of the apron.

Larger French Puma Reaction Force transport choppers were crouching in the white-hot sun with their side doors wide open. Paratroopers from 1 Parachute Battalion carrying R4 assault rifles, kitted out in compact, high mobility combat vests, with Velcro tear-down reflective ID patches on their backs for the chopper pilots and especially the door gunners to see them clearly from the air, were hastily embarking. They would be transported in all likelihood to some godforsaken grid reference, where highly trained insurgents capable of running at least twenty miles per day with full battle packs, were spotted, confirmed, and reported by a routine infantry patrol after a brief skirmish.

That was the standard order of the day. We noticed hurried last-minute adjustments to gear between buddies. Logistic support troops scurried around clutching clipboards, each man checking his own domain and fuel tender operators rushing from chopper to chopper, while maintenance teams were performing last minute engine and rotor blade checks on the apron.

Three body bags, with thick yellow-brown fluid dripping freely into the dust from one with a partly opened zipper, were offloaded from a Puma into a small military truck with a red cross on either side that drove away to a well-known building at the end of the apron. The air was heavy with the strong smell of aviation fuel. The paratroopers were preparing to drink their bucket of blood for the day.

I cupped my hands over my mouth and said as loud as I could, 'Let's get out of here, Sam, this is no place for any mortal.'

We walked through the boom barrier and straight to where a sign on the left indicated 'Water Hole' marking a sandbag protected underground shelter where we were hoping to find some water or beverage so as not to dehydrate in the intense heat. The thermometer against the wall announced that it was a sweltering 45 degrees C.

Sam asked the duty barman for two lemonades and as he dropped his bag on the gritty floor a voice called from the shadows, 'Whichever way you slice it, you must for sure be a Spook; only Spooks drink lemonade.'

The voice offered his 'hand', an artificial mechanical arm tipped with a small convenience hook, and said with a clear voice, 'Ray, Major, and who the hell are you?'

I noticed the lemonade on the table in front of him and that he had two artificial arms. His face was marked black where the residue of an explosion had embedded itself in his skin. He was dressed in a modified infantry uniform with sleeves cut short and trousers hanging loose over well worn but recently cleaned distinctive special forces boots, with those canvas panels on the sides showing signs of brown shoe polish. He smiled with a wide grin and it was immediately clear that this was a man one could like.

Sam downed his lemonade in one gulp and asked, 'Will you walk with us to the Snake Pit?'

Ray smiled and answered, 'Sure, it's close. Hope you have your measurements handy for your coffins.'

He muttered something in Portuguese to a black man in nutria who came forward out of the shadowy background in the Water Hole when we stood up. Paolo nodded to a quick introduction and left the dimly lit water hole.

Ray explained briefly, 'I am leaving for the Cuando Cubango province within twenty-four hours. Paolo has to pack my things.'

I instinctively realised, with some excitement, who we had just met. He was dr Savimbi's closest ally, the UNITA training officer and the highest decorated soldier in our army; controlling on any day of the year at the very least 10,000 rebel troops. Paulo was The Doctor's personal choice as Ray's 'batman' after a mine explosion that ripped his arms away some years before. He literally threw himself on the Claymore anti-personnel mine to protect his men. He paid a massive personal price for his bravery on that day.

As I would find out much later, Ray was also somewhat controversial, especially amongst those illustrious members of the armed forces and government who focused on a slightly more self-centred approach, homing in on more masterfully planned and brilliantly executed operations for personal gain rather than the cause for the survival of *die Volk* (the people) back home in South Africa, better known to the troops as 'The States'.

Little did I know how this focus would lead to a clash of fundamental values that would ultimately destroy a leader and enslave a nation. In time Sam would be at the centre of this conflict.

Ray accompanied us to the intelligence centre, a dusty upside down 'half-tin-can' building squatting in the centre of the base.

Rows of white chalked stones outlined the different operational centres and all walls were sandbagged. The intelligence centre was the most unimposing of the lot. Ray excused himself abruptly at the door and disappeared with an excuse of pressing responsibilities elsewhere - had I only known at that time how little he wanted to have to do with the intelligence centre - while Sam and I entered through the spring-loaded mesh outer door banging behind us and then through the rather shabby inner wooden door.

I felt concerned as I showed him ahead into the CO's office where you were lucky to leave with your skin intact every time you entered. I had been around for a while and was used to the cavalier self-serving importance that hovered in the dimly lit and smoke-filled room. Jake the Snake - the colonel in charge of military intelligence UNITA operations in Sector 20 - sat behind his desk surrounded by his 'inner circle'. I introduced Sam to all the members of the team and within seconds the atmosphere turned heavy with unanswered questions and meaningful stares. No one in that room knew what the hell Sam was doing there and he was not really telling.

The only thing he said during that whole fifteen-minute 'audience' was that he was there 'to learn' and 'to possibly travel to Cuando Cubango and Mucusso'.

The silence in the room was deafening. I broke the atmosphere with, 'I will help where I can, Colonel. Maybe we can try to accommodate him?'

At that time I was unsure of why I chose to stir the Snake Pit. Today though, I am very sure why. I liked Sam the instant I met him and somehow I trusted him. He had that quality. Not everyone liked him immediately, mainly due to his self-assured manner. In years to come most people I knew in the defence force however respected him and trusted him explicitly.

No one in the room reacted but just stared at me. Jake had to leave and managed a muttered 'welcome' and 'I will see what is possible' before he stood up and asked me to take the commander to his sleeping quarters and show him the dining hall. He then left abruptly.

All and sundry including my arch enemy captain Montague - a macho bush fighter with torn-off shirt sleeves, a low slung holstered, large full steel frame 9 mm Parabellum Star and an even bigger fixed blade knife - followed and literally left us standing alone in the Snake Pit.

Sam smiled and said, 'I know that guy. He has a bit of a chip on his shoulder. My navy buddy Lieutenant Commander Ernie and I once beat him to the target during a night march, compass training session. Imagine sailors beating a paratrooper.' Somehow it seemed Sam and Ernie had the best route to the target figured out well beforehand.

Slowly but surely, I was beginning to understand the situation we were in. Sam knew some of these guys and they knew him. They were not comfortable with one another. 'Oh, my God', I thought to myself, 'what have I done to land in a conflict between a bunch of crooked brown jobs and a self-assured ice-cream suit and mixing it with them in the dust?'

Sam turned to me and said with a wink, 'Alistair, let's drop my bag and will you then please join me for an early dinner, sir?' I laughed and thought quietly, navy spy through and through plus the good manners and nodded my acceptance. These inconsequential self-serving bastards had measured Sam and they did not like what they saw. He was not a smuggler or a thief because he did not venture onto any quick access-routes into the inner conspiracy sanctuary of the Snake Pit. He was clearly different. I suddenly remembered Ray's earlier pitch-black humour about 'measurements for a coffin' and held my hand out as if measuring Sam's height.

He grinned while muttering, 'Go away, Alistair.'

We laughed together and walked through the door and into the blazing sun despite the late hour.

He turned and I still remember to this day the sun shining

on his shoulder straps and said, 'Thank you, Alistair. I will not forget your support today. One day I will invite you to walk with me in Scotland, a place a mathematician I once met described as 'silent excitement.' Maths teachers don't lie, you know. He had that place figured.'

I would only really grasp those words about Scotland much later, but they signalled the beginning of our friendship. We left his bag in his sleeping quarters and went straight to the dining room. We ate in relative silence while only exchanging a few generalities about daily routines and my schedule. After agreeing to meet at my office, which was situated adjacent to 'Bambi' - the UNITA military intelligence training facility in Sector 20 - I left to have an early night. I tried to sleep, but could not forget what transpired in the Snake Pit. I never trusted the people there and I was concerned about their reactions towards Sam. I did not know it then, but his journey towards Highway 61 had already commenced.

The next morning I was hoping to find Sam at breakfast, but he wasn't there. I caught up with him when I drove into the vehicle park adjacent to 'Bambi', nestling amongst thick vegetation away from any prying eyes. Sam was standing with Ray and I noticed the excited discussion that was taking place.

'Good morning, Alistair! Ray has just invited me with him to visit Cuando Cubango. We leave as soon as the final approval comes from HQ. Would you be so kind as to chase it up for me? It will benefit me greatly to see the requirements and training situation on the ground as soon as possible. Will you be able to join us?'

I noticed Ray's broad smile and heard him say laughingly,

'Careful, Alistair. There are creepy crawlies in that pit.'

It was clear that any protestation from my side would be futile and I agreed with a mutter and left to survive, evade, resist and escape the fangs in the Snake Pit. As I walked away we chuckled together at the vehicle service yard sergeant major screaming a deliberate obscenity that had to do with a sister, mother and grandmother all nicely put together at a soldier who had just driven into the yard with a Ratel IFV after a training run.

A tree that would just not give up distinctly bent the vehicle's rapid-fire cannon. The soldier was immediately found guilty and ordered to run to where the sun sets with a UNIMOG tyre tied around the waist. It was so simple. Bad performance leads to bad punishment. No delays or politics or dancing with your hand on the girl's tail the whole evening instead of inviting her to your room straight away. It was an uncomplicated system run by competent, trained men that worked quite well thank you very much.

My eventual arrival in the Snake Pit was less than comforting. I sat staring out of the window at a slow turning Puma rotor blade as it finally came to rest after landing. I felt months of frustration with this excessive control and internal secrecy clutching at my throat. The heat in the office was stifling.

Jake was explaining to me how vast the risk was that a newcomer would run on entering a war zone and in any case, 'What the fuck is he really doing here? He's a sailor, for God's sake. And why does he also want to go to Mucusso, Alistair?'

I explained my relative non-involvement as the 'messenger' and that Ray actually supported the proposal originally issued by Pedro 1.

The phone rang and I just overheard the words, 'Roger, understood.'

Jake was livid and banged the phone back on the receiver.

He turned to me and spoke very loudly and angrily, half out of control, 'that was DCI. General Henry supports Pedro 1's damn proposal. Tell him he can go. The risk is his. I cannot take any responsibility. Tell him the visit to Mucusso cannot happen though. There will be no time with this Cuando Cubango madness.'

I pictured DCI (Director Counter Intelligence) sitting in his office in the intelligence headquarters with his feet on his desk, cleaning his fingernails with a massive pair of scissors. It was his trademark stance whenever he was taking any decision.

Quite silly actually, bearing in mind that he was a major general and did not need to impress anyone with nonchalant symbolism in an attempt to show his power. He already had the power and authority and he applied it without hesitation.

He once confronted Sam in a lift at HQ accusing him of taking unnecessary risks intentionally. Sam replied with, 'if you have a problem with my work and the risks I have to take out of necessity, please take it up with Pedro 1. How else do you expect us to do the task General? Someone has to run the gauntlet.'

I found it somewhat irritating although, from afar I regarded him as one of the most professional senior officers in our outfit. I also know that during later years Sam and general Henry built a sound relationship based on mutual respect. That was the way we did things.

We sorted our relationships based on respect after proof of ability. I excused myself and contemplated the whole messy business while driving back to the forward base 'Bambi'. These bastards are keeping him away from Mucusso because they are afraid he may stumble across evidence of the guns they are running and the ivory they are peddling with the Portuguese traders in Rundu close by and Jim from Grootfontein - the 'commercial partners' in this filthy little military scam - under the guise of logistic support to UNITA involving weapons, ivory and war fuel siphoned away along the route from Walvis Bay and then sold to farmers along the way for personal gain; all covered by crooked NCO's cooking the books on both ends of the supply line.

What in the name of God am I doing here working with these people? I suddenly remembered the so-called 'terrorist' attack with a RPG–7 on four army officers on the road between Sector 20 and Sector 10 close to the White Horse Whisky Bridge - the line between the operational sectors - the previous year.

The bridge's name refers to a story that a truck and driver with a load of whiskey once drove off the structure - it is rumoured that on a clear day the labels are visible through the brown river water from the new bridge ... The officers were burnt alive in the vehicle and all their paperwork was destroyed.

They were investigating possible gunrunning and I suddenly remembered that a naval officer originally reported the allegations to Pedro 1 directly. The investigation and all findings died with those men that day. And what is Sam really doing here that would provoke such reaction? I was utterly disgusted with myself for my impossible position where I would be damned if I talked about what I knew and ultimately damned if I did not. What a mess.

We grabbed our gear and left that same afternoon in two Samil 100 trucks on our five-hour journey to the east. I drove the one truck with Ray sitting in the left and Sam in the middle on the gearbox 'seat' modified with an army pillow.

Paulo travelled in the second truck taking care of Ray's 'personal body parts' - the term he used for his mechanical arms - as well as other special equipment to be transported to UNITA. Sam never complained once although it certainly was the most uncomfortable seat in the house. I felt relieved to be away from all the intrigue. Ray and Sam's lively discussion about the war and the do's and don'ts of 'black ops' and revolutionary military activity while driving through some of the most beautiful countryside in Kavango gave me a renewed sense of purpose. This is what we were really here for.

We were here to fight an enemy and not to attack our own ranks. Or were we perhaps not? I was jerked back to reality when Ray called out above the din of the large ADE diesel motor and the constant grinding of the tortured gearbox, 'Thirty minutes to go and we are close to the turn off to Tigre, Alistair. Watch out for a sharp turn in the road amongst a clump of trees and a white road beacon on the right.'

Tigre was our last forward base camp before crossing the 'cut-line' - the thin strip of cleared land indicating access into enemy territory - into Cuando Cubango. We would spend the night there and gather weapons and ammo - mostly AKs - before leaving early the next day to enter Ray's world of revolutionary warfare.

Chapter II

Spyker's Backyard

The journey into the rebel-controlled Cuando Cubango province in south eastern Angola took a full day. We departed at 06h00 the day after our arrival at Tigre and drove to the north along an inconspicuous deep sand track that became increasingly difficult to follow as we progressed through terrain varying between savannah and thick bush.

Massive tree roots criss-crossed the track that made it difficult to hold the large vehicles steady while sitting was clearly becoming downright impossible. This was not made any easier by the ever-present fine dust that penetrated everything and made breathing quite difficult. It was well over 45 degrees in the shade. Sam and I opted for standing on the back where the heat was slightly less intense because of air movement.

We travelled in relative silence with the odd remark about the surrounding scenery and the wild game that was in clear abundance. Every now and then we had to squash a tsetse fly on an arm or leg by hitting and rubbing to break its back.

We were right in the middle of an area where sleeping sickness, caused by the bite of the tsetse fly, was prevalent. Ray opened the rear window of the cabin and asked us to be vigilant as we were entering the so-called 'affected area' and there were many UNITA patrols in the vicinity to prevent enemy incursions. It would be unwise to draw any unwanted attention, as they were nervous even though we were friends.

Within the next two clicks and precisely at a turn in the track we were unceremoniously and suddenly stopped by a UNITA special forces patrol in dark blue battle fatigues. They were well armed with assault rifles, hand grenades, semi-automatic pistols and several RPG 7s and took up position around the two trucks within seconds of a soldier stopping us with an AK-47 pointed straight at our windscreen. I noticed a soldier on the left with an RPG 7 aimed aggressively at the side of the truck. I looked around and saw the same pattern repeated with the second truck behind us.

The rest of the platoon was positioned around the vehicles. The platoon leader came to Ray's side of the truck's cab and smiled unashamedly when he recognised him. He mouthed the words 'man of steel' in Portuguese. Later I would learn that this is what they called him throughout the whole war in recognition of his persona and his two 'steel' arms. He waved us on and saluted Ray when we passed. The words 'man of steel man of steel' rang out again and again and the whole platoon of about forty men waved enthusiastically with AKs held high above their heads.

Ray nodded and smiled while holding his right artificial arm against his forehead. This was clearly 'his world' where he was known and respected. It seemed so far away from the mindless political machinations back home and the apparent deeply entrenched corruption at Sector 20 headquarters. This was war and there was no place here for personal benefit beyond the requirements of 'kill or be killed'. This is where Ray honed a peasant rabble into a fighting force for freedom that would eventually, hopefully, be able to wrench power from the corrupt Luanda horde and hand over the power to 'Spyker' - the code name for Doctor Savimbi - the UNITA leader. I felt strangely at home.

We drove a further seven or eight clicks and suddenly came to a clearing with two rough wooden gate posts and a boom. Two soldiers in green fatigues stopped us and after checking that it was their 'Instructor' the boom was raised.

They saluted Ray smartly while we drove through. I stared at a magnificent, very large and to me quite scary, black snake curling through the thick vegetation cut vertically close to the gate to allow easy passage. I had the strangest feeling about this clear mix of nature and steel and wondered about the outcome. This place was not really any different from other quite recently established forward army bases. The people and location were just different. We drove on a neatly prepared pathway past a parade ground where all training stopped the moment we passed. One of the gate guards ran down to the parade ground and alerted everyone to Ray's arrival. AKs were raised above heads and the words 'man of steel' once again rang out with a steady rhythm.

All this activity did not surprise me as UNITA was in the process of intensifying its guerrilla campaign against the MPLA. The path was lined with low placed lanterns and I noticed well-camouflaged grass hut dwellings alongside with low wooden beds with neatly rolled sleeping mats.

Ray pointed at the 'piss lilies growing' amongst the huts and said half jokingly, 'We simply have to try and maintain a semblance of hygiene with such a concentration of men.'

I laughed a little to myself and remembered the story of the visitor who once thought the piss lilies were real flowers and was quite embarrassed to learn afterwards that these 'flowers' were actually plastic pipes with funnels buried in the sand to prevent the men from relieving themselves in the bushes. This was a well-disciplined and clean base, in the best tradition of what we had grown used to back home. In some of the huge trees with massive low-slung branches extensive tree houses with intricate stairways were now becoming clearly visible. We stopped on a neat clearing in front of a large army tent. A small notice board read, 'HQ'. Several young instructor officers in familiar brown battle fatigues came out of the tent to meet us while others walked down from the tree houses. Ray opened the truck door and stepped out.

After having greeted each officer enthusiastically and asking about their personal wellbeing, he turned to us where we were still standing on the back of the truck and said with a wide grin while pointing at the pitchers of fruit juice standing in the shade of the mess tent front cover, 'Welcome to my town. Let's rest, eat and drink some sumu.'

It was late in the afternoon, but the sun was still an unchanged hellish fireball. We each drank a glass of sumu and ducked into the adjacent mess tent and settled around a neatly prepared table. A young lieutenant handed Ray a warm glass of tea to fit his mechanical hand with the warning that the tea was freshly prepared and quite hot.

Ray's sharp sense of humour, that I will always remember and appreciate to this day, shone through when he accepted with a 'thank you' and a loud exclamation of 'ouch, that's hot' as if he had burnt his hand.

We all laughed and slapped knees and the table and the meal was immediately relaxed and all the officers were keen to sit as close as they could to Ray to hear all the news from Sector 20 headquarters and the outside world. Sam sat next to Ray and listened intently to the lively conversation that went on until 21h00. Ray stood up and stretched his shoulders.

'Let's go rest, gentlemen. Tomorrow we work.'

I rose at 05h00 after a dreamless, deep sleep. It was still quite dark. I quickly washed in the bucket that was placed on a rough wooden stand in the tent the previous night by a UNITA soldier, dressed and followed the path lined with low-slung lanterns to the mess tent. I heard soft voices from alongside the tent and followed the sound. Ray and Sam were sitting next to a small fireplace sipping coffee from slim mugs. All drinking utensils here were slim to fit Ray's steel grip. The air was filled with the aroma of strong coffee brewing in a dented pitch-black enamel jug.

I heard Sam say, 'They will not listen to me. I have provided sound intelligence. The smuggling and stealing will continue and that will ultimately harm our position. All this continues, despite the fact that I advise the president unofficially.'

Ray was staring into the fire and I heard him respond angrily, 'I will never trust these people. Several of them are involved and they will destroy all our honest efforts to help UNITA expand their influence towards the west and north. Will they at least allow you to visit Mucusso after we have familiarised you with our training activities and requirements here?'

'Negative. There are a lot of nervous people at HQ and they are watching me like hawks,' Sam replied.

I stepped into the circle of the fire and they both looked up at me and smiled.

Sam said, 'Just in time for coffee, Alistair. Good morning! There's a good spot to sit on this log next to me. What do you think, Alistair?'

I sat down and poured some of the strong black coffee into a mug. I took one sip, grimaced and answered, 'Maybe we should feed the bastards this black poison. If they do not die on the spot they should accept our viewpoint even if just to get away from the coffee. How can you guys drink this stuff? It will kill you if our enemies don't succeed in doing so!'

Ray roared with laughter and Sam smiled and pressed on, 'Seriously now, Alistair, what the hell do I do?'

Ray interjected, 'Come on, Alistair. Sam told me how you stepped right into the snake's fangs on his behalf during your 'audience' with the CO.'

I looked at both of them and knew I was cornered, I leant forward and spoke softly, 'You listen and learn and work with what you've got for now, Sam and then you act once you have enough information. You will have to work from the outside. The inner circle will not allow you access to a place where they are in all probability storing contraband and trading from. Remember the four officers who have already died since the report you handed in? We do not want to search for your eyeballs in the trees.'

Sam looked at me with some amazement and said, 'So you know about that report to Pedro 1 and the suspected killing of the four officers?'

I nodded, stood up and started towards the mess tent. I stood in serious awe of Sam's apparent access into areas of political power. I also felt a strange sense of responsibility for this man who spoke softly and did not show the slightest signs of having an ego, especially in this testosterone-laden hellhole where one had to be especially careful not to tread on so many macho soldiers bullshit crooked personal agendas. Somehow I trusted this quiet man. Ray? He was just how I imagined him. He was immensely strong, quick as a whip, clever as a fox and straight as a ramrod with a sense of humour, despite his horrendous physical injuries. He was someone to go to war with.

That day Sam and I witnessed infantry training in the raw that included repeated assault rifle and mortar training, coupled with a familiarisation session with young men crouching low in trenches while instructors fired random assault rifle automatic fire bursts into the trench edges.

I saw more than one wet their pants out of sheer terror. This was coupled with repeated detailed field stripping and cleaning of Heckler &Koch G3 assault rifles which was complicated, as some of these men were quite young and uninitiated with their cultural and behavioural roots still embedded in strictly rural traditions. They were noticeably unfamiliar working with modern weapons. All activity was accompanied by extensive briefings on the run to Sam, ranging from training aid requirements to weapons preference for the specific conditions, to medical needs, communications and general logistic support difficulties. Ray was a fountain of knowledge and clearly right on top of his subject. I was surprised by the bare necessities the training staff got by with.

As the day progressed the program developed into lecture sessions focused on teaching the recruits why they were there, and motivating them for their freedom struggle against their oppressors in the capital Luanda where their power was focused.

Ray delivered his training in a calm but determined voice speaking in fluent Portuguese from behind a heavy wooden table with a pile of neatly stacked notes. We were seated in an open thatched roof 'classroom' with rows of rough benches made of tree trunks. Sam and I were at the back watching proceedings. The heat was overwhelming and the recruits were struggling to stay alert. I was amazed at Ray's resilience despite his injuries and the commitment in his voice was contagious.

Suddenly I noticed a bright green tree snake slithering across the roof rafters. I pointed it out to Sam and the next moment the snake lost its 'foothold' and dropped straight into the middle of the class and then slithered into the tall grass. The class was empty within seconds and everyone was wide awake. Ray laughed heartily and the recruits joined in with broad smiles and jabbing each other in the ribs while pointing at the rafters. Ray calmed everyone down and reminded the class of the dangers that lurk when one loses concentration. The lesson was well taken.

Ray dismissed the class as it was past the last training hour and they fell in and marched away energetically singing a resistance song. The three of us sat down in silence while he poured sumu from a jug on the side of his table.

I asked, 'How do you know the president, Sam?'

He looked at me and then at Ray, hesitated for a few moments and then commenced speaking as if slightly detached, 'I know his son. Trained with him in 1968 at the naval gymnasium and the naval college. William and I served on the same Type 12 Rothesay Class frigate as bridge-watch-keeping midshipmen. We come from similar personal backgrounds; we were both born with golden spoons in our mouths and are part of only a small group of so-called high society kids who actually became actively involved in the war. The rest are either studying overseas or are on active sports duty elsewhere in the world.'

The sarcasm in his voice did not escape my attention. Ray was very quiet and sat sipping his sumu.

'What happened to him?' I asked.

Sam gazed into his mug and spoke softly, 'He left the navy at the end of our training and is now a businessman.'

I was not satisfied and kept prodding.

'What can you tell us about president Burton?'

I saw instantly that Sam was uncomfortable and Ray said softly, 'Don't go there, Alistair. You have no idea of the pitfalls that leads to.'

I tried to answer and to apologise, but Sam started speaking in a soft voice without missing a beat, 'The president comes from a profoundly brave family background. His father Pieter - named 'The Tiger' for his prowess - was a scout in the great war of 1899 against British imperial expansion and he and his brother, Ampie, were the quintessential guerrilla fighters with highly distinguished war records.

They were fearless, disciplined men with high personal values. Ampie spoke fluent English and formed a special scouting unit with an aura of daring surrounding it to this day that caused havoc amongst the enemy especially in the pastoral Free State. He even wore a British Colonel's uniform enabling him to access the British ranks and observe their movements very closely for later pinpoint attacks. He had a ransom of several hundred pounds on his head. He was eventually killed by a group of black soldiers in British uniforms under the command of a white traitor called Bergh. Their whereabouts were revealed to the British by a goat herder who chanced on their mountain-hiding place in Doringberg, near Senekal in the Free State. They were surprised one morning before dawn and when they attempted to escape on horseback the smallest man in the commando team, Antonie, fell when his horse was shot. Ampie turned to save him. He pulled him onto his horse and as he spurred him on the animal stumbled on the uneven ground and eventually fell. Antonie crept into an aardvark hole and was the only man to escape the massacre.

He would give his eyewitness account of his great-uncle's death to William in later years while attending his great aunt's funeral, asking him to remain true to his grandfather's and uncle's reputation of strength and honour. William never forgot that. Ampie resisted during the attack, but was shot seven times and his arms were cut to the bone by assegai and axe blows. All this was done while the white Afrikaner traitor Bergh stood watching. Some years later Bergh died of tongue cancer. The old people of the town who survived that terrible conflict and who knew Pieter and Ampie said that Bergh deserved that for betraying his own people and that he could be heard screaming with pain in his house while dying… When Pieter eventually fetched Ampie's body he was lying with his handkerchief behind his head with his clothes drenched in blood. He never forgot that moment.'

'President Burton's mother Hendrien, was made of similar steel. The president's father Pieter, once saved her life when he and his group of scouts stopped at the farm to gather food and water.

He walked into the kitchen and found a rogue black British

army drifter attempting to attack and rape Hendrien in her home while her husband was serving in a commando away from the family farm. Soon after this event and when she was alone on the farm again, another drifter attacked her in her house.

These attacks were frequent occurrences and often ended in rape or murder of womenfolk who remained behind on the farms while their husbands fought against the British. She and her children and a young house servant girl Let, who always slept with her in the house in front of her bed on a mattress covered with a 'karos' - a soft cover made of cowhide with a goose down filled quilt attached - woke deep into the night during a bitterly cold winter and found their attacker already in her bedroom.

She diverted his attention by pretending and indicating that one of their neighbours, Kerneels, was entering the house behind him. While the attacker investigated they fled through the window to the servant's house where she spent the next several hours with Let's father, Jantjie and his family. After discussions amongst themselves they decided to run for their lives to prevent her daughters and herself from certain brutal physical abuse and rape by drifters and white and black imperial soldiers.'

'Hendrien left the house and while evading the attacker who was still lurking about, she went out into the cold and rain to the stable to prepare the horses and cart while Jantjie and his family were packing necessities to be able to survive. The attacker was however waiting for her and when she walked through the door he struck her from behind against her head with a heavy bundle of ropes. She fell to the ground. The attacker then went to the house and stole food and some of her husband's clothing. While he was in the house Jantjie, who was by now quite distraught about her long absence found Hendrien where she has fallen into the freezing water in a furrow close to the stable. They carried her into the stable and covered her with blankets on the cart, packed their few belongings, prepared the team of horses and ran for their lives. They hid in a cave for six months until one day when a British patrol arrived on the ridge above the cave and her one young son heard the footsteps on the roof of the cave and mistook it for goats. He ran outside shouting at them 'bok-bok' ('goat-goat'). Hendrien was summarily seized and interned with her children.'

'During the process of transportation to internment at the infamous Winburg concentration camp in the Free State 80 miles away, she refused to ride on an enemy wagon. A British officer rode up to her after she had walked nearly 50 miles, stepped off his horse and with his khaki helmet in his hands went down on his knees and said, 'I beg of you as an officer and a gentleman, please ride on the wagon Your feet are bleeding and you are clearly exhausted. I would expect the same kindness shown to my own mother'. She accepted graciously and climbed on the wagon. Several of her children died in the horror of the concentration camp where sickness, poison and glass deliberately inserted in food were commonplace. After the war Pieter's wife died and Hendrien's husband died. He went back to find the woman whose life he had saved and married her. They never changed their ways and maintained their belief in what was right to the end of their lives.'

'The president was the only child born out of that union.

His parents instilled high personal values in him from a young age. Unfortunately, 'resourceful advisors' with personal agendas now surround him. Meanwhile he has to bow to the demands set by the church and secret Afrikaner cultural organisations. I fear deeply this may well eventually be his downfall. I believe he is inherently an honest man. I can only hope that all the power that he has accumulated around him will not lead him into a situation where he starts choosing soft options partially created by a cushioned and privileged ten years in power.'

'What about his children, Sam? How do they handle their position in such a high profile family?' Ray asked in a barely audible voice.

'He has five children', Sam answered, 'The oldest daughter holds the traditional position of first born and is first in all things. Together with the youngest daughter and son - who were both born into a later better position of social standing due to his political promotion following his loyalty to the party, are clearly the favourites, especially with their mother. They willingly enjoy all the benefits of status. The eldest son William and second daughter hold significantly lesser positions in the family because of their preference for privacy and honesty untainted by outside interests. The relationship between them remains based on trust and shared values.'

'How did you get to know all this and how did you become an advisor to Burton?' Ray asked.

'I know because that's what I do, Ray, and he knows that and he trusts my actions. I met him through his son. He talks to me through a back channel. I try to fill in the holes that his advisors leave when they are attempting to score points or win benefit for themselves. It's complicated, though. My access is covert and not regular enough.'

Ray winked at me and said with a nasal twang, 'Comprendo!'

I still do not know why, but at that very point and just when the wup-wup sound of a chopper rotor with that familiar whiplash reverberating through the bush every now and then broke into our sound circle, it felt as if someone had just walked over my grave.

Ray stood up and calmly announced laughingly, 'That must be Jake the snake man, arriving for his weekly check-up on the revolution. Come on comrades. Let's be diligent snake charmers.'

Somehow I knew that this visit spelt the arrival of a serious future shit-storm.

Chapter III

The Visit

Ray was already waiting for Jake when the Puma settled down and he and a junior officer jumped out and ran bent over through the thick dust cloud kicked up by the rotor blades. They sat down on their haunches in the shade of a clump of thick undergrowth and a heated discussion ensued. Sam and I remained standing out of earshot. Jake held some pages in the air handed to him by the junior officer while Ray was gesturing with his right mechanical arm in his familiar way. After a few minutes Jake stood up. Salutes were exchanged and they hurried back to the chopper. Unprotected aircraft were always a target this far beyond the cutline and within minutes the chopper lifted wheels and with screaming turbines amid a massive dust cloud, skimmed away with tail in the air and nose well down. The aircraft's heat wave distorted shape disappeared within seconds. I saw Ray walking away in the dust towards the main base without as much as a glance in our direction.

Sam looked at me and said in a soft voice, 'Let's go and find out what transpired. It looks ominous. There has to be a problem.'

We found Ray in the mess tent. He was not amused and

answered in short, clear sentences; something we were becoming used to and did not question. This was after all his backyard. A large group of government officials, cabinet ministers and VIP's would be arriving at Jamba, the headquarters of UNITA in southern Angola, during the last week of the month for a twenty-four hour public relations visit. Sam and I were required to attend. Pedro 1's orders were clear.

Ray would not attend because as he put it, 'I will not waste my precious time with irresponsible louts who have nothing better to do than drink whisky and embarrass professional soldiers.'

I tested the water with some hesitation. 'What did Jake say when you refused to attend, Ray?'

'Nothing! This is my domain, he only reports back to HQ. He knows how I feel about these people and their wasteful ways. But, let's not concern ourselves too much now gentlemen. We have much work and I have a lot to show and teach you, Sam. Don't stress, Alistair. It's only politics and public relations. It does not really affect us here now.'

I felt uncomfortable, but let it go at that. I did not want to spoil the time we were enjoying watching something constructive being done for a good cause. Little did I know how precious this time would turn out to be in future when this world would be turned upside down and much more blood would flow into the burning hot sand of Angola.

Our days during the ensuing weeks were filled with early mornings, incredibly hard physical and mental instruction work and never-ending blinding heat and choking dust. Ray's mornings were always challenging and Paulo had his hands full trying to provide sufficient sun-charged batteries for his artificial arms.

Paulo always reacted with quiet resolve to help the major with dedication and visible respect. Our high regard and respect for Ray grew day by day as we witnessed his persistent professionalism under unimaginably complicated personal physical and environmentally challenging conditions.

Our many activities were spread out over three forward training bases and Ray and Sam made me question their sanity by insisting to run between the bases dressed only in running shoes, T-shirts, shorts and infantry floppy hats to, as they both described it so elegantly, 'remain in touch with reality, experience the wild game and stay fit'. Ray would take off his artificial arms and Sam would carry an AK-47 with two inverted-taped magazines for 'defensive' purposes. I had to travel with the truck that would depart two hours after them to give them a head start. I resented the fact that my backside would be exercised vehemently and regularly in a truck, but the alternative was running in deep sand and that was not my field of activity. Everyone had to start earlier as they also insisted on actually departing at 05h00 hours on these running days to beat the sun at its game. I was horrified and could only hope that the UNITA special forces operatives in the field were aware of this incredible insanity.

As it were they were actually warned beforehand and our two intrepid runners were welcomed with loud cheers and wide grins whenever they passed a patrol or entered a base. It became quite a wonderful thing in these crazy times - instead of the FUBAR situation I thought it would develop into.

Our sojourn in this beautiful stretch of virgin, lush land with its early morning and late afternoon crimson skies was exciting and inspiring. The friendship among the three of us strengthened, despite the constant threat of stupid outside meddling, which persisted despite the overriding requirement for a concerted war effort.

Even though we once earned Ray's serious displeasure and sharp reprimand for the danger we exposed ourselves to when we went walkabout along the river with our special forces protection team and only returned after dark, I began hoping that it would never end. It was as if we were in the eye of a storm where it was calm, disciplined, clean and decent and although we felt it we did not say it for fear of losing the magic moment.

The end to our visit came all too soon.

Ray shook our hands silently and then I heard him say to Sam in a muffled voice, 'Thanks, I'll remember your visit, Sam.'

He then stood completely alone that Saturday morning - four weeks after we had arrived - while we boarded a chopper that was sent in to fly us to Jamba. The Puma's turbine shrieked and with fast increasing rotor speed Ray disappeared alone on the ground standing ghostlike in a massive dust cloud.

Last thing I saw was his right artificial arm raised in a wide wave. The chopper flew away with its tail in the air at treetop level and the violent uneven ride reminded me of a journey by truck. The side door was open and praise the Lord, the rush of wind prevented me from being sick. I always marvelled at how the infantry fighting men handled this jolting ride. Within an hour we abruptly banked to port and descended at high speed to evade the lethal thirty-degree attack angle of enemy missiles. I gazed through the side window and saw a sprawling village appearing as if from nowhere. We were directly over Jamba.

I had never visited Jamba before and even though it seemed to be a place straight from an adventure story on some Caribbean island, I was fascinated by the neat rows of huts - very similar to the ones we visited at the training bases - and the orderly and purposeful way in which people seemed to be going about their business. We passed over the village and landed just outside the perimeter on an open sandy space among the trees.

Sam and I nodded to the pilot who was looking to the back from the cockpit and shouted, 'Thanks, buddy', through the ear-piercing whine of the engines. We jumped to the ground holding on to our hats and kitbags.

He responded, with his hand briefly touching his helmet. Apparently this was just standard procedure. These guys were doing an incredible job as if it was nothing while they were so often right in the firing line. Many of us regularly owed our lives to them.

We headed for a waiting Land Cruiser with two heavily armed UNITA rebels standing on the back and one man waiting closer to the landing area. I noticed the extra wide tires for sand work. The chopper engines screamed briefly behind us and its familiar shape disappeared over the treetops leaving only a huge dust cloud.

Right, we were in Jamba. Now what?

We briefly greeted the men waiting for us and with a 'we go now?' from one of them we scrambled onto the back of the Land Cruiser with our bags and leant forward grabbing hold of the roll bar.

The men's open admiration for Sam's golden navy lions on his shoulder straps amused me. But of course, I thought to myself, lions are a serious symbol of strength here. This visit is going to be interesting because only naval officers wear these and I shudder to think how that would go down with the mostly brown job top brass.'

My thoughts were interrupted by a bone jarring thump as we careered over a tree root and Sam's voice calling out, 'Watch out, Alistair. Tree branch.'

I ducked wildly while we laughed like two youngsters. I quite enjoyed the wild ride amongst the low hanging tree branches with the growling diesel powered vehicle sometimes drifting wildly over the thick sand track while the driver painfully double-clutched his way through the willing but whining, grinding, overworked gearbox. I felt alive and I could see Sam was also in his element.

We came to a sudden stop in front of a low thatched roof building buried halfway in the sand to beat the heat. The dust settled and we noticed a row of neat wooden steps fashioned out of horizontally placed tree trunks, leading into a noticeably spacious 'dugout' meeting place. Extensive and intricately woven reed seating against the walls and a large wooden table in the middle of the room surrounded by military issue steel chairs completed the picture. Clearly this was the place where most things of any importance happened.

A voice called out from the other side of the table. 'Gentlemen, welcome. Step closer and join us here.'

It was CSI - Pedro 1 - the man the US Secretary of State called 'The Ratcatcher'. This name emerged after Pedro 1 made such an unmitigated nuisance of himself at the South West Africa settlement discussions with the Americans that the Secretary of State requested that he be removed from the meeting. He was dressed in army fatigues with a British military issue jumper with canvas squares on the shoulders completing the picture. This was one of his peculiarities.

His lieutenant general insignia sat oddly on the shoulders of this 'foreign', non-South African military regulation gear. I always suspected that this assumed behaviour was due to a seriously misplaced ego reminiscent to that of a Patton, albeit that he would never be qualified to tie that famous warrior's bootlaces. Next to him and also dressed in infantry fatigues sat major general Niels - director of military intelligence operations. He was a slightly overbearing, and clever man, with a quiet disposition.

They served together in Paris in covert intelligence roles and I always wondered about their so-called convenient 'closeness' to the DGSE. They were an exclusive shady inner group within the so-called 'French Connection' - an influential informal 'brotherhood' in the defence force with mostly unknown special responsibilities and privileges - made up of some really good men whom I respected and knew quite well. Slightly to the rear a well built black man in a striped camouflage uniform and a purple scarf leant back in a large armchair.

Low and behold, on his shoulders he wore three narrow and one broad gold stripe. The physical similarity in rank insignia between The Doctor and Sam's three naval commander rings were both interesting and alarming in an amusing sort of way, in this part of Africa that was steeped in tribal tradition and mysticism. I briefly wondered again how that would sit with our generals. It was a worrying coincidence. Next to The Doctor, on the table lay his beret adorned with a metal badge depicting a red circle with a small black star in the centre. His baton of rank was made of deep brown hardwood with a brightly decorated knob.

He rose with a broad smile as we approached while Pedro 1 and Niels remained seated. I found that not only strange, but actually quite rude. Clearly they were supposed to take the cue from their host. I noticed the broad leather belt with a large brass buckle and a stainless steel revolver riding in a right-to-left open cross-draw leather holster. We saluted and he greeted both of us with a soft voice and welcomed us in Jamba.

I was instantly aware of the fact that this man had poise, personality and presence. There was immediately some strange 'brotherly chemistry' between Sam and The Doctor. I had the distinct feeling that he immediately saw Sam as someone who could possibly make some difference, especially when he inquired very discreetly how Ray was. I suspected that there must have been some information provided to The Doctor regarding Sam's activities and arrival in Jamba. He sat down and looked intently at us and listened while Pedro 1 explained our role as accompanying officers for the dignitaries that were expected to arrive the next morning first by executive jet - for the smart ones - and C130 Hercules - for the mere mortals - at the airbase close to Rundu in Sector 20 and then at Jamba by Puma chopper. I listened to the clearly self-assured, but irritatingly pedantic instructions that always ended with some stupid little joke and remembered with regret the constructive period we had just experienced away from all this bullshit that was so easy to step in. I knew whom I liked and respected more in that meeting hall.

When we left that day to find our shared quarters and have

something to eat and drink, I could not help but sense the marked difference in presence between the two officers and The Doctor. An overwhelming and stifling sense of foreboding took hold of me.

The simple meal of river fish with potatoes and vegetables was deliciously well prepared by chefs trained by the South African army and served on white linen in a spacious tent, by immaculately trained and dressed rebel waiters - all with white napkins folded neatly over the forearm. I was astonished at how they managed to keep up standards under such difficult circumstances. Night came and we turned in and slept fitfully in neatly prepared huts with en-suite bucket and water drawstring release bush showers, waiting for the morning and the arrival of 'our SA leaders'.

The next day we ate breakfast hurriedly and armed with only our 9mm service pistols we positioned ourselves under a tree in the already blistering heat close to the landing site. We were surrounded by at least one hundred battle-hardened UNITA rebels well armed with AKs, Tokarev semi-auto pistols, RPG7s, hand grenades and tactical blades. In the distance the familiar sound of the approaching choppers broke the silence. I looked at Sam and noticed a slight smile.

'What?' I asked.

He adjusted the Tekna knife click-sheath next to his holstered 9 mm pistol and said softly, 'I hope they are mostly sober, Alistair, so that we will not be shamed in front of our gracious hosts.'

We were accompanied by a major Jan from directorate counter intelligence. I did not know him, only that he was responsible for security and counter intelligence during the visit.

The two aircraft landed several metres apart and switched off engines. After the dust settled the doors opened. To this day I will remember the white, wide open eyes of the first 'dignitaries' clambering quite tentatively from the aircraft on seeing the ferocious looking rebel fighters surrounding the landing site. 'These guys are completely out of their depth in this place,' I thought to myself. First on the ground was Rangle - our cock-sure minister of foreign affairs. With his long black fringe hanging over his eyes and prevalent bad body odour, he reeked of widely rumoured infidelity and appeared dishevelled and distinctly unstable on his feet. Next appeared Christopher with his pencil moustache - the smooth acting, but speech challenged, member of the cabinet aspiring to be responsible for constitutional affairs. His secret claim to fame I suddenly remembered was his rather unsavoury attempt many years before when he served as the member of the provincial council to influence a certain very influential party apparatchik in his constituency – Mrs Hoven - to support his candidacy for Member of Parliament in secret while the serving MP - now President Burton - would be accommodated elsewhere.

He was ultimately and unbelievably forgiven by Burton and survived this act of treachery. God help us in such hands. Following them was general Max - minister of defence. He was a brash and pompous 'military micromanager' with little or no operational experience, who allegedly failed his marine course years before and hated the navy passionately forever after for this humiliation. His single most visible and irritating characteristic was his continual meddling in military operations to the utter frustration and desperation of most senior officers.

Next the seriously overweight defence force surgeon general Nelius stepped from the aircraft; a man who somehow always reminded me of a vulture after a particularly big feast; a man who actually sat on a little raised platform in his office back home - possibly so that all visitors would look up to him.

The polished Dr Becker appeared next - the national intelligence chief with a doubtful academic background and thesis on the 'communist threat' vigorously promoted and supported by secret Afrikaner cultural organisations rather than by serious academic minds. He was known for his ability to subvert and grab power. His operational experience when he was appointed in this powerful position at the tender age of thirty-four, was as an army intelligence officer in the SWA territorial army, physically sweeping enemy bases for paperwork and other information after the fight. His strategic operational experience was doubtful from day one and Pedro1literally had to take him by the hand ever so often and guide him through the pitch dark and dangerous maze that was the intelligence world. It was also suspected that his appointment was really owing to a recommendation by his home province party chief minister Kobé, who was afraid that the good Doctor would become his political rival for the provincial leadership. Then the medical battalion brigadier (dr) Bana with his disturbingly threatening physical appearance attributed to a prominent nose tilted slightly upward appeared. This time he was without his shadowy forensic expert friend general Nicson at his side. These two men were more than anyone else the driving force behind the chemical and biological warfare programme 'Project Coast' - originally approved by President Burton.

The following two persons to appear in the chopper door

were colonel Jake from 20 headquarters and a junior medical battalion dr Philip who attended to take care of any 'casualties'. I knew Philip. He was bright and friendly enough, but one was never quite sure of his real personal agenda. My slightly tainted opinion of him would in years to come be confirmed, unfortunately to Sam's incredibly cynical disadvantage.

Then, junior minister Baier appeared. His eyes were wide and he was clearly on unfamiliar terrain. Major Jan shouted some remark to Sam. I could only guess that he was making fun of how scared this man looked. I did not realise that at the time, but this scared man would one day in the not too distant future, be instrumental in the sell-out of our country at Kempton Park.

He would be one of the prime movers in the constitutional negotiations - just another term for 'sell-out'. We introduced ourselves and ushered these men to two waiting vehicles. As they drove off Sam and I turned and noticed President Burton and his suave, slippery ADC, captain Ailes, standing next to a Land Rover close to the second chopper talking to The Doctor and Pedro1 while entering the vehicle. We saluted from afar. I noticed an unexpected and on the spur of the moment, informal wave from Burton directed at Sam as they drove past. Sam did not flinch for a second. He saluted and snapped his hand down as the vehicle passed us. I thought nothing more of it. Sam was after all his back channel adviser.

What an odd selection of guests.

I thought and immediately chastised myself for my uncomfortable sense of suspiciousness about people. However, had I known what I know today, I would have been even more attentive on that day. The majority of them were powerful and they were all politically and some even physically dangerous, like an elite hit squad surveying their mark. Unknown to me, the hunt for Burton's life was already on.

Chapter IV

The Party

The rest of our day was spent accompanying the dignitaries, seeing to their personal needs and acting as 'facilitators' between them and the UNITA personnel while they were shown the different aspects of activities in Jamba.

That included the mechanical workshop, clothing and uniform manufacture, schools, medical facilities, agricultural activities - especially the irrigation system on the outskirts of the village - and the varied training facilities that were also in operation here. They were kept away from the headquarters planning area for reasons of security. Burton - accompanied by The Doctor - was however taken to the more sensitive aspects of the operation.

It is important to note at this stage that during that time there already existed a profound suspicion amongst some of the support and operational officers involved with UNITA that even amongst our own people a sinister threat existed, which consisted of high level 'moles' that co-operated especially with the CIA and the French DGSE.

A small section of the French Connection - for all their power and influence - featured high on the list of suspects. Certain former military special forces operators organised themselves into a sinister, highly paid 'special task privatised army', commercialising warfare and specifically co-operating with the state sponsored CCB (Civil Co-Operation Bureau - a deeply suspect organisation with primary hit list objectives to eliminate 'enemies of the state') - were operating as 'strong arm executioners' with the ability to contract even criminals to do their filthy work for them.

This organisation operated outside of the law with complete impunity. In the future this private army would directly work for the demise of UNITA, their leader and death and destruction in Sierra Leone by introducing Ebola into water resources. Subsequently even high-ranking officers and especially politicians who did not have any direct involvement with UNITA were kept away from sensitive activities and core aspects of the revolutionary campaign.

There were also discussions later that afternoon with The Doctor and his senior staff where Sam and I were not involved and I cannot say that we felt excluded. Sam was especially relieved as I noticed Rangle - minister of foreign affairs - cornering him earlier in the general assembly hall. He was clearly pressurising him for more information. In fact we were thankful to be able to walk away from these people and mix with our counterparts in the rebel movement. That evening however there was to be a party that would be attended by all senior officers from both sides and of course by The Doctor and his senior staff. We felt uncomfortable about this event, but had no alternative but to attend.

We assembled at the same meeting hall where we met The Doctor earlier that day. It was late afternoon and the sun was already quite red in the west. Lamps were lit and the interior of the hall looked impressive in the semi-light with tables and chairs carefully laid out in grand fashion in a large horseshoe shape. All officers from both sides were present, dressed smartly in clean combat fatigues.

We were shown to our places at the table with the visitors sitting on the left leg of the horseshoe and the senior UNITA officers on the right while the more junior officers like Sam and me were seated facing a single table in the middle of the opening where The Doctor, Burton and the Ratcatcher - Pedro1 - were seated. The meal was well prepared and the service was excellent given the bush environment. Two-thirds through the evening people were beginning to move around and several individual officers were sitting on haunches or moving their chairs around with them and chatting to colleagues seated elsewhere.

The Doctor suddenly called to us over the floor, 'Commander, please join me for a moment?'

There was a surprised pause in the din of conversation as Sam stood up, walked to the main table and sat down next to The Doctor, who immediately smiled and took his one hand in his and commenced talking to him quite softly and confidentially. That is when I noticed for the second time that day the brief smile when Burton looked towards Sam.

Again I thought nothing of it. Conversation was picking up again - Rangle was specifically quite vocal and already drinking heavily. After a few minutes Sam got up, shook The Doctor's hand and took his place next to me again.

'What did he say, Sam?' I asked.

'Oh, he asked amongst other things how Ray was and whether I was satisfied with my visit to the training bases. Nothing much, although...he did tell me that he knew what my task would be and thanked me. Ray must have spoken to him.'

I did not venture any further questions. I knew this was sensitive stuff and did not want to even attempt to force Sam into telling me anything more. The meal was nearing its end. Burton had already retired to his lodgings, as did The Doctor. All the UNITA officers were still present while we remained to oversee the departure of all the dignitaries.

At that very moment I noticed Pedro 1 standing directly behind us.

Bending over Sam's shoulder I heard him whisper, 'You see that drunken man over there?' while pointing at the minister of foreign affairs, 'He will ultimately betray us and cause our defeat in this war. Please do not tell him anything. Not a word, Sam. I smelt the liquor on his breath.'

That same chill I felt before ran down my back and I could not help noticing the faint smile on Sam's face as he said to Pedro 1, 'He has already asked me questions about my activities earlier today sir. I said nothing and just walked away.'

Pedro 1 turned on his heel and with a brief good night he walked off with a slight stagger to one side in the company of general Max, who was also clearly under the weather, and accompanied by general Nelius and colonel Jake.

We remained standing in the back of the hall. Rangle was seated closer to us and already acting like a drunk skunk. He was taking swigs from a half bottle of whisky while laughing, talking loudly and shouting wild profanities in a drunken stupor.

He was only starting to party. In the middle of all this he asked Philip for some painkillers for a painful ingrown toenail to be fetched from his hut. Sam and I looked at each other and together we noticed the stern looking faces of the surrounding UNITA officers.

I was deeply embarrassed and quite angry at this unseemly behaviour.

'Please fetch the bastard the painkillers, Philip,' Sam asked in a muffled voice. 'Will you go with him, Alistair? Then take Rangle to his bed before he destroys all credibility we have left here. I will wait here for you to come back.'

Philip and I went to the minister's hut and started searching for the painkillers. Eventually we found a pack of tablets in his shaving kit. While searching for it, a handful of condoms fell on the floor.

'Jesus,' Philip exclaimed, 'What the hell is this, Alistair? The stupid idiot was planning to have sex in Jamba. What the hell else will he attempt for amusement?'

'Smell this, Phil' I said, holding out the foreign minister's water bottle. 'He has whisky in here. That's probably why he was already half drunk when he arrived.'

We stood there for a few minutes, shocked beyond reason about the man's sheer immeasurable audacity bordering on the obscene, in of all places, a war environment which required sincerity and focus. We were working with soldier's lives, for God's sake. We then rushed back to the meeting hall.

When we arrived back the scene was completely surreal. Rangle - who was now mindlessly drunk - was thrashing about and cursing and shouting. All the UNITA officers were still there and staring at the drunken scoundrel's antics.

Sam seemed relieved as we entered and while Philip fed the drunken man a handful of painkillers he took me by the arm and said, 'Get the drunken sod out of here and to his bed now, Alistair. He is not really worth our anger even though he actually deserves to be beaten to within an inch of his life for this misbehaviour. Please go with him, Philip. This is a disaster of tragic proportions in front of all these men. We are trying to fight a war with this kind of political leadership. God help us all with these kinds of lowlifes floating around.'

Philip and I each took hold of an arm and half dragged the drunken minister to the door and out into the night to his hut while he wailed and sobbed wildly that he was not drunk and wanted to have one more drink. He was a big man and it took all our efforts to get him to stay on the pathway.

'Maybe we should throw him in the river. Do you think the crocs will eat him, Philip?' I whispered.

Philip answered in a measured voice, 'Nobody will miss him. I doubt however that the crocodiles will have an appetite for bad food that resembles garbage and that will accost anything that remotely resembles a female.'

We both snorted loudly while manhandling the big man and burst out laughing at the thought.

'So much so for our great foreign affairs champion and our people's so-called noble cause', I thought to myself. It was just another glaring example of how far these idiots were removed from the reality of war. I profoundly envied Ray who took a firm decision and simply refused to attend the 'occasion.' We dumped the great unwashed on his bed, took his shoes off and killed the lamp. He smelt of liquor and sweat and urine and I needed to get out of there to wash my hands. I felt incredibly dirty. So the first day of the visit ended in precisely the fashion that Ray had predicted, with a drinking orgy that shamed us in front of our foreign brothers in arms. When I told Sam about our finding the condoms earlier in the evening he just shrugged his shoulders and shook his head in total disbelief.

The same feeling of foreboding I felt earlier took hold of me as I lay in my bed that night, looking at Sam sitting at the table with a lamp and reading from Martin Gilbert's biography of Churchill. 'Is it a good book, Sam?' I asked.

'Yes. It's about a great man who understood the subtleties of most things, Alistair. As he so rightly said, "Good cognac is like a woman. Do not assault it. Coddle it and warm it in your hands before you sip it." It seems that our minister of foreign affairs understands only the assault on both.' Sam was clearly upset.

I had not seen him like that once during the previous weeks. He was visibly shaking with emotion as he went on speaking.

'He is clearly a bloody swine, although we should probably not be surprised about his behaviour. It's all true to character. When he served as our UN representative he was apparently caught in bed with two call-girls in an upmarket hotel room, all very efficiently arranged and photographed by the CIA, and then used to convince him to work for them against his own people. All of course very cleverly hidden away from the public eye and unbelievably stupidly ignored by the present government.'

Sam then interrupted himself, 'Please Alistair, you cannot talk about this, ever. They'll kill you.'

I did not know who 'they' were and quite frankly I did not want to know.

That night I was extremely restless in my sleep while I dreamt of war and dead men with their fingers clenched claw-like, grimacing at me with blood and soil between their clenched teeth while a drunken man in a black suit was screaming obscenities. I woke up in the dead of night in a cold sweat and for the first time in many years I prayed to God to show me why I was in this situation.

I was emotionally drained because of what we saw happening around us, mostly because we understood the risks that good men were running daily, while this kind of nonsense was being perpetrated with utter impunity by dangerous politicians.

The next morning, after a brief breakfast session, all the guests left in two choppers that arrived at dawn. It was an unimportant event devoid of any relevance or importance to our work and we withdrew the moment the two aircraft skimmed away over the trees. A third puma arrived shortly afterwards and Sam and I departed with no further ado. We wanted to get back to Sector 20 as Sam was set to depart that same afternoon. We did not talk during the journey back.

At 14h00 I shook his hand and I remember his words to this day, 'It's not about the cause, Alistair. It's about the man next to you. Thanks for your support. I will not forget. Please give my very best regards to Ray. Take care of yourself, buddy.'

I nodded but did not have the words to answer him. He boarded the C130 and as the engines roared into life I walked off the apron and back to my desk in Sector 20 intelligence headquarters. My heart was empty with the same incredible emptiness that I always felt on Sunday afternoons at the now disbanded 11 Commando training unit at the battle school in Kimberley.

There was nothing to do and only miles and miles of dusty open spaces to stare into, followed by the inevitable feeling of desolation that regularly crept into my soul. I felt deeply uncomfortable about all that had happened, but somehow I knew that it was important in ways that I still did not fully understand.

Although we saw each other a few times at our HQ back home, I also had more extensive private contact with Sam on quite a few occasions between 1980 and 1987. We spent some time together when he and Jackie invited me to join them for outdoor excursions with their children. These were precious experiences where I would see Sam and his wife do the things they really loved, far away from the throng of the city and its bright lights. I especially developed a deep-rooted respect for Jackie who discreetly appeared more and more to be the adhesive that kept their underlying stress-ridden lives together.

Within the context of our work, Sam actually disappeared from sight for long periods. I saw him briefly again in Jamba during late 1985 when he was rewarded by The Doctor for services to the people. This meeting occurred one night at a huge campfire when he was given a special ivory gift with his name, the date and the UNITA and SA flags proudly adorning the item. It was described in the citation read out as being 'for services to the people'. I knew by then that he was deeply involved with UNITA's war effort, but it was not until this chance meeting at Dover that I came to understand the full extent of his activities, which took him way out into the full force of the storm. These activities were interspersed with intelligence support for the Comores and Equatorial Guinea; electronic monitoring operations directed at our enemy on the African continent as well as pre-military strike negotiating work in neighbouring states, such as Lesotho and Botswana. His main activity however remained a weapons supply line as it required the skills that originally brought him into the military - a conventional business sense with an intrinsic feel for the unorthodox and the uncanny ability to work anywhere, anytime and anyhow as a single operator. These served to cover the main activity of moving vast quantities of eastern bloc weapons over huge distances to friendly resistance movements in Africa, such as UNITA, right under the noses of the major international intelligence services. The personal risks were enormous, but he seemed to perform these activities with a humility and efficiency that bordered on the unbelievable. That is how I knew him. Down to earth with no nonsense attached, hardly ever using his rank and always introducing himself merely as 'Sam'. I liked that and I was increasingly modelling my own actions on this understated reality. Sam became a mentor to me and I sought out his company whenever I had the opportunity. He seemed to trust me, most likely because I managed to keep what we spoke of very quiet, as simply we were becoming good friends and I did not want to betray that trust. That did however not preclude regular arguments about critical aspects of the job. That was part and parcel of our professional relationship and friendship. It was as easy as that. He was now the man next to me, as he had put it that last day when he left after our shared experiences at Jamba in 1980.

In exchange I was beginning to understand the analysis of the storm as we lived it between 1980 and 1987. The core of this analysis lay in Sam's growing sense of impending danger because of perceived conflicts within the security establishment. It was clearly becoming increasingly complicated to hold a purist view of warfare and its short and long term ramifications within an environment that was rife with infighting and sheer distrust. Gradually, it was becoming clear to me that Sam was even more concerned than before about the conflicting interests within the government, manifesting itself in several intrigues with internal and international ramifications and involving both politicians and senior military officers. It was as if the growing security risk for the country that was fast bordering on chaos was motivating people to steal, lie, cheat and connive on both the political and commercial fronts.

After the ceremony we had sat talking and drinking coffee on the fringes of the fire's circle. Sam was responding to some questions I had been asking regarding his activities. I had become increasingly concerned about some dubious movement of goods between west coast ports and Grootfontein. Equipment was normally moved by truck or air to military destinations. The financial arrangements for these consignments were buried deeply in Europe and were for all intents and purposes untraceable. For several years Sam was the core intelligence link with the suppliers and he handled the whole process with a handful of backup operatives. The problem at that time was that a massive breakdown was developing among the powerful intelligence agencies in South Africa. Sam and specifically his backup team in the Pacific Rim, had a particularly hard time evading their own people who spied on them internationally, based on their quest for power and their fear of the military's growing international influence far beyond the country's borders. In one instance they all barely escaped capture when the national intelligence service team contaminated their route by tailing them and some of Sam's people had to run for their lives. I would only learn the full implication of this incident much later when Sam took me into his confidence. The man who made all of this happen was dr Becker, our over eager, poorly qualified, national intelligence chief.

Then he delivered the bombshell, 'You also have to remember, Alistair, as I have told you before, Pedro 1 and director military intelligence operations general Niels, know each other from their covert stint of duty in Paris. During that time there was enough opportunity to set up bank accounts and build networks with a view to their ultimate goal of self-enrichment. Pedro 1 is the only senior officer I know of who drives a Porsche, owns a farm and several other properties in the capital and Niels is the only senior military intelligence staff officer I know of who owns a farm that I believe is fully paid for. They built a considerable network apparently including certain operational officers such as Jake, who are in critical positions from where they are able to drive the smuggling network through the Portuguese trading link in Rundu, and Jim in Grootfontein, who, by the way, supplies 'all' of UNITA's logistic support other than weapons, which I handle. I find myself in the awkward position of covertly procuring weapons, which are then partly traded for ivory, indigenous hardwood and diamonds from the Cazombo bulge in the northeast where UNITA has significant military and political influence. I believe they are personally becoming wealthy men and that is the reason why they originally killed the four investigating officers and placed the blame on so-called SWAPO 'insurgents'. They were protecting their business interests. They are lining their pockets should the situation back home ever change and the South African Freedom Movement eventually win the struggle.'

'Jesus, Sam, can this be? What about your position of trust with Pedro 1 and the president?'

'The president?' Sam answered with a slight smile, 'He is mainly dependent on dr. Becker and his intelligence crowd, while Pedro 1 is gradually being levered towards Rangle, who has his own agenda with the Americans. In all likelihood based on his own dirty little secret of the video and his assumed personal political agenda. I am gradually being pushed aside and the president's personal aide Captain Ailes is ensuring that my appointments with the president are becoming less frequent. My associates and I suspect that Pedro 1 is talking increasingly to the CIA and the DGSE for personal strategic and economic reasons. These personal considerations place him in a favourable position to be drawn in by Rangle.'

'How does Ailes fit into this perfect little domestic disaster, Sam?' I asked in a hushed voice while leaning forward.

'Ailes has close links with the Knights of Malta based in the Seychelles, which is rumoured to run the Roman Catholic Church's international business and finances. He is heavily involved with supplying foreign oil to the Seychelles. I believe that through this organisation he is also involved with several Italian businesses of uncertain origin that in turn, use him as their conduit to the president and the government. I am aware of his exorbitant personal tastes in clothes and cars and I am told his fridge is packed with Italian chocolates and many other delicacies. He has apparently also accumulated considerable financial wealth for a mere navy captain.'

'So, how does this all influence your position with the president?' I asked.

'He may just be in it for the money, Alistair and by apparently leaning to the unethical side, he will deal with anyone as long as it brings him personal wealth. Since 1978, a secret organisation within the National Party called Club 2000, has been working tirelessly and in secret with the Freedom Movement back home to promote their idea of majority rule at all cost, while preventing the president's ideal of establishing a confederal system where minorities would be protected with the right of secession in the event of irreconcilable constitutional dispute. In these efforts our largest father and son commercial tobacco conglomerate, as well as several intellectuals apparently specifically supported Club 2000. I believe Ailes is assisting them by supplying confidential information from the president's office to Rangle's greater political-commercial network in exchange for the promise of money. He is probably just a common crook and he is dangerous, Alistair.'

I felt quite alarmed at all of this and then remembered our discussion some years before. 'Sam, slowly but surely I am beginning to understand why you warned me in Jamba all those years ago to be careful and that I could be killed,' I said as if to myself.

He smiled and continued, 'I also believe that general Max and his surgeon general as well as the boss of the military chemical warfare program, dr Bana, general Nicson and dr Becker are also involved in some way and that this may well turn out to be the undoing of the president. Dr Becker is warming to the conspiracy within the party and I believe he is talking to the enemy and outside intelligence organisations without the president's knowledge. This is due to the fact that I am unable to get close enough to the president to test the water. Becker has established an incredibly powerful position for himself.'

'Can't you reach the man through his son, Sam?' I asked.

Sam looked at me with a faint smile, 'William has been pushed further and further away from the family due to his expressed personal disgust with the internal betrayal that is becoming more evident by the day. I attempted to see the president one evening, Alistair. I was given a sensitive report by a friend and senior brigadier in the military intelligence directorate regarding the internal security position and specifically regarding the growth in so-called national 'liberated' areas in South Africa. After I had to argue and eventually threaten my way past the gates and the police guards at his home one night, I told him that we were well on our way to losing the war internally, forget about South West Africa and Angola. I similarly warned him about Becker and told him that this man was not to be trusted. Jackson - his press secretary - walked in on the discussion unannounced and he blurted out the name of one of my key Pacific Rim network people in an attempt to show me how well informed he was. To this day I do not know how he knew the name. I suppose someone from within our already porous intelligence community gave him the detail where betrayal was already at that time the order of the day. I stood up and approached him saying, 'I will kill you for that, Jackson. Do you want to get my guys murdered by your arrogant and reckless behaviour, you stupid bastard? The president unexpectedly entered the room and shouted at me to back down immediately and leave Jackson alone. Jackson laughed out loud in my face and the president asked me to leave. The president once again supported the wrong man. After all of that he still did not believe me and my position is now weakening daily. I do not believe he ever read the report. He probably gave it to Jackson who handed it to Becker and his cronies. He never was a good judge of character. And now, to crown it all, Pedro 1 has been promoted to run the state security council, a toothless body. Becker's power is growing by the day. Our new military intelligence chief Vice-Admiral Andreas is a well-meaning and bright man, but unfortunately too weak to make any real difference. I have noticed him visibly losing interest during several important meetings.'

As an intelligence officer I was unfortunately also painfully aware of these last facts and suddenly felt quite helpless.

'This is 'snafu', Sam, isn't it?' I whispered.

'Indeed Alistair, 'situation normal all f-cked up."

And then he uttered words I could hardly believe, 'I now fear for the president's life.'

I suddenly felt as if I wanted to be sick and as we sat quietly, I remembered our time with Ray some years before when everything seemed clear and focused. There was literally no one left to trust. I felt incredibly uneasy as we walked to our huts along the half lit pathway that night. I did not want to be shot in the back or feel a blade across the throat, or even worse, to be blown apart by an RPG–7 - remembering the four luckless officer's fate years before - at my tender age of thirty-five years. I believe today that that was the moment I really decided to become a journalist after all this was over and if I was still alive. I wanted to dig for the bloody truth and show it to the world in an attempt to make a difference.

The next morning we travelled back to Sector 20 intelligence headquarters by chopper and Sam left on board a C130 freighter within minutes of our landing.

We shook hands and Sam said, 'Remember Alistair, it is

important to do the right thing to stop what's happening, even if you are the only good man left standing.'

I briefly remembered Edmund Burke's words to this effect during the 1700s; *The only thing necessary for the triumph of evil is for good men to do nothing.*

Several body bags and stretchers with wounded soldiers were loaded into the back of the aircraft after all the passengers had boarded. As I stepped from the aircraft's rear ramp after seeing Sam to his seat I noticed as before the thick yellowish straw-coloured fluid dripping from the one body bag and slowly running down one of the freight rails in the floor of the ramp and dripping into the dust. So much for our war effort and I wondered what in the hell we were doing there. For the first time I really worried about our government's commitment to the war effort and whether we were just there as a delaying action. Prophetic words indeed.

We were used and we were ultimately betrayed. We were so much cannon fodder and so expendable. We were indeed good men left standing. However, at that stage I already no longer believed that we were able to prevent the evil from engulfing us all. The words 'damn them all to hell' drifted through my mind. I felt utterly helpless against the unseen hand of money and betrayal steering our lives.

Eighteen years would pass before I met Sam again - quite by chance - in Dover.

Chapter V

The Invitation

Monday 4th December 2006. I am off on my visit to listen to Sam's story. As it turned out I stayed for over a month. It was a bitterly cold day with wisps of clouds hugging the far south-western sea horizon. Narrow winding country roads led me to a remote part of South West England where nestling on a hill amongst a scattering of trees stood an old sandstone house with a black slate roof. Smoke from a tall chimney stack showed that there was life. I turned left into the narrow road leading to the house and noticed some Kavango ethnic masks on the inner wall of the white painted veranda when I pulled up. Several sturdy wooden steps led up to the front door. I left the car on the far end of the parking space in front of the house and walked towards the entrance.

A voice called from under a clump of trees, 'I see you found me alive, Alistair. Fortunately Highway 61 does not pass by here.'

Sam sat in a wooden armchair in a pile of cushions. He had his feet on a low stool and there was a table with several books, a notepad, pen, a huge pile of hand written notes neatly bound in a black ring binder and of course, a large pitcher of juice.

He pointed at a similar chair standing opposite him and

said, 'It's not the Sector 20 Water Hole, but at least it's safer here, buddy.'

It was all so damn familiar and I suddenly felt welcome. He stood up with his right hand on his walking stick and I embraced him like the brother he was to me. We laughed out loud and then talked a while about my journey. Sam then excused himself and limped away - he again reminded me of my old limping tiger - while I sat talking to Jackie who had appeared from the house.

'Sam has been taking weekly chemotherapy injections plus daily oral medication for several years to keep the enemy at bay, Alistair.'

She spoke openly and without even as much as a hint of affectation and as if I had never been away. I knew her to be that way.

'He is quite unwell and tries to manage it as best as he is able to. Sometimes I struggle to cope though, simply because he is often uncomfortable and the condition tests his willpower and my ability to understand and endure, on a daily basis. He has always had a fast and sometimes quite dark temper, especially when incapacitated.'

'What really happened, Jackie?' I asked softly.

'He should rather tell you the whole story, Alistair' she answered.

'You may find it quite enlightening although I cannot guarantee that you will enjoy listening to a tale of such indecent betrayal.'

'What are you two talking about behind my back?'

Sam stood in the front door resting on his walking stick.

'I hope you are discussing our walk tomorrow. We both

need the exercise. Come Alistair, let's eat. Jackie has prepared a feast for us.'

I instantly felt a warm glow of welcome as if I had come home and the treeline skirting the house strangely reminded me of Cuando Cubango.

Later that day - after a hot meal and coffee which reminded me of our meals back home - we sat down in huge armchairs in front of a roaring fireplace in Sam's working room overlooking a valley that stretched right to the edge of the sea cliffs. For several weeks I would oscillate between my armchair, the dining room, the living room briefly in the evenings after meals and a daily walk for an hour. During this time Sam would regularly give me selected notes from the packed black ring binder. I found these to be deeply emotional accounts of what had happened and more than often than not, the words were so poignant and succinct that I simply copied it straight into the relevant sections of the subject matter at hand. His writing style was to the point and sometimes even rough. I often sat with him late into the night to discuss certain sections of his written work shaping and sharpening it to precisely what we wanted to say. During this time my tape recorder would be working overtime while I struggled to keep up with a man with a walking stick who still insisted that staying fit is the only way to live. What he told me during that time was related with a certain restraint and sensitivity for graphic detail, but it was still so monstrous that I mostly listened carefully and only interjected to confirm some aspect and to catch up with my own memory notes delivered into the recorder or to change recordings.

Sam spoke as if slightly detached from our setting. It was a strange, almost surreal situation given where we had come from so many years before. It gradually became clear that my friend, Sam, was always a sensitive and very private soul. Once driving along the deserted beach with his parents on a threatening overcast late Sunday afternoon during the winter of 1955 and gazing at the dark, threatening cloud mass hugging the horizon, he felt prematurely estranged for an eight year-old boy, as if all his childhood fears were locked into all that tangled darkness. He was lonely, unsure and scared of things he had not even seen yet. And, somehow found no solace in his parent's presence. They were talking about things that did not remotely interest him and never really would. They saw the world through politically ambitious eyes, clearly far removed from the honestly fearful observations of a child. He would cross his arms around his knees - the corduroy fabric of his trousers soft against his hands - in an attempt to find safe comfort with his woollen knitted cardigan warm and soft around him. Now the dark clouds were shut out. He wished they were home where he could ultimately escape into his warm, wooden floored room with all his familiar things around him.

The only time he witnessed memorable, real, raw emotion from his parents was when he was quite young and again travelling with them to his maternal grandfather's home after he unexpectedly became ill. His grandfather was a uniquely talented man who studied for his PhD in theology in the USA and the Netherlands, who spoke fluent Greek and was an accomplished astronomer. To pay for these extended studies he worked as a cowhand on a cattle farm in the northern USA during holidays. The whole family loved and respected him for his intelligence, ingenuity, sense of adventure and his inherent kindness as a human being. It was raining quite hard during the journey and suddenly as if from nowhere, a small bird hit the windscreen with a loud thump and then fell from view with a fluttering of wings and leaving a cluster of feathers and a thick smear of crimson blood. It gradually spread over the whole windscreen under the wiper blades and then faded away to the edges of the glass. Sam's mother cried out in anguish, sitting upright in her seat and clutching her throat. 'Oh my God, oh my God, my father is already dead. This must be a sign.'

Sam will never forget the ensuing soft tone of his father's voice half in tune with the sound of the wipers attempting to allay her fear. It would remain with him always and would help him to refer to his parents with at least a semblance of understanding of their complex relationship in years to come.

'There, there. I am sure everything will be all right. Sit back and close your eyes and try to rest a while. We will soon be there. The bird hitting the windscreen was just an unfortunate accident. It could have happened anywhere.'

On their arrival his grandfather was indeed very ill, but he lived for some time still. In a way and specifically in Sam's mind, his father saved the day and his grandfather during that rainy journey.

Somehow the inherent darkness remained hanging over Sam for many years and contributed to him embracing an ascetic self - protective lifestyle that ultimately formed the foundation of his carefully nurtured ability to perceive the world from the shadows with a hidden and somewhat mercenary outlook; the so-called unseen eye behind the eye. A child man with many fears, not always knowing how to overcome them and ultimately hiding and training mind and body while merely appearing from time to time to address life's problems and accept reluctantly whatever meagre merit was considered by so-called superiors; becoming more suspicious and reclusive, always doubting the motives of politically well connected individuals who wanted to please by rewarding the chosen subservient few. Ultimately he became a quiet, serving, monk-like personality in a mangled world where he was increasingly being drawn into the safety of life's shadows, only appearing and acting out of necessity.

He was born with the proverbial golden spoon in his mouth at the end of the 1940s in our post-colonial country, into a family firmly based within new nationalist sentiments, interests and ambitions. His life was always adventurous and clearly different, in the broadest sense of the word. He was a moderate student at school and despite much expectation for a brilliant public career in the best traditions of nationalist fervour, he never really excelled above average in his studies. His lack of appetite for all things bright and public led to his early departure from his parents' home, partly because of a newly acquired public office his parents had taken on, which necessitated moving to another more suitable environment. He took up lodgings with the ageing, streetwise and controversial poet, Abraham and his quite pedantic and strict author wife, Lulu. His life alternated between study to better his grades and long philosophical discussions in the evenings and during fishing trips with Abraham. This is where he learnt first that life was about doing and not about showmanship; whether it was catching the fish with excellent technique or enjoying the meal with all the unique finishing touches such as positioning of the fish on the plate, with the head to the right and the tail to the left; adding salt to food and a pinch to the beer. These meals were a major event in as much as it was nourishment as it was a private ritual in honour of the fruit of the sea. Sam never forgot these culinary sessions that were marked by soft but intense discussion about seafood and other matters regarding life in general.

It was during the late 60s that compulsory military training in the navy followed. He enjoyed this experience, as he previously trained as a sea-cadet officer while at school and he felt at home in this structured world. Signs of a natural talent for this kind of life with a certain unique flexibility and certainly an unorthodox approach to all problems, was becoming clear. He subsequently attended university to prepare for his life as a budding practitioner of nationalist aims. It was a profound mistake and in later life he told me that had he joined the army at that time his life would have been much more focused much sooner. This unfortunate early lack of focus and search for his real strength was often mistaken as career indecisiveness, an accusation from his family with which he struggled for many years as a young man. His career at university was as profoundly complicated as his school career, no less because of constant questioning and badgering about his privileged past and his family's politically advantaged position in a country where revolution was already on the cards. Apart from a growing interest in all that was extreme and difficult in outdoor pursuits, despite not being a natural athlete, his three year stint at university ended in him leaving that institution without a qualification. His failure and utter disappointment was now underscored by total disgust with the 'nouveau riche' privileged academic environment that perfectly matched the superficial company and affected lifestyle frequented by his family. He systematically commenced his private life of seclusion where discipline and dedication were the priorities. This would become his trademark profile in later years. He worked in several places and expanded his insight into the commercial world while he remained consistently involved with the military to satisfy an underlying quest for something more meaningful in life, and disappeared at regular intervals for lengthy periods to learn about covert warfare.

He did something else to remove any doubts about his abilities to focus his mind. He studied and very discreetly and on his own terms, gained a degree in political science. He furthermore honed his ability of not only seclusion, but actually 'disappearing' from the public eye - something that would stand him in good stead in later years - while he followed his natural instincts and started participating in physical endurance challenges with a dedication that bordered on the impossible. This is where for the first time Sam really showed his significant ability to withstand extreme physical exertion while retaining his mental focus. Despite his family's constant badgering about his lack of a 'public spirit', his moral and ethical stand on most matters were never in question. I found that out many years later when I met him and worked with him. Somehow his growth as an athlete participating in outdoor and athletic sport bordering on frenzied, but disciplined madness seemed to strengthen his focus day by day. Sam was now gradually escaping from his past and his mind was racing against time to find a place where he could deliver his honest contribution for the cause of the Afrikaner. His single biggest mistake though, was that he initially honestly believed in this cause and that instead of being wary of causes and staying with the disciplines he knew, he plunged into a whirlpool of betrayal and deceit of enormous magnitude for which he ultimately paid dearly.

It was the early 1970s and political conflict was growing steadily in the country. It was the end of a post-colonial era of glorious minority control and incredible abuse of power and the majority of people, simply referred to as the masses, were growing restless. Ordinary middle and lower class young men were being called up for national service, while those from wealthy families either studied in the professions and became the so-called 'thinkers', or applied for international study and sport bursaries that placed them effectively beyond the reach of the military. National Service was however the glorious and very public cry of the day, especially for those who did not have to face the enemy. This enormous and scandalous misplaced patriotic fervour troubled Sam deeply and he became further estranged from his family who revelled in this glorious enterprise at the expense of less fortunate mortals.

Then the war broke out in all its fury. The country's borders were under attack while internally the enemy commenced with subversion and acts of violence to overthrow the government of the day. Politicians and their henchmen were flourishing; power and money was an all encompassing driving force while soldiers were bleeding their lives away in the sand on the northern border. There was fire everywhere. A massive car bomb exploded in the centre of the Jakaranda City (Pretoria), right in front of the air force headquarters causing utter chaos and panic. In the rural areas life for ordinary farming folk suddenly became so much more complicated with random land mines being placed on remote farm roads. The government reacted with brutal force. By this time Sam's flexible personality profile was identified and during 1977 he was recruited and he joined the war effort as a covert operative in the shadowy world of military intelligence. With that action his personal detail was removed from all public records and as a reborn personality he was poised to carve out a place for himself in this sinister world of military activity where his specific blend of work ethic, or honouring yourself does not count, and rather taking care of the man next to you had been unique for centuries.

The murky cloud that hung over all of this action packed drama was known as 'our cause is right' with all the profound madness this slogan brought into the arena. Sam's personal battle between inherent strength, honour, honesty and professionalism and the backing of a national cause by others, behind which self - honouring and an insatiable lust for power and money was carefully hidden, started here. In the process his own kin jettisoned him, with glaring differences in approach and beliefs between him and his parents and everyone that 'walked in their ambitious light'. He had finally successfully escaped from the narrow minded societal condition where he could hardly breathe and where his parent's status prescribed his every move. His self - perceived modest image made way for his real capabilities that enabled him to work on his own in a high-risk environment, with only his own capabilities to support him. He was now utterly alone as he embraced the world of shadows, snakes and rat packs. The tiger was ready to feed.

'What about your relationship with the president?' I asked.

He frowned and said, 'During the war years it was still reasonably intact, Alistair. But you may remember when we met in 1985 I indicated to you that I was concerned about a possible plot to kill the president. Between that 1985 and 1989 that possibility became a reality.'

I kept on probing.

'What happened to his son during this time, Sam?'

'He was rejected by his family and ultimately paid a massive personal price for his refusal to trust his father's 'confidants.'' Sam reacted softly.

'Where is he today, Sam? Would it be worth my while to speak to him to determine his insights?'

'I doubt it,' Sam replied. 'He's gone to ground and I would not be surprised if he is dead.'

He went on as if he was conducting a military intelligence briefing, speaking softly and in complete command of his subject matter.

'The reality of William's life was that having left his home when he was still quite young, he was exposed to a more everyday set of life experiences than anyone else in his family.'

I heard Jackie chuckling while placing cups of steaming hot chocolate in front of us and touching his cheek with the back of her hand as she walked away.

I heard her say the words, 'Lonely old tiger' as she walked away.

Sam looked at her as if he would never take his eyes away from her. That undeniable admiration for her always surprised me about him. He was a hard man who struggled with weakness and inefficiency in others, but Jackie clearly was the one person who made his life worthwhile. I remained astonished at the tenderness with which he regarded her after all that they had been through together. My attention was quickly refocused when Sam spoke again.

'Three of the other children became extremely comfortable with their privileged position of newly found status and publicity in terms of their father's rise to power, while his one sister who agreed with William's practical and honest lifestyle set of values of being himself, was also thrown to the wolves. Meanwhile his parents heaped benefits and attention on the remaining children. The president had become intolerant of criticism especially since his advisors - who secretly started conspiring against him and picked up on his son's isolation within the family - were feeding him information that led him into a profoundly dangerous political 'comfort zone', that would eventually become a political trap. His son tried to warn him, but by this time he was so isolated in large part by the clever machinations of people around the president, that his attempts to help his father were brutally scoffed at. As William and I agreed on many issues, my position became equally impossible and by the end of 1988 the president hardly ever listened to me. The time was right for the internal attacks to commence.'

'My friend Madala was the first of many to be subjected to such an attack.'

Sam took a measured sip from his mug and told me the fascinating tale of Madala's close encounter with death as a result of growing betrayal in the system.

'Parallel to this timeline and our own struggle for survival, another drama was unfolding in Europe. It involved Madala - the name given to him by war buddies who respected him - who would become my best friend and ally when several people were baying for my blood. His career spanned several years from when he was a theological student and when BOSS (Bureau for State Security) recruited him to work as an agent on campus. He would later qualify as an engineer before joining the ranks of the intelligence community when the war grew in its complexity and intensity. Madala and I had much in common, cemented by a willingness to run risks for our country and for a greater cause. We were also both grossly mistaken in our early assessment of our duty. I am sure had we known better we would have taken alternate routes instead of hitching our horses to the greater cause wagon.'

Chapter VI

The Rebirth

'The 9 mm high powered Browning semi-automatic pistol was Madala's weapon of choice,' Sam resumed.

'After having oiled the firing mechanism and slide thoroughly, he wiped the inside of the barrel, pushed the loaded magazine in place and cycled the gun. He stowed the loaded weapon with two additional fifteen-shot magazines and suppressor in a small black canvas sling bag, ready for his departure to the target site at 23h00 on that fateful day during late June 1970 in Marseilles. His deadline was 23h45 with zero hour 23h50. He checked the four-inch benchmade Spike tactical folder clipped into his right trouser pocket and briefly glanced through the room for any traces of oil or rags. He grabbed his dark brown leather jacket and checked the pockets for his gloves and woollen cap. The pedestrian bridge close to the bus terminal was a street block away. He had thirty minutes to get there - time and distance paced out earlier - and into position with fifteen minutes to spare.

'The mission to neutralise a senior KGB agent stationed in France, who was a threat to our electronic surveillance interests in West Africa, was elementary for a man with his training and experience. He was extracted from Havana only six months before and remained behind in London during the return trip, while the two man briefing team, after having prepared him for Marseilles, supposedly went back home. His two year posting in Cuba was a special surveillance operation to observe and report on troop movements to and from Cuba in terms of an earlier agreement reached between the United States Intelligence Services and us. He worked as an engineer in the sugar industry and was ostensibly responsible for solving a problem with pipes in their irrigation system continuously bursting under pressure. What he was actually doing, was to fix the pipes during the day and sabotage them during the night. He was responsible for at least two complete crop failures during that period. Madala had spent the previous year and a half training with the US Rangers in the USA where he honed his weapons and field skills, preparing for his assignment. He also built lasting relationships with two CIA agents, Robert and Donald. These men would play a significant role in his life from then on. London would ultimately be the staging point for the operation in Marseilles following his timely departure from Cuba.

'His two year stay in Havana came to an abrupt end when his name was blurted out during a staged commercial telephone call to Havana. His position in Cuba was immediately compromised, as he was well known in government circles. His director was a close collaborator with the secret pro-freedom movement faction in our government; functioning at all levels as well as within the core of the ruling Nationalist Party caucus. The director was becoming increasingly aware of Madala's links to the CIA and wanted to prevent him finding out about foreign minister Rangle's indiscretion in New York while he was l stationed there as a diplomat and his subsequent forced contract with the CIA. The commercial telephone call to Cuba mentioned that Madala was in the paid employ of the Americans. He was immediately targeted by the Cubans while the same story was discreetly spread in his own agency by his director.

'They also very cleverly arranged a routine meeting between the CIA and Madala at the point where he was supposed to execute the hit. He was patently unaware of this secondary plot that would place him in direct conflict with his CIA partners.

'As far as he was concerned, he was ready to neutralise a KGB agent in France. The earlier secret co-operation agreement reached between the USA and South Africa had casually been swept under the carpet. At the same time Madala's mission to kill the Russian in Marseilles was duly leaked to the Russians. They immediately withdrew their man. He unexpectedly had made several 'enemies'. The stage was set for Madala's life-changing experience.

'The information about Madala's whereabouts reached Cuba within a week and he was warned by a local paid asset that he had 48 hours before the information would reach the security police. He had no option other than to burn each and every shred of evidence in and around his house on the outskirts of Havana. What few indestructible items remained he placed behind a secret wall panel. Madala surveyed his handiwork and then poured himself a hefty mug of rum, which he downed in one gulp in an effort to help calm his ragged nerves. He slept for two hours. When he woke up he cleared his head with thick black coffee, some leftover food and a long hot shower. Then his full extraction plan from Havana kicked in and he fled as fast as he could first on foot, then by car and then by boat. After the deeply disturbing and life changing incident that would follow in Marseilles, Madala would make it his mission to find the person who betrayed him and deal with it in the only way he knew how. He was a professional assassin with special knife skills, a qualified semi-automatic 'point and shoot' specialist unequalled in his training squad - full firing range scores being his normal standard - and was a highly proficient master practitioner of Aikido. Added to this, he was one of twelve candidates who were chemically-psychologically prepared to react on keywords delivered by telephone. Madala proved to be the most resilient of all the South African assassins trained in this way. Eleven of them died during the course of the war; several due to side effects of the conditioning drugs they were treated with. Such were the times we lived in and the considerable personal price some of us paid; all in the name of the great white Afrikaner cause.

'The fake mark came walking down the deserted street at 23h50 that evening as planned, his hands tucked deep into his coat pockets and a soft baseball cap pulled low over his face. Unbeknown to Madala, a CIA agent instead of the KGB agent was on his way to meet him at the pedestrian bridge, as previously arranged by his director. From his vantage point under the narrow pedestrian bridge Madala could see the large frame of the man that he would have to kill. He quietly and smoothly attached the suppressor to his pistol barrel. At ten metres he stepped from the shadows and pulled the trigger twice in quick succession. The gun thumped twice through the suppressor. The mark sank to his knees instantly and when he rolled over on his back Madala saw him clutching his head where the two subsonic 9mm bullets struck. Blood was streaming through the fingers of both hands. He walked closer and went cold. 'Oh, sweet mother of God. It's Andy Flax. He had killed the wrong man and a CIA operative at that.

'Madala turned away immediately and started running flat-out in a southerly direction breathing rhythmically through pursed lips. His only purpose was to put as much as possible distance between himself and Andy Flax lying in a pool of blood on the pavement. He suddenly heard a car approaching from the rear. He noticed a bus terminal on the opposite side of the road. He swerved sharply to the right, crossed the street and positioned himself on the far side of the terminal. His hands were shaking after the fast sprint. The car approached at high speed and stopped abruptly with screeching brakes right opposite the terminal. The right window opened and the suppressed muzzle of a rifle appeared. He instinctively went for his gun in the sling bag, but as his hand closed around the butt he noticed one member of his briefing team behind the steering wheel and he hesitated for a split second. As if in slow motion he saw the flash and then simultaneously heard the suppressed thump of the Dragunov SVD. He felt an incredible blow and burning sensation on the right side of his head as the hastily aimed shot ripped through his skin. He instantly crashed to the ground to one side and lay slumped over the wooden bench in the terminal. His last sensation before losing consciousness was hearing the car pull away at high speed.

'He lay there for some time with blood pouring from his head when in the distance several dark shapes appeared and started running towards the terminal. The strong and soft hands and voices of six nuns in black habits were all around him and one of them whispered to him in French. He was lifted up and he could feel soft shoulders supporting his arms and legs on both sides carrying him gently. He opened his eyes and saw the distinct shape of a nun walking briskly before him. He felt the surface changing under his feet and then noticed that they had turned and passed through a narrow gateway into a dark and thickly overgrown garden with trees and shrubs. A large dark building loomed ahead. A door opened and a nun appeared carrying a paraffin lamp. He heard soft whispering everywhere and more hands were now helping him through the door and up a narrow staircase into a dimly lit room where he was carefully helped onto a narrow but comfortable bed. He was bleeding profusely from the open wound in his head where the bullet had opened the skin to his skull. Soft hands and the ripping of sheets were underscored by the sound of water in a bucket. He felt a warm soft cloth against his head while someone held his hands; there were whispering voices everywhere. The last sound he heard before closing his eyes was a French voice asking everyone to speak softly. Madala was in a convent in Marseilles. Madala was in God's hands.

'He was woken by a sound at the door well after midnight. He slipped from the bed onto the floor and positioned himself close to the door. His head was throbbing and he felt dizzy and disorientated. The door opened and Madala struck. He grabbed the intruder by the throat with his right-hand forefinger and thumb and fought with him into the passageway where he landed on top of him struggling to retain control. But he was feeling weak and within seconds he was lying on his back looking straight into large and visibly innocent dark brown eyes.

He noticed the long black dress and the white edge around the hood. She helped him to sit upright and whispered to him while gently helping him into the room and onto the bed. 'I am sister Isabel. Do not be afraid. You must rest.' Madala felt embarrassed and tried to explain that he reacted out of fear. She held her hand in front of her lips and pushed him back against the pillow. He closed his eyes and fell asleep with sister Isabel holding both his hands. She gazed at the small black sling bag on the table and wondered about the gun she found inside, the knife in his pocket, and the speed with which he reacted when she approached the door to check on his condition. She sat with him until he fell asleep. She never forgot that episode and especially Brother Francois' concern after they called him in and he saw to Madala during the night. She feared that the worst was still to come. Madala would never forget her eyes and how she watched over him.

'Madala woke up early the next morning as a ray of sunlight, shining through a narrow opening between the two white linen curtains covering the small window, touched his feet. He lay completely still and deliberately recalled all that had happened the previous night. He decided not to attempt to analyse everything but to rather just get through the immediate aftermath and the injury. He glanced at his small sling bag on the table next to the bed. He raised himself onto his left elbow, and was just able to reach the bag. He pulled it towards him and immediately checked the contents. Everything in the bag, including his Spike knife that sister Isabel had removed from his pocket, was just as he had arranged it the previous night.

'The door opened and sister Isabel followed by three monks

entered the room. They greeted him hastily, but politely and two of the men left. The slender, third man who remained behind appeared to be a senior person wearing an immaculately pressed habit. His head was clean-shaven. He wore small round steel rimmed spectacles positioned to the middle of his nose bridge. Madala noticed that he had the curved hands of a martial arts practitioner. Sister Isabel closed the door softly and they sat down on two wooden stools. This process that went on as if he was not really there fascinated Madala. Sister Isabel smiled and nodded towards the monk who immediately offered his hand and commenced speaking with a heavy French accent. 'I am Brother Francois. I represent The Order of the Rose in Marseilles. What is your name? So, you will have to stay in the convent until you are fully healed. What is your name?' Such was Madala's rebirth on that day in June 1970 - through an intervention that was not yet clear to him - in a convent in Marseilles, where he entered into the inner sanctum of one of the most powerful secret international organisations serving within the Roman Catholic Church - The Order of the Rose.'

According to Sam, Madala was still unaware of the other scenario's that were developing around him and that everything back home was in a state of flux. What was written was that he would save Sam's life in the most extraordinary way within a few years and that together they would attempt for the last time to stop the sale of a country and the demise of its people. His link to the righteous Rose would also create a conflicting potential power base for the ultimate attempted counter move against the deeply corrupt efforts by captain Ailes and the money hungry Knights of Malta - the Catholic Church finance organisation stationed in the Seychelles - which backed Ailes.

The Knights enabled Ailes to perpetrate several self-enriching actions such as selling oil to the president of the Seychelles and personally pocketing a healthy profit, while the rest of the traitors were already far down the road with their efforts to remove president Burton from power. To this day the key to this dichotomy, good versus evil in the Catholic Church eludes me. The uncomfortable truth was that the operation against Burton was already so far developed that everything that was done to stop the immoral actions against him, would in the end prove to be inadequate.

'And that', Sam said, while stretching his arms out about his head, 'is the strangeness of this story. It's like rivulets after a storm running towards a stream that became unstoppable and utterly destructive towards the end of the 1980s.'

Then, in a complete change of direction that seemed really quite odd at the time, if not for the fact that it felt so profoundly foreboding, Sam said, 'By the way, Alistair, if you ever need to talk to me in future, this is a secure telephone link where you may contact me from a 'clean' instrument on your side.'

It was a satellite phone number. I did not know at that time that that would become the communications portal for the next phase of this story starting in the year 2009. I could only guess that Madala had made this link possible before he was killed simply because he cared about Sam and Jackie. We were entering a whole new game of drawn knives. As I would find out much later, Madala knew what was coming.

Chapter VII

The Plot

Sam stopped talking and leant forward to put some more wood on the fire. I was changing the tape when Jackie walked in with hot drinks and announced that she was off to bed.

Sam touched her hand and she remarked, 'Don't let him keep you up all night, Alistair. This man never rests. He's always walking around the house and growling at something that may possibly irritate him.'

Sam laughed and excused himself for a short while to lock the doors and close the windows.

I thought I sensed a hint of sincerity in Jackie's apparent joke about Sam and I suddenly realised that life must have been complicated for her having had to cope with the earlier uncertainties of Sam's profession and then the health issues and his often impossibly difficult personality that became harder to handle as time went by. During time spent with them amid the war years, I recall being present at a discussion where Sam and Jackie were speaking about his work - something that hardly ever happened. At that time Jackie was adamant that she understood why he was involved in covert work. It was however clear from her remarks about some of the people that we worked with that she had doubts about how Sam's idealism and loyalty would stack up against the self-honouring and self-enrichment that was then already prevalent. She was a professional in her own right and never looked for any handouts during her life. She required dedication, loyalty and hard work from people that worked with her but she gave as much in return. Jackie was never someone who tried to be clever at subjects that she was not involved with, and she always had the ability to read people and did not require constant recognition and reward like so many of the ambitious men and women we had to associate with during the course of our work in the military. She very much kept her life and their children away from army social life, rather ensuring that their family always had a private aspect that no one else was ever really given access to. Jackie also had a deep-rooted distrust of the political social system and always felt uncomfortable with the high society Sam's work sometimes required him to participate in.

Jackie's loyalty to Sam came at a significant personal price. Her origins lay in a profoundly creative family with an essentially self-made business and farming background resulting in considerable means. Her family participated in World War II and chose to follow careers in the defence force after the conflict. These origins stood in stark contrast to Sam's family who were steeped in National Party ideology and who strongly disapproved of participants in the 'English World War'. These objections referred back to the Boer War and were so fundamental in their essence that Jackie was never really accepted by Sam's family. Instead they chose to keep her isolated on the outer fringes of the family for the greater part of her life. This family class war was underscored not only by political rank, but also by an acquired nouveau riche societal status in Sam's family. The result was not what her opponents had hoped for, namely her unconditional surrender. Instead she became deeply committed to become all that she could ever be and in the process be a force to be reckoned with on her own terms. She succeeded with her initial chosen career as a teacher specialising in guiding and empowering people to cope with new life challenges. Many a young person had the good fortune to be guided by this single minded and deeply private woman who understood the art of winning confidence and steering talent. Later in her life she would move into creative photography, underscored by a passion for sketching images she loved.

Sam's position was clear from day one. He resented his family for their deeply flawed conduct and chose right from the beginning to associate with Jackie's family who knew commitment and loss in practical terms similar to the ordinary families of sons who fought the war while the wealthy connived to create bolt holes for their precious offspring. For this choice his family mercilessly condemned Sam and that would eventually lead to a situation of complete distrust and removal of his participation in family matters.

He shared this fate with William, president Burton's son, who also associated with mere mortals who died for South Africa while the privileged ran for cover. The upper classes were making money while the underprivileged bled for the cause. This fundamental principle of class distinction became the single most devastating factor in the outcome of the South African war in that unity of the people was a mere figment of someone's imagination right at the top, created for exclusive gain and ultimate positioning under a new black government which seemed inevitable even at that early stage.

I knew all of this ever since I met Sam and then Jackie. I looked at Jackie where she stood close to the fire and said that I should watch the time as I knew that in the morning he would want to walk again starting 06h00. I needed to rest if I wanted to keep up with his pace.

Jackie turned and said in a barely audible voice, 'Alistair, he always did his very best and mostly at significant personal risk to life and limb. He does not deserve what has happened to him. I am trying to prevent his collapse by supporting him with his efforts to keep going for as long as possible. You have to realise though, there is no cure for the illness that is destroying his body. Eventually he will collapse and he will in all probability become an invalid if he does not die before then. That is the reality I have had to cope with since the late eighties. One would have thought that he would get a fair deal after his contribution during the war. There is no fairness in all of this Alistair, there is only our personal effort to make the last years we have together the best ever.'

Sam walked into the room and stood quite still behind Jackie. He had clearly overheard her last words. He said nothing and just looked at me. She noticed him and turned and walked away without a further word. I immediately realised the importance of that spoken demonstration of unquestionable support I always suspected she had. She kept Sam going without fanfare and without demanding to be seen. She did not have to be seen. Her quiet presence, influence and constructive criticism were always there while she coped with everything that ever happened to him. He could never do it on his own. Suddenly I felt somewhat awkward being witness to two people struggling to cope with something that was so much bigger than they were. That was what made their relationship extraordinary. They were just two ordinary people, but their loyalty towards one another - despite many differences in the way they saw things that I was aware of - was precisely the one thing that made them special.

I was switching tapes while Sam looked at me patiently.

He then picked up our discussion while handing me a few hand written pages with some words written in pen that he had fetched when he left the room, 'Read that later, Alistair. It will show you the depth of my physical breakdown and my complete inability to manage it on my own. During 1985, as you know, operations against UNITA were escalating. We countered, but our gradual withdrawal from Angola weakened our defences. That kept the army extremely busy, while back home people were living their carefree lives as before with the war effort far removed on the borders.

'At that time the creeping onslaught internally was intensifying. A secret organisation with its core hidden within the National Party caucus, Club 2000, was deeply entrenched in all areas of government and politics from the lowest to the highest levels. Members' diverse backgrounds made it possible for them to function in commercial, civil service and military circles. Cultural organisations and church groups were influenced and slowly but surely the message of the so-called futility of military action took hold.

'Simultaneously, these same people worked with core elements in the largely diluted national intelligence organisation consisting of agents drawn from the old BOSS (Bureau for State Security) and even disgruntled members (for a variety of personal and professional reasons) of the defence force's military intelligence division as well as large numbers of new recruits. The organisation was led by an uninitiated intellectual, dr Becker. This organisation was notoriously unstable and continually subjected to investigation, especially for political meddling, resulting in regular subsequent organisational changes. Amazingly though, their powers increased as their influence with president Burton became more substantial. This growth in influence was due in the main to director Becker's ability to impress the president with his pseudo intellectual prowess derived from his Afrikaner backed sojourn at the University of the Orange Free State, the same institution where the president spent some years when he was a young man. It was a curious liaison as one would have thought that Burton would lean towards the defence force which he transformed and came to adore during his tenure as minister of defence. National intelligence won the fight for the president's attention though and this signalled the end of well-balanced intelligence reaching his desk. Ultimately national intelligence would acquire the rights to scrutinise all intelligence reports and to deliver the final product to the president. Through these developments the defence force became beholden to national intelligence and sadly lost the real ability to influence national strategic security and defence policy.

'This resultant new conglomerate of civil and government organisations, operating under the auspices of national intelligence, was covertly intended to promote a liaison with our enemy - the Freedom Movement - both internally and on the borders. Co-operation with regard to training and strategy and tactics between the security and civil elements were now a given. During this process our enemies expertly infiltrated military intelligence and it became nearly impossible to operate from our headquarters without deliberate precautions not to alert them. In 1987 it became clear to me that we were not planning on winning the war and that military operations were merely holding actions intended to allow the politicians to plan for a negotiated settlement in Angola and back home. By 1989 when the withdrawal from the border area was imminent we were already mostly fighting on our heels and against the ropes. There were two obstacles blocking the 'way forward' to a negotiated settlement, UNITA and president Burton.'

I smiled and remembered how we had considered throwing the helplessly drunken Rangle to the crocodiles in Cuando Cubango years before.

Sam took a sip from his hot chocolate and resumed, 'I was known to have had a direct personal link to The Doctor and through Ray to the UNITA organization, even after my departure from the defence force two years earlier, while the president and The Doctor had continuing close ties. The freedom movements inside and outside the country were experiencing difficulties in securing a victory for the government forces in Angola. Such a victory would shrink the border safe zone to the national borders after a South African withdrawal, first from Angola and then from Namibia. Ray was still in place and supporting The Doctor and my channel to UNITA through him remained secure. Our enemies within had no choice - they had to neutralise the president, Ray and me, since we stood between them and a handover of our country to our enemies. The Doctor would be dealt with later in cold blood in 2002 through a covert multinational hit team led by our defence force and after betrayal in his own ranks.'

Sam stood up and stirred the fire. He looked at me and said in a soft voice, 'You know, Alistair, president Burton was deeply concerned about minority rights in our land and he believed that a confederal system would secure those rights. The opposing hidden group within his own party, Club 2000, were however at that stage so deeply involved with secret discussions with the enemy in close co-operation with foreign governments that it was simply too late. The plot that was then hatched and executed changed everything forever and we would soon all become refugees in some form or other.'

At the end of 1987 when Sam realised that the war was over and read the signs of political deal making at the expense of the soldiers, he resigned from the defence force. After refusing a position as personal aide in the defence minister's office he went into business as a strategic business advisor for large international companies attempting to access developing markets specifically in Africa. He however still helped the defence force with certain 'complicated equipment procurement' wherever he could, but ultimately slowly came to the realisation that this was also drawing to a close when his access to key decision takers became more difficult.

'It was one Saturday at about 16h00 at the end of 1988 when dr. Philip from the medical battalion arrived at my doorstep.'

Sam was speaking quietly, but quite deliberately in that measured voice I knew from earlier days.

'Although I knew him well, I was deeply concerned about this unannounced arrival. Philip was always a bit of a dark horse with his own secretive private agendas and I was always unsure of his intellectual insight and originality. It seemed as if he was forever searching for new mentors. I was however sure of one thing, he was always a good messenger boy. Jackie offered him a coffee as we were just sitting down after having been out the whole day. He looked at me and then at Jackie and said, 'Long time, no see Sam. You look fit as always. Things have changed on the political horizon, haven't they? How close are you to Ray?' I was completely taken by surprise by this side-by-side shotgun approach and my inbuilt professional paranoia kicked into place. I instinctively answered in the time tested delaying-to-allow-time-to-think fashion the Chinese taught me, 'I don't follow, Philip. I am slightly confused. What do you mean?' He immediately sensed that I was cautious and started explaining, 'Against the background of our changing political landscape it has become so important to create the right climate for negotiation for peace. We should rid ourselves of any suspicious aspects of our former activities that may hamper our way forward.'

'I have always loathed this kind of political correct speak that had become the custom of the day in our changing country with a passion. This alone, quite apart from Philip's insolence, triggered my temper.

'I felt Jackie's hand on mine as she tried to calm my growing irritation. She was perfectly familiar with my views on the new peace-at-all-cost approach in our country and she had noticed my body language showing a growing annoyance with this person lecturing me about things I had forgotten thirty years before. The medical battalion had always purposely and deliberately breached the operational dividing line into the intelligence domain over the years and even broke into special forces operational responsibilities. This led to several embarrassing moments both nationally and internationally. I restrained myself and said in as calm a voice as possible, 'What is it that you want from me, Phil?' He looked at me with a slight hesitation and said, 'We need you to help us to remove Ray from his position of trust with UNITA. You know he is a wild card. He is arrogant and dangerous as he believes that he is able to control and direct UNITA. His attitude is becoming an impediment to the peace process in Angola and Namibia and further peace and democratisation initiatives in the rest of Southern Africa.'

'You could hear a pin drop in the room. I stood up slowly with Jackie still holding on to my hand and said as calmly as I possibly could. You know that I still have close ties with all these parties, don't you?'

'Yes, that's why we need you to help us get rid of this irritation,' he answered.

'So what you want me to do is to betray the position of trust I have with these people, or what, Phil?'

'He looked at me with a clearly aggressive attitude and said, 'If you agreed with the changes happening in our land you would not hesitate for a second to assist us.'

'Jackie was standing next to me holding my hand in a firm grip. I pointed at the front door and said in quite a deliberate tone, 'Get out, Philip, before I throw you out, you son-of-a-bitch.

'I was trembling from head to toe and slammed the door shut behind him while he was turning to say a last word.

'That was the quite sudden ending of that friendship and the beginning of the focused persecution by the government that would destroy a life that I had built up over many years, destabilise my family and nearly kill me.'

At the end of 1988 Ray was to receive a military decoration for services to the country in the international arena during the Border War. His wife Gretel looked at him throughout the whole ceremony with open admiration and affection, as did all of his loyal comrades in arms. She had nursed him back to life after the horrendous explosion that nearly took his life earlier during the war, while his former relationship with a woman he loved evaporated amongst the horror. When he was back on his feet they got married to stay together forever. Sam and Jackie were invited to attend the ceremony and the ensuing function held at the state guesthouse in Waterkloof Ridge, in Pretoria. Sam was politically close to the already discredited and unpopular Burton, mainly through his friendship with his son William and he was already well known to differ strongly from the hidden agenda of handing the country over to the Freedom Movement. With his contacts right across Africa and his significant influence with many key players he had to be neutralised. There was also the distinct, albeit totally unreasonable fear amongst Sam's enemies that somehow Burton's circle of influence would be transferred to him. That would give him serious power that could lead to resistance to change. Ray's dinner after his medal ceremony was the perfect place to get to Sam. A detailed plan was hatched and Rangle's attendance as minister of foreign affairs provided sufficient believable cover to be able to deny any possible wrong-doing. Ray was in the limelight during the proceedings and could not be targeted. Dr Bana had provided a custom designed chemical weapon in a small inconspicuous vial with a snap-off top - intended to induce a carefully selected autoimmune illness from the defence force secret chemical biological weapons program - Project Coast. Sam was the mark. Phil was the hit man. Despite his training and alert professionally paranoid nature Sam never saw this curve ball coming. He was after all amongst his own people.

Phil sat next to Sam, a situation Sam felt skittish about, but nevertheless accepted. Phil excused himself right after Sam had ordered his fruit juice. He hovered close to the service hatch where the drinks were being left to be served after preparation in the bar area and deftly delivered the chemical weapon into the glass of juice that was Sam's favourite and clearly identifiable amongst a group of people who were mostly drinking hard tack or red wine. He stepped away briskly as the waiter collected the drinks and rejoined the table guests. Sam quickly emptied the glass of juice while Phil referred to his non-alcoholic lifestyle. Later that afternoon they all said their goodbyes with much back slapping and loud laughter. Sam and Jackie walked with Ray to his car. His wife Gretel held Sam and Jackie's hands while Ray stood there with his new long overdue medal on his chest and looking at Sam with that 'what the hell are we doing here and why are we not where we really belong under the open sky' look on his face.

He just said, 'Thank you for coming, Sam. You know I will never forget you.'

They would not meet again until 2005.

'Minister Rangle remained behind. We speculated that it may well have been for whatever unsavoury R&R with some unknown local slut in the VIP suite while Phil crawled back under his rock where he rekindled his dubious inspiration with the rest of his murderous gang.'

I looked at Sam as he completed this part of the story. It suddenly became very quiet with only the burning fire crackling in the background. He was not saying anything and his eyes were suddenly incredibly sad and he looked so tired.

He started speaking in a barely audible voice, 'It took nearly a year for the weapon to kick in properly, Alistair. At that time I was still unaware of what had happened to me. It took Jackie and me several years to piece this attack scenario together. I ignored the persistent earlier signals and kept on 'trucking' as a committed long distance runner. It was 1989 and I was running a 100-mile race and Jackie was seconding. I struggled throughout and finally broke and fell completely apart at 70 miles when - with the benefit of informed hindsight - my red blood-cell count fell dramatically. I stopped running and simply could not continue. I still remember the vast field of pineapples on the left side of the long and winding east coast road. Jackie rushed up to me from the seconding vehicle and removed my Oakleys. I remember her saying, 'Now, Sam now, look at my hand, oh God, Sam, your eyes are broken, your eyes are not focusing.' I will always remember her voice in the late afternoon howling wind on that hot but grey-hazy day, the voice of the one person I have loved my whole life sounding as if she was losing me. Strange how I then remembered the chopper rotor blade sounds and the sight of body bags in Sector 20 and in the confusion I felt so terribly lonely to be losing the one thing that always inspired me deeply, the ability to remain upright and to fight back with body and soul. I never really recovered. From there on it was all downhill. I summarily walked away from the event, totally confused and utterly devastated by the unexpected sudden disappearance of my physical endurance and conscious ability to survive.

'That was the end of my amateur sporting career and the start of the darkest time of my life that initially lasted for two years. From then on I slowly started the attempted mending process while hanging on to Jackie who was by then and by far the strongest and most supportive of the two of us, despite my impossible condition and the fact that I lashed out at her time and again just because she was the closest to me. I still do not know how our marriage survived the impossible situation we found ourselves in. The sophisticated chemical weapon in virus for designed by dr Bana and his co-criminals for use against enemies of the state delivered to me during the function at the state guest house during Ray's medal ceremony, had finally slammed home with massive effect and my immune system went into overdrive under the pressure of an auto-immune disease. I was the victim of a chronic progressive degenerative ailment that would slowly destroy my body. It was the beginning of pain akin to being sliced up with razor blades permeating all my waking and sleeping hours. My life was forever changed.'

I had no way of knowing that this story was to be so severe and I felt the ice-cold sense of anger I always feel when good men are hurt by bad men, creeping into my heart. 'You swines,' I thought to myself. I sat there with my notepad and pen and completely forgot to stop the tape recorder. I suddenly remembered the story of experimentation done in our operational area during the war when terrorists in captivity and even some of our own black troops were subjected to some of Bana's 'medications to facilitate co-operation during interrogation'. The failed scientific attempt that resulted in deaths by brutal strangulation with cable ties, were handled in a typically efficient military way - 'dump the deadly evidence'. Patrick Haynes, the ex- special forces operator, paratrooper and pilot, flew the plane with the sealed oil drums far out to sea. Only the content of the barrels was not oil but the 'failed attempts' literally forced into the drums in foetal posture. Read in conjunction with the attempt on reverend Frank's life - the same man who later ran the president's office in the new South Africa - the whole picture started to come together. It was in fact an all encompassing program of experimentation and extermination of identified resistance at all levels of society ran by murderous criminals we had tolerated within our own ranks. Sweet Jesus, and then we talk about the Nazis'. I felt sick. Sam looked at me and said, 'Alistair, you look knackered, stop the tape buddy. Let's go to bed. Tomorrow at 06h00 we walk.'

I went to my room and while sitting on the side of my bed I read the heart wrenching raw poem in the hand written pages Sam gave me earlier. Jackie had written *The dance of the Tiger* about Sam and left it on his table one night after the pain completely enveloped him and he screamed at her in complete anguish at his growing physical weakness just because she was there, but clearly refusing to allow her access to his nightmare.

> *You think I have forgotten it all*
> *or do you think that I have never known*
> *that when midnight comes*
> *when the blades start slicing at your bones*
> *and you are hardly capable of dragging one foot before*
> *the other,*
> *that you then jump on the back of the tiger with the long*

white teeth
which leave bloodstains on your soft white skin
The tiger that rips your joints asunder
as it lunges at your body
That I do not know of the red hot flames licking at
your soul?
I stand and I look and I hope that one day you will allow me in ...

This poem more than anything else starkly depicted the horror of what had happened to my friend and how the creeping monster of his illness was creating havoc between him and Jackie. Sam was like a wounded animal, snapping at anyone who tried to help him. Jackie was deeply hurt in this way several times when Sam completely lost self-control, not knowing how to cope with the invisible enemy in his system. After such clashes he would withdraw in a tactical way that he was familiar with in military terms - to survey the land and to lick his wounds only to reappear weaker every time and then to find that she was still there, waiting to help him, always patient and always loving him and always trying again to get through his armour.

She persisted doggedly, specifically on one critical occasion after Sam woke up one morning and was unable to walk. He underwent two surgical procedures to restore the use of his leg. A few weeks later Jackie and their son bundled him into the 4 x 4 and drove him to a vast farm in the northwest 'wet' Karoo where they knew their friends would protect their privacy at all cost. Here they helped him to regain some of his self-confidence by painstakingly walking forty kilometres over a rough hiking trail. Jackie initially encouraged him with small cups filled with an energy drink carefully placed at one kilometre intervals until he regained his rhythm and slowly won back his physical freedom. These excursions became the saving grace during a dark time convincing Sam that Jackie would never forsake him. His life was out of control and he could not go it alone, and eventually win the fight as on so many previous occasions when he worked as an intelligence operative. This was a cruel reality that he had to learn to cope with.

I folded the piece of paper away and my emotions got the better of me. I cleared my throat in an attempt to stem the sadness that was in my heart. I remembered better times and better people who were our true friends, before the darkness and cruelty and murder at the hands of our own sub-standard political masters engulfed us and sent us into exile for ever.

That night I slept the sleep of a tired soldier as I remember it from Sector 20. Dead to the world. No dreams. Just numb, dead sleep.

Chapter VIII

To Kill a President

The next morning I was woken by the rich smell of toast and coffee. We walked after breakfast and enjoyed the fresh morning air backed by the growing light in the east. It felt surreal to have to talk about death and destruction in a place that was so beautiful. Out of nowhere came the familiar sound of chopper blades and Sam and I stopped and looked towards the sea. A Royal Navy SeaKing helicopter rose above the cliffs overlooking the Atlantic, dipped its nose and swept over us. The sound of the rotor blades was unmistakable. Sam and I held onto our jackets and hats as the moving air rushed over us. We waved excitedly at the young pilot and laughed together as he smiled and saluted back briefly with a gloved hand and walked back through the short grass to the house where Jackie waited with the customary after-walk eats and drinks. It was like 'brunch in the bush' and once again the food reminded me of our meals in Sector 20. Sam looked tired and after the meal he withdrew for his injection. I had a feeling of incredible discomfort and could not help but notice the suppressed anxiety with which Jackie oversaw all of this as if she was going through a well-known pattern of tasks that was intended to console both of them while they knew what the inevitable outcome would be.

Sam was ill and he was not getting better. The meals, the walks, the talks were all meant to stimulate and relieve pain through structured ritual, exercise and analysis and compilation of factual material, but the end of the line was the end of the line and once the rope had run out there was no more to hold on to. Maybe just a serrated blade would then remain to free him from the suffering as the 'last stricken climber' hanging over the precipice, so to speak. I decided to walk straight into this whirlpool of emotion and try to show some backbone in the face of this unnecessary sadness - something I have always struggled with - by asking and moving ahead with the story despite the pain I was witnessing.

Sam walked into the room and saved my sorry ass.

'Let's sit in the sun, Alistair and let's talk softly together as old friends.'

I hastily grabbed my pen, notebook and tape recorder I had fetched from my room. But I dropped the pen and the notebook and Sam - without looking - amazingly caught both before it hit the floor.

'I still have some of my old life saving reflexes, Alistair, albeit heavily laced with luck.'

We both laughed sincerely, but when I took the items from him I saw how his hand shook and I grabbed hold of it and steadied it and I felt quite upset about this undeserved and uncontrollable condition inflicted on him by tepid low lives who were supposed to be our brothers-in-arms.

'It's okay, Alistair. Ray lost both his arms you know. Toll is dead and gone. Ed's wife was stricken and broken by stress. Twenty-three senior officers in total were fired and emotionally broken through the opportunist actions of a pompous jet jockey general that I will not even name and give recognition to. This man who knew nothing of the fight on the ground and showed it at every occasion when he was caught unawares in private discussion, after which his lack of ground level experience of the war lay exposed. At least I am still alive and still have all my limbs. Even though they are a bit dodgy, I still have them.'

We walked down to the chairs under the trees. Sam sat down and smiled at me busily arranging the tape recorder on the low table and positioning the microphone and my notebook and pen.

'So Alistair, where was I?'

The die was cast and the irritation that dr. Phil referred to regarding UNITA and associated areas were now in line of sight. The most important target was the president himself.

The telephone call from Uncle Paul came late one night in 1989. He was a wartime colleague and previous director of military intelligence who had gradually moved politically to the far right. Although Sam had no reason to distrust him at that stage, his political leanings were a concern. The conflict potential in South Africa was severe enough and could simply not absorb dangerous uncontrollable fanaticism.

'Sam, I need to see you, now. Get over here my friend. It has begun.'

Sam slammed the 4 x 4 truck into first gear and worked his way as fast as possible through the slow utility gearbox until he reached the double carriageway from Johannesburg to Pietersburg in the north. There was no time to play with. He literally had minutes to get to Uncle Paul's house where he would get the evidence of what he had suspected for months.

He struggled to find the dimly lit doorbell at the house that lay just off the highway. He was relieved that the two massive very aggressive Dobermans were locked in the backyard. The door opened and Uncle Paul stood squarely against the light. The white blemishes on his face, the result of his fighter jet crash-landing and burning when he was still flying actively - partly covered by a white chin beard - showed clearly in the half-light.

'Thank you for coming, Sam. Please step inside and go directly to my study. I will join you in a minute. Would you like a cup of coffee?'

Sam nodded and climbed the narrow, steep staircase to the study.

Uncle Paul walked in with the coffee and handed Sam a cup. He turned around, closed the door, and switched the radio on in the background.

He took a seat directly opposite Sam and started talking, 'I hope you are okay. Are your wife and children well? Please, give my warmest regards.'

Sam nodded and sat forward. Uncle Paul started speaking again, only this time more softly, 'There will be an attempt on the president's life. I have the names of the conspirators.'

He suddenly leant forward and handed Sam a sheet of paper. The notes were scribbled in hurried handwriting, the name of a chemical substance that takes approximately twenty-four hours to activate if taken orally, its effect on blood pressure, typical symptoms, the further cumulative effect on blood pressure when taken with other medication and then the names of a number of prominent persons. These men were all serving in senior positions in government. They were suspected of involvement in the plot to kill the president. Sam went ice-cold. The one name was that of a prominent person in president Burton's office, captain Ailes. If this was true, it was very close and it was very late, as the president trusted this man with his life. Sam folded the piece of paper and placed it in his shirt pocket.

He looked straight into Uncle Paul's eyes and asked in a whisper, 'Do we know who supplied the substance?'

He looked back at Sam with wide open eyes and said in a barely audible voice, 'CIA. They use a cocoa leaf derivative that will probably be added to a meal taken at his office. Without a single doubt the perception afterwards will be that he has suffered a stroke.'

'You probably need to get to him immediately. We do not know precisely when they will strike, but it could be as close as within the next twenty-four hours. Deep down the president trusts you and will listen to you. You must isolate him physically and give him the names so that he will be able to act against these men. We do not know the detail of what they are planning.'

Sam explained that he had an appointment in Cape Town the very next day and that he was planning to see the president. What he did not know at that time was that Ailes had only given him the appointment because he knew that even if he knew what was happening behind the scenes, he would probably be too late. There was total silence in the room. An old Chris Blignaut song from way back when ... *Ou ryperd* ... drifted through the room from the radio positioned on a dark wooden bookcase. Irritatingly the song kept reverberating in Sam's mind while he drove back home to pack his bag and catch a few hours sleep before leaving for Cape Town.

Sam left the next day on the 13h00 flight from Johannesburg International Airport. He arrived in the Cape just before 15h00 and first made his way to the minister of defence's office in Parliament Street to discuss shoulder launched missiles from the Far East destined for special forces and to gauge the climate.

He had arranged this appointment for 16h00. His appointment with the president would be at 17h00 at Tuynhuys close to Parliament just across the street from the minister's office. After having worked his way through the traffic in the centre of Cape Town, he parked his vehicle in the Plein Park parking garage close by. He checked in at the security desk in the foyer to the minister's office at 15h45. This was as always a long-winded affair with millions of questions being asked by security officials, filling in masses of paperwork that was never looked at ever again. He had to wait a while and finally only entered the minister's office at 16h20.

He walked in and just as he stretched out his hand to greet the minister, who never said a word, the red phone on his desk suddenly rang. The minister picked up the receiver, spoke briefly and then pointed to the telephone close to the door behind Sam.

Without pulling a muscle he said, 'You had better take the call.'

Sam thought nothing of it. He had known general Max for several years and was accustomed to his mostly undiplomatic dealings with people, sometimes bordering on the downright impolite.

Sam picked up the receiver. The voice on the other side was that of the president's eldest daughter. Sam knew her from introductions on previous occasions. She knew his earlier position of trust with president Burton. She decided to phone him because she had no one else to contact and said as much to him.

'He has been taken to the ICU at Wynberg military hospital, Sam. He apparently suffered a stroke. Please get there as fast as possible. I called your home and Jackie told me you are in the Cape at the ministry.'

Sam put the receiver down. He turned and looked at the minister.

He started talking and said the words, 'The president is ill'... and then stopped because he noticed that the face in front of him was completely devoid of emotion.

Then he saw Max's mouth open and these words came out, 'I suppose you had better go. I trust you have transport?'

Without saying a word Sam turned and walked out. He remembered the names on the list Uncle Paul gave him the night before and specifically the general's name. He went straight to the lift and out of the building to where his car was parked in the parking garage.

He realised with complete desperation that he was probably too late. The front wheels of the small hire car spun and shrieked irritatingly as he exited into Plein Street from the parking garage. He drove towards Table Mountain and took the turn into De Waal Drive, the fastest route to 2 Military Hospital in Wynberg situated in the southern suburbs on the Cape Peninsula. He switched on the car's emergency lights and pushed the accelerator pedal to the floor.

Sam did not bother to park his car in the allotted public car park. He stopped in front of the main entrance and walked straight into the main passageway. He made his way down the long passage at a brisk pace and stepped into an open lift at the far right-hand side and pushed the button for level two, the ICU. The doors opened and he noticed a group of doctors dressed in immaculate white coats standing in the centre of the ICU. In the middle he noticed the overweight hulk of the surgeon general major general Nelius. They were talking in soft voices and as he approached they turned towards him.

One Sam did not recognise stepped forward and asked in an emotionless voice, 'Who are you? Can I help you?'

He brushed past him and started walking towards the motionless shape lying in a bed in the centre of the ICU surrounded by medical apparatus. Suddenly he felt an arm on his sleeve.

'Sam.' He turned and recognised dr Van Burgh, the prominent heart surgeon from 1 Military Hospital.

He wanted to trust this man. This was the man he consulted about all medical matters over a period of many years. Van was also his physician at 1 Military Hospital in Pretoria. This man was his friend. Van took hold of Sam's arm and they walked to the far side of the ICU.

'He is very confused and not coherent at all, Sam. We believe he may have had a stroke. We are unsure of what happens now. The director general is demanding that the appointment of a possible interim president only be authorised following a mass of detailed legal inquiries before anything happens. He has already taken up a lot of time. He seems to be stalling. He is pushing a different candidate to the president's known choice - Christopher. The doctors are delaying. I asked them to proceed, but they do not want to inject him to relieve the pressure on his brain. General Nelius seems reluctant.'

Sam immediately reacted, 'When and where precisely did this happen? Who was with him midday, yesterday?'

Before dr Burgh could answer, a scream of pain and profound desperation rang out from the motionless shape on the bed in the middle of the ICU and then the words, 'Oh God, please God, help me.'

It was the desperate scream of a man in agony and close to dying.

Sam walked across the ICU to where he noticed the short, overweight, bald-headed controversial former senior jailer dr Rowan, the director general in the president's office, standing in a doorway leading to an adjacent room. He was dressed in a grey striped suit and of course, grey shoes, the quintessential dress of an official of this time. He had a thick file clutched tightly under his right arm.

Sam walked up to him and said in a clear voice while pointing his finger right at his small round nose, 'You, little man. Go inside I want to have a word with you.'

Rowan looked up at the tall man, his round eyes shocked behind large gold-rimmed glasses. He was clearly afraid of Sam whose no-bullshit reputation preceded him. The fact that he knew of the distrust Sam felt towards him based on several previous encounters in the president's office did not help to calm his immediate and growing anxiety. Rowan was not a brave man. He was a crooked, scheming political vulture with a dubious professional past that mainly used his official position to feather his own nest. Sam followed Rowan into the room. The president's wife, his political advisor Daniels and his press secretary, Jackson, were all present.

The president's wife looked haggard and sat with her hands

clutching a rumpled handkerchief in her lap. Her eyes were wide with fear. She looked tired and her lips quivered when Sam walked in.

He looked straight at her, gave a brief nod, and asked in a soft voice, 'Are you okay, Mrs Burton?'

She immediately acknowledged with her eyes, but started crying softly. All the signs of a frightened and confused person were quite evident. Daniels stood in the corner with his empty pipe between his teeth. Sam did not like this man much, mainly because he was mostly unwilling to listen to advice or informed input from elsewhere. Jackson, the oily, seedy opportunist with the slightly shifty eyes, stood in the opposite corner with a typical cynical smirk on his face. Sam did not like either of them and he certainly did not trust them.

They were part of the president's inner circle. Their individual attitudes had been consistently negative and even belligerent over past months. Sam always feared that the inner circle was in fact part of a larger attempt to isolate the president from the reality of the escalating border war and township unrest and consequently the real state of the nation.

Jackson was a former journalist of doubtful moral origins known by his several sets of principles and widely rumoured incessant womanising. Sam clearly remembered at that moment how he flaunted security measures and specifically how he had blurted out the name of a sensitive associate in the intelligence structure for which Sam promised him a sound beating.

Daniels saw himself as very well informed and was perceived to be reluctant to listen to advice from other specialists. In later years he would write president Burton's biography. The book would reflect Daniel's academic style and would although well researched, not be a great piece of work and in consequence not reflect the real story. The mere fact that they were there worried Sam. Their apparent condoning of Rowan's commanding position irritated him.

Sam cornered Rowan and immediately confronted him with, 'You, Rowan. Why are you playing this game? Why are you delaying the interim succession process? What legalities are you talking about? Why do you want this president to die before Christopher can step in? Whose agenda are you following?'

Rowan grinned defiantly and opened the thick file he was still carrying around, 'Here are the reasons I am waiting for the state legal advisor to call me back. There are rules and regulations to be obeyed here you know.'

He waved the piece of paper in front of Sam's face. Sam decided to end the discussion at that point.

He brushed the paper aside and said in a clear voice for everyone to hear, 'I am going to take you away from here and I am going to rip your f-cking head off. You are a stupid ambitious little runt with an over-inflated ego. You want the president to die to enable you and your cronies to push for an alternative candidate as interim president. This is unacceptable behaviour. I am fully aware that he has made his choice before he became ill.'

Sam somehow suspected that there was a link between this former jailer and the rest of the conspirators. This would become clearer in time as Ailes' and Rowan's roles were exposed.

As Sam stepped forward to grab Rowan by the neck, he suddenly felt two arms closing around his shoulders.

'Sam, don't. It's not worth it soiling your hands with this little bastard.'

It was dr Masters, the president's eldest daughter's husband. Sam had conflicting feelings towards this man. He always appeared to be in a superior dimension of his own far removed from mere mortals while being hopelessly lost in shallow political insights, driven by his financial success. This appeared to lead him towards the wrong personal political choices for himself and his family. However, he trusted his abilities as an accomplished private practice surgeon who cut his medical teeth in blood up to his shoulders operating in Sector 10 during the war. It was almost possible to like this man, but Sam's years of experience with self-centred individuals at the top of the white supremacy ladder, who never reacted in kind to a genuine positive attitude prevented that. Sam ultimately realised that Masters would always be a most capable doctor, but utterly incapable of clear political insights.

Masters turned Sam around and held him with both hands on his shoulders. He said calmly but in a quite determined, trustworthy voice. 'I will fix this mess.'

In fact, he then did just that and Sam would always remember that outstanding deed when thinking of this man during the years following the event on that fateful day. Dr Masters turned away and approached the doctors still standing around Nelius and talking in hushed tones.

He said, 'I will inject him. Please prepare the syringe.'

Nelius looked at him, and with his fat fleshy jaw quivering with anger and his round belly suddenly protruding further than usual, he shouted, 'You cannot do this. This is an army hospital. This is official and you have no right. He is the president.'

Masters looked straight at him and said in a clear calm voice,

'Yes he is, but he is also my father-in-law.'

Despite all the opposition Masters acted and saved the life of a man, however thankless a task that would turn out to be later. Within minutes he injected the president and two hours later he was stable and awake and signed for Christopher to act as president in the interim. The queue of people standing ready to welcome the president back into consciousness grew rapidly and before Sam could even move to get closer Ailes was standing in front of him.

He bent down and Sam heard the president say in an almost saintly tone, 'Oh, look at the little head with hair neatly combed. Come here, my dear captain Ailes.'

Ailes, the polished servant who was always immaculately turned out with his carefully chosen brand name suits, shoes, belts, shirts and ties and other ancillaries stepped forward like an obedient dog. The president lifted his hand and placed it on Ailes' head as if bestowing a benediction on him. This appeared to be the final confirmation of Ailes as the chosen one. Sam felt an eerie, sinister sense of foreboding of biblical proportions. It was as if by mistake a blessing was given to the enemy. Then it was Sam's turn to be greeted. It was quite official and visibly an abbreviated moment. Sam knew finally that he had lost the president's trust. He turned on his heel, and with a brief glance at the hovering circle of political vultures and other inner circle beneficiaries of the self-honouring political glow that shone forth from the fallen leader and as if they were waiting for some final godlike blessing, he left the ICU.

It was now Sam's turn to find the origin of this darkness. He knew that his position was not secure once the old leader was down. He would have to travel back north and work all the sources he knew to get to the truth. Sam walked from the hospital straight to his car. As he turned the key he glanced in his rear-view mirror and straight at the dark front door of the hospital. He shuddered at the sense of evil and the impending dark threat lurking within those walls. What Sam did not realise at that time was that the events would eventually overtake even him and that he would ultimately have to struggle for his own life - to use a politically loaded word. There was still a significant fight ahead. As he drove through the hospital gates, the dark words from Revelations that would haunt him for the rest of his days kept reverberating through his mind, *And I looked, and behold a pale horse, and his name that sat on him was Death ...* He remembered his own personal credo with some amusement as all that he had seen until now was so much in direct conflict with this belief of Strength and Honour. This was Strike 1 and the president was still alive. The next strike would follow within days after he was stable and moved to his home. That would give a clear indication of how deliberate and focused the process of removing the serving leadership would be. Sam was old fashioned in more than one way and his personal references to old-worldly sayings were testimony of that. History did count after all, however far back it went. Darkness would soon envelope Sam in physical and emotional terms. He was quite alone.

Chapter IX

Pillars of the Party

In order to understand the conspiracy that now played itself out one needs to analyse the mechanics of how the party structure was traditionally held together. Because of his long close association with these different elements Sam had a deep insight into this dark maze of intrigue that was held together through politically tenuous associations, which eventually succumbed to a very efficient internal revolution that changed the political landscape in the country forever.

Sam contemplated how the second strike against the ageing president came with unexpected suddenness and emphasised the depth of sheer naked animosity against the man. This animosity was long in the coming and had to do with the nature of the governing party beast.

What were the origins of this hostility? Sam took a large blank page from his writing pad and with a black pen drew the lines of a flowchart showing clearly how the web of governmental, religious and cultural organisations formed a foundation aimed at maintaining the integrity of the state. As the picture took on a recognisable shape Sam spoke in a voice reminiscent of a well formulated military briefing. 'The pillars on which the political power system rested were the party caucus, defence force, police force, intelligence organisations, church and secretive Afrikaner cultural organisations and their youth subsidiaries (designed to take care of the upcoming youth being prepared for their future roles as saviours of 'Die Volk') If any one of these pillars were removed the power base would disintegrate.'

'Many years before, during the late seventies a group of young Turks, not unlike in the early 1900s within the Ottoman Empire, commenced a secret plot within the National Party caucus to form alliances with influential academics and large business conglomerates to create a new and younger governing elite. This new approach was in broad strokes the result of years of continuous training of the young white privileged minority. They were supposed to take over from their old guard fathers as the new guard. Unfortunately for the old guard, their children were subjected to subtle intellectual influence by academics that had experienced the wide international world. They gained new insights mostly through extensive studies at overseas institutions of higher learning, no less through the benefits enjoyed during white rule with subject matter both morally and ethically correct, but in revolutionary terms, spot on. Here they were identified by and briefed by enemies of the state and ultimately placed very carefully in strategic positions within universities as the new leaders of thought who were inspired by a post second world war fervour to find the truth. The very people who were supposed to train the new young cadre of leadership ultimately became the enemy within acting out their role as the Pied Piper of the old South Africa. Their agenda was one of gradual change from within and was inclusive of sympathisers and the enemy, albeit very well disguised and hidden from clear view. Participants in this process included ambitious clergymen with a new fangled revolutionary view of their God and businessmen who came from meagre beginnings making money off ordinary white people's salaries - who now became the nouveau rich core of the business world. They were able to think and act more broadly in support of professional politicians who mostly just wanted to ensure that they would have a seat and the accompanying benefits when the music stopped. They all wanted a slice of the expected cake once the old guard was disposed of. As I mentioned before when we discussed the origins of the plot leading to the handover of South Africa to its enemy, they called themselves Club 2000 and their vision was set firmly on the new millennium. The end result was that the party caucus was gradually brought to accept a handover as the only solution by means of a mix of threats based on influence with the enemy standing waiting in the wings and far reaching promises of political reward.'

Pointing at the specific element indicating the defence force on the flowchart he said with some emotion, 'We supplied the threatening fist, which meant that all senior military positions were essentially party-politically motivated appointments. These men were supposed to carry the torch of political survival with armed force if required. The foregoing process of gradual capitulation ultimately led to serious discontent, simply because the junior ranks were fighting the war and resented going to war with one hand tied behind their backs. This was mainly due to the fact that there was continual meddling from the defence force's political leadership (often burdened by personal and personality issues such as general Max's lack of battle experience and doubtful military academic record that led to a constant ambition to personally lead the fight) and the mover and shaker part of Club 2000. This ultimately led to the question being posed whether the country was involved in the war first and foremost to win the fight, or merely to act as a holding action for some tenderfoot politician's treacherous political agenda. In this sense the defence force was always the prime target for the young Turks who continually attempted to curb the force's work. The Special Forces units and associated units such as 32 Battalion and the parachute units formed the real hard core of the fighting force and carried a superhuman physical and mental load right throughout the war. Their numbers were never very high and as could be expected, the first and last man to die during the war were special forces operatives. These men were special in more than one way and everyone who ever worked with them only had the highest regard for their sheer tenacity, ingenuity and proven bravery. During the war it was difficult to penetrate them simply because of the relative secrecy that surrounded their activities. Of course in what was to follow after the 1989 betrayal they were naturally also the first units to be vilified beyond any reason, simply because they were feared as people who did the right thing under all circumstances. If anyone could unravel and show the truth of the unspeakable ongoing political treachery - in association with hard-core intelligence operatives - they could. So, they had to be silenced by breaking up their units and merging it into a mindless amorphous brigade structure without real military soul. Their true spirit would never really return despite an effort at restoration in later years. Many of their former members work very efficiently elsewhere as paid specialists to this day. The defence force remained hamstrung and indeed had to fight a war with one hand tied behind its back.'

Sam remained quiet for a while and spoke very softly but deliberately, 'The police force was responsible for containing crime and the rising internal tide of political discontent underscored by rampant poverty leading to incredible hardship in the townships. They mostly did that with unspeakable brutality. The police were always less sophisticated in their approach and any attempt by the enemy to penetrate them would be not only dangerous, but also pointless. Any attempt at curbing their methods would not only be futile, but also life threatening. In the end the South African police actually came to grief, mostly because of the sheer disgust that people felt for their brutality throughout.

'As you well know, Alistair, the military intelligence corps worked to maintain factual sanity and reporting, while guiding the system with advice based on the perceived truth supported by facts and not some incredible fabrication to fit the political agenda. We never tweaked the facts to fit a desirable agenda. While we understood the importance of support for political aims, we constantly and throughout tested each aspect of the agenda against the facts as we uncovered them. Our ranks were swelled with academically qualified and mostly liberally minded individuals that brought a semblance of sanity, but regrettably also the seeds of possible treachery that could be exploited. Hidden deep within our ranks and mostly unnoticed because of overworked operatives and in consequence inefficient counter intelligence activity, enemy agents worked tirelessly against the war effort while some of the critically placed operatives were in fact working for more than one intelligence organisation internally, something which directly fuelled the 'rot' in the system.

'Some of the senior staff officers sold their services to foreign espionage agencies and in so doing secured for themselves futures beyond the survival or in this case, the demise of 'die volk'. The leadership of this organisation started in the late seventies with a practical visionary general Fritz, who created both the intelligence corps as well as the reconnaissance units that would do the practical fieldwork to provide the defence force with the facts to plan, justify and execute their military strategy and tactics. He was succeeded by a man you are familiar with, general Heinz, who was an intellectual at heart who used the organisation to set himself up in later life as an academic with elder statesman status 'taking care of his own interests. The slippery Pedro 1 who created an empire especially serving his own interests then succeeded him. He was always suspected of actively participating in the sell-out of his country and taking money for it after which he joined the foreign affairs service and used that to build an international business for personal gain. The decline in the fortunes of our organisation continued with the subsequent appointment of admiral Andreas who I respected since the days he was my navy training officer, but who regrettably ultimately resorted to alcohol to solve whatever problems he may have had. This decline in the quality of leadership of military intelligence did nothing for the status and ultimate role of our organisation.

'Also hidden within the bowels of this organisation there were civilian faced organisations such as the Civil Co-operation Bureau consisting of front companies that initially contributed to the war effort but later on proved to be a mere killing machine and more often than not, money generators for the people who ran them. Many of these front companies were either plundered dry or simply converted into purely civilian businesses with original state funded capital after the 1994 ANC takeover.'

Sam's voice indicated total disappointment when he referred to the next group, the national intelligence service. 'The NIS would always serve whoever paid their salaries while bending to the incredibly naive strategies and methodologies created by the intellectual who was appointed with a substandard academic record and who had a limited understanding of the real war. In time he would turn on and become a massive danger for all covert operatives who were still attempting to act sensibly within the war effort by authorising massive internal and international surveillance on our own forces. This organisation represented the treachery factor that sold out the rest of the security establishment for their own financial and ideological survival. It gradually became known that immediately before the 1994 takeover they handed all covert operational files they could lay their sticky fingers on to the enemy. Many of the operatives involved are still running for their lives today.'

Stabbing aggressively at the next block on the flowchart with his pen, Sam stood up and I could sense the naked anger in his voice, 'The security police were in essence the covert arm of the police force. They had a free hand in most things and ultimately, mainly due to untrained, unintellectual and flawed leadership and personnel, which ultimately proved them to be a mere blunt instrument. They were responsible for many violent deaths of resistance fighters even in captivity, and other fabricated threats to the state under often dubious and corrupt circumstances, characterised by incredibly brutal methods. In doing this they did not keep track of the post war factor which ultimately led to their leadership running for cover while drawing state pensions to this day, with many of the foot soldiers languishing in jails for many years.'

Sam was clearly deeply distraught and left the room momentarily. I regrouped and marked the end of that session on the tape recorder while I waited for him. He was back within minutes and apologised for his outburst. I merely nodded and kept quiet. I understood by now what the hell was happening. Sam was reliving the whole mess and I for one was not about to distract him with any interjection whatsoever.

He went on speaking in a clear, but still quite emotional voice and I lengthened my recording stride, so to speak, to keep up.

'Once the attack on these pillars of the system was well under way to being completed successfully, all that remained was for the leadership to be removed before the freedom fighters could take possession of the country. The second near fatal attack on Burton came within weeks of his discharge from 2 Military Hospital. This was launched to complete the first failed attempt. The physically weakened president was recovering at his official residence in Rondebosch, in the southern suburbs of the city hugging the mountain. The house was surrounded by a large and beautiful garden and one would have thought that such a surrounding would be ideal for a recovery. But that was not to be the case at all. This process was being monitored very carefully by a team of doctors under the auspices of Lt. Gen. Nelius - the surgeon general of the defence force.

'One doctor Sweeny, quite a pedantic little man, was specifically designated to take responsibility for the president's recovery. His methods were at best clearly less than subtle and his attitude was at worst clearly belligerent. President Burton was suffering from the after effects of a perceived stroke including difficulty to perform simple tasks. He would have to relearn to do certain things like tying his shoelaces and fastening buttons. Relearning these things would take the honest and dedicated efforts of an occupational therapist who would in time build a relationship of confidence with him. His brain was not affected, but certain of his motor functions were and because he was no longer a young man the recovery process was slower. Sweeny homed in on this and constantly delivered sharp criticism and comments about his slow improvement that irritated the old president beyond reason. The emotional impact had the added benefit of creating an unstable and stressed environment that was detrimental to a fast recovery. In fact, Sweeny was purposely driving the struggling patient mercilessly and that gave rise to increased emotional irritation and subsequently more physical strain. He developed a urinary tract complication and Sweeny prescribed medication and inserted a catheter to assist with emptying the bladder. It is believed Sweeny quite brutally ensured that an unsanitary catheter was used and within twenty-four hours the president had a raging infection that led to fever with the resultant uncontrollable shaking of both his hands. The frustration and discomfort led to screaming matches during which the president accused Sweeny of attempting to harm him.

'His wife was deeply concerned and contacted his loyal son-in-law Masters, who advised that he be moved to his holiday home on the southeast coast where Masters would personally oversee his treatment. The day he departed by military VIP flight his shaking hands were clearly visible on the television news. It was now clear that there was a plot to kill him and his family was doing whatever they could to minimise further medical battalion life threatening involvement in his treatment. Under the guidance of general Nelius this proved to be one of the most dangerous units in the defence force to be subjected to for treatment, especially if you were a political adversary. The reality was that the defence force as a whole was by now so totally and completely politicised that they intervened directly in many matters that would otherwise be the domain of civil government. Their strategic ranking in the state structure and many special powers made it nearly impossible to fend off any attack on one's person. At his holiday home Burton made a steady recovery, but the harm had been done. Although the plotters had failed twice to kill him they were powerful and audacious enough to try again.'

Sam did not miss a beat and plunged straight into the rest of this dark narrative as if he wanted to talk before he lost the opportunity to do so.

'The president was never a very popular man. He was egotistical and quite direct to the extent of often being blunt in the extreme. This behaviour came from strong parents and a self-centred personality as he was an only child within a large family of half brothers and sisters who smothered him with attention, which in turn led to a deep seated, personally perceived higher destiny drive. That certainly contributed to his position of increased vulnerability towards the end of his reign. Those members of his family that were integrated into the leadership circle of influence spoke regularly of the so-called golden years. I always believed that this referred more to the privileges enjoyed by so many hangers-on rather than to the real substance of the presidency. The fact that there was a larger picture and an international plot to kill him followed by a subsequent failed attempt became patently clear. What is not always so clear is the fact that there was a growing mood of self-importance by the man himself that led to abusive behaviour towards anyone who opposed him. Many enemies were made out of an ever shrinking circle of loyal friends.

'The questions that linger to this day are, was he a giant amongst similar potentates, supported by a system which recognised his appetite for power, self gratification and self-honouring, which realised that he could be manipulated for their own gain, or was he a real giant amongst international statesmen and a man of destiny who was quite simply betrayed? Many of his actions point to the first, but there are many political commentators who to this day believe that he was in fact a giant amongst true leaders. Despite a few moments of true greatness as a statesman that I witnessed from afar and some examples of efforts to endear himself to his closest and most loyal friends and especially towards his eldest son, William, who remained an outcast because of his repeated warnings against a self-honouring approach and a lack of attention given to the plight of ordinary people, I remain sadly unsure.

'Added to this is the fact that the president's son William's alienation within his family was so extensive that even officials were aware of his diminished status and more often than not he was prevented from seeing or talking to his own father. He was subjected to the same appointment regimen that all other mere mortals were subjected to. This worried me and was a clear demonstration of the growing isolation enveloping the old president. The last significant effort William made to defend the old president was when he advised him to consider firing his cabinet, disbanding parliament, dividing the country up into military sectors under the control of military governors and finally to declare martial law. After that a period of ten years would follow, during which time the two opposing parties would be given time to reach a settlement with proper safeguards for minorities. The president refused to go down this route, ceased any further discussions along these lines and eventually William stepped away from him in total despair. The country was now irreversibly in the clutches of international interests and their in-country political and business allies.'

Sam stretched his arms above his head and explained that, after an all too short rest period Burton had returned to work and was confronted with an out of control political storm. It became fundamentally clear that he would have to step down. The howling wolves were closing in to force him out in favour of the Club 2000 candidate. It was widely advertised in most all newspapers and on national television that the president was not physically or mentally capable of running the country's affairs. Burton ultimately resigned during a last defiant television appearance. The new messiah who would lead the country into the light was Craven, a weak man whose father was suspected of an inherent sexual appetite for minors. Years earlier his father was thrown out of the teaching profession because of these sexual escapades, after which he was taken in by the National Party and eventually promoted to the position of cabinet minister. Craven himself harboured the history of an apparent shaky professional law career in a rural town before also entering the protected world of exclusive white minority politics. It is also rumoured that Craven possibly had his first wife murdered for dubious reasons.

Sam was a professional and he subsequently pursued a line of inquiry with all the intelligence techniques and contacts he possessed immediately after the president was stricken the first time. In order to access certain channels available to him he had to call in quite a few hard earned favours. His inquiries led to an alarming reality. The names he had been given by Uncle Paul were confirmed and linked directly into a secretive plot to kill Burton and to hand control over to a Club 2000 controlled puppet president who would execute the deal that was a struck with the freedom fighters years before during secret overseas negotiations. These were subsequently ratified in some specific detail elsewhere. This handing over process was apparently actively supported by the governments of the USA, UK, France and Germany while their intelligence organisations played a major part in the construction of a detailed plan to murder the serving president and prominent members of his family and specific advisors who moved quite close to him and enjoyed his trust.

Then, he delivered the bombshell that left me completely speechless.

'The main players in this plot were in part, according to Uncle Paul, and also according to other research completed by Sam, Pedro 1, aka The Ratcatcher - chief of staff military intelligence. He was apparently a sophisticated double-agent with strong ties to the DGSE and the CIA who left military intelligence during the late eighties to become the Secretary of the State Security Council, a body with significant oversight powers within the military dominated government system, after which he was pulled into Rangle's dark side circle of friends and became the ambassador to Chile. Rangle - the reckless minister of foreign affairs - who was actively supported by his director general Neville, a calculating man and as sly as a hyena; general Max - minister of defence - unspeakably inefficient, overbearing and meddling; dr. Becker - director of national intelligence - a political system supported and undeserving amateur with flawed insight and dreams of personal political grandeur as the faceless man behind the throne; Captain Ailes - the former naval officer and ultimately the president's personal assistant and the suspected hit man who administered the drug in his food during one lunch break in his office. A Greek bearing gifts who came from meagre beginnings and was apparently deeply corrupted by the Knights of Malta based in the Seychelles, and who subsequently developed massive materialistic ambitions; dr Bana - a medical specialist with suspected cruel leanings who was widely believed to have perfected a significant variety of large scale artillery, missile and individually administered chemical warfare weapons from which he also apparently personally benefited financially; general Nicson - the brilliant but easily misled police forensics chief working in close association with Bana and last but not least, dr Phil Burgh - a family member of general Max who was deeply involved with the CBW (Chemical Biological Weapons) program. These men apparently planned the strikes on the president's life and they promoted Craven who knew all the detail, but was left to one side because he was too much of a weakling to hold a knife.'

I sat motionless and for a moment the silence in the room was quite deafening. Sam looked at me with the palms of his hands turned upwards as if asking me for some explanation of this outrage. I felt my blood run quite cold.

Chapter X

The Real Enemy

During this time Sam made an appointment to see Pedro 1, who had resigned as Secretary of the State Security Council and was on his way to take up the position as ambassador to Chile. They sat down in the living room of the temporary house in Monument Park in the Jacaranda City where the general resided before departing for Chile. The discussion was short and uncommonly stilted bearing in mind that these men were supposed to be very good friends and colleagues during the years before.

Sam started by outlining his concerns without hesitation, 'General, I am here to ask for your help in an attempt to prevent the handing over of our country to our enemy. Craven is betraying our people and with his personal ambitions in the forefront he will not hesitate to place all minorities in jeopardy in his quest to create a personal international reputation for himself as the great peacemaker. Will you use your influence to help stop this madness?'

Pedro 1 seemed strangely detached as he squirmed away from the issue. He referred to the negotiations that were now a fact of life and that the new president was attempting to create a new, free and peaceful country. His answer was at best a weak compromise in the extreme which screamed 'leave me alone, I have to survive this personally'.

In the years to come he would prove to be a true coward who ran away from his responsibilities as the former CSI, while soldiers and his former colleagues in military intelligence and the state security council had to carry the full weight of the accusations the enemy would throw at them after 1994. Sam left that day with a feeling of deep resentment, disappointment and a deep-rooted sense of unidentifiable concern.

Sam received the phone call out of the blue during the middle of 1989, two years after he had left military intelligence's employ. It was Chief of Staff Intelligence general Whitlock's personal aide. He was to attend a meeting with the general to discuss 'certain matters'. Sam was irritated by the prospect of having to meet with this character. He regarded Whitlock as somewhat of a low-life as he knew full well what his personal history was and to what extent he was believed to be involved in corruption and the abuse of power in the operational area during the war.

Sam stepped into the entrance lobby of the Military Intelligence Division HQ. He smiled at the slightly shabby surroundings of a typical government department as he went higher with the escalator leading into the even dirtier and bleak reception area. On the left was the familiar x-ray scanner that was still the same ineffective rubbish equipment that he beat so many times with 'official contraband', the guards visibly - as always - rushing around and incapable of handling the workload. The metal detectors directly opposite the peculiar tube-shaped access swing gates that required either an escort or electronic swipe card. He walked through the metal detector, which as per normal picked up all the relevant metal pieces and commenced shrieking. Sam produced his car keys that was promptly accepted as reason enough for the disturbance and walked straight through to the reception desk with his .45 ACP semi-automatic, two extra magazines plus a five inch blade Spyderco tactical folder still on his person, undetected and untouched by the badly trained and harassed security guard. He smiled to himself and thought that this was enough reason to understand why the war was already lost. He was glad that he was no longer part of this badly managed environment. He announced himself at the desk and gave his full name with his rank. The guard saluted half-heartedly and handed him the same badly designed security questionnaire that had been in use for the best part of ten years. He completed it and handed over his national identity document as assurance that he would exit through the same door.

After spending nearly thirty minutes in the dingy and foul smelling waiting room the general's personal aide arrived with a lame excuse, 'I am so sorry Commander, as you know the General is terribly busy.'

Sam did not react but thought to himself, 'Yes, busy stealing the defence force's money.'

As he entered the lift Sam remembered some aspects regarding this man that he was about to meet. He was a schoolteacher before he landed on his feet in the defence force - no doubt a position arranged by influential decision takers with ulterior motives. He quickly rose through the ranks and was eventually appointed as CO of Sector 10 in the operational area during the Border War. There he carved a reputation for himself as a hard, but also incredibly unfair leader, who very often threatened officers and men with cancellation of home leave should they not perform to his exacting standards. He in fact often executed these threats. This home-leave formed a vital part of surviving the dragged out cat and mouse 'campaign' against SWAPO in this isolated part of the country and was cherished by everyone.

I also remembered how we would move in to win the hearts and minds of the local population only to be replaced afterwards by our friendly neighbourhood SWAPO political commissar, who would enter in our tracks and arrange for some of the townsfolk to be 'convinced' of their loyalty by cutting off their ears, noses and lips and then reinforced the message with the very public and very brutal rape of preferably the chief's daughter in the village square. Everyone of any influence on South Africa's side of the fence knew what was going on, but no one was prepared to say out loud that 'the king was in fact naked' and everybody went along with the politicians' utterly stupid belief that we were in fact going to ultimately win an election against SWAPO. During this process general Whitlock created the saying 'our cause is right' and he did whatever he felt like doing to serve that brainless slogan in a world that no longer served anything else but its own interests. He once visited Sector 20 and landed his chopper halfway back to Sector 10 to enjoy a hearty lunch of sandwiches and cold chicken washed down with some chilled wine. The infantry group who was instructed to provide peripheral defence for the 'lunch in the bush' had already been there for nearly two weeks living on rat packs and could only look on in total disgust as the general feasted next to the helicopter.

Whitlock was subsequently appointed as Chief Staff Intelligence when admiral Andreas retired. He immediately commenced screaming his particular brand of military madness at the members of military intelligence, often insulting senior officers over the public intercom system in the military intelligence headquarters. He was also a heavy drinker with a pain psychosis that drove him to chew handfuls of pain tablets washed down with water several times daily, in order to manage unidentified and non-specific pain, frustration and a general sense of psychological malaise. This loser was now in a most sensitive position of authority and he would make many people pay dearly for his seriously flawed personality bordering on complete psychological imbalance and for his resultant inability to manage a sophisticated organisation. A veritable madman was in charge of a very powerful military-political machine. This was the man that Sam had to face within minutes regarding matters that were still completely unknown.

Sam had to wait once again when they arrived at the general's office. He was sincerely glad to see his somewhat self-conscious and ungainly friend colonel 'Tall' Williams who was his operational security chief when he was still working for military intelligence as a covert operative and who would attend this 'discussion'. Sam did not really feel like facing the psychotic Whitlock on his own. Williams greeted him with sincerity while asking about his family. Sam remembered the gift that his friend gave him the previous Christmas, a book, the *Navy's Fighting Ships Past and Present* by Allan Du Toit, with a sincere Christmas message to him and his family written in the front. This was not the customary thing for the man to do and somehow when they met on the day Sam understood when he suggested cautiously to 'be careful' because things had changed considerably since Sam had left the defence force.

These changes were soon to be demonstrated quite brutally. The door to the general's office opened and his personal aide approached them and ushered them into the office and to a low table with some army regulation chairs arranged around it. General Whitlock was busy talking on the phone behind his desk while opening a packet of Lexington cigarettes. He lit a cigarette and inhaled deeply while proceeding with a heated discussion with some hapless colonel on the other side who had clearly irked the great general. Whitlock screamed at the luckless officer to stop wasting his precious time and to 'get his fucking ass into gear and make the action happen or face the consequences'. The general slammed the phone down unceremoniously and grabbed a bottle of pain tablets on his table. He shook several tablets from the container and threw them into his mouth. He proceeded to chew them with an open mouth and took a swig from a large glass of water to wash the medication down. Sam's suspicions about the man's sanity grew in leaps and bounds. The general gazed over to where Sam and Williams were seated.

'Yes, yes, and how is the commander?' he said in that typical superior parade-ground voice that Sam loathed for its obvious overbearing and patronising intent.

Sam never subscribed to this kind of military superiority and always referred to the essence and power of intellect to conclude his tasks quietly and discreetly. He suddenly understood what it was that Williams was trying to tell him when he gave him the book before, but never got around to saying outright for fear of his own position in this changed environment, where screaming abuse took precedence over brainpower.

Williams immediately stood up and said in a subdued voice, 'Good day, General. Thank you for taking the time to see us.'

Whitlock ignored him flatly and walked across to the table and chairs. He sat down and threw a stack of passports on the low table.

One by one he took each passport and paged through them and said in the same patronising voice, 'You were quite busy during your time in the service Commander, travelling almost everywhere.'

He threw the passports in front of Sam on the table. Sam was unsure of what this was about and simply said questioningly, 'Yes General?'

He felt Williams' hand clutching his shoulder and heard him whisper, 'Stay calm.'

Whitlock resumed, 'I understand that you do not agree with the negotiations at Kempton Park and that you openly criticise president Craven and what he stands for in his quest to create a new and free country. You apparently feel that not enough is being done to protect minority rights and that the president is a traitor with personal international ambitions.'

Sam did not say a word and instead just looked at Whitlock with a slightly amused expression on his face. Somewhere in the back of his head he remembered his last discussion with Pedro 1 and it worried him that very similar words were used during that interview. Whitlock was clearly irritated, but also somewhat out of his depth. He had an infantry background and was never during his career exposed to the intricacies and subtleties of covert intelligence work. His appointment as CSI was once again one of those decisions taken by politicians, in this case general Max, for purely military political reasons and because he could control Whitlock apparently being a 'brother in crime'. Whitlock on the other hand was up against an accomplished and experienced covert operative and he did not really know how to manipulate Sam.

He screamed at Sam, 'Is that true, Commander?'

Sam looked at the general's red face under a strand of blonde hair swaying over his left eye, swathed in a cloud of Lexington smoke and the cigarette with a drooping ash tip between his fingers and simply said, 'Yes.'

Whitlock was becoming visibly flushed in the face and he said quite loudly but very deliberately, 'You have a wife and children, don't you? You love them very much, don't you? Also they are quite safe now, are they not? Well, we will change all of that for them if you refuse to support this presidency striving towards building a new country.'

Sam looked at the general and muttered softly but just loud enough for Williams to hear, 'The crazed f-cker is threatening me. He is in fact threatening to harm my family.'

He looked straight at Whitlock and said with a trembling but clear voice, 'You are the great general and I am sure that you have all the power required to take such decisions and to perform whatever acts you wish.'

Whitlock was clearly perplexed at his inability to lure Sam into a fight.

He simply said, 'Well, you think about that very carefully, Commander.'

That was the end of the discussion. Sam stood up and left the office without speaking to Whitlock. He was deeply upset and trembled visibly as he walked towards the lift bay. Williams ran after him, grabbed him by the arm and begged him in a suppressed voice not to do anything foolish.

Sam turned to his friend who was perspiring and showing physical signs of significant personal pressure and said, 'I will kill them all if they touch my family, Colonel. That is a f-cking promise. He will come to grief eventually. This is not how any of us were trained to behave.'

Prophetic words indeed. Some years later this same excuse for a general would be working as a security detail supervisor at a woman's clinic in the Jacaranda City. 'How the mighty hath fallen.'

General Vanziel phoned the day after this episode and asked to see Sam. He had been requested to do so by former president Burton who was still in touch with him and said that Sam was apparently under some pressure. The president wanted to find out what the problem was. Vanziel was an elder clergyman who served in the defence force as the chaplain general for many years. At one stage he indicated to 'informed observers' what a great believer the former president was and how he once found him on his knees and deep in prayer during a visit to The Doctor in Angola. Sam always had a bit of a problem with such a tasteless publicising of president Burton's private religious practices. This was especially strange coming from a man who became known over time as having 'taken care' of the wives of absent soldiers at the military academy when he was stationed there, before being promoted to the position of senior spiritual leader. In one well founded account he was surprised one evening by a returning battle weary soldier husband. He fled through the back window, with his pants trailing from his hand, after having 'comforted' the lonely wife. This story came directly from the horse's mouth so to speak. Sam's father-in-law - a man he adored for the sheer guts he displayed right throughout his life from serving as a navy coder during WWII in the perilous North Sea convoy escort on the Murmansk Run, up till the day he was appointed as a senior admiral in his home navy - was a senior officer serving at the Naval Gymnasium at the time and Vanziel was well known to him.

Vanziel sat down in Sam's house facing the window with the sun in his eyes. Sam was quite deliberate when he placed him there. He wanted to be able to see precisely what this old religious conman had to say.

He started with the well known platitudes of 'How are you, how are your wife and children?'

Sam looked at him and without answering merely said, 'What is it that you want, General?'

Vanziel knew Sam well enough not to push the politically correct angle.

He got the message and went ahead nervously, 'Former president Burton is concerned as he has heard that you are under pressure from the government because of your political stance regarding the new policy for a new country. He asked me to visit you and inquire about your well-being. As you know he is also now under considerable pressure to re-evaluate his own critical position regarding the new country.'

Sam looked at the man and listened to his typically overly saintly voice. He did not know whether to throw him out or talk to him. That's how far removed this situation was from reality. He reached in under his khaki waistcoat and pulled the .45 ACP from its holster with a leathery thwack.

He slammed the heavy loaded gun on the table in front of them, pointed at the weapon and said, 'That is my fucking answer, General. You go back to your mates in the security services, specifically Whitlock and Becker and tell them that if they as much as touch one hair on the heads of my wife or children I will kill the next man I see behind me. I will furthermore deliver his dead body with a personal note explaining my intentions jammed between his teeth at the front door of whichever service he represents.'

Vanziel looked at Sam with an expression of shock and horror on his face.

'Please do not do anything irresponsible, Sam.'

Sam looked at him and shouted as loud as he could, 'Irresponsible? How is anything that I may do irresponsible? That bastard of an excuse for a general, Whitlock, threatened to harm my family. How dare you sit here and ask me not to act irresponsibly! Tell the old president I am trained to use a gun and that I am extremely angry. That is all he needs to know.'

That ended the discussion. Vanziel left somewhat subdued as Sam showed him to the door. He attempted to shake Sam's hand. Sam purposely ignored the gesture by this useful idiot.

Within days of these two incidents Sam received a phone call from colonel Anthony, a former colleague at military intelligence and a man he had trained with during the late seventies. He indicated to Sam that he had to see him as soon as possible as he had news for him that could affect his life. By this time Sam was under so much strain and still unsure of the reasons for the pressure brought to bear on him that he immediately booked a flight and departed the very next day. Anthony was stationed on the east coast where he was working as the military intelligence chief for one of the black homeland states.

Sam arrived late in the afternoon. Before driving to Anthony's house he had another meeting to attend as arranged by Madala. He asked Sam to meet with Uncle John who previously commanded 32 Battalion and to test his viewpoint regarding ongoing political developments. This would assist both Madala and Sam to take the correct political positions. His reputation for fierceness and doing the right thing preceded him. He agreed and a meeting place in a parking lot in a seaside resort was arranged. Sam waited in vain for nearly an hour. Uncle John never arrived and Sam decided to leave since it became clear that the man had probably been warned not to talk to him. Bright red lights were flashing in Sam's head, but he pressed on.

When Sam arrived at Anthony's house, his dark haired wife was somewhat cavalier when she invited him inside. She spoke with that 'I am in control of my life - voice' and projected a devil-may-care attitude which was quickly interpreted by Sam as in line with the reckless attitude he knew Anthony by, combined with a suitable and so typical 'I am a macho army man' slight disregard for women. However, her attitude quickly changed into nervous anticipation when she found out who Sam was. Anthony was on his way and she offered to make Sam some tea while he waited.

Just then lieutenant colonel Anthony walked in and with a typical, 'Yes, yes' he walked over to Sam and shook his hand.

Before Sam could say a single word Anthony drew Sam towards the far side of the room and out on the veranda and said in a hushed, but severely agitated voice, 'What the fuck have you done, Sam? You have got the combined security services on your tail in the form and shape of two teams of twenty-seven operators each with a modified, powerful Datsun vehicle with full surveillance kit installed. They regard you as a threat to the new presidency since they believe that you will inherit the full circle of influence and support base from Burton now that he has left the political stage. They believe that you will use this to assist with a coup against president Craven's new country initiatives. Your previous colleagues at military intelligence, specifically your friend colonel Dan at directorate covert collection, have been instructed to freeze you out of any further contact with the division.'

Sam finally understood the reasons former friends and colleagues were shunning him. After he had left the defence force his association with the Corps remained intact for some years and he assisted them with 'special international tasks' whenever he could. This relationship was inexplicably terminated some months before.

The same colonel Dan's wife would bump into him years later after the new government also rid themselves of her husband. She summarily pointed her two oversized breasts and cleavage prominently at Sam and asked whether he could help Dan to find work. At the time he was amazed at this lack of shame on her part after her husband blatantly refused to speak to him for so long. Sam seemed to remember that Dan was always a bit of an idiot with a 'non-intellectual personality who ultimately made it through the ranks to senior staff officer' chip on his shoulder. He would never let any opportunity slip to get close to any willing young female officer at impromptu late-night parties at the old observatory, where the corps training facility and covert housing for special guests were situated. Sam sometimes wondered how many times Dan had stayed over in one of the houses to rearrange some skirts after these casual functions. At the time he simply shrugged off Dan's wife's request and walked away.

He was somewhat caught off balance by this direct approach by Anthony, but tried not to show his anxiety. He was concerned about his wife and children, especially after the direct threat levelled at him by Whitlock at the time of their meeting. He believed Anthony even though he knew him to be somewhat of a rogue, with an unconfirmed reputation for summarily taking out unwilling prospective assets. Although they were not friends and never really worked together, Sam knew that Anthony was a solid intelligence operator who hardly ever got his facts wrong and that there could be no other reason for his openness other than unit loyalty and the sense of brotherhood that came with that. After having told Anthony his side of the story they agreed that Sam was in trouble and that the best way forward for him would be to simply take evasive action and lower his profile. They parted company amicably, but Sam knew that this would be the last time they would meet. From now on he was entirely on his own.

Sam arrived back home late that afternoon and he and Jackie sat down and he told her in how much trouble he really was. He was now an enemy of the state and the official machinery would ensure that he remains that, because that simply was how the system worked. Any new suspect, guilty or not guilty, would provide work for idle hands and a reason for existence for the system's operators. It was not important that Sam merely warned openly and honestly against a dictatorship of the majority and the dangers for all minority groups. This was a new dawn and the political playing field had to be cleared of all hindrances. Power and money now determined the day. Soldiers, living and fallen, were all forgotten as the political scavengers moved in to demand their portion of the dead carcass, which was the beloved country. As they sat together in the afternoon sun, trying to assess their desperate position, Jackie asked, 'When did you see Pedro 1?'

Sam sat quietly for a moment and then everything became crystal clear. His hands felt wet and as always he tasted the danger in his mouth. Pedro 1 The realisation hit him foursquare between the eyes. His life started imploding after his discussion with Pedro 1. He was betrayed by the general that he would 'walk through the fire' for. How else did his words to Pedro 1 come back to haunt him via Whitlock? This was a brand new ball game and Sam was not playing in the winning team. Sam and Jackie sat quietly for a long time that afternoon until the sun disappeared in the west. Soon total darkness would envelope them.

Chapter XI

Invisible Fire

It very soon became clear that Sam and his family were under considerable pressure. It remained complicated though and with all that came the darkness that Sam and his family attempted to evade for so many years by living a discreet life. They felt the fiery heat, but they could not see the flames or the enemy that started it. First there was a major break-in at his offices with severe damage to entrance hall windows. When Sam investigated he found traces of a surveillance device in the form of a microphone cradle taped to the underside of his desk. The cost of the damage and electronic sweep to clear the area plus additional safety measures started soaring. Then his board of directors were influenced and ultimately convinced to terminate his services as managing director. I would only understand the full impact of this ultimate life-threatening occurrence when Sam told me the story of his 'Crossroads' experience in China, which should have alerted him to what would follow in later years.

He left the employ of his own company, which he started, after an acrimonious conflict with his board and with only a small severance fee, ostensibly to enable him to find work elsewhere. Sam tried everything and spoke to everyone he knew.

After thirty-three attempts at new job prospects he gave up because the same answer kept coming back at him, 'We are sorry, we cannot help you, your military background is not applicable for this line of work.'

However hard Sam explained the professional nature of his international work experience as a military operative the jobs remained unavailable to him. That was clearly just another way of saying, 'We do not want you close to us as we have been told by the government that you are bad news and critical of new government policies and that we should not touch you with a barge pole.'

Simultaneously Jackie began noticing strange goings on in her immediate vicinity. Their children were still quite young and it was necessary, especially in those years with the war still underway, that they were not allowed to go anywhere unattended. She became aware of cars following her day and night with just enough visibility to create uneasiness and ultimately fear for the children's safety. Their post was being tampered with and after a particularly badly resealed envelope arrived, Sam inserted a few hair cuttings in an envelope and mailed that to himself. On receipt he noticed that the hairs were gone. Their mail was being intercepted and scrutinised regularly. Then suddenly in one month their telephone bill rocketed to about four times the normal monthly amount. Sam called the telecommunications company. When the technician arrived Sam confronted him with the situation and explained that he understood how an electronic link had been established to his line with an auto-dialer running up huge bills. The man tried to deny it but Sam persisted that he would blow everything wide open in the media if the situation was not resolved immediately.

After this the bills returned to normal levels within a month. Sam's nerves were ragged and Jackie was beginning to show strain. He noticed with some considerable alarm how her thick black hair had inexplicably turned distinctly grey within a few months. A sickening, stifling darkness was slowly enveloping him and his family. He was against the ropes and as an enemy of the state he had nowhere to turn to. His nights were again regularly filled with terror as his war time experiences working alone outside the country for months on end, came back to haunt him. He regularly woke up with Jackie forcibly holding him and struggling with him to calm him down.

Eventually they were forced to sell their house and move into a lifelong friend's house since Sam's funds were running out. This friend, a senior government official and his wife were in the Cape for the parliamentary session and these months would provide an opportunity to be relatively safe, because they were able to simply disappear from all known locations. Their friends wanted no money for this favour. All their earthly possessions were stored in one of the two garages on the property. They did not have much left after Sam was declared an enemy of the state. He was regularly forced to sell some of their more valuable possessions to pawnbrokers and second hand furniture dealers for money for food and to pay bills. Living in this house also gave them an opportunity to find new income and to consolidate their position. For the first time in his life Sam did not know where to turn to. One afternoon during an exercise run to clear his head he was standing on top of a hill overlooking the city. He sat down on his haunches and was overcome by a feeling of profound darkness and utter desperation. Sam knew that he could not really defend his wife and children efficiently. There were simply too many fronts and too few hands to cover all. They were at the mercy of the government who was bent on at the very least hurting them and at worst killing them.

He remembered the brutal murders of the financier dr Roberts and his wife years before, which was according to Sam's information apparently ordered by the former finance minister dr. Nicholas who was deeply involved in stealing state funds and sending it out of the country. Roberts took part in the investigation and stumbled on information that directly implicated dr Nicholas and his deeply corrupt family. His son apparently made a habit of engaging regularly in three-some sexcapades. Roberts' wife was brutally knifed to death in her home and her husband was shot in the back when he arrived home shortly afterwards. Sam's information was that dr. Nicholas was apparently standing quietly behind the door and witnessed the killings in silence. The words Rau Tem were spray painted on the wall to create the illusion that some radical group was responsible. According to Sam's sources it was a hit executed by the former bureau of state security - the forerunner of the NIS. It was never clear whether the then prime minister Balthazar knew about this or whether it was planned and executed covertly by BOSS under instructions from dr. Nicholas who was an incredibly powerful and deeply corrupt man.

Sam stood up from his haunches and stretched to his full height while consciously attempting to do a simple mental exercise he regularly used when he was under pressure working overseas on his own.

He said softly to himself and repeated the words several

times, 'To give in now would be to die. Plan, plan and then plan again. Do not allow the darkness in to find the light.'

Amazingly he felt emotionally slightly stronger after this familiar exercise. The road home was a little easier to negotiate than before.

He took a decision there and then to call in some of his former colleagues at the directorate of counter intelligence. They set up a sting operation with a fake far-right letter addressed to him asking for a meeting close to the war memorial on the hills overlooking the city. Sure enough, the mail was intercepted and they set off on the prearranged meeting date with a panel van rigged with cameras and a fast chase vehicle close by. The purpose of all of this was to establish the intensity and identity of surveillance on Sam. The state machinery was gullible enough to buy into this make believe meeting and they arrived with a surveillance vehicle that Sam's associates picked up on the perimeter. It had all the tell tale signs about it. The car was white and missing a hub cap, with a broken tail light and false number plates. As soon as their presence became evident, a wild chase through the entire city ensued with the state surveillance team running for cover and eventually escaping. Sam knew that his life had become seriously complicated and he was at a bit of a loss as to what he should be doing to get himself and his family into a safer position. The pressure was building.

By now Sam's health was in serious decline and Jackie was showing alarming signs of strain and a creeping exhaustion trying to stay ahead of the massive emotional load of the number of government intelligence operators unleashed on their personal lives. This was a worrying aspect as she always had the capacity to deal with nearly every situation that presented itself during Sam's time in the defence force. Her reaction seemed to reflect the severity of the relentless pressure on their lives. Their children had no idea of what was happening except that they were visibly disturbed by the fact that they had to sell their antique furniture and Jackie's jewelry to stay ahead of his creditors as Sam's money was running out. Jackie went back to work part-time to keep the family afloat. Then one day the bank refused to cash her small salary cheque. Jackie was completely distraught. At about the same time the bank also commenced exerting pressure on Sam. The only way they were able to stay afloat was through the interim and unexpected kindness of two friends, a wealthy American who in earlier years flew black ops flights for military intelligence and a wealthy Canadian financier who campaigned years before for Canadian Indian civil rights. Both of them were intimate friends of Sam and his family and both simply refused to see him sink into bankruptcy. With hindsight, if they had not come to his rescue Sam's situation would have been catastrophic.

Then out of the blue, Sam's luck turned and he was fortunate enough to be appointed by an electronics company to take care of communication with the government since they were deeply involved in Air Force Avionics programs. Simultaneously he would assist their business development in African markets. While in their employ and seemingly out of nowhere Sam was contacted one day and told that the state prosecutor's police investigating section wanted to interview him regarding the death by execution style shooting of two of the company's technical employees in the country's eastern province. They indicated that they had half a fingerprint that could help them with the identification of the killer. Sam suggested that they compare this fingerprint to his records at the central firearms register (CFR). He also requested them to check the commercial flight lists to and from that destination to verify his movements. The police official requested instead that Sam provide them with fingerprints. He refused because he insisted that he had nothing to hide and that such an act would clearly make him a suspect. After some considerable time, several aggressive arguments and a repeat interview the police admitted that the half fingerprint did not match his CFR fingerprints. The investigation against him was dropped. In later years Sam would suspect that these two innocent men were probably simply killed in an effort to frame him, but that the plot failed because the information given to the police to contaminate him was sketchy and they could not place Sam at the scene of the crime in Port Elizabeth at the time.

Despite nothing ever being proven he was also regularly accused of weapons smuggling and his name was once inexplicably linked to a weapons stash found at a place called Muldersdrift between the Jacaranda City and Johannesburg. General Whitlock furthermore summoned Sam for an inquiry into a laughably small amount of R850 that was apparently missing from a secret account. This accusation evaporated when Sam arrived with a fiery redhead female lawyer who had an appetite for a good fight and a reputation for discouraging creative persecution with brilliant legal argumentation. These fabrications were all widely publicised, but none were ever proven to be true. They were simply all intended to destroy Sam's credibility. The pressure was gradually turning into a profoundly dark process of undermining all aspects of Sam's life.

It was late on a Saturday afternoon when his phone rang. It was captain Murray, a 32 Battalion and 1 Recce veteran who trained with Sam some years before. He wanted to meet with Sam. They agreed to meet at a quite well known coffee shop and that changes to the venue would be made once they were together to ensure that they were alone. During this meeting Murray told Sam how during the previous months he had become witness to a carefully worked out plan to neutralise Sam as a perceived threat against the state by increasing the invisible pressure on him and his family. This plan would fuel Sam's concerns and strain after the threats from the apparently mentally disturbed general Whitlock.

Murray was a highly talented, multi-disciplined, energetic and loyal friend and Sam told me in some detail of their time together during training. It was a real soldiers-on-training mischievous undertaking, albeit with worrying undertones. The specific security training course at 11 Commando at the battle school in Kimberley was one of those events that one attended with some hesitation as it involved masses of detail with no recognition whatsoever of the experience level of the officers attending it. Murray and a few other fellow special forces operators and border strike specialists, in particular one decorated 61 mechanised infantry battalion group officer who wore a distinctive black dagger on a yellow background badge, embossed with a red thunder flash for cross-border operations, were becoming tired of the mundane repetitive aspects of the course. The training was done under the auspices of an overbearing intelligence corps officer, major Brown, who was hell bent on showing these truly gritty, battle-hardened soldiers just how clever he was. The situation came to a head when the ambitious major wanted the course members to answer a question consisting of eighty individually listed security check task items that had to be reproduced in a written test. This impossible and utterly useless exercise proved too much to bear for the battle hardened Murray and Co., since everything could be read from an official checklist anyway. They threatened to walk off the course if the standard of lecturing did not improve. The outcome was that an investigation was ordered with changes to future courses promised but not before the major had a field day with failing individual officers and causing all concerned general untold misery with different petty administrative matters. This plus the fact that he treated operationally experienced officers like school children made for a quite volatile atmosphere.

Murray and his band of special forces brothers waited patiently until an expected general security check of the training base was ordered as part of an exercise. That night they took all the highest classified documentation from the CO's safe, rapidly and quite violently overpowered the munitions depot guards, tied them up like snared game and snatched the very latest highly sensitive and hugely expensive night vision equipment and hid the whole lot on the back of a truck in the bush under a camouflage net. This whole undertaking caused enormous enjoyment amongst the embattled students and discussions about this act of downright mutiny went on late into the night with loud bursts of laughter drifting into the darkness from the sleeping quarters.

The major had to come crawling back before Murray and his cohorts agreed to hand all the missing items back together, with a scathing security report indicating all the miserable failings in base security. After that the course became significantly more mature. This was Murray at his best. This was the same man who, some years before, had broken a gate sentry's jawbone late one night. The soldier insisted with several unmentionable obscenities on inspecting the cargo in the back of a canvas canopied Samil truck. This against the stern advice of the two-man team which had just hours before extracted Murray and his special forces team from a long and arduous, highly sensitive cross-border three week reconnaissance mission. The sentry chanced upon the grimy group of recces in enemy uniforms and holding AK-74s crouching in the back staring at him with white eyes. I was told that Captain Murray flew out the back horizontally and sent the luckless overzealous soldier straight into hospital by severing his jawbone with his fist precisely where it links onto the skull with a loud thud and the words 'Fucking idiot, you know nothing' reverberating through the dark. His subsequent words to the investigating team were, 'He was too persistent and I was too tired, Sir' Murray was let off with only a slight rap over his already bruised knuckles and a stern instruction to the Sector 20 CO to brief his sentries more thoroughly when special operations teams were deployed and especially when being extracted. Yes, that was also Murray at his very best.

During their meeting at the small coffee shop on the fringes of the city that midday, Sam took the opportunity to hand back a stainless steel pen that he 'acquired' quite by accident during a discussion session on the course he and Murray attended together in Kimberley. Murray's name was inscribed on the side in shaky lettering. Sam always treasured the pen and this was a welcome moment to hand it back to his friend.

Murray took the pen with a smile saying, 'Hell, this is excellent I wondered where I had lost it and all the time you had nicked it, Sam.'

He was clearly relieved to receive it back since it had been a gift from someone else that he treasured. The pen was certainly a good luck charm and Murray was pleased that he had found it again. They laughed together for a while like only men from their background could, with happiness and sadness always carefully balanced and showing clearly in the lines on their faces. Sam made it clear that if it was not for the pen that he had nicked they would probably not have met again. The pen was not even valuable, but in a world of blood, guts and much tears something so simple had the same meaning as the dearest good luck charm. It shone like the brightest diamond where it lay on the table and they were both looking at each other and then at the pen several times.

'Yes, Sam,' Murray said pensively 'where has time gone and what will still come over our paths?'

Murray told Sam how he had overheard two drunken men speaking in a bar one night. He had just completed a discussion and was on his way out when he heard Sam's name mentioned in the course of the slurred conversation. Murray, loyal friend that he was, moved closer and within seconds he was accepted as part of this inebriated group.

The two drunks were one Louis C. and Koskas Du P. who both worked for the national intelligence service. They were laughing wildly and referring to Sam and his wife Jackie and their children with a variety of filthy obscenities while hitting the liquor smeared table with their fists in a fashion akin to only a specific type of white South African trash. Several years later Louis C. would end up in a Mozambican jail for cross border gunrunning - a sojourn arranged by Sam and Madala through the Mozambican intelligence Service when they learnt of his activities in that part of Africa. Hopefully he was duly taken care of in that jail environment by some really big overly affectionate jailbird mamas. I really appreciated that little gem of a black op perfectly arranged by Sam and Madala. That however still lay in the future and would be part of Sam's ultimate effort at getting back at the people who destroyed his life.

Murray was pretending to participate enthusiastically in this drunken orgy and very soon they were telling him the whole story in all its grotesque detail. They were tasked as a result of a joint operational decision by dr. Becker of national intelligence and general Whitlock of military intelligence. This followed a private briefing by Pedro 1 - indicating Sam's criticism of the government and his belief that this constituted a threat against the state - acting on direct instructions from the president's office after the failed attempt on Sam's life. President Craven knew the detail and gave the go-ahead for the state agencies to terrorise Sam and his family. This betrayal by Pedro 1 was quite shocking given the fact that Sam served him with loyalty when he was chief staff intelligence. How was Sam to know that Pedro 1 would betray him when he confided in him some time before these events took place regarding his concerns about the road Craven was placing the country on? Sam would never forgive this cynical action taken by Pedro 1 and he swore in years to come that he would take revenge on Pedro 1 wherever he found him. The attempt on Sam's life was driven by dr Bana under the auspices of the surgeon general of the defence force and executed by dr. Philip during the medal ceremony that was held for Ray some years before.

The two drunks explained to Murray in some detail how they were instructed to destroy Sam financially while exerting all manner of pressures on Jackie to place strain on her and through her on their children. The idea was that Sam would collapse financially and ultimately psychologically and that he would then be unable to support any kind of resistance against Craven and his fellow traitors, who were hell bent on handing the country to the enemy without securing any real political rights for minorities. Murray confirmed all the pressure signals that Sam was experiencing in precise detail. These signals entailed car tails, the break-in at his office before he was fired by his own directors, telephone taps, running up his phone bill, intercepting and reading his mail, exerting pressure on the bank to close his accounts, refusing to cash Jackie's cheques and contacting all potential employers with negative reports, all perpetrated by two substantial intelligence teams with two cars packed with electronic surveillance devices and money to burn.

Murray recalled how Sam told him about the weird circumstances under which another man close to a leader died of complications after contracting chicken pox of all things. This man was prime minister Balthazar's son Peter, who protested against his father's known political assassination and alienation from the party inner circle by Burton and his political cronies. Sam was pretty sure at the time that dr Bana and the medical battalion killed him under instruction from Burton. It would have been only one of the strange deaths that occurred during this time that remained cloaked in a haze of uncertainty for years to come. There was a sick irony in all of this whereby when leaders have run their course, advisors or close allies are always attacked when the stakes are high. He could not help thinking at the time that all politicians seem to attract this kind of behaviour. Deceit and murder seems to follow in powerful men's footsteps as if they pave the way for death and its disciples. When they die like all humans do, their empty ambitions die with them and all they leave behind is darkness and cruelty and the nightmares that come in the night suffered by the men who simply tried to do the right thing.

Sam and Murray agreed that running and hiding would for the time being be the best solution to the problem of possible injury inflicted on his family or himself. They stood up to leave the coffee shop.

Sam said, 'You go first, Murray. You do not want to be seen with me.'

'No', Murray complained, 'screw them, Sam. Walk out with me. I am not afraid of Craven or for that matter any of his henchmen. They are a bunch of fucking weaklings anyway. Keep your ammo dry and your gun cycled, my friend. They will kill you if they get the opportunity under the guise of the proper cover story.'

They hugged each other briefly and went their different ways.

It was the third day of my working visit with Sam and Jackie. Sam and I were sitting with our backs against a tree after a very long walk that particular morning. Sam had just completed a detailed description of the surrounding area to me and commented how content he was to be able to walk and savour the clean air and open horizons. Then he sat upright and plunged straight into a new part of his story.

'Strange how fortuitously you sometimes meet someone so extraordinary that makes a huge difference to your life. I met Madala during a social gathering at Uncle Paul's house during middle 1991. Uncle Paul's son - a wild young man who served in the infamous Koevoet (Crowbar) unit during the Bush War - was very vocal about his personal prowess. That evening I noticed a man of stocky build in gold rimmed glasses with the look of a soldier about him, sporting a neatly trimmed short grey beard with sinewy inwardly arched hands showing clear signs of significant martial arts activity. He was looking at the young fool with an amused smile. The same young man shot and killed an innocent black man some years later and was charged with murder. He escaped with the help of an imaginative, but treacherous Frenchman - who cut his teeth in Algeria as a Foreign Legion soldier - and hid away in Portugal until his mother died tragically. He went back home and was arrested and still languishes in jail.

'This was an unbelievable story and psychologically quite complex, albeit stupid and indicative of the madness of our time and our insanely religious based ideology. This ideology allowed untrustworthy and unethical people amongst us to assist criminal elements who broke the law, with the exclusion of all personal values of right and wrong. I steered away from the discussion and eventually escaped and sat next to the stranger. He introduced himself and we exchanged some ideas. It quickly became clear that we originated from similar backgrounds and that we held similar views on several pressing political and military matters of the day. At the end of the evening we agreed to meet again. Just before he drove off

Madala said to me, 'Based on what you have told me and what subsequently happened to you, you will never work in this place ever again. Contact me, we can possibly work together ...'

'Some months after this meeting I was invited by Uncle Paul who had by then retired from the Bureau for Information - the previous Government's propaganda organisation where he was transferred to from Military Intelligence - to attend another meeting at a dr Williams' house one evening in late 1991 to discuss the direction the country was taking under Craven's 'new country' initiative. Dr Williams built our nukes, a few other retired fellow officers and some scientists who previously worked with him on Project Kilo Tango and the full nuclear program at Pelindaba attended. Madala was also there. Everyone present was so confident and arrogantly self-assured and a plan of action was outlined to attempt to stop Craven from selling the country out to our enemy. The leader of the movement also represented one of the far right resistance groups. A brief outline was given as to the strategic aims of the group; to act as resistance to Craven's already fast developing handover to a newly elected government after a democratic election that was planned for 1994.

'Uncle Paul was always confident and quite vocal in his utterances about Craven and about how we would stop him with a popular armed uprising. I was horrified about all of this because as you know I spent a large part of my military career working with revolutionary organisations in Africa in a black ops environment and I had a fundamental understanding of the requirements for such actions. These people were clearly not prepared for what it takes. Uncle Paul took a deep breath after one such long explanation of how we would take over the government and how we would kill all our enemies and gazed across the room directly at Madala and asked, 'Do you agree?"

'I caught his eye just before he started talking. We already had a tacit understanding stemming from earlier discussions about working together, after we met that evening at Uncle Paul's house. We were also quite clear about the circumstances under which we would be prepared to get involved with this kind of subversive activity. I need not have worried. Madala was quite accurate with his reaction amongst all those so-called revolutionary experts. He came upright from his chair and said, 'Uncle Paul, if you want to destroy yourself and your group and all hope, you have to pursue this ill conceived and probably badly executed plan. If instead you are not willing to start with proper counter intelligence orientated activity that entails all of us undergoing security scrutiny first, you will fail. If anyone was found lacking in honesty all of you will have to accept personal responsibility to remove traitors. Combined with that, you will then have to consider all possible peaceful approaches within South Africa and internationally first, before embarking on a road of violence. If this is a problem, we may as well all go home. You have to send a strong message of no tolerance to determine what causes do to loyal servants of the state, while striving constantly to stay alive. Causes are actions reserved for politicians and other idiots.' Madala and I said our goodbyes and left these men with their immature plans that would in time come to nothing and land the majority of their followers and most of the original perpetrators in jail. It was one thing to theorise about rebellion. Executing it was quite another matter and best left to professionals, who understood the total, brutal price of such actions and that failing was never an option.

'Madala was an exceptional and resilient man and had survived similar persecution as I was experiencing twice during earlier years, but only in worse form. He escaped the attack in France, but was not so lucky in his own country. After his return from Cuba and Europe and the failed attack on his life, he was appointed as the Army Chief in the same black puppet state where Anthony was active as Intelligence Chief. The two men did not see eye to eye. This was in all probability due to the fact that they both essentially came from intelligence backgrounds, although Madala had extensive international experience and had suffered brutal experimental chemical preparation before he was deployed as a professional international assassin. Anthony however, was essentially trained as a spy handler working in and immediately around the country. This led to major differences between them not only regarding strategic matters but also tactical aspects. Anthony had an intense dislike of Madala and pronounced him an intelligence whore, based on his extensive international exposure and contacts. There was however never any doubt in my mind that Madala was the superior operator. He was not only older and more experienced, but he had also seen action in a far bigger international arena while the experimental part of his training exposed him to dynamics, capabilities and techniques far superior to and far more brutal than Anthony's training.

'The experimental training entailed a selection process during which the former theological student and qualified engineer was chosen to be prepared for single combat as an assassin with eleven other men from a significantly larger group of hopefuls.

The failure rate was significant. The selection process entailed psychiatric profiling and a variety of physical and mental tests. Eventually the final group was selected and their training began. The training course was divided into four distinct phases. The first was a psychological process during which time the student was first broken down to a basic level of being through a combination of physical challenges to the point of exhaustion and brutal suggestive therapy throughout, concomitant with a chemical treatment regimen. The aim was to produce an operative who was initially psychologically and chemically prepared and afterwards regularly conditioned through a quite severe medication regimen. The result was a constant haze of headaches and insomnia when inactive. Throughout this phase he was conditioned to accept and react to certain closely guarded long distance delivered trigger words - by telephone or radio - that would propel him into action at predetermined levels of proficiency. Secondly the candidate was trained in the full complement of the counter intelligence and intelligence gathering disciplines. The third phase focused on unarmed combat, martial arts and weapons training, the selection of personal weapons, sniper training and ultimately dedicated assassin's field craft. Madala excelled with the handgun and knife. This was followed by the last and final phase, which was a practical test phase in the company of a senior operative. Madala passed with flying colours and was internationally deployed to ply his new trade against carefully selected targets.

'Things are however never that simple. Some of the debilitating side effects of the 'preparatory drug treatment' were worsening headaches coupled with insomnia and once asleep, very dark and deeply troubling nightmares. Eventually eleven of the twelve initial candidates would die of suspected related causes after being operationally deployed and having experienced increasingly severe physical problems and eventually psychological side effects, which in combination was quite deadly. Only Madala survived and I remember clearly how even he struggled well into the nineties - many years after this conditioning and training. He always used to say to me, 'Sam - the monsters come in the night. Then I have to fight to stay alive.'

'During his time as Army Chief in the black puppet state a military coup was planned against the reigning and increasingly autocratic political leader. The plan was hatched between our country's Defence Force and the Department of Foreign Affairs, more specifically Minister Rangle, who had an underhand political escape route and get out of jail free card in the shape of Madala, to safeguard himself and his political career in case of failure. The coup went horribly wrong and the blame for the mess was placed squarely on Madala's shoulders. He was arrested and put on trial and jailed for a year and eventually transferred to the infamous C-Max prison in South Africa. Eventually after a massive legal battle he was released. Despite his self-discipline and strict physical training regimen in jail, the strain - especially in jail - eventually proved too much for Madala to bear and he succumbed to a stroke after his release. He fought back and within months he was on his feet but without a job, and as he often jokingly put it to me, 'minus my ability for instinctive calculus.' In jail he was incarcerated right next to and befriended a man who would play an important role once the revolutionary movement took over the reins in 1994. He was Conrad, a young white theological intellectual who supported the revolutionary action against white minority rule. This same man would play a momentary but important part in my life some years later after Madala arranged for me to meet him.'

'Our Government had jettisoned Madala and he was now entirely on his own. Except, The Rose was still interested and he stayed in touch and was again approached by his contact in Europe. Once he was reactivated, he was regularly deployed for missions in the international arena. He was very upbeat about the fact that he always did very well in the yearly Rose Pistol Shoots in Switzerland where the operatives competed in weapons handling.'

I was perplexed by this part of the story and asked Sam how it was possible for this man to work on two fronts without compromising his loyalty to his country and his own organisation.

Sam looked at me and said calmly, 'Madala was not your ordinary covert operative. He had a sense of what was really necessary to do at the time. He was a consummate professional whose capabilities far outstripped his home-grown training and activities. He saw light-years ahead and formed alliances to help him in his professional life while always retaining a fundamental loyalty to his own country. It started with his exposure to US Ranger training and his subsequent contact with the CIA. He never betrayed his country. He simply worked in a much bigger theatre. After the attempt on his life in France and his subsequent arrest and persecution for someone else's bullshit political agenda, many things changed though. Madala knew that his own country betrayed him and in a sense that set him free. That however still did not mean that he would betray his own country. It simply meant that he was able to sell his services to the highest bidder as a full-blown mercenary while maintaining a uniquely sympathetic and purist approach towards his own countrymen - amazing though it may seem after they tried to kill him. I believe he was a patriot his whole life long. He just chose to do his work in a most unique way. The Rose for one recognised that in him and was prepared to trust him.

'So, Madala and I found ourselves completely isolated at that stage. The white resistance movement was dissatisfied because we refused to involve ourselves with any actions that would end in disaster for sheer lack of basic planning and attention to detail. The last white government was very concerned about me and what role I would be able to play while they were certainly very suspicious of everything that Madala was involved in after his release from prison. Against this background we followed the only logical path left for us to follow. We consciously agreed that we would form a loose partnership in everything, namely commercial enterprise and political views and that from then on we would follow a strictly mercenary approach. In short, we worked only for money and left the rest to the politicians, their adversaries and their gods, each clearly uniquely suited to the many Afrikaner splinter groups.'

Chapter XII

100% Sale

When the constitutional negotiations at Kempton Park's World Trade Centre commenced between 1991 and 1993 all experienced operational military personnel who knew the opposition intimately were specifically excluded. This was partly due to Craven's inherent pacifist personal make-up, underscored by his fear of a white-based military coup once his betrayal of his own people became clear. His mind was set on keeping the military at arm's length. That created a situation where certain crucial information that the military obtained never featured during the talks. The core of the information that was confidentially given to the military and that the ANC wanted added to the existing agenda was as follows: - the white Afrikaner minority would be given a piece of land enabling them to practice their unique culture; - similarly other minority rights would be constitutionally guaranteed; - furthermore the principle would be accepted that should full amnesty be granted to the ANC, they would similarly not prosecute anyone linked to the white government after they took control. With the exclusion of the military from the peace talks the government negotiators were none the wiser and consequently these specific points were dropped from the ANC agenda. This would ultimately have profound implications for the white minority in the eventual peace settlement. Under scoring this was a secret financial reward arrangement whereby all the white government conspirators were paid eye-watering amounts of money with the help of international interests.

The negotiations were a complete and utter farce and compromised all minorities in the country. It was also the mechanism by which all individuals who could have assisted with a better dispensation for minorities were effectively neutralised. While the preparations for the Kempton Park negotiations were being made, Craven had to ensure that all possible resistance was squashed and that all knowledgeable people - especially in the defence force - were neutralised as he feared a coup more than anything else. Sam's persecution was based on the white government's fear of his influence in terms of his long-term relationship with Burton. This was an early example of several such operations that were undertaken to 'remove' anyone remotely capable of assisting with the launching of a coup and dismantling of the peace negotiations.

The reality was that Sam always found it quite unthinkable to subvert the state. The persistent persecution he was being subjected to - however deeply contradictory his experience might have been in view of his career as a soldier - literally forced him to get to the facts of the matter. Such action was however always problematic for him, having been grounded in an intelligence discipline underwritten by vigilance and knowledge and more than anything else, loyalty to the government of the day.

This was especially significant since all of the high-ranking politicians of the time who were involved with the negotiations had subsequently received typewritten threats that they would be tracked down and eliminated if they persisted with their efforts to betray the country. The intelligence community took these threats seriously and a long and arduous investigation followed. The members of a shadowy organisation 'Die Binnekring' (The Inner Circle) who sent out the letters - the emblem of a rifle telescope crosshairs and the words 'Die Binnekring' adorned the top of each letter - were however mysteriously never identified. The documentation had been meticulously sanitised and mailed from several different locations. With no fingerprints, no DNA traces and postage origins dispersed, no clear pattern emerged. Whoever did this knew were technically astute. The threats from this apparently small grouping however came to nothing since the time for revolt had long since passed and even the most ardent of Afrikaner patriots were already jockeying for positions within the new political dispensation. Faced with this reality clearly none of the members of 'Die Binnekring' would be prepared to risk their lives for a cause that was no longer relevant.

To add to the chaos within the military Craven furthermore used a former Air Force general specialising in personnel matters - and newly appointed as Secretary for Defence - to eliminate opposition to the sell out. General Petrie, a man who was known for not being able to hold his liquor and a loud braggart at heart, identified twenty-three senior officers that needed getting rid of. The charges against them were mostly trumped up and it was quite evident right from the start that they were intended to be paraded as examples to any other soldiers who would dare to oppose the betrayal orchestrated by Craven. Most of these men lost everything they had and the wife of a former commanding officer of special forces had to be committed to a psychiatric institution following a complete mental breakdown after the cruel and calculated persecution of her husband. Sam's friend general Christian was paraded in due course as the main culprit and was fired from his position of Military Intelligence second in command.

Simultaneously Craven reneged on a promise former president Burton had made to the former Namibian Territorial Force and 'Koevoet' (Crowbar) members. The promise was that they would be given safe passage to South Africa after the war and that they would be able to live out their days there in peace. This never happened. Craven betrayed all these men except for a few older 32 Battalion soldiers originally recruited from Angolan rebel groups who entered the country earlier and who still live in South Africa, where their position remains deeply uncertain if not downright tragic. It is said that many of these former allies of the South African forces in Namibia who were not taken to South Africa in time, were ultimately hunted like animals and routinely shot in the back while being chased with military vehicles in the rural areas as they fled on foot after the SWAPO take-over of Namibia.

Craven's despicable betrayal of specifically military personnel did not end here. During a quite sad farewell function for a fellow and already quite ill persecuted friend, Colonel Moore, one evening at a military mess in Pretoria, Sam met Colonel King who was responsible for processing all formal approvals for special forces 'black ops' during that time. He would personally and regularly take the paperwork from 'Die Kop' (Swartkop) to Craven's office in the Union Buildings. Craven would sign it after which the operation went ahead. During the later hearings where the new government tried to establish the truth, Craven denied all knowledge of these operations or the papers he signed. He effectively hung his soldiers out to dry by blatantly lying and refusing to admit any knowledge of these operations. What made this occasion even sadder was the fact that Moore ignored Sam completely during this function, despite the fact that he supported Moore quite openly under often arduous conditions and instead thanked everyone around him quite conspicuously. Sam left the function early and never spoke to Moore again. The act of betrayal was clearly no longer reserved for politicians.

General Christian ultimately decided to take legal action against Craven following his unfair dismissal. The matter was settled and the tale of the final meeting between them in the presence of their legal teams after Craven had already left office is now the stuff of legend. So it was that Christian finally walked into the room with his lawyers and came face to face with Craven and his legal team. The lawyers spoke and the message was that Craven would pay him R1M (about £89,000) to keep the whole unpleasant dispute about Christian's unfair dismissal out of court for Craven's political gain and to prevent unwanted publicity. Craven stepped forward with his usual pacifist smile and offered his hand to Christian.

Christian looked at the man he despised as a traitor and said, 'I will not shake your hand and I do not want your money. I only want an unconditional apology signed by you so that my family will know who I am and who you are.'

He then turned to his lawyer and said while sniffing the air, 'I cannot breathe this foul air. Can we please go now?'

Needless to say, Craven signed the apology and in the end

Christian got some restitution and his children knew who he was and who Craven was. General Christian - a proud, brave, professional soldier - never forgave Craven for what he had done and to this day he despises the man and everything he stood for.

During this time of the persecution of senior military officers Sam visited the offices of the then finance minister Bartholomew to discuss with him his take on what was happening and to assess not only his own position, but also the extent of a negative atmosphere in the higher echelons of government.

Sam related to me his meeting with Bartholomew as follows. 'As I sat in the waiting room at the ministry I thought about my relationship with this person. I knew him as a chance friend during the time of president Burton's rule as he was to be the crown prince earmarked as a possible successor after the president's retirement. I originally met him at a function I was obliged to attend at the president's invitation during better times. That was however all in the distant past and the intended succession never happened since Craven was already in control after the silent coup was executed against president Burton. Craven merely stepped forward as the conspiracy group's front man. I knew that Bartholomew was not a courageous man and that he would probably be reluctant to resist any wrongdoing by the Craven government. This referred back to a surreal incident several years before during an elephant hunt where I was present as the occasion happened under the auspices of UNITA in the southeastern province of Angola and I was an accompanying officer with practical hunting and tracking experience. Bartholomew was given an opportunity to shoot an elephant cow at the back of the herd. He eagerly took aim with the .458 caliber rifle at about 150 yards and hit the animal in the spine from the rear. I saw how the rear of the spine bone sections jumped up starkly in the air like a snow-white house of cards as the heavy caliber big game bullet tore into the animal. Her rear quarter collapsed first after which she fell to the left with a huge sigh. We walked closer and I said, 'Shoot the animal, Bart.' Bartholomew looked at the wound and the tears streaming from the stricken elephant cow's eyes. He could barely conceal his complete horror at the damage the bullet had caused. He said in a barely audible voice, 'I cannot do that, Sam. I simply cannot do that. You please see to it.' I looked at him and said, 'You are the hunter, Bart. This is it. It is nothing more and nothing less.' I held up one of my rifle cartridges between my fingers. 'This is the reality of the hunt. You have to finish what you have started. You cannot delegate this solemn responsibility to me.' Bartholomew simply could not face the situation and he turned on his heel and walked away from the wounded animal. He was brave enough to take the shot from one hundred and fifty yards, but he could not face up to the reality of having to finish the job standing right next to the animal. I was angry at this display of cowardice. I cycled the .375 H&H Magnum I carried in my role as backup, pressed the barrel lightly against the elephant's head between those two wet eyes and pulled the trigger. The rifle thumped and I stood and watched silently until the eyes had lost its shine. I extracted the empty cartridge case, slammed the rifle bolt forward, engaged the safety catch, cursed softly to myself, turned and walked away. Around me the butchers were already closing in with loud whoops of childlike joy, ready to dissect the carcass with long bladed knives and eager to distribute the meat amongst the men. I wanted to be sick and I could never hunt with any dedication again after this incident. In the distance I could see the cowardly Bartholomew standing, nervously fidgeting with his rifle. I never forgot this display of cowardice. It was a stark reminder of how politicians were very happy to send soldiers to their deaths from afar while never being remotely capable of facing up to the realities and mostly the worst consequences of their deeds up close and personally. In my book his actions or rather inactions were clearly deeply cowardly.

'I walked into Bartholomew's office and remembered that I was always slightly amused at the conspicuous splendour with which these offices were decorated. There was very often more than one expensive carpet overlaying another while the walls were covered in expensive artwork, clearly not always reflecting the depth of artistic sensitivity of the person who inhabited the specific space, but rather the touch of some money-grabbing interior decorator. It was quite evidently a display to impress others. Similarly the furniture was modern and lavish and displayed a certain other worldly character in a country where poverty and suffering were so prevalent.'

'Bartholomew rose behind the desk and called out, "Hi Sam, M'friend, how are you today?" That use of the phrase 'm'friend' always irritated me beyond all logical comprehension for the invasive casual closeness it suggests. Bart smiled his familiar affected smile and laughed just that little bit too loud, indicating his self-importance in his surroundings. I watched his eyes and the unfeeling expression displayed did not escape me. I thought, 'I am not your friend, you damn coward.' But of course, always being the polite intelligence operative who needed to get results while setting personal preferences aside, I reacted with a well-practiced smile while hiding my real thoughts behind my eyes. Bartholomew gestured towards the large and lavishly furnished informal discussion area to the side of the office overlooking the city. Through the large windows I noticed the clear view of the western and northern suburbs where so many of the soldiers came from - mostly working class or self employed families. Their rich counterparts - who most fortuitously for them did not serve the fatherland as soldiers due to the evasive efforts of their rich and influential parents - mostly hailed from the eastern and southern suburbs where the professional, corporate and government members of the white society lived in the lap of luxury. The utterly chaotic, red dusty sidewalks filled to the brim with peddlers sitting underneath the Jacaranda trees were clearly visible and evident of the difference between these areas and the carefully manicured environs of the richer suburbs. There was a wind blowing that day and the twitchy dust devils skirting the streets reminded me of Sector 20, Cuando Cubango, Luanda, Maputo, Bata, Kinshasa, Harare, Khartoum, Abidjan, Franceville, all places I knew like the back of my hand, all with the inevitable surrounding slums and desolate outlying areas where death and brutality were always prevalent. These places resembled mindless killing fields from some surreal half poetic Faustian underworld. Doomed bodies seemed to be everywhere, gasping for air and retching forth filth with huge mournful sighs with blood pouring from gaping wounds, severed limbs and wide open silent screaming mouths lined with white teeth soiled with blood and dust. All the different smells of plants, people, vehicles, fire and smoke and noise seem to merge into one amorphous mass that is the

Africa where we lived for so many torturous years and that seemed to be represented by those sidewalks. It is so complex to describe the strange mixture of memories of neat military training, home and strike bases and the chaos and bloody reality of war and ensuing mindless killing for gain after armies have passed through. What chaos have we released on our land and how did we survive the bloodletting and where are all the promises? How did we not see the lies and the eternally cursed money underscoring everything?'

Sam looked at me with staring eyes. I realised for the first time since we met all those years ago in Sector 20 that my knowledge of what he had seen over the years was less of a shock than a revelation to me about the state of man in a so called modern western world, that is consistently oblivious of what is really happening in its distant filthy underbelly that used to be the European colonial stomping ground. It seemed suddenly as if the prevalent darkness had changed Sam forever, having brought him to the brink of his own destruction where the smell of death and decay became so overwhelming that breathing had become just about impossible. Before I could contemplate the depth of this darkness any further Sam resumed talking about his surreal albeit revealing meeting with Bartholomew.

'Bart spoke with his familiar deep semi-intellectual mathematics teacher's voice when he asked, "what is there that can I do for you today Sam? How are Jackie and your children?" I ignored all of these feeble attempts at being civil and went straight to what I wanted to tell him. I was irritated with the man and I clearly remembered the incident with the wounded elephant cow. 'Listen here, Bart, excluding the defence force from the negotiations at Kempton Park will create an opportunity for the opposition to grab all of the spoils simply because of lack of knowledge on the government's side. We both know that Craven is a weak tenderfoot with no real-world pre- or post-armed conflict negotiation experience and that the government negotiation team does not possess the wherewithal to complete this task successfully. They have not had the same exposure to the enemy the soldiers have had and the real risk exists that many critical aspects that may affect several minority groups in the country may simply slip through the floorboards. The illustrious leader of our team, Baier, has never seen any action but instead served his time in the armed forces in the official Air Force choir, the Canaries. He will lose by default Bart, simply because he is too inexperienced and was never really exposed to the enemy. The opposition will have his guts for garters and I implore you to use your influence to obtain permission for some experienced soldiers to assist with the negotiations.

'For good measure I repeated the story of how I once waited for Baier in Cuando Cubango. He was on an official visit. I was surrounded by an experienced protection squad of some fifty UNITAS armed to the teeth with assault rifles, hand grenades and RPG 7s. I explained to Bart my impression of Baier's eyes when he stepped from the chopper after the dust settled. I saw in his eyes that he was scared witless that day and how the counter intelligence major Jan standing in the shade of a thorn tree shouted at me when he saw Baier, drawing my attention to the scared look on his face.

'We cannot have a scared man negotiating on our behalf, Bart. We need real experience in that firing line. The opposition is not stupid. They have several well trained minds waiting for us.'

Sam took a deep breath and continued, 'I purposely held back on the information I had regarding the land and amnesty issues and decided to give Bart a chance to react first. I had no idea what his reaction would be.'

'Listen here, Sam,' Bart said while spreading his well manicured fingers with distinctly long black knuckle hair on the backrest of the armchair, 'these matters are best left to the politicians and other experts who are knowledgeable about the affairs of state. You Military Intelligence types, and the idiots from National Intelligence, are always dramatising matters while talking so much bullsh-t. You are unable to contribute anything of value to the debate. In any event, you are specifically soldiers and you do not know about these sophisticated political matters.'

'There was nothing more to be said. Any attempt to convince this man would have been wasted simply because of Bart's inability to comprehend an environment where he never worked and consequently could not grasp. The meeting was over and Sam left without revealing the information about the land and the general amnesty the opposition was contemplating.

Almost at the same time dr. Becker of the NIS decided to hand over all the operational files of covert operatives from NIS and the Defence Force to Craven's new government. This started a huge witch hunt as it coincided with the negotiations at Kempton Park and especially the Truth and Reconciliation Committee's activities that started during this time. These files would ultimately be handed over to the future new black government. After that the witch hunt deepened with leaps and bounds.

It was important for the last white government to create an environment where the outside world would be convinced that the country was on its way to becoming something shiny and bright, while the new white government officials and politicians raided the money coffers and pushed the country into near bankruptcy, something the black government would be blamed for after the take-over in 1994. The new catchword for most everything that was happening was 'new'. So much so that many humorous stories were fabricated and spread around regarding the 'new country' slogan used ad nauseam by Craven. Commercial advertising latched onto this and designed all their advertising to fit in with the new nation-building frenzy. Beer advertising became such a near national symbol that later on it was difficult to distinguish between advertisement and reality The song *Shozaloza* rang out loudly over most radio and television stations.

But, underpinning the euphoria was a dangerous and brutal political darkness that would ultimately place minorities in the country in enormous danger while a fortunate few at the top of the social ladder were making millions. The dawn of 'true democracy' and 'true capitalism' had arrived for this new 'rainbow nation' the name the aged leader of the revolutionary group who was released from jail after having been incarcerated for twenty-seven years gave the land. Old scores were settled right across the country and political groupings jumped up right across the political spectrum.

The election followed the near one-sided negotiations at Kempton Park and with the ensuing 100% sale, it was all over within what seemed like days and 342 years were gone as if it had never existed. The outcome of the election was never in doubt; the majority won and all minorities were now at the mercy of the opposition Freedom Movement who were forming a new government. Craven was part of that first government, but it was soon clear that he would not last. He was a treacherous man and immediately clashed with the new governing elite. Eventually Sam would warn the new government against him through a back channel to the then Minister of Justice and that would ultimately contribute to Craven's dismissal from the cabinet. This first black government had no problem with accepting what Sam said to them. They understood Sam's background and respected him for that. It was not difficult to accept when he told them that Craven was a traitor to his own people and that he would betray them too.

It is strange how combatants ultimately tend to accept each other's word more readily, especially when a politician is in the crosshairs. This respectful understanding was clearly demonstrated some time later after the election when a meeting - arranged by Madala - followed between Sam and Conrad - a prominent white member of the new government.

Sam was quiet for a moment and then said softly, 'I suppose I could have expected nothing else from Bart. He did not have the guts to kill a suffering elephant that he had wounded and subsequently in later years - after he was a party to the sale of our country in the company of other weaklings - he turned to extreme religious convictions to soothe his rotten conscience. I sincerely hope that when I meet him in the afterlife that elephant cow will be waiting for him with me. I will not stand in her way when she decides to trample him into a pulp.'

I answered with 'Sela', and held out my hand to Sam to help him from his chair.

We walked to the house from where Jackie called us for a warm meal and some rest. We had a lot to talk about the following day and I was exhausted.

Chapter XIII

The Real Friend

Strange happenings were the order of the day over the following years during which time Sam and Madala oscillated between several extremes in the course of their daily lives. Sam was still working for the Avionics Company, but he was struggling to stay afloat mainly because of the ongoing government harassment. Madala's marriage to a religiously fanatical and political extremist woman was gradually failing. This woman - Mabel - would play a devastating role in the future in both his and Sam's lives. Madala's close association with an attractive and astute business woman - Rowena - did not help matters. He did however find some solace in this relationship and Sam always felt that this business association that became much more than that, and would later sustain him during the most difficult years of his life.

Sam was always prepared to give Madala the benefit of the doubt. The profoundly cynical background of international black ops and espionage they shared taught him succinctly that self-righteousness was a luxury that he was not entitled to. During their entire time together Sam often differed significantly from Madala. They however maintained their deepening friendship and Sam regarded him as his mentor during a very turbulent time in his life.

Their friendship never faltered and there was never the slightest indication of disloyalty or distrust. I suppose in a philosophical sense they were truly blood brothers. They had some business successes in the security advisory environment in Africa, but they mostly struggled to compete in a new marketplace where the new government dictated the rules and where corruption and nepotism were fast becoming the norms underscored by impenetrable black tribal loyalties.

Sam was consistently trying to keep his head down, but it was clear that the intelligence agencies watched all his activities with a paranoid precision that was typical of an acrimonious handover of political power, so success remained elusive. Sam's health was deteriorating progressively and that did not help him with his efforts to rebuild his life after the disastrous eighties. None of the medications seemed to help him as the chemical weapon administered to him at Ray's recognition lunch created havoc in his body. Sam was given a new drug administered intravenously. The effect was immediate, but relatively short-term and when he developed an allergic reaction and nearly died, far greater care had to be taken with his condition.

He told me how on that occasion a former military nurse saved him and the military doctor who rushed into his room at the hospital and appeared on the scene where he was literally suffocating after an allergic reaction. The doctor consulted in the hospital and the nurse was on duty in that ward on the day. He told me how when the doctor stood next to his bed he heard her ask the nurse, 'Is he ex-military?' The nurse who knew Sam well said, 'Yes, many years service', Sam came upright and tried to breathe. The doctor pushed him back and said softly close to his ear, 'Lie back soldier. I won't let you die.' It was like old times where the reassuring hands of military medical personnel were always close by to save the day. He never forgot that. At this stage no one, including Sam, even remotely considered the possibility that he might have been attacked with a chemical agent. This reality would only surface after Sam and Jackie had already fled the country to live in Europe.

Sam had already left the defence force in 1987, but something significant now occurred that would place him in an interesting position to observe the process during which the country was handed over to the Freedom Movement. Just before the take-over in 1994 he was recruited by a colonel Dan to work for military intelligence in a civilian capacity as an undercover intelligence operative.

The first project that he was asked to tackle was the obtaining of the detailed plans for a project in one of the neighbouring states. This project entailed the building of a military strike base of significant proportions that could potentially pose a major threat to the safety of the country. He had indirect access to the plans and successfully intercepted and photographed all the airbase drawings and consequently provided a major database to military intelligence for the complete development, namely physical layout and avionics installations of the airbase. The drawings were originally requested and made available to the avionics contractor for planning purposes. This was a major security breach on the part of the contracting state that could be exploited. The uniquely modern operating principle of the base was that troops would be housed on the base and processed from their living quarters through all the different phases including rest, ablutions, meals, medical check-ups, issuing of weapons and gear and then embarked for air transportation to the battlefield. This time saving process presented a real threat to all neighbouring states simply because of the potential for rapid deployment of any potential attacking force based on the international relations of the host state.

The twist to this tale is that the handler Sam worked with during this time was one of three traitors. Two of them were Sam's handlers at different times and one an intelligence colleague responsible for handling target identification with special forces with whom he had occasional contact. The three sold intelligence to other agencies right throughout this period. Sam was always at risk and so were all other operatives that were exposed to these men. Such was the dark time we lived in and such were the bribes that once loyal soldiers turned traitors were prepared to accept in an attempt to buy their new political master's confidence while also enriching themselves. This betrayal would only show much later and would add to Sam's exposure in an already totally prostituted intelligence community. One of these men was the Englishman Keys, who was slippery and treacherous, the ex-colonial Portuguese Ant, who was soft spoken and believable; and the Afrikaner West, who mainly served with special forces in a target identification liaison role. He was a drunken, often dishevelled looking, boaster with absolutely no conscience and once proclaimed that he would personally assassinate a high profile opposition politician. A Polish foreigner, under the guidance of a local far right fanatic, subsequently shot the man in the driveway of his home. These two men were ultimately both caught and incarcerated for life. This was the madness of that time. The three traitors caused the defence force immeasurable harm, but they would never be exposed for what they really were. Sam would only determine the true facts many years later through a later trusted associate, Oscar. Sam respected Oscar for his diligence, honesty and bravery. He was able to ascribe most of Sam's ill fortune and near escapes from the intelligence services that were always on the prowl for new cases and file creation – accentuated by so-called threats against the state which were mostly based on unfounded, untested and often fabricated evidence - to these three men.

General conditions in the services remained atrocious during this period. Even where loyal soldiers worked diligently for the intelligence service, they would still be prone to surveillance and possible persecution through the direction of higher authorities that would ultimately use them for intelligence work and blame afterwards once it became clear what the political spoils really entailed.

Something completely out of the ordinary transpired that was to give Sam a final insight into the extent to which the country was already compromised internationally. It was after the 1994 intelligence deactivation period. Sam had already been re-hired as an undercover operative after a brief interlude during the elections. At this time all similar agents were paid substantial amounts in advance and put on hold and out of reach temporarily pending the outcome. This allowed the election process to run its course, after which they were reinstated by a command structure that remained largely intact.

Late one afternoon Sam was being debriefed regarding recent projects at one of the outlying military intelligence safe houses.

A discussion ensued about British intelligence involvement in the country and Sam confirmed that he was aware of the activities of a certain British national, Riley, who came from a position elsewhere in Africa and who consulted for the same electronics company Sam was employed by. In addition to this work with the company that brought him close to the heart of government through mainly defence force programs, Riley was now also involved in a major recruitment drive and training program for British intelligence in the country. This was the beginning of a significant double operation. Sam would 'work' for British intelligence by offering them so-called qualified information which they would hopefully regard as the real thing and in so doing military intelligence would be enabled to get closer to and ultimately expose collaborators and British agents that - together with other international agencies - were using the country as a springboard for African-wide operations. The country was rapidly losing its independence and sinking back into colonial serfdom that would prevail when Craven completed his betrayal and once Burton was attacked and deposed. Strangely enough, the handler that managed this project was the same overweight officer major Brown that Sam, Murray and their mates had been subjected to years before during the training course and equipment 'theft' incident at 11 Commando.

During this project discussion, Sam felt oddly detached as he was then quite far removed from the core of military operations. Despite his inherent concerns about the safety of the state and the value of the operation to counter any national threats having to work for the 'enemy' was complicated and hard to maintain. Brown asked, 'How serious do you believe the threat against the state to be, Sam?' Sam gave him an expressionless stare and the thought did occur to him that this fat man could not possibly be aware of any of the real threats against the country, simply because of his inability to be socially mobile enough to observe the different theatres of operation that were already activated in commerce, parastatals, the religious community, trade unions and universities. Sam did not respect this character and more than anything else, this probably placed increased strain on the operation. For any double operation to be successful the relationship of absolute trust and confidence between the operative and handler was crucial. 'I believe the threat to be quite significant,' he answered.

He left it at that, because Brown mentioned to him that he would be replaced by a new handler who ultimately proved to be professional and clearly the real deal. Sam was relieved that Brown was out of the immediate loop, but it did concern him that he would remain in an oversight position at the intelligence covert collections headquarters. His replacement was Oscar, a man Sam immediately trusted because of his uncomplicated and direct approach to all matters.

So it was that Sam travelled west one windy day. Shadowy red dust swirled angrily around the shaking truck on the neglected road to his destination. Sam was lost in thought about the war and the fast changing times. He suddenly realised with some irritation that he had taken the wrong turnoff and missed the road to the rendezvous point where a new and alarmingly threatening chapter in his life would begin. He slammed the brakes on, turned sharply to the left, the ageing off-road vehicle's unforgiving rigid rear suspension gave way and the wheels spun awkwardly on the gravel road shoulder. He was angry at allowing his mind to wander off into the past. This was not true to his carefully honed and observant professional nature. Riley was waiting, with all his apparent intellectual superiority, suave style, his carefree colonial demeanour and knighthood for hunting KGB operatives in Eastern Europe and back home, and Sam was now quite late for the meeting.

He turned the vehicle onto the narrow road and started racing back to the point where he had missed the turnoff. In his mind he was already beginning to run through the 'agenda' of the most devious operation of deception he had ever attempted, luring Riley into paying him to 'betray' his country.

He picked up the mobile and dialled Riley's number, 'Hi Mr Riley, apologies please, I am a bit late. Be with you in twenty.'

He turned into the hotel parking lot, stopped and checked for a cartridge in the cycled .45 ACP semi-automatic under his left armpit with a smile. He hooked his left index finger under the lower front of the slide and pushed back just enough to be able to see in the chamber before re-inserting the weapon in the holster. What an insignificant and slightly out of place reassurance in this intensely complicated web of intrigue. He rushed past the casino where dozens of glazed eyed hopefuls yanked at one armed bandits and leaned expectantly over alluring gambling tables and eventually reached the reception desk where he inquired briefly as to Riley's whereabouts. He hurriedly entered the plush resort hotel dining room and immediately noticed the man.

Riley was lounging at a window table, his muscular frame as always carefully hidden under loose fitting brushed cotton garments. He cut the figure of the typical English gentleman who was apparently completely at home in Africa. Even his thatched roof house situated to the west of Johannesburg displayed that self assured colonial atmosphere where a large Land Rover Discovery stood in the shade of the lush trees outside; the relaxed atmosphere of the house furnishings and his graceful young wife who always seemed eager to please the great white English African hunter at all times. All too frequently though she appeared to be more of an expert assistant than a wife.

He grinned broadly and called across the room, 'Hi Sam, good to see you. How are things at the Company?'

Sam nodded and said, 'Everything's okay, thanks Riley. We miss your presence.'

Sam thought that was enough said as he wanted to steer the discussion into the direction of the 'training program'. Riley appeared relaxed and a broad smile spread over his sun tanned face. Sam sat down, rolled over like a well trained dog and immediately allowed Riley to start manipulating his erroneously inferior, misguided persona while observing him with his unseen eye behind the eye, suddenly quite relaxed and with each carefully honed sense alert and not missing a beat.

This relationship was always complicated. Riley was an expert trained operative and Sam had to watch him like a hawk. What surfaced here by virtue of Riley's ever so slightly over-inflated ego though, was an extensive operation whereby he acted as the coordinator of a recruitment and training program for a new 'super police force' - the 'Scorpions' - that would mainly investigate major commercial crimes committed within the state system and the associated commercial world. Riley's ego could simply not resist the alluring questions from Sam about his important role. He let slip several items of information simply because he completely underestimated Sam's abilities and consequently missed the battle signs. The candidates for the 'super police force' were all selected by a combined state and private consulting panel, of which Riley was the leading player. The selection process was reinforced by a carefully planned recruitment procedure, during which most of the successful super-police-force candidates were also signed up as sleepers by British intelligence to be activated at a later stage. Huge rewards in the form and shape of large amounts of cash and gifts such as luxurious white goods and TV sets, accompanied this recruitment drive.

Sam's specific offer to Riley entailed providing apparently significant, but instead carefully edited, intelligence regarding African Freedom Movements thereby luring British Intelligence into exposing greater detail of their spy network in the country. He succeeded in doing this by convincing Riley of his apparently underlying far-right and thus willing-to-deal-for-a-price sentiments by confirming in discussion that he would never support any new political dispensation. In this process and through his ongoing contact and association with Riley, Sam and his associates at military intelligence succeeded in photographing and documenting most of Riley's network members as he contacted them over time.

Sam very soon warned the government about the danger of a consistent penetration of the country by major foreign powers. With the USA, Russian and French (who supplied the white government with weapons for many years) intelligence services already underway the country was fast becoming fertile ground for foreign intelligence activities, while its own intelligence capabilities were declining fast. This episode gave Sam a valuable insight into the extent of foreign espionage in the country and how that defined everything that happened from then on. Ultimately however, Sam's double operation was torpedoed by a macho black general, who changed the reporting structure from a quality to quantity-based format. More reports implied increased payment, which quickly led to a proliferation of fabricated intelligence reports with questionable content to fit the intelligence requirement. Sam's role came to a halt under these conditions as, he was unwilling to exchange quality for quantity. His activities were stopped and he withdrew into the woodwork. A few years later his handler 'Juliet' would contact him and relate how she was asked during a reporting session what had happened to the agent that supplied the initial intelligence and whether his double operation could be restarted. She stood up, collected her files and replied quite bluntly, 'You let him go, General.' She offered an apology citing another meeting and walked out the door. A few weeks after that incident she resigned. Like so many good operators she disappeared and the country became more vulnerable for it. Thus during 2002 Sam's undercover position with the organisation finally came to an end. The operation had eventually failed, because of a lack of training and insight within the new military intelligence and British intelligence remains entrenched in the country in an ever-stronger guise to this day.

As soldiers we always believed that the reality of operational conditions very often changed the way you approached problems. Whatever the planning beforehand, once you were on the ground, you often had to take decisions without the luxury of a quick brainstorming session in an air-conditioned office in the safety of your HQ. To make matters worse, as intelligence operatives we were entirely on our own and without any assistance or recognition if caught. We were told just that in no uncertain terms, 'We do not know you', when we left to perform a task in some godforsaken part of the world where our interests were apparently at stake.

That is in fact the main difference between working on one's own under cover and being a regular infantry soldier in the field. In the last instance there is still the possibility of discussion amongst team members. As a single operator such benefits do not exist. You have to work with what you've got. No amount of planning can cater for all the different scenarios that could develop and especially as operatives of one of the most hated regimes in the world (Apartheid) we had little or almost no recourse to any authority or protection in other parts of the world. We simply had to make do and live and work with the situation as it presented itself.

Sam never forgot that lesson and once the election was over he understood that he could hardly rely on any of the previous associates he had in the armed forces or elsewhere in circles of influence. New loyalties had already been forged and especially soldiers did not feature in this new political landscape. With regard to most soldiers the words used by an old forgotten sailor, *selected, trained, used, abused, accused and discarded* come to mind.

Sam now had to establish contact with the new government to declare his position as a loyal citizen and a non-supporter of any sedition against the state. He also had to indicate his wish to stay and work in the country as a businessman. So it was that Madala arranged for him to meet with Conrad. When Madala was thrown in jail after the failed coup in the black puppet state where he was appointed as the defence chief, Conrad was held in the cell next to his. It was only a question of time before they became friends. Madala quickly realised that Conrad would eventually be rewarded and accommodated within the new government for his role during the revolution and that this was an opportunity to befriend a high-ranking member of the revolutionary movement. He was one of several young white intellectuals who refused to accept the ways of the National Party government. He was given a jail sentence for his 'efforts'.

Sam thought a while longer and then started describing to me how he met with Conrad.

'The Golden City (Johannesburg) was always a strange otherworldly place. This atmosphere was probably the result of the development of the mining industry, which was - because of the foreign element streaming in to benefit from its riches - always slightly out of touch with the mood in the rest of the country. When we fought the British for three years during the late eighteen hundreds The Golden City was always a festering island of foreign influence and political resistance. That never really changed and when we were ultimately involved in a fight for our survival during the seventies and eighties that old city remained ever so foreign. That was precisely the eerie feeling I had when I walked from the parking garage to the Carlton Hotel that night to meet Conrad.

'The entrance to the hotel was plush as always and once again the contrast between rich and poor in our deeply dysfunctional society caught my attention. I marvelled at the discreet lighting that was reflected by the highly polished marble walls and floor. I was amazed at the mass of humanity gathered there and the obvious wealth that oozed from everything they displayed; shoes, clothes, jewelry, handbags. I found it rather obscene and remembered with some amusement how I struggled to identify or deal with the obvious social discrepancy it represented.

'Conrad's dimly lit office was on the first floor down a long dark passage on the side of the building. There were people milling around in that passage and in front of his office. On my way to the office, walking over a very soft crimson carpet, I was frisked at least twice before I was allowed to enter. I was told to wait as Conrad was travelling to the Carlton from a previous engagement.

'After some thirty minutes there was a shuffling noise outside the door. He walked into the office, smiled at me and said, 'Good day. Please sit down. What can I do for you?' I referred to Madala who arranged the meeting, mostly because I did not know how else to start this discussion with a man who had been my faceless enemy for so long. Conrad suddenly looked quite pleased. 'Of course, how is my good friend? Please convey my very best wishes to him when you see him again. How can I help you?' I explained to him in broad terms, but with considerable discomfort since I did not really know him, what had happened to me and Burton and that I could not support the new ANC government, but that I would not subvert them as they had been elected through a democratic process. He looked at me with a slight smile and delivered this bombshell, 'We know precisely what they have done to you and president Burton. I found evidence of this in a filing cabinet in my new office. We also know your background and we have no problem with you. You are free under the sun in this country. No one within our freedom movement will harm you or your family.' I did not know that at the time, but those words would prove to be an inverted prophecy of sorts since the far right eventually turned on me and tried to kill my family and me because they believed that I supported the new black government politically - my former enemy - who actually turned out to be a real friend after I was betrayed by my own people. We exchanged a few more words and then I left to try to pick up the pieces of my life.

'Conrad went on to become a minister in the newly elected government. After a difficult time working in such a strange environment after the struggle, Conrad accepted a diplomatic position in Europe. I am unsure of his fate after that, I only know that he was accused of corruption during later years. Maybe he was eventually disregarded like so many former sympathetic white and mixed race people who were often used by other African revolutionary movements before, simply because they were quick witted and familiar with the deeply corrupt ways of the western business based world; only to be thrown out after the fight was over while the spoils went to the indigenous people. For all I know he may have stumbled of his own accord because of the alluring glitter of newly found power. Whatever happened to him, I find the disloyalty even amongst enemies profoundly disgusting and I refuse to judge him simply because he treated me decently and with respect during that terrible period of my life. I will never forget that.'

I looked at Sam and struggled to hide my realisation that the man I met in Sector 20 and then again in Dover were completely different animals. Sam was clearly cynical to the point of possibly even discarding all principles he previously believed in.

'You are very negative about all of this, Sam?' I said softly.

And then with my journalist hat on, 'Have you no positive inclinations left?'

Sam looked at me with a slight smile and said, 'I have to admit that I have changed a lot. I have become impossible to live with in more than one way. Jackie struggles to stay with me and to work with my daily bouts of pain and general unstable physical profile and the devastating effect that has on my psyche.'

He cursed under his breath, 'F-ck it Alistair, I have just about lost everything I ever had. I am left with only memories and a few core principles on which I base my life. So what do you expect of me? Craven and his in-country and international partners sold us out after refusing to listen to the soldiers who knew the enemy. Then he turned his back on the people who fought with us in Namibia. Most of them were killed like animals. Then he turned his own security services on his own soldiers who refused to accept his betrayal. During that process I was attacked and I nearly died. My family was harassed and after I became ill only Jackie's stubborn tenacity and sheer fucking guts saved our children and me. Apparently close to four million white people have already left our country. Only the very old, very poor or really stubbornly tenacious, remain while white farmers and their families are still being attacked and often killed on their farms. These attacks are commonly marked by unspeakable cruelty and torture including the repeated gang rape and subsequent murder of all womenfolk by attackers who often carry the AIDS virus. Not even their workers escape this fate. Thousands of former special forces soldiers have left the country and are now working in the Middle East for either

American or British security companies. Refugees from other parts of a neo-imperialist violated Africa are streaming across the country's borders. At the latest count 4.5 million illegal refugees from Zimbabwe alone have already crossed the northern border. It will take only one farmer with far right leanings to shoot one of these refugees to unleash massive civil unrest in these parts. As it is, civil organisations are patrolling the border because the government has no intention or means of performing that task. How could I stay the same man you knew all those years ago? I have become someone I at times do not even know anymore.'

I just looked at him and honestly did not know what to say. He was a very different man. I knew that I would accept that fact simply because Sam never said anything without having thought about it carefully. I had to give him that at least.

I thought about how under white elitist upper class rule, the most visibly devoid of any intellectuality and with the big stick of an artificial middle class officialdom, white lower classes were protected before black people received any benefits. Meanwhile a small group of black, mostly intellectual expatriates, plotted and prepared in other countries right across the globe for their day of reckoning. Then when that day came the white upper class left the country with their money. There was still a huge white and black lower class while the black expatriates came back and replaced the white upper class and only took care of themselves with the help of a new artificial liberal middle class officialdom, many of whom are white. No members of the lower class would ever move beyond their desperate state of deprivation. The film quote *God has left Africa* drifted through my mind. Nothing has changed. The old system of lower class deprivation still exists and frustration is always mounting.

Chapter XIV

The Faithful Wife

The slow systemic decay in the country had manifested itself in people's personal lives. The Burtons did not escape this cruel fate.

Burton's wife was deeply unhappy before her death and spent much of her time away from her husband, residing with her sister in a small town nestling in the folds of the southern region's mountains. She remained deeply hurt by the unceremonious way in which she was publicly blamed for an air force flight that was to be arranged for former official friends to attend a respectful farewell from the armed forces for which she cared sincerely. The relationship between Burton and his wife was also sadly quite loveless at that time. The informed opinion was that the strain of their unceremonious and brutal eviction from office and Burton's impossible temper and refusal to grant her an opportunity to travel the world and specifically to Scotland, that she so much wanted to see, drove them apart. It happened very often that he would invited her to accompany him to visit the smallholding where he had spent much of his time while recuperating after the two failed attempts on his life. She was sadly overweight due to severe diabetes and sight impaired as a consequence. She moved with some difficulty with a walking stick. It was not uncommon for him to wait until she reached the top of the stairs leading to the driveway and to leave just when she started down the stairs. She would be left standing pathetically while he left in a fit of anger after having waited for her.

Such was the incredibly insensitive behaviour of this man who had no time for anyone but himself and who always revelled in playing the lead role in his own play. In earlier and 'happier' days this disrespect also took place in hidden fashion. William once confided in Sam that when he was a small boy he witnessed an occasion when Burton hit her for arguing with him. William sat on a low stool in the main bedroom when she made some ill considered remark about his family. Burton scrambled across the bed like lightning and slapped her across the face. She cringed in shock and agony and cried for hours afterwards. This act of brutality was burnt into William's memory forever and has remained hidden to this day. His mother was a bright and musically talented woman with a solid academic background, which was never put to any real use. She always served Burton's cause as the ever faithful wife, a concept of female servitude that was quite specific and especially religiously acceptable in the Afrikaner nationalist society of the day. William also remembered with huge affection and some pride that she was a crackerjack driver who understood the secrets of safe broad-siding and mostly wore racing gloves when she was younger and loved challenging him to impromptu time trials over complicated routes especially when they drove to holiday destinations separately. She mostly won the challenge. She had exceptional interpersonal skills and above average judgment of character. She could smell insincerity and dishonesty a mile away and throughout Burton's public career she was the one who constantly warned him against the approach of enemies with her tactical and strategic insights. Her eventual death meant that he was totally defenceless.

These tragic events were exacerbated by the fact that she had inexplicably chosen to embrace three of her children mainly because they keenly participated in the public domain with their parents and apparently flourished in more ways than one because of that. Two of the children, William and his second sister, were however alienated from the family for superficial reasons that confound the imagination. Their embracing of a far more realistic approach to life based on reason and a fundamental belief in privacy in all circumstances, unfortunately did nothing to secure their positions in the family.

William's second sister, a sensitive, but fiercely independent person with a mind as sharp as a razor blade, was rejected as a young child after a brutal and apparent random physical attack for which she was blamed, instead of being nurtured when she arrived home one evening from a church function with blood on her clothing. The only reason why she overcame this incident as well as unspeakable personal tragedy suffered later in her life, was because in more ways than one, she represented the best and strongest characteristics of her forbears. She was the strongest of all the children. William was witness to insensitive, unfair and often disrespectful, treatment handed out to her by Burton at regular intervals over their youth years. In later life she would become a highly skilled trauma therapist. This describes best the skilled and brave actions of this woman who always chose engagement before withdrawal. She was ultimately thrown from the family's inner circle because she was unwilling to conform to the superficiality of the family's self- honouring lifestyle based on politically acquired status.

The eldest son William was rejected because he similarly refused to praise Burton's non-existent clothing and instead stated outright that just as the king in the fable *The King's New Clothes*, that he was naked and that he would be betrayed from within his own ranks. He was furthermore singled out for rejection because he predicted against popular belief and very accurately throughout his adult life how the country would ultimately be handed over to international political interests, with the energetic assistance of big business and academic experts backing the actions of several high level traitors within. This was underscored by government's lacklustre attention to political and administrative detail in later years, which ultimately led to the party political structure being gradually infiltrated by ruthless and lowly qualified individuals who were simply in it for the money and personal status. They would sell the country for a pittance to the highest bidder. International political interests would ultimately control the country through second tier positioning supporting the new black government that was carefully prepared for their proxy role over many years of political struggle and exile. This permanent division in Burton's family would have a profound effect later when they were faced with irrefutable evidence of their father's final neutralisation through a cunning strategy clearly driven by the intelligence agencies conniving behind the scenes.

According to Sam, Burton's wife died while enjoying sincere, but inherently flawed relations with three of her children based on her vision of what they were and what she wanted them to be and become in later life. For all her practical political insight she could not distinguish fact from fiction regarding her children. William and his second sister would form an alliance in years to come based on their joint belief in old values underscored by the truth or at least the perceived facts that were as close as possible to the truth. William could never accept the fact that his second sister was utterly alienated from the family. He tried to compensate by offering kindness, but ultimately the sadness would linger unresolved. She would maintain in later years that she did not see herself or William as victims, but actually as survivors. Very often they would remember their days as small children with sincere happiness when they played under the fig trees close to the tall pine trees and small round-leaved decorative shrubs at their home in the old and culturally rich Oranjezicht part of the city overlooking Table Bay. Their recollections of this place were bright and good and the truth was simple to recognise and the sky mostly blue and clear. These memories served to largely drive some of the vicious societal predators out of their lives and would add to a feeling of inherent calm.

William and his sister remained close friends through many years of challenge and heartbreak and enjoyed moments of happiness whenever the darkness lifted. Despite differences that occurred mostly through circumstance rather than intent their loyalty towards each other never faltered.

When his wife collapsed in a bathroom one evening Burton phoned his youngest son to come to the house to see what had happened to her. He was somehow incapable of going near her body after she did not return after having excused herself earlier. The young man however walked straight into the house to where his mother had collapsed and confronted this immensely challenging situation directly and fearlessly. William always respected him for that act of sheer bravery. These strange circumstances left unanswered questions lingering in William's mind for years to come. He remained unsure whether she died of natural causes or whether perhaps Burton was somehow involved. He always preferred to believe that his mother just gave up after her and her husband's public humiliation that lasted for several months and simply left this earth forever.

William attended his mother's funeral. It was a strange affair with a diverse group of people travelling vast distances to attend. In a way it proved that she was after all inherently a respected and talented person without whom Burton could not survive. After the church service held deep in the mountains overlooking the lakes in the southwestern district, William turned around to leave the church.

Dr Becker came walking from the front and put out his hand, 'I am so sorry, William. Please accept my condolences.' William looked at the man whom he always distrusted deeply as his father's enemy and said, 'What are you doing here? You are not welcome. Get in your car and leave this instant.' Becker withdrew without a word.

William then joined the pallbearers in the graveyard and he remembered in years to follow how he struggled to help carry the coffin. It was as if for the last time he had to bear a physical burden that became symbolic of the verbal distance he had suffered for so long. While he struggled to carry his corner of the massive coffin containing her large frame he remembered how she shouted at him so often when he disagreed from his father and how she undermined his position as the eldest son by allowing his eldest sister and his younger brother to give his names that he inherited from his father and his profoundly respected grandfather, to their sons so that their positions in the family would be inherently stronger. William felt nauseous as he reached the grave. The joints in his hand that were previously broken ached and he could hardly open his fingers. He muttered under his breath, 'Oh God, why did I even come here.'

After the ceremony refreshments were offered to all guests in the church hall. He stood around for a short while and then returned briefly to the grave, which was by then already covered. He picked a pink hibiscus flower from a bush close by and put this on his mother's grave. Standing there he felt incredibly lonely. That was his only, final private moment with the woman who gave him life. As if a moment ago, he would always remember this fleeting experience with sincere sadness in years to come.

He then joined several other special guests who were invited to the house for refreshments, an old tradition intended to provide sustenance for farmers who travelled far in the early pioneering days to attend a funeral in remote parts of the country and who had to return to their farms afterwards. He took the opportunity to walk into her bedroom before joining the other guests. He noticed her two golden pens with her name inscribed in black on her desk next to a small pile of neatly stacked documents. He enjoyed the quiet moment and with only the slightest hesitation he took the one pen and put it in his inside jacket pocket. He had a feeling that the pen would be important one day. This was indeed the case. William treasured the pen and would give it to his sister years later to keep as a reminder of the mother she loved, but who did not recognise or return that affection and did not protect her against her father's wrath.

That night William sought out the company of his mother's sister at the house since he believed that she would know at least part of what had happened in the years that went before. She lived up to his expectations and as he sat down next to her while offering her a glass of wine, she said, 'Your mother spent much time with me these past years, William. She gave me a message for you. She asked me to tell you that 'she understood." William believes to this day that with those words she gave him some belated credit for shunning the limelight when his father was president. Somehow albeit it small, that was some consolation to William. At least he knew that his mother tried to understand him towards the end of her life. William thanked his aunt. That was the last time he would see her.

As he walked downstairs and into the main living room he noticed several people amongst which general Max and general Vanziel, were seated around his father, both people William despised deeply for their personal and professional deceit and treachery over many years. Max looked up and said while laughing out loud, without greeting him, 'Just look at him. He is still wearing those strange clothes and scraggly beard.' William was always known for his distinctly casual and individualistic way of dressing while being fiercely proud of his neatly trimmed beard as part of his naval tradition and now his civilian trademark. For William this was an enormous affront given that it was his mother's house and that it was her funeral.

He walked over to Max and placed his finger under his nose without touching him, 'You are not a general's a- and I no longer work for you and I have a good mind to kick the crap out of you where you sit. Have you no respect? This is my Mother's house and this is her funeral. At least respect that and my position in this house.'

Burton jumped up and rushed in between the two men. He shouted at William, 'What are you two doing? Stop that this instant. Behave yourself.' William never forgot this incredibly insulting incident, more so because his father did not defend his position against this arrogant conniver who preferred taking what he thought he was entitled to whatever the cost.

For a brief moment during, but especially after the encounter, William remembered the time when a good friend in counter intelligence was tasked to investigate the great general because there were significant rumours that he received a farm as payment from a businessman who supplied aircraft transportation hours on contract to the air force in an untoward manner, for which he was eventually prosecuted. He investigated the matter to the bone and found the farm and all relevant proof of the bribe for business. On handing over the file and after scrutiny of the detail he was summarily moved to another directorate and the file was lost. Such was the power of this man who clearly had no respect for the law of the land or common ethical behaviour.

This growing breach between William and his father was now a reality and because Sam was close to William it would ultimately also affect his relationship with Burton. Burton not only lost his wife he also lost his son and Sam, the one man that would, as he once openly declared, never lie to him. William immediately left in total desperation and deeply hurt that night while Burton sat drinking whisky with his pals who insulted his son in his mother's house. None of the other family members living in the vicinity invited William over after the funeral. He stayed in a guest house and left for home the next day. His alienation from the family was now final.

The subsequent transformation of former president Burton was quite sudden and fully underway. William had expected that he would be more of a changed man after his wife's death, but he did not expect the change to take hold so fast. It was as if she had never been there and he put several of her prized possessions on auction instead of allowing his children to take what they really wanted as a reminder of her. Burton was now entering a world of make-believe with new friends that would in time and unbeknown to him, place him firmly in the position of the symbolic protector of the far right.

Despite the fact that by now I was prepared for just about everything that could still come to the surface during the course of this narrative by Sam, I was still troubled by the increasing inherent darkness that came to the surface with monotonous regularity. I tried to describe this journalistically to Sam, but quickly fell into the trap of regrettable superficial comment that did not really address the core of the problem.

'Why is it that everything you describe now is becoming more and more dark and sinister, Sam? Was it not merely a matter of sour grapes after a system failed and people started losing their influence? Were you and William and your families merely paying the price for your associations with the system or is there a deeper truth?'

Sam looked amused and said, 'We were not only losing our power and status, we were also losing our souls. You have to see this in a broader panoramic context, Alistair. Yes, the betrayal of the state affected all of us. But more than that we were now starting to question each other's loyalties and instead of closing the ranks against the enemy at the gates in true Machiavellian style we were working against each other in smaller groups and as individuals. That meant that whole support systems came undone and people were running around in circles trying to make sense of why we were losing everything after nearly 350 years in Africa. In parallel we lost our value system since all traditional support groupings such as the church and cultural organisations - however misguided, still presented a certain safe refuge against all the new attacks on our lifestyle - were compromising to retain some semblance of credibility in a fast changing and now nouveau African secular environment. In essence it was not firstly a fight for geographical and political control, it became a fight for people's hearts and minds and our people were not ready for that. There were no carefully honed plans to protect the people. They were on their own and without a leader in the true sense of the word. The smooth talking Craven was already suspected to be a sell-out after his period in office during which time he ensured that everyone knew that the transformation was irreversible. He simply did not provide for a stable political structure to take care of our people after he had gone. Certainly it looked like a fairy-tale ending for the rainbow nation, but just under the surface a brutal reality started to unfold as the price of minority constitutional loss started showing in people's frame of mind.'

I thought about this very carefully for a while, while my counter revolutionary training came back to me slowly, but surely. I remembered the inadequate feeling I regularly had when realising that a certain carefully planned and immaculately executed military operation brought no result. Instead the enemy had just walked in behind our infantry patrols in South West Africa's northern regions and messed with the local population's collective mind through physical and psychological means after which it was all over. Ordinary folk could simply not deal with the big-time conflict between major political adversaries.

Then Sam interrupted my thoughts.

'It was becoming downright impossible to live with what was happening around us. Our small micro existence became threatened by our unwillingness to compromise with the enemy and in the process even families imploded and turned on one another. My life was certainly becoming a sinister and very dark affair. I remember once sitting with my head in my hand in front of a window. The sunlight caught my arm and I noticed from the corner of my eye the small rhythmic movement of my heart projected into this one single vein. It suddenly gave me an incredible sense of vulnerability and I realised again how tenuous life was. I cannot say that I never contemplated whether it was worthwhile carrying on with my existence. I sometimes felt as if my life was simply over and I certainly did not always have the willpower to make it work.

'Every time I was pulled back from the brink by Jackie, despite regular massive disagreements, arguments and incredibly damaging shouting matches with her, borne mostly out of my incalculable frustration with my affected and profoundly weakened body. This was especially prevalent at times when I illness peaked and I did not see any way out of endless medical procedures focused on improving my life after the invisible and unidentified attack. I had no one I could really trust except Jackie, whom I often treated unfairly, while my physical condition was visibly in decline. I knew that I was starting to lose my links into government and the gradual loss of my specific access to Burton was only a symptom of what was really going on under the surface. My life was rapidly spinning out of control and I did not really know how to cope. I remember feeling as if I was sinking into a deep black hole and it was impossible to grab on to the sides to pull myself to safety. All the old war monsters came out to play, not only at night, but even during the day. I was utterly and completely lost and I must have become increasingly harder to live with.

'By now there was also a gradual and noticeable breach looming between Jackie and me. For several years to come this potential breakdown lay under the surface. At regular intervals this latent conflict threatened to break us apart and on several occasions we came so close to ending it all only to decide to try again and again and again. It would only resolve itself years later when we gradually rediscovered the reasons why we teamed up originally and only after we had left the country. During this time we decided to try to forget what went before and to find separate and combined ways of accommodating each other's individual needs. By doing this we would forgive each other the mistakes we made under severe pressure and rather focus on the few common areas of interest we shared.

'More often than not Jackie forgave more than I did. She was always more determined to save our life together for the right reasons.

'These occurrences were precisely what my enemies wanted. Extreme pressure was exerted to break down our personal relationship and our family unit and in so doing any possible ensuing united front with other like-minded people was highly unlikely. The physical attack on my life may have been unsuccessful, but the later consequences for me seemed to be very close to the real thing. The pain Jackie and I experienced was far more severe than any chemical weapon or poison could ever inflict. It was the pain of fear for our children's lives, running away, not knowing where to hide and who our enemy was and in the end the regret and anger at losing so much of nearly twenty years of our lives. How do we ever justify or explain such a loss to ourselves Alistair? It sometimes feels as if one's heart is wrenched from one's chest and thrown, beating, into the dust from where it can never be resurrected. So, that was us and we are still together, hanging on for dear life to what little remained. Now let me tell you what happened to Burton.'

Chapter XV

The Trial

'After his wife's death Burton was pushed politically to the right and it became apparent very quickly that it would only be a question of time before he was brought before the Truth and Reconciliation Commission to explain his part in what went before when he was in control.'

'If she was still alive Burton's wife - despite her own failings and dreams of grandeur - could well have prevented him from destroying himself so thoughtlessly through her sheer presence and insight. Burton refused to testify before the Truth and Reconciliation Commission after he was betrayed and then deposed by Craven who simply handed the country to the enemy. During 1998 he was ultimately put on trial that served as a grim showpiece occasion. This was done in an effort to show the power of the new democracy and to crush any future efforts to rekindle the flames of a deeply flawed previous political system, where a minority group ultimately overstepped the boundary of decency in all matters of humane governance. This public display was enormously damaging for Burton's image and even more so since his behaviour during the procedures was less than proper. This left him open to persecution and condemnation, and his enemies seized the opportunity. Chaos reigned supreme.

'This was a process with many hidden agendas and no one knew for sure how it would end. He was ultimately convicted of holding the TRC in contempt and given a sentence of R10,000 or 12 months jail sentence, plus a further 12 months conditionally suspended for five years. This political showpiece conviction was ultimately overturned on appeal. But, the damage was done and he would never regain his full public image, where some people hated him passionately and some loved him as passionately, while all respected him for his baseline convictions and determination. He had effectively become the rejected Christ figure who paid the overall price for his people's biggest failing, losing the political war, following a military victory at best and a reasonable stand-off at worst.

'Before and throughout the trial he maintained that the Commission and the court case were farcical and that ultimately minorities would pay the price once the majority took control of the country. His trial was exacerbated by his rather strange behaviour during the court case. Right throughout he persisted with not paying attention to the proceedings and throwing small paper balls at people he knew in court and joking loudly about the proceedings. This embarrassed not only his legal team, but present and absent family members and friends. It complicated the task of the prosecutor who told his eldest daughter before the trial that he would at all times treat the accused with respect. His son William knew this man as they attended the same high school and Burton's complete disregard for the legal process - in itself a denial of the very system he had helped put in place - was sad and simply improper in the extreme. I believe that if he had acted in a dignified manner throughout the court case it would have served not only his, but all of his people's case.

'Initially when he was put on trial Burton had nowhere to go for legal advice. His son William used his fortuitous and significant contact with the legal fraternity to obtain a reputable law firm with access to the very best in senior legal counsel. Burton regrettably treated these people with disrespect and ultimately, after they had won an appeal against the conviction, they refused to have any further contact with him because of his public rudeness towards the team on more than one occasion. Amazingly though, he walked away from the trial with only a slightly bruised ego. For the rest he remained the same old self-centred persona everyone knew. I always had grave misgivings about what had transpired at the trial and I believed that Burton could have acted in a more dignified manner.'

I was amazed at the depth of the darkness that Sam felt in later years here in the Isles. True intent of action and ultimate responsibility for the disaster that ensued after the two attempts on Burton's life, followed by Craven's bloodless coup and his subsequent departure as Head of State at the end of 1989, still needed clarification. Sam remained quite deliberate in his comments in discussions mainly with Jackie who remained his confidant throughout. Burton was the chairman of the State Security Council for many years. The work that this organisation performed was in reality superficial and publicly insignificant. Under the surface this Council in fact acted as a force outside and independent of party political organisations, caucuses, government departments, the cabinet and even the law courts. This organisation consisted of a core element of the important cabinet ministers acting quietly within a highly organised coterie of officialdom representing the security and defence community. It became an impenetrable policy making body within the government executive, with hidden powers applied on a strictly need to know basis amongst a select few. It was in essence a government within a government. Any political scientist or person with insight into principles of sound governance will confirm that this could never be acceptable. Within this structure Burton ruled the roost with an iron fist. Decisions regarding both people and innate objects and projects involving both were taken here while implementation of some of the harshest measures were reserved for an inner circle of trusted lieutenants within the select few. They acted in terms of a grid based management system, allowing for several cut out points that provided the required plausible deniability for the man at the top.

Burton in all probability knew just about everything that was decided and implemented with possibly the exclusion of the detailed plans, but no one would ever be able to prove this, simply because the management system of the State Security Council specifically protected him by withholding operational detail within the carefully compartmentalized structure. Operational detail was always shrouded in political and military euphemisms such as 'eliminate' and 'take out' used in place of words like kill and assassinate. This was similar to the escape doors that were installed in the walls behind his desks in all his offices, so that he could make a quick and smooth departure in the event of a penetration of his inner office sanctum and a possible ensuing attempt on his life. I always felt deeply troubled by this cynical final escape solution. It reminded me so much of many of the ultimate solutions that dictators such as Hitler and Mussolini would subscribe to with no thought whatsoever to the ordinary folk that would remain behind to face the enemy.

William specifically had serious misgivings about some of the methods used by the Civil Co-operation Bureau and the security police during this time. Methods applied during interrogations and the manufacturing and use of chemical biological weapons were sometimes so horrendous that he struggled to accept his own position within the system towards the end of the war. These misgivings would haunt him for the rest of his life and would be strengthened by his continued return to the subject matter of a deeply disturbing film *Music Box* written by József A. 'Joe' Eszterhas, which in its essence questioned the underlying truth about Burton that kept eluding him as his son. He never really knew whether Burton was a deeply guilty party to all the horrors or whether he was really innocent. As his son he often hovered between exposing him for what he suspected him to be or for defending him.

William vividly recalled how he raised his concerns at table during Sunday lunches where the whole family was often present. These concerns became stronger as his personal involvement with the war effort increased and were directed at policies, methods and personalities. More often than not these concerns resulted in acrimonious confrontations during which he was often belittled and bitterly criticised as being not adequately qualified to comment on these matters, despite his training and sound insights into subjects of the day. Because of Burton's inability to reach out to his children or anyone else, and to show real affection, these confrontations systematically grew in ferocity and soon it became quite impossible to attend family meals without it resulting in a shouting match. This inevitably led to William's regular swift departure while endured ill use, accusations of disloyalty and advice to his wife to assist him to seek psychological help with 'his problem'. William now began questioning his father's inherent psychological make-up. At this time he was still loyal to the hilt, but the doubts regarding Burton's abilities as a leader began gnawing at his conscience. He fought with this mainly because he still believed that at some point Burton would see the light and that he would begin an examination process to identify the problem areas and stop the decay within the political system. Regrettably however William did not reckon with the inherent unique personality make-up of the man.

Picture a child growing up as the centrepiece of a large family's attention, developing all the traits of a self-centred individual who always wanted to be accepted as being right and who never really mastered the art of wise compromise. His parents were already older people who came through the horrendous Boer War against the British and who held strong views on foreign influence and who were understandably reluctant to forget the pain they were subjected to. The world was changing rapidly between the end of the 1920s and the early 1930s. On the whole and with the exception of the European dictators the horrors of World War I, became the driving force behind a new, albeit unsophisticated, international negotiation methodology for preventing confrontation. Burton remained psychologically stuck in an inherited late 1800s mind set and as a result proceeded with a life of neo-fascist nationalistic absolutes, instead of embracing new ways of solving problems however under-developed they were at the time. By the time he became the prime minister in 1978 he was fully immersed in a party political system that practiced blind leader worship in its worst form. Re-elected with acclamation and applause became the adulatory nationalist cry of the party congress faithful year after year. He also failed to develop a successful international communications strategy and in consequence he was typified from day one as a hard-liner who would never in the words of many a seasoned living rock climber, *run away to climb another day.* As a consequence his only fully successful international forays were those closely aligned with old French and Portuguese colonial protagonists who were soon to be cast aside as African revolutionary movements rapidly swept over the continent to seize power from their hands. These colonial powers however, in turn and quite cunningly - with some considerable difficulty - secured international political deals to remain in Africa mostly in second tier government positions from where they still exerted considerable influence. When time ran out and the bell ultimately rang in this game of political musical chairs Burton was the only man left standing without a chair. He never learnt the lessons that the French and Portuguese paid such huge penalties for. He very quickly became the pariah of the international world, which seemed intent on only focusing on his wagging finger, instead of highlighting the many positive things that he also spearheaded.

This inability to deal with reality within politics as the *science of the possible,* also showed itself within his family relations. He chose to embrace those family members who supported him blindly while apparently completely ignoring the value of the discreet voice of reason behind closed doors. This inability to make the right choices in his personal life would ultimately erupt into a tragedy for his family long after his death. Burton did not fail in his task as a leader because he was unintelligent or incapable of learning. He failed because he was a self-centered person with a massive ego who was incapable of accepting the signs of the times that could lead him to make the right choices. This resulted in his ultimate downfall while his countrymen and children remained behind to pick up the pieces because he failed to make the better choice of securing minority rights through a more harmonious negotiated dispensation.

All of this transpired while he was already aware of the fact that ruthless men of money, in particular the tobacco magnate Bear - showing increasing odd mannerisms such as tilting his head while approaching submissively by bending forward and smiling in an affected way in his dealings with people (clearly symptomatic of a twisted effort to show humility) - in the company of armchair politicians in the guise of nouveau-secular philosopher academics and more specifically the southern academics; prof. Willie the amateur 'spook', dr Johan the misguided philosophical preacher, dr Andrew the logical philosophical fanatic, prof. Simpson the Free State know-it-all and Gago the Willows wine connoisseur, were discreetly planning his downfall with the country's enemy. The influence of these academics were ultimately so profound that their actions reverberated into the inner circle of political life and especially the back channel driven negotiating between warring foes.

In typical selfish fashion he only took care of his own interests. Burton also failed to warn William and his second son in law. They were both deeply involved in government related activities in advisory and support roles. They proceeded with their businesses in good faith until it was too late and they also became the victims of a system that was ultimately bent on destroying the king and the princes. After having failed to save himself he also failed to save his sons from this fate of being branded as outcasts and thrown to the dogs. It was as if Burton knew all these things, but still decided to play the Samson pillar card and take his family with him into the abyss so to speak.

Burton fell increasingly into a profound state of self-pity and depression. He was understandably lonely notwithstanding his poor behaviour towards his deceased wife at the end of her life. After a failed relationship with a well endowed woman of doubtful moral character - who apparently just before meeting Burton warmed the bed of the town's traffic chief - from a small town some distance to the northeast, his one daughter introduced him to a person she met through shared religious activities and who expressed interest in her father. Regrettably she was politically naive and publicity struck, introduced them without once questioning the sudden appearance of this complete stranger. Amazingly innocent as this may appear to be, there was a far more sinister background to this story.

Within months he married this lady with extreme religious convictions. She immediately took the added position of personal assistant to Burton and since it was part of his retirement package, the state very conveniently paid her salary. No one knew where she came from, so Sam started doing his homework and very quickly determined that this woman, Beatrice, was not as innocent as she appeared to the outside world. Her suspected extreme religious fervour would tie in very conveniently with the development of a suspected dangerous far right religious movement, controlling more than seventy far right political splinter groups during the early years of the new millennium. This group believe that they are the descendants of the Thirteenth Tribe of Israel. They apparently remain quite willing to kill for their religious-based political fervour. It was well known that they had a hit list with names of people they believed to be traitors to the white cause and with that a danger to their particular extreme brand of religion.

This would provide the backdrop for a most cynical, but utterly successful double operation where the state would use Beatrice as an agent provocateur to portray one image, but to steer towards a completely different end result. She literally conned a grieving Burton to believe that she would care for him, while she paved the way for his ultimate demise. Beatrice very quickly established herself as the person who controlled everything around Burton. She firmly managed his personal life and any of his children who did not agree with what was prescribed were restricted from speaking to him or seeing him. Cloaking her real intentions in pseudo humane utterances, she said openly that she was sent to ensure that, 'This proud man would be humbled.' Her fanatical religious fervour was the cornerstone on which his life would be based in future. She very quickly and regularly began leaving him alone during several sudden and extended travels. William's second sister, a street-wise and gifted violence victim therapist, once found him lying in a semi-conscious state on his bed during an unannounced visit. The only food left for him was a flask of tea with some sandwiches. This strengthened her suspicions that Beatrice was ensuring her control over him by giving him some form of calming drug that would have the effect of keeping him in a semi-conscious state most of the time.

William told Sam that he once received a message on his mobile phone where his father's voice was barely audible, calling out his name, 'William, William, are you there?' This one message would haunt William for the rest of his life; despite the harsh emotional treatment he suffered at Burton's hands over many years. Beatrice's impromptu trips away from home would be to visit the financial advisor Henno, who was reported to be a friend to both of them, but was soon suspected to be much closer to her. Other visits seemed to be more like secret meetings with members of far right religious based organisations and of course her state employer. All in all this was a distasteful, sordid relationship in which Burton was being firmly controlled and manipulated. Similar suspicions were also raised by Burton's concerned personal bodyguard, who was treated like garbage by Beatrice. At one stage William reported this strange behaviour to a friend of the family and the chief at the regional police HQ, in the hope that he would see the inherent danger for the weakening old president. They were unfortunately - or perhaps conveniently - reluctant to commence tailing Burton's wife to check on her dubious activities.

All food cupboards in the house were routinely locked, while she very swiftly fired the servants that had taken care of Burton for many years and prepared all his favourite and tasty old-fashioned meals. His diet was changed to a strict health food based regimen. He soon became quite emaciated and only a shadow of his former imposing figure. Treatment for any ailments was often restricted to natural healers and herbal remedies, while visits to professional doctors were becoming increasingly limited. Ultimately their relationship quickly descended into chaos and at one stage he asked William for assistance to divorce Beatrice. William obliged, but Burton regrettably left the proposed paperwork for possible divorce proceedings lying open on his desk. Beatrice chanced upon it and that escape option soon evaporated. Their relationship darkened after this. When William's second sister once visited Burton unexpectedly she eventually found him at some natural healer's consulting rooms where he was being treated half-undressed and in full view of the public. She decided that enough was enough and requested all the children to co-operate to have their father removed from the house by court order and placed under special care at a frail care centre. Only she and William agreed on this matter while the other children incomprehensibly chose to allow Beatrice to proceed with her control over him.

The relationship between the other three children and Burton clearly became increasingly shallow as he struggled to communicate his deepest thoughts, hopes and fears to them with his inherent inability to do so sincerely with those people closest to him. The lack of honest discussion between him and these children became more evident as time elapsed. He attempted to reach out to William and his second daughter; he would often allow her partly into his isolated world of increasing solitude and desperation, only to withdraw when the pressure from his controlling wife overwhelmed him. The relationship between him and William remained tragically strained until the very end, mainly because of a complete lack of shared interests and ultimately mutual trust.

William and his second sister were desperate. They called Sam and requested his help to attempt to get to the truth and spare Burton further embarrassment and possible harm. It was clear to Sam, especially after in depth discussions with William and his sister, that there was something amiss. His homework through intelligence channels revealed that Beatrice was apparently in the employ of the National Intelligence Service. Her cover of being Burton's personal assistant was merely an extension of her work as covert operative for the government. Her orders were to control Burton by creating tension between him and his children while ruining him financially. Simultaneously, between her and the financial advisor, they convinced Burton to sign away public company shares worth at least four million rand. It is widely believed that she then promptly sold the shares and pocketed the money. By doing this, the state in effect took his financial independence away from him and thus he would be less enthusiastic about continued opposition to their plans for change, while his children, some of whom had some considerable influence, would be left with very little inheritance. No money, no power base, no resistance. Simultaneously she drove him closer to the far right, specifically The Thirteenth Tribe of Israel, by pretending to be a religiously motivated far right supporter herself. Several religious fanatics with far right leanings were paraded through Burton's house to keep him occupied with this mindless pursuit of an illogical and historically challenged political rebirth of the country. This further isolated him and labeled him as a far right fanatical power symbol, and providing them with considerable emotional justification for their ill conceived and badly executed resistance plans.

Beatrice also made contact with Madala's estranged wife Mabel who (it was probably carefully planned) lived close by and who shared the same apparent religious inclinations. Mabel had a close connection with government and performed various other tasks for the national intelligence service. According to Sam she became estranged from Madala because his broader international agenda had no space for this kind of extremism, real or fake. Beatrice had found her accomplice in crime - Mabel. Together they formed a formidable witch-like killing squad.

These two evil women were the ideal front for a whole plethora of evils. They had the perfect religious cover story - whether real or fake is really irrelevant - with which they hid a deep, dark political agenda underscored by a deep-rooted passion for money and material wealth that would stop at nothing.

To understand their thinking their origins are important. Mabel was the person who masterminded Madala's release from jail after his conviction on coup charges in the black state. She was not only ambitious, but had deep, strong links to the revolutionary grouping that would eventually take over government. As a sympathiser she was eventually assured of contracts as a personnel trainer and PR marketing specialist. The new government would need such people to prepare a new cadre of civil servants. This was only a short hop away from being recruited for intelligence work. Madala had long since divorced his first wife due to the sheer pressures of covert intelligence operational realities as well as his adventurous and slightly roguish nature. These realities were driven home very specifically when Madala was stationed in Cuba, where a casual relationship with an attractive young Cuban woman developed. The designated operation in France led to the eventual attempt to kill him in Marseilles. There was no communication between him and his first wife for extended periods and their marriage simply could not survive that. Mabel was his second wife who went through the horror of his arrest and first imprisonment in the black state and subsequent longer incarceration in South Africa. By the time she stepped in and secured his release with the expert help of the very best far left lawyers, Madala was already under enormous emotional pressure in jail. He was incapable of taking care of his life immediately after his release, as he suffered a stroke that was a severe emotional and physical setback. Mabel's religious beliefs enveloped him and it would take him years to escape her smothering control both financially and emotionally.

Beatrice was identified long before Burton's wife died and kept ready for insertion as soon as it became clear that Burton was vulnerable. Burton the statesman and Madala, a knowledgeable and international operationally astute soldier, were under direct threat. This reality would however only play itself out much later.

Previous successive white governments in the country used opposition groups to divide and rule. The new government did precisely the same. They supported the far right covertly by inserting agents that were seemingly promoting their own cause, while actually actively spying for the state. Government benefited by knowing the inner workings of these organisations, and at the same time discrediting these activities through blaming them for everything that went wrong as well as all associations with them. Beatrice and Mabel were carefully selected and placed close to Burton to drive this process. Government remained concerned about Burton's circle of influence. They had to ensure that his position remained tenuous and contaminated in the eyes of the public at large. The Thirteenth Tribe of Israel had the scope of control in the country to ensure that Burton was kept busy with meeting several religious extremist far right dignitaries to enhance their status amongst ordinary people. Between Beatrice and Mabel they managed his ultimate demise. It is also relatively certain that the members of the Thirteenth Tribe of Israel did not suspected Beatrice or Mabel of complicity with the state but instead, like so many times before, were merely useful idiots.

In conjunction with her task to keep Burton under control Beatrice was also tasked to ensure that Sam who was known to be close to the old president and also Madala's closest friend, was kept in line. The method she employed was as old as the mountains. She used the far right movement she associated with to contaminate Sam's image and to brand him as a traitor to the Afrikaner cause since he associated with the new black government. She used the same methods to estrange William from his father. The clock was ticking relentlessly. Sam's time was up, again.

Chapter XVI

Poisoned Gulf

It was never a given that the Afrikaner would fight for his freedom. As a matter of fact it was always highly unlikely that they would be that brave as to actually oppose the taking of their country. After all, history tells us that during the Anglo-Boer War (Second Boer War) fifteen thousand of them worked for the British against their own people as so-called joiners or 'witbande' (identifying white armbands were worn by Boer men who joined the British forces). The Boers' reputation as brave and honest men were however saved by the 'Bittereinders' (men who fought to the bitter end), ten thousand Cape Rebels and a few thousand commando fighters from the Orange Free State and Transvaal Boer Republics, that carried the flag for these persecuted people right until the end of the war in 1902. The new millennium dawned with a mere whimper. No change to the deep-rooted skewed character of the Afrikaner ensued after 1902. It was however a given that after the betrayal during middle 1990, nearly a century later, many of them would work tirelessly and without shame, internationally in registered offices in Syria to secure as much as possible money for their personal use.

During my recording of Sam's experiences I remembered

with some amusement a story he once told me in Angola about God and the Devil. The Devil approached God with a request to attempt to 'corrupt' the Afrikaner. God was amused, and ever so slightly irritated, but allowed the Devil to proceed. It was the time of the Great Trek to the north of the country during 1838 in an attempt to flee from the enslavement of British Colonial rule. The Afrikaner came through this ordeal with some effort and ultimately formed the two Boer Republics in the North. The Devil had clearly failed in his first attempt to entice the Afrikaner to 'submit to sin'. Then after some years the old Devil approached God for a second time. This time God was rather irritated by the Devil's attempts to lead the Afrikaner astray. The Afrikaner was particularly busy at this time fighting the full might of the British forces during the first and second Boer Wars and participating in the ensuing First World War and the Rebellion against the country's participation in the First World War. Once again the Afrikaner came through the ordeal a little worse for wear, but nevertheless morally intact. Some years later the Devil tried again. By now God was very irritated and told the Devil to get on with it and to stop wasting his time. The Afrikaner was in the grip of the 1930s depression, which was then followed by the Second World War, and despite incredible hardship they survived and in fact took control of their destiny during the middle 1950s and commenced running their own affairs. Sometime later the Devil took his chances again and shuffled closer to God to ask for yet another chance at corrupting the Afrikaner. God was furious, but his undying trust in the Afrikaner people convinced him to give the old scoundrel one more chance. The Devil then gave the Afrikaner affluence and money in the years that followed and contaminated their will to do the right thing at all times. In so doing Old Nick finally broke the Afrikaner's moral back. The message is crystal clear. The Afrikaner loves money and that has been their final downfall.

In this spirit of personal financial gain, one such a financially driven man, doctor Dutton and his group of scientists in fact went so far as to hand out visiting cards depicting their Syrian office address in Damascus in precise detail. Given the subject matter of his work it was astonishing to say the least. Maybe they were attempting to hide their deed behind a so-called open trading business. Eventually they would be found out and that is why it is possible to write about that here today. It may be that no one will ever pay for this transgression, but at least it should serve as a grim warning to other people who decide to steal from their own country and sell secrets to international political criminals and in so doing contribute to the creation of a conflict that would ultimately cost thousands of lives of both soldiers and civilians in countries like Iraq, Afghanistan and Syria. This gross transgression would fit quite neatly into the existing category of artillery capability specifically in Iraq. Years before South Africa covertly sold heavy G5 artillery pieces to Iraq. It would only be a small step from there to manufacturing an artillery missile that would have a chemical warfare capability that would in turn endanger all Iraq's neighbours.

This part of Sam's narrative was both surreal and frightening. He spoke softly, 'I never know which of these aspects is more terrifying, the surreal nature of the deed or the fear. I can work with fear because in most instances I can give it a name and substance, but surrealism has a quality that suggests a lack of control over one's own thoughts. I find this disconcerting to say the least, simply because we always dealt in factual content to provide a stable departure point for all actions whether military or civilian. These people's actions demonstrated that part of our people's soul, that cannot be explained and which I can only depict as the all or nothing, or the Samson principle, which is devoid of any hope or consideration for others. I suppose in the end one just observes and wonders at the incredible lack of loyalty and conscience that some people displayed. I for one never believed in doing to others what was done to you at all cost. Especially if so many innocent lives were at stake. There has to be a point where sanity prevails and where the better man walks away from the madness.

'I was visiting Madala one afternoon during late 2001. The moment I walked through the door I knew something strange was afoot. Madala was waiting for me with a stack of documents. He invited me to sit outside on his private veranda overlooking the large lawn at the back of the townhouse. I walked past the cage with the huge pet Indonesian constrictor Ounooi, that Madala always said really liked me. I was unsure of that and always gave the lady a wide berth. He was known to let the snake out of its cage to rid him of unwelcome or difficult guests since she would, according to him, inevitably always seek out warm company by slithering underneath the table and suddenly appearing in the lap of an unwanted guest. He fetched coffee and some tasty biscuits and he commenced showing me detail of chemical weapons technology, an electromagnetic pulse weapon system design, already further developed than a similar American design and a laser weapon system design; all experimental weapons systems technology I was wholly unaware of and said, 'Sam, today I want to introduce you to the most exciting opportunity we have ever had that will set us up and secure our positions internationally when the balloon finally goes up here."

'He showed me Dutton's visiting card with the Damascus address detail and indicated that the project - manufacturing and marketing - would be managed from there. Madala always maintained that our country would not be any different from any other failed African state and that ultimately all would go to waste. Consequently such a project could not be driven from inside the borders of the country. I listened in silence as he explained to me how he and his group of associates were planning to covertly sell this technology internationally. He explained the pricing structure and asked whether I was interested to be involved with this project. That is how we worked. One man would bring a proposal and the other would have the chance to speak his mind and to either stay within the process or to decline. I explained to him that I was concerned about two of the men who were, according to him, key associates, and that I had met before. As a matter of fact I indicated that I did not trust them and did not want to be associated with them. The one man - apparently a former special forces operator - a title many people took for themselves without any military record in that field of expertise and consequently no merit whatsoever - was intrusive and rude and his constant questions about me and what I do made me feel distinctly uncomfortable in his presence. The other man was obese and blubbery and was presented to me as a doctor of economic studies. He was a seedy personality with a profoundly dubious state intelligence services background none of which could ever be confirmed.'

'So, it was that Madala and I decided that I would not be involved with the Gulf poison project. Madala always had a sense of reality and he ultimately clearly believed that my involvement would complicate my life and that no value would be added to an already deeply complicated activity. He did however mention Donald and Robert - the same CIA operators that he worked with in Central America - and that they would be involved in a central role. That was the cue. I knew Madala and his special relations with these men and that he would only involve them if there was a panoramic plan that took careful note of their first loyalty - the USA. Simultaneously such a project would propel him into a position of trust where he would once again be able to work with his old friends. With South Africa in the state it was then, it was only logical that Madala would cash in all his chips. That was the morality we lived during those days. Hounded by our own government, survival became of paramount importance. Well-intended principles would be rationalised and adjusted if needs be in the face of new realities. However, it gradually became clear to me that Madala was running a carefully planned sting operation that was intended to expose the far right in our country that was set on delivering some of our finest military technology to strange powers for huge amounts of money at the expense of everything we had always stood for. Ongoing discussions with him containing carefully worded messages and information gained independently in years to come would ultimately confirm my deductions with frightening accuracy.

'Madala, Donald and Robert would run the intelligence and liaison part of the operation and the far right group would be convinced that they were in fact doing the business. The deal would then be cancelled right at the end of negotiations and all the guilty parties would be eliminated. Simultaneously the CIA would know the detail of the operation, all middlemen involved and precisely where the weapons were to be built and delivered. This was classic black op stuff and typical of the sort of high-risk double operation Madala was most adept at conducting. Madala gave me a copy of all the documentation and as was our agreement I undertook to guard it in a safe place without my direct involvement. The operation went ahead and ran from late 2001 and well into 2003. He would have been paid well and his position with the CIA would be secure while I am sure that The Rose would also have been satisfied with the ultimate removal of the weapons and the neutralisation of dictatorial powers in the Gulf region.'

'What went wrong, Sam?' I asked.

Sam looked at me pensively and replied, 'Madala's life was incredibly complicated at this time. On 23rd February 2002 'Spyker' - The Doctor - was killed in Angola. This operation was a joint action led by a special forces team - detailed plans for such an attack were apparently drawn up at 'Die Kop' by special forces operators and officers who fought with The Doctor in earlier years, in co-operation with the CIA, British Intelligence and the Mossad. The driving force for this operation was mainly the continued access to oil and diamonds. The new political masters in the Jacaranda City, (Pretoria), had spoken and special forces did not miss a beat in their execution of this plan despite their longstanding alliance with him in earlier years during the Bush War. The Doctor was betrayed by a close bodyguard detail who took a fair amount of money for the betrayal. Apparently he fought like a man possessed and died fighting with two AK 47 assault rifles in his hands. Blood curdling instructions were that he was not to be shot in the face unnecessarily, so as to ensure clear identification by the media. A collapsible coffin was close at hand and he was buried in an unmarked grave immediately after the required photographs were taken for the benefit of the international press. So much then for the honour of our soldiers who did not hesitate to turn on a previous ally. This betrayal shocked Madala as he was also instrumental in introducing certain moderate conservative white groupings to The Doctor over a period of time during Craven's reign, in an effort to create a Southern African strategy to benefit minorities in our country as well as UNITA. The Doctor had to be killed to allow the liberation process in Southern Africa to be concluded. The continued instability in the southern regions of Angola did not fit the picture of a liberated Southern Africa.

'At this time there were several international military conflicts raging and in Somalia the situation, following the 1993 US Ranger and Delta Force catastrophe characterised by the shooting down of USA helicopters, was rapidly deteriorating. 'The Rose' - the Catholic Church's international disciplinarian group dealing with wayward mortals - contacted Madala through their intermediary -The Englishman- who worked closely with Sally, Madala's slightly wild, but loyal Spanish gun-runner friend of many years. The Catholic Church wanted him to go to Somalia to deal with a specifically messy situation 'The Rose' was experiencing there. He accepted, especially since the fight in our country was lost and he was looking further afield for work and income. Madala was not a man to say no to a challenge, however complicated. Several of The Rose's agents who were sent in to take care of pivotal and destructive warlord elements were being expertly killed by an unknown enemy and Madala was the best operator who could possibly effectively penetrate and operate in that God-forsaken and violent landscape. He would access Mogadishu and determine the enemy's capability and deal with it as best he could. Bearing in mind that he was a trained assassin with all that it entailed, it was not an impossible task. The environment would however prove to be a severe challenge. Movement in the city was a nightmare and staying out of sight and effectively evading the ever-present RPG-7s applied against anything that moved by hitting the walls and creating lethal rock shard projectiles in addition to the shrapnel proved to be extremely difficult.

'He ultimately came out haggard, utterly exhausted and severely strained after the operation of finding and neutralising the Catholic Church's enemy. For reasons that I am unable to determine to this day he then decided to see his estranged wife Mabel immediately following this horrendous excursion. He arrived in the Golden City (Johannesburg) and travelled to the southwest Coast to spend some time with her. At this stage I had completely lost touch with him.'

Sam leant forward and showed me the large red garnet set in a white-gold Egyptian Christian 'ichthy' (Greek for fish) frame that this strangely complicated man had given him as a gift many years before. He wore it on a silver chain around his neck next to a small but bulky silver cross with a small diamond and interspersed with a vertical onyx insert.

'Jackie gave me the cross years ago, Alistair. After what happened to me on Highway 61 I have never really been able to take it from my neck.' I was amazed and amused at the mythical angle I saw in my friend's personality for the first time. I would never have thought that this matter-of-fact, efficient soldier would be given to such fancies. He noticed my amusement and spoke to me in a very deliberate but soft voice, 'The attempt on my life and the threats against and persecution of my wife and children ripped the foundations from under me initially and filled my life with a profound sense of ever-present evil. Especially at night I would wake up screaming, groping for my gun and reliving all my experiences over the years working alone in really bad places. I found solace in a small Catholic Church where I regularly went to think and pray to my God while promising to do my bit every inch of the way. It helped me to focus and to regain my perspective.' I always knew that Sam had broken with the Afrikaner Church years before and immediately after the infamous Broederstroom Church conference during which the war effort and by implication all soldiers were simply cast away when the church distanced itself from the conflict. I was however not quite prepared for what he said to me next, 'My God represents a reality that I believe my grandfather lived. He survived the Anglo-Boer War against the British by believing that God helps those that help themselves. If we do not work with what we have to survive we will perish, not through some divine intervention, but through our unwillingness to use our personal abilities in a responsible way. We lose God through negligence Alistair, not through some bullsh-t man-made church dogma that plays politics in the company of the political upper class. The cross and the fish constantly remind me of how one good man once also worked with what he had.'

I nodded and suddenly felt that I began to understand the

clarity and logic of it all and especially why that 'working with what you've got' brought Jackie and him to Europe where they could restart their shattered lives after Craven and his cronies had finished with them and cast them aside like rubbish to be lost forever.

'I can only guess why Madala actually risked seeing Mabel,' Sam continued, 'She controlled most of his shares in their previously shared business and I believe he was trying to convince her to release some funds to him. Mabel refused to share anything with him after his affair with Rowena came into the open. The Gulf Project was still in progress and he was running low on personal funding. I am aware that his creditors were continually harassing him and subsequently his life became more complicated. It was September 2003 and about that time I lost contact with him. All I know now is that according to Rowena, he stayed with Mabel for three days and then departed to rejoin her in the Jacaranda City.'

'That first night of 9th September 2003 after his arrival back in the north he became violently ill. Rowena woke up with Madala complaining of nausea and a severe headache, typical symptoms of some types of poisoning. His condition worsened rapidly. He became violently sick and within minutes he had lost consciousness. Rowena attempted frantically to revive him with mouth-to-mouth resuscitation, but to no avail. He died within an hour of waking her up and immediately became disproportionately swollen to twice his normal body size. These events sent me into shock for several months to come. I had lost the only loyal friend I ever had and I knew my existence would be much more complicated in the future. I felt as if part of my life had been cut away with a knife.'

Sam suddenly stood up and stretched his legs. He gestured to me and said, 'Alistair, come with me, I want to show you something.'

We walked into his workroom. He opened one of his two very plain wooden cupboards and took out a small soft padded bag. He unzipped the bag and produced several medals and military insignia. He handed the items to me one by one and said, 'These belonged to Madala. I took it from his uniforms after his death. His children were not interested and I kept it as a reminder of the man's life.'

Sam handed me the red and silver full-sized South African Paratrooper Instructor jump wings, US Army Airborne Master Parachutist Jump wings, US Ranger badges, Attack Diver badge and Demolitions and Salvage Diver badge, as well as a handful of other medals and shoulder flashes. It was as if I was holding a full and adventurous life in my two hands. The fact that Sam had these very special items in his possession demonstrated to me how close he was to Madala and I began understanding how severe the loss must have been for him. When Madala disappeared from the scene Sam lost the ability to test information and insights with him. That new reality would seriously complicate his life in years to come.

'Madala's body was apparently cremated within days and I still do not know whether he was buried or whether his ashes were simply scattered in some unknown place. Rowena remained most secretive about all of these arrangements. I found that most disturbing.

'What was profoundly worrying was that several days after his death, I received an email from my friend who always wanted to be a yachtsman in some tropical paradise, addressed to 'ye olde cleric' (his words for me) telling me that he was under pressure and wishing me the sun on my face, the wind in my sails and the seas calm. Somehow it felt as if he was simply saying goodbye and that he was running as fast as he could, rather than expecting some assault on his life. Since then I have always been looking in crowds trying to find his familiar face. I have also consistently retained a dream to visit Madala's Netherlands Antilles, his favourite place, to sit and look at the sea and just maybe, maybe see my friend again and the yacht that he always dreamed of. I remember him saying with a laugh in his voice how he would sail on the blue water and do exquisite body painting whenever an attractive young woman asked him to.

'Disappointingly Rowena teamed up and formed an unhealthy relationship with a mostly drunken and incredibly aggressive apparent former special forces operator who quite unexpectedly turned up in her life and took possession of my friend's US Armed Forces ring and his Breitling diver's watch. He could not refrain from insulting Madala's legacy as 'fraudulent and meaningless'. I never quite understood his role and to this day I believe he was placed in that position to oversee the final dismantling of Madala's remaining positive legacy. I always saw that as the ultimate insult to a life that was both adventurous and meaningful. Rowena became increasingly isolated and when I last spoke to her she appeared to be afraid of her situation and the clear threat the overbearing 'wannabee Recce' posed in her life, demonstrated when he wrote her car off and afterwards coolly lived off the money she had saved during her relationship with Madala.

'I believe Madala was poisoned with a weaponised chemical substance administered by Mabel who was apparently in the employ of the government and who in all probability probed his ongoing double operation activities while he visited her. I also believe she was briefed beforehand. This poses the question of whether the SA intelligence agencies were aware of the project, and to what end? At that stage Madala's activities were poorly coordinated and controlled because of the strain he was subjected to and it would only have been a question of time before he was compromised. I remain convinced he was exposed by one or several of the extremist religious far right representatives he was working with during the sting to expose the sale of weapon systems to Iraq - systems that would be manufactured and shipped across the border into Syria as the Allies invaded Iraq. I remember distinctly noticing a CNN broadcast as an on-screen news line clearly unearthed by some brave, diligent newshound stating that chemical weapons were swiftly moved across the Iraqi border into Syria - a claim that has since been corroborated publicly as a significant by-product of the Syrian uprising against Bashar al-Hassad. I firmly believe this to be a fact and that the USA was unable to react since that would place Israel under direct threat from Syria. It would also create yet another front in the Middle East that would place USA and allied forces under enormous strain. Understandably this news item was never repeated on CNN. It remains a horrendous thought that our people may well have been responsible for one of the single most devastating military confrontations of modern times through their sheer greed.

'As Madala's closest friend for many years the extremist group now came after me to find the documents he gave me and to ensure that I would remain quiet. A deadly game of cat and mouse ensued. What I however did not know was that Burton's new wife and Mabel were already working together and the aftermath of Madala's failed sting, his death and Beatrice's efforts to remove Burton and destroy me, were one and the same operation. With the ease of hindsight it is possible to ask whether the new political masters in South Africa were sadly as deeply immoral, flawed and brutal as the actions perpetrated against loyal soldiers and critical citizens in general under the old white government, while the ever present far right religiously driven movements only added fuel to this fire already raging out of control. I was deeply saddened by the thought that the new president whom I had befriended after 1994 was also being systematically undermined by deeply corrupted officials and white liberal advisors who worked for their own personal interest underscored by apparent sheer philanthropic drivel.'

Sam now became aware of the constant movement of people around him busily observing his every move. 'On one occasion I set up an appointment to meet with the instructor who helped me update my gun handling skills that were becoming rusty after my resignation from the defence force. We were scheduled to discuss my continued participation in activities during a time when gun-control was being tightened for reasons of both crime prevention and political expediency by the government that was becoming concerned about threats from the far right. I was suddenly experiencing increased rude references to my person and visible singling out during shooting sessions at the shooting club, mainly due to my perceived positive relations with the government. My position regarding these matters was known to those close to me. I was always a professional and not prepared to participate in any way, shape or form of sedition after a democratic election. In fact, after the 1994 election I became friendly with many senior officials including all three of the presidents in the course of my business activities. I knew that I was trusted by my former enemy and respected for my professionalism and honesty. However, I frequently said during discussions that I would never vote for them and more importantly that I would never betray my country or the president.

'On the day of the meeting with my gun handling instructor I quickly became aware that I was being followed. As we sat down to commence talking the person following me came directly to our table and asked whether he could join us. I was utterly surprised at the man's audacity. He exchanged platitudes and then summarily left. He was clearly simply checking up close and personal that I was the right target. I asked my friend in a hushed voice who this person was. The instructor quite glibly identified him as a former 'Koevoet' (Crowbar) operator with far right leanings. I left soon after and realised that I could not trust this man either. The chance meeting with the operator was simply too convenient. At that stage I was still painfully unaware of Beatrice's involvement with Mabel, the influence she was exerting over Burton and how she was in the main responsible for the far right action against my family. This action varied from cars following my family members and me and aircraft with clearly open photography bays flying low over our house and several attempts to penetrate the property deep into the night for months on end. I would respond with the largest possible commercially available handheld searchlights and messages delivered through a former well-connected army friend to the far right movement, to leave me in peace. Jackie and I were woken many nights by intruders attempting to penetrate our home defences. These were so numerous that I could no longer keep track. Our son slept with a semi-automatic rifle and pistol on his night table. A pump action shotgun was within reach of my wife and I with our pistols close by. We were harassed and tired and confused about who our new enemy really was.'

This sequence of events would ultimately culminate in Sam and Jackie leaving South Africa to find safety in Europe. It would however take them the best of three years before they actually left and another three years before they found relative peace in a quite cynical new environment where strong xenophobic sentiments would become gradually more prevalent. They sold most of their earthly possessions while sending their children into the wide world in different directions to find safety and a future elsewhere. Fortunately Jackie found employment in Europe and they scraped together what money they had left and she simply boarded an aircraft. Sam stayed behind to wind up their affairs before leaving. That was however not so easy. He was still under such enormous strain from his enemies at this time that his health continued deteriorating and he was forced to undergo extensive medical examinations and treatment before he was able to leave.

It is difficult to explain to Europeans how different life in 'modern' Africa is. For the descendants of settlers that went to Africa hundreds of years ago, now carrying pistols, knives, combat flashlights and telescopic batons routinely and sleeping with those items on your bedside table, in a house with burglar bars and contact and beam alarm systems is so incredibly far removed from the cushioned and pampered life in Europe. In Europe people are discouraged from defending themselves and everything is left to the police. The closest people in Europe come to carrying anything remotely protective are iPods, shoulder bags and umbrellas. In Africa and specifically South Africa, the police are very often, especially in certain dangerous areas, part of the significant criminal threat against the citizenry. They are the very last - if at all - people to call in case of a threat or attack against your person by a majority black population criminal element often under white guidance; now wreaking brutal and often inhumane vengeance to the point of animal-like behaviour on the white population for fifty years of political abuse, as well as on their own fearful middle classes who have accumulated some possessions and money. Nearly 2000 farmers and family and workers have already been slaughtered on their farms with recent evidence of farmers forced to sit in a bath and their heads being sawn open and their brains removed and stacked beside them as their wives and daughters savagely raped and then killed. The state in the meanwhile is gradually strangling private gun ownership. The illegal gun trade is soaring with nearly one million AK 74 assault rifles and incalculable numbers of handguns out on the streets.'

Jackie and Sam - despite his now distant experiences as an international covert military operative - were the quintessential wide-eyed pioneers from the colonies who had to attempt to calm themselves and 'detoxify' in a new environment that was so far removed from their country where danger lurked in every shadow and potentially in every car that followed behind you after dark. It was as if they had stepped out of a time machine into a world where not wearing a yellow jacket when your car breaks down and not helping a drowning person or attack victim before having applied all the health and safety paraphernalia first - a completely incomprehensible modern European creation, which is totally foreign to the pioneering mind - is clearly important to a point of total despair. That plus an immensely closed society made for total isolation in their new land with no kiewiet calls at sunset, no grey loeries clowning crazily in the trees to make you smile at dawn, no ten minute thunderstorms that make you sprint for cover to escape the dove sized hailstones and masses of water pouring out of the heavens. Their leaving Europe in 1679 to escape civil unrest, wars and famine and their return during 2005 were surreal and miles apart in its essence, to say the least of it.

Sam and Jackie were out of Africa and relatively safe, but they left their old country in disarray and apparently bereft of God. It was not easy. It was difficult at best to say the least and close to impossible at worst.

But like the mountaineer Sam used to be, he took a decision on the dangerous and insurmountable rock-face and climbed down and ran away to fight another day.

Chapter XVII

The Brotherhood

So it was that during a second visit in mid 2007 that I understood for the first time in my life what it ultimately meant to give someone a gift. In this instance it was a Spanish knight, a symbol of respect, trust and loyalty. This reality was portrayed in a story that Sam told me of circumstances that were so terrifying that a mere effort in reconstruction without rounded edges would probably have torn his heart out. The story was about Sam the Tiger, Raphael the Fox and Alejo the Knight. The story represented Sam's unique, rather old-fashioned, way of shrouding the terror and revisiting old and worthwhile values. Without a conscious effort on my part it was as if the story took on a life of its own through real life occurrences while I was only required to record what was happening. Seemingly insignificant things became the inukshuks within a reality that overshadowed everything that we had planned before, as if the story wanted to be told at all cost. I was ready with the first few chapters of the proposed book when I visited Sam and Jackie again but I was also somewhat apprehensive of what was still to come.

The Fox met the Tiger for the first time during late winter of 2007. It was a frightening experience since he had never before seen such a formidable being in a place where he had always been in command of most of everything. It was quite late - in fact it was already long past midnight - and Raphael, the urban fox, was on his way back to his home in the woods on the farm from a long regular scavenge-hunt through the fields and the town. His route took him through the hospital grounds where there were always lights and noise and where vehicles with loud sirens and blue lights constantly kept coming and going. It was a particularly dangerous area for a fox to navigate through and he always felt relieved once he reached the dimly lit back garden of the old hospital annex. Many people now lived there and from there he could reach the park skirting the old hospital that would eventually lead him to the narrow dark alleyway past the chapel and then down to the river. However, between the church and the final steep pathway down to the river lay one more obstacle, Highway 61. Now our Raphael was not a faint hearted fox. In fact he was quite a courageous and intrepid urban lad with many scavenge-hunt excursions to his credit. But crossing that Highway 61 was always a big enterprise and every time he survived the ordeal of sprinting across before the next wave of cars came roaring past, he felt a rush of energy and took that quick look around to see whether he was really safe.

On this particular night a bitterly cold wind swept in from the far northeast and Raphael hugged the buildings, shrubs and trees wherever he could in an attempt to stay warm. He had already swung by the river and was on the second leg of his journey having successfully crossed Highway 61 for the second time that night. He entered the old annex grounds and ran past the chapel on the edge of the car park. He rounded the corner of the building and slunk into the shadows to leave his scent to keep the little cats that frequented the house with the flower baskets busy and on their toes and to sniff around for some tasty bits to eat. He only had a short way to go before he could cross back into the woods on the farm where he lived. He stopped for a brief moment and as if inspired he looked up at the building. There, framed in the lower window of the flower basket house he looked straight into the eyes of a tiger.

His first thought was to run for his life, but then he noticed the lined sadness in the tiger's eyes and the slight smile as he said in a measured voice, 'Good evening, Mr. Fox. How nice to meet you at last. I have sensed your markings and have seen your footprints and have been looking forward to this meeting for a long time. I hope we will be able to share some time and thoughts so that I will also understand your world. Will you perhaps be my friend?'

Raphael was caught completely off guard.

He smiled nervously and said, 'I am surprised by your kindness and would like to consider your offer. You must know that tigers are very big and fierce and that foxes are really small and with only cunning on their side, they would be well advised to take great care when chancing upon such powerful felines.'

The Tiger smiled and Raphael noticed the Apache obsidian tear encased in a thin metal frame and carefully strung from a neatly woven lace around his neck. 'Surely,' he thought, 'someone who wears the symbol of such grief suffered by the Apache maidens so close to his heart with such care and sensitivity must have a reason for not wanting to cry again. I wonder what tragedy this tiger suffered in his life. I think he may be a good tiger to know and that I will be friends with him.'

Raphael looked the tiger straight in the eyes and said, 'I would like to be your friend, Mr Tiger. What is your name?'

The tiger looked at him and said, 'Sam.'

Raphael smiled and repeated the name. 'Sam, and mine is Raphael. It is a pleasure to meet you.'

He glanced around nervously because his attention had been drawn away for some time now and danger could lurk anywhere outside.

He smiled at Sam and said, 'So, until another day then, Sam. I have to reach home before the sleepy people with their dogs come out to play.'

Raphael turned to run into the night, but not before he noticed in the background behind Sam an impressive large shadow shape on the back wall of the room. It was a shape long since forgotten on the Isles and only displayed in a few very old places nowadays. It was the shape of something his grandfather always spoke of in a soft voice and with great respect and admiration. It was the shape of an armoured knight. Raphael thought to himself, 'Oh, what a good friend I have made. Surely a tiger who asks to be my friend, who respects Apache maidens and their grief about their men who were driven over the cliffs by soldiers and who wishes not to cry again and who has a personal knight to watch over him as well, must be a good tiger.' He smiled at the tiger, backed off a few paces and hurried off. Sam watched as Raphael disappeared into the night.

He closed the window and as he drew the blinds he looked towards where the small shiny metal knight from Toledo stood overlooking the room from the bookcase with his detailed shape projected majestically and full size by the light on to the back wall and said, 'We have made a new friend, Alejo. I think the intrepid and brave little fox Raphael will bring us much joy.'

The next night Raphael passed by the Tiger's house again. It was a very dark night. He glanced up at the window but for some reason Sam was not there. Raphael thought nothing of this since he knew and understood that tigers very often moved about and sometimes stayed away for some days. So, remembering that there was a third party to this newly formed brotherhood, he jumped onto the window sill in an effort to see the Knight since he accepted that he may well be in the house guarding Sam's possessions.

The window was slightly open and the blinds were drawn.

Raphael laid his head on his front paws and whispered through the window, 'Are you there, Knight?'

A deep voice answered from inside, 'Yes, I am here.'

'It is Raphael here. I am a fox and Sam's new friend. Maybe you have heard of me? May I ask your name?'

The voice replied, 'I am Alejo, a Knight from Toledo. Yes, Sam told me about you and I am delighted to meet you, Raphael.'

Raphael smiled and said to himself, 'Surely I am the luckiest fox in the world. I have met a tiger and a knight within two days and they are both prepared to be my friends.'

Alejo smiled quietly to himself and said, 'Do not underestimate the importance of your willingness to be our friend. Sam and I have been lonely for a very long time and appreciate all goodwill we are shown.'

Raphael crept closer to the open window and asked in a soft voice, 'Will you please tell me about yourself and the tiger?'

'Now where will I begin with this story? Ah yes, let me tell you about the beginning when Sam was still young and I met him and Jackie in Toledo during their holiday after they were married during 1972. I lived in a brightly lit house in Toledo with many other knights and horses and items depicting armour and weaponry. Sam walked up to me and I remember him saying to Jackie, 'I think my friend Burton will like this beautiful knight. It will symbolise his life's work and will inspire him and hopefully it will remind him of me when life gets lonely and fragile in his high-office.' Sam took great care to request the attendant to make meticulous travel arrangements so that I would arrive safely after the long journey. So I left my home in Toledo and travelled for many hours to a place called South Africa where the air was filled with strange new exotic smells and noises to the Tiger's first home and from there to the coast where I was given as a gift to Burton - a leader of the country - who would later become president.'

Raphael was not a fox to be easily impressed, as he had seen a lot during his adventurous life. But he was still only a little fox and this was a most important event in his life. 'Alejo was a knight to a president?' he thought to himself, 'I am indeed honoured to know such a distinguished warrior.'

He lifted his head from his paws and said, 'Please tell me more, Alejo. I am listening with great interest and in awe of your strength.'

Alejo paused before answering, 'I stood guard in a place overlooking Burton's private workroom. There was a large working table and chair, a comfortable soft armchair for him to rest in and a narrow but comfortable bed to sleep on when he became tired of his most arduous work of managing the affairs of that troubled country. This room contained many memories of the president's life work and I was always impressed by the neat and unassuming way in which he displayed the objects showing the essence of his life.

'I remember many occasions of triumph and defeat as I stood watching over him. The tragic conflicts with his son William and friend Sam - who tried in vain to warn him against many of his closest allies and friends who conspired and conspired with the enemies of the state behind his back - stand out in its stark reality.'

'I remember especially the time of his departure from office after he was ultimately betrayed by people who attempted twice unsuccessfully to kill him after having visited him in that same office before to swear allegiance to him. The cowardly behaviour of general Max, who declared his loyalty and then betrayed him, distinguished himself in this treacherous regard.'

'I regularly observed the woman giving him a substance to dull his mind while she controlled all those who ever came to see him. All the time she was pushing him into the hands of extremely ruthless people who wanted to rebel against the state. By doing so she destroyed his reputation as a man of reason. I am sure he would never have supported anyone with such radical beliefs out of his own free will.

'Deep into the night of 31 October 2006 I heard a terrible sound from his bed chamber which was right next to the study where I stood guard. I heard Burton shout fearfully for help against an evil I could not see, but I was unable to reach him in time. I regret to this day that because of my physical bondage I was unable to reach and protect my charge. I was always deeply concerned that it would come to this, especially since his heart only kept working because of a small device setting its rhythm. His screams were such as I have never heard before and reminiscent of a wounded cornered animal thrashing about for his life. Then everything went quiet. Directly after that the woman walked from his chamber and into his study. As always she was dressed in black and I thought that she looked more like a witch than ever before. She picked up the receiver of the telephone and dialled a number to report his death to his children. She was ice-cold and calculated. I noticed the powerful magnet she placed on the table in front of her and did not fully understand what that meant, although I suspected that it had something to do with the small device supporting his heart. I was so sad because in a way Burton and I were so alike in our vulnerability, both firmly attached to the same solid pedestals from where he could never escape his structured origins to oppose the evil that surrounded him, while I could not escape my physical bondage to help him. I failed my old friend and I blame myself to this day because I believe he deserved a good death. After all - despite his failings he did give his best for his country and his people as he saw it. I respected him for that and I will miss him for the good things he represented and also for our many silent conversations when he looked at me as if to inquire about simpler less politically convoluted times.'

Raphael was completely stunned as he crept ever nearer to the window and asked, 'What happened after these terrible events, Alejo?'

Alejo stayed silent for a while and replied, 'His son William and second daughter were pushed away from the sibling inner circle. William lost his position as eldest son while his friend Sam was prevented from seeking the truth. The other children wanted to keep the myth of their father's apparent faultless life intact and came to an arrangement with the woman dressed in black. Almost everything Burton owned were either sold or given away or taken by the other children. I was the only valuable item to be handed back to Sam after he asked for me. The rest of William and his second sister's inheritance were siphoned away by the other children and the evil woman.

'I am so thankful to be home. I travelled alone and over a very long distance to Sam and Jackie on these Isles. When Sam finally met me again I was dirty and tired of years of work, but I was so very pleased to see them again and to take a place of prominence in their house from where I can oversee their lives. After Sam was nearly killed crossing Highway 61 in South Africa he is sometimes so unwell, but he tries to stay upright. Jackie is here and I love so much seeing her every night and to listen to her calming words when she speaks to Sam when he is incapable of working through the unfairness of what happened to them and especially when the pain devils grope at his soul.'

Raphael was quite shocked and lay completely still for a while and then realised that it was time for him to go.

'Alejo, I am so thankful that you have told me about all of this. I have a better understanding of your brave and strangely tragic lives and I promise to remember that. Have you told the Tiger all of this?'

There was silence from inside the house.

Then Alejo said, 'I am afraid to tell him this. It may break his heart and I want to spare him that.'

'That is not for you or me to decide, Alejo', said Raphael, 'you must promise me that you will tell him soon.'

Again there was a long silence and then a soft, 'I promise. But tell me Raphael, what is your story?'

'I am a fox of ancient local origins Alejo. I come from a long line of foxes that roamed these hills for centuries. My world is becoming smaller by the day and we mostly earn our living by hunting rodents and insects and by raiding the town waste piles that humans leave in their wake. Our lives are happy, but not always. Sometimes we dream of the open northern country, but fear of humans and their machines keep us pinned between the farm, the hospital and the town. We try to be friendly foxes, but not everyone appreciate us. Sometimes fast cars kill us and sometimes farmers distrust and hunt us down. We are so fortunate though that the horses and the hounds and the sharp shrill sound of the horn have been absent for several years now. Then sometimes we meet tigers and knights and then our simple lives are richer for it. That is all I can say about that, Alejo.'

A dog barked somewhere. Raphael looked around nervously and stood up stretching his legs, 'I have to go now. I am so glad you are both my friends. Maybe together we can try to make this better? Please give my regards to the Tiger. May I see you again tomorrow night?'

'But of course. Be careful as you return to your home Raphael.'

Raphael gave a sharp short bark and ran off into the dark. Alejo looked down at his hands gripping the heavy sword planted firmly between his feet, anchored permanently into the base of his wooden pedestal and his shoulders shook uncontrollably as he cried softly because he remembered that however hard he tried, he could not break free of his bondage high on the bookcase to resist all the enemies that came to Burton's house to conspire and conspire and plot and plot against him over time or to stop the evil woman that night when Burton screamed for help. 'The fox believes I am so strong and brave.

Little does he know how small and vulnerable I really am.'
Small teardrops fell on his sword and ran down onto his pedestal. The little Knight was standing as if fixed in his sorrow and tears.

Sam came home late that night and as usual he walked into the room to ensure that the window was locked.

Alejo looked at him as Sam whispered, 'Oh, my heavens, I forgot to close the window. One day I will come home to find our little fox inside.'

He turned to Alejo and briefly touched his helmet and breastplate.

'Good night, Alejo.'

Alejo replied softly and unheard, 'Good night Sam and thank you for always noticing me. I am so sorry but you just missed Raphael.'

Alejo smiled slightly at Sam's 'exemplary' language. It was exceptional because often Sam would swear at his own mistakes, just as he, Alejo, could. It showed simplicity of personality and lack of pretence. He liked that. As always he felt slightly guilty about not keeping his promise to the fox and telling Sam what happened on that night in president Burton's house. But, he shrugged it off since, as always he firmly believed Sam had to be protected against this horrible truth.

A long time passed by. The strangely inspiring brotherhood of tiger, fox and knight was firmly in place. Sam would wait for Raphael whenever he could during the night and when they missed an opportunity to talk about their days, the fox would speak to Alejo before Sam closed the window at night. Only the fox and the knight spoke about the past though and only they knew the full tale of the dark night of 31 October 2006 in the house anchored between the lake and the sea. These facts were still hidden from Sam. Other than that the content of the conversations were about the daily experiences of tigers, foxes and knights.

It was the summer of 2008 and it was a particularly hot evening. A sleek and shiny young fox rounded the corner where the Tiger lived. He noticed the two flower baskets on the wall just as Raphael taught him and he headed straight for the windowsill and the slightly open window.

He lay with his head on his paws and whispered through the window, 'Mr Knight, are you there?'

'Yes I am', replied the Knight.

'Who am I talking to?'

'I am young Alejo the Fox and son of Raphael'

'What a pleasure to make your acquaintance, young Alejo. I am surprised that we have the same names.'

'Yes' the Fox replied, 'my father gave me the name and told me to carry it with care and pride since it was the name of a brave knight. He told me how and where to reach you. Are you Alejo, the brave Knight?'

'I am a knight, yes, but I can unfortunately not answer to the question of whether I am brave. That is for others to decide.'

'My father told me that you are the very best of the best and that no one can find a more true friend anywhere in this world. I am honoured to be able to meet you at last, brave Knight Alejo.'

Alejo was suddenly concerned and asked the young fox whether his father was well and when he could expect to see him again.

There was a long silence and then Alejo the Fox said in a sad voice, 'My father has died, Mr Knight.'

At first the Knight did not know what to say.

Then he whispered, 'When? Where? How?'

'He died last night, Mr Knight, on Highway 61. He was hit by a fast car. He was tired and too slow to evade the speeding car on his way back from the river. We found him late in the night when he did not return and we went to look for him. He looked so sad where he fell with his eyes open, but lifeless and only his shiny hair moving in the wind.'

'I am so sorry, young fox Alejo. Your father was a good friend who brought Sam the Tiger and me much happiness with his presence. I will keep you in my heart.'

The young fox barked his appreciation, promised to return and then ran off into the night. The knight remained behind alone with only his sadness while he remained cruelly bound to his pedestal.

Sam walked into the house that night after a day of travelling to a far place to walk and look at the sky and smell the fresh air of the hills in order to strengthen his weakened body. He entered the room and closed the half open window, drew the blinds and turned to greet and touch Alejo. He was profoundly shaken by what he saw. There on the high bookcase the Knight from Toledo sat on bent knee with both hands on his sword handle with his shoulders shaking with the grief of a great many years.

For the first time in a long time the Knight was really alive and Sam could only make out the words, 'Raphael is dead, Highway 61, the young fox Alejo came and I have to tell you everything, Sam, because I promised our friend Raphael.'

That night the Knight from Toledo told Sam the Tiger what

had happened all those years ago in South Africa when Burton died at the hand of an evil woman in the house anchored between the lake and the sea. This was then how for the first time Sam was given 'insider' confirmation of what had really happened to his friend Burton.

The Knight and the Fox and the Tiger were now bound forever by a tragedy that would remain a secret until I visited Sam and he told me the story that I have now written on these pages. The power of the seemingly lifeless symbols and apparently unimportant living things that surround us often brings the truth to the surface, especially when they are seen together for what they were, a brotherhood for the truth against the incredible evil that surrounded us during that time and that we survived.

Sam and I walked outside to enjoy some fresh air and look at the stars before turning in for the night. I asked Sam how he really found out all that had happened on that fateful night. As we stood near the trees I noticed a young fox moving seamlessly into the night. Just before he disappeared he looked around and his eyes glistened in the house lights. I looked at Sam. He was smiling quietly to himself and I heard him say the name 'Alejo.'

'The fact that the Knight came back to me proved to me that what I suspected was the truth. After all, a knight would not lie.' Sam stuck to his fable of the 'brotherhood'.

I suspect it helped him to work his way through the cruel tragedy that took place. The story of the three unlikely friends and what it represented in terms of observation from afar and the symbolism of gifts and their meaning gave me the feeling that we were living as if in a dream and that represented the escape to real freedom that we all wanted, but that eluded us all for so long. Escaping from reality into dreams was now also part of my life and I decided to accept Sam's answer without further questioning.

Chapter XVIII

Changing Continents

I thought about the events Sam related during these several days while working on my notes and I started realising slowly but surely that it was not the detail that really mattered. It was the devastating effect on his life that alarmed me, probably more so because he was my friend and our relationship was determined by old-fashioned values that were fast disappearing in a world of incredible uncertainty and shallow self-serving agendas. I felt helpless because I could do nothing to help him while he struggled to stay afloat with a cruel regimen of injections and large quantities of tablets. I tried to stay with the present moment, but could not get away from the memories of our time together in Kavango and everything that went with that. A feeling of déjà vu and a haunting sense of melancholic sadness held me spellbound whenever I walked out of the house and noticed the Kavango masks and the trees and the skyline. It was as if we were back in our familiar surroundings, but only without any of the familiar sounds of aircraft and vehicles and voices and heat. We were reliving our experiences as if escaping in a dream, where we were looking in from the outside and investigating our lives to see what we could possibly have done better. Thinking about it now I believe we both realised that it was all in the distant past, but that was the only reality we really knew and consequently we repeatedly referred back in an attempt to find some answers and hope.

Sam interrupted my thoughts when he walked into my room and said cheerfully, 'Now, now, Alistair, although you are clearly very busy with your notes it is very important for your perspective to remain physically active.'

I looked up from my laptop and gazed at him as if begging for mercy. As always though, Sam got what he wanted and I agreed to join him for a long walk. He drew me into his world and away from my work. I understood the importance of these walks since many a crucial aspect of our discussions originated in the open where he felt at home. We decided to leave the next morning after breakfast and immediately made all preparations. Rucksacks, water bottles, some food, first-aid kit, boots, jackets and hats were the main items.

Sam vividly reminded me of major general Christian always saying, 'Prepare for every eventuality before stepping into that chopper. However innocent the journey, should anything happen you need to be self supportive.'

We laughed softly as if we were sharing a secret. Suddenly I looked forward to our little adventure.

We drove to Padstow and left the Land Cruiser in a secure parking area. We set off carrying our medium sized day sacks. After forty-five minutes walking we gazed out across a wide sweeping bay of calm seas framed by green and beige hills and white and grey clouds supporting a blue sky. At that moment a sea-rescue helicopter swept in low and flew over us just as before, long ago. It felt uncanny and as if once again our outdoor exploits were underscored by well-known images.

We reached the stone Daymark Tower, built as a lookout post during the days of the Spanish Armada, just before commencing the descent to Trevone Bay. We sat down for a moment close to the tower and its dark menacing shape reminded me of the tree houses in Cuando Cubango at the end of the day when the shadows lengthened. I had a distinct out of body feeling as if looking down on the two of us with some sadness and a longing for that time that was long past. With the fresh wind on our faces we took in the view and had some refreshments. My mind raced back to our days spent together in Angola when Sam suddenly, as if sensing my quiet reflections, started talking in a quiet voice.

'I never once would have believed how difficult transplanting our lives to Europe would be, but we had no choice other than to leave South Africa after all that had happened. We were so threatened by a variety of political groups with different political agendas while I was unable to walk the streets or even drive through the city without sensing that curious threatening lack of ownership after the take-over by our previous political and military adversaries. Even sidewalks, familiar stretches of road and well- known neighbourhoods seemed somehow inaccessible. I did not know where to go, what to do or who to trust. It felt increasingly as if our inner sanctum of private experience of many years was invaded and somehow desecrated.

'My health was deteriorating fast, mainly due to inadequate medication and the mounting pressures - both physical through intrusions into my property at night and psychologically by the destruction of my political and business networking - from extremist far-right groups who were bent on destroying me. In the light of all of these pressures, as I described to you, my wife and I decided to encourage our children to leave the country as fast as possible, after which she left. I would follow much later after having closed down our life in South Africa. These events had an extremely damaging effect on my life. Unavoidable as it was, it was that part of leaving the beloved land, the actual physical separation and resulting loneliness that nearly broke me. Jackie's departure came as a massive hammer blow that nearly killed me. We argued the day before she left and I simply did not have the wherewithal to mend the breach before she boarded the aircraft that night. I was sick and weak and these testing circumstances worsened it. I felt sorry for myself to the point of total collapse, especially when the doctors suddenly suspected that I might possibly have suffered a heart attack, which thank heavens, was later proven wrong. This added to my stress and I felt that my life was spinning out of control. New drastic medication that was intended to calm my body down and restore some kind of equilibrium had massively adverse side effects and I would wake up in the middle of the night with exaggerated heartbeat brought on by being unable to breathe. I would fight my way through locked doors and into the darkness outside - cycled Glock 23 semi-automatic pistol in hand - responding to my built-in sense of self-preservation of many years and thus not wanting to venture into the dark without being able to fight; furtively sucking in the hot December air with thunder flashes around me, while cursing and shouting my anger at the gods and weeping because Jackie was gone. I could just as well have died then, I was so helplessly weak and so lonely, filled with a growing sense of utter desperation. Only my sense for the factual and my built-in sense of survival based on discipline through training kept me going.'

Sam sat quiet for a while and I thought to myself that to transplant overseas is always so complicated. To transplant to a highly developed country from a place where in later years it became commonplace to survive with often only basic senses to rely on as early warning devices, is more complicated as far as mindset is concerned. Add to that the risk of highly trained persecuting operatives making your life difficult to the point of complete exhaustion and desperation, such a change becomes a completely different matter. I clearly recalled how difficult it was for me to move to South America - without any outside pressures exacerbating my position.

Sam leant back against a flat rock face overlooking the sea and while pointing to the dark tower and as if he could read my thoughts he said, 'This ancient tower reminds me of my life that no longer fits the modern idiom and the apparent lack of commitment to anything valuable. I am struggling to explain this to you, but the best way of describing my dilemma here is probably to refer to a small, but frightening experience with a few new friends who objected vehemently when I dared to express positive sentiments about The Doctor and my work with him in Angola. It was one evening at a small private function, despite the fact that the hosts merely knew of Savimbi, but never met him and certainly never worked for or with him. This experience was made all the more devastating when it was suggested that after my revelation I was no longer really welcome there and that I was merely being tolerated.'

'That was probably the worst display of sheer disrespect and profound dislike of whatever I represented in their opinion, I ever experienced on this beautiful island. I had finally come full circle. My status as a spent force and forgotten soldier was completed by this seemingly insignificant, but quite vehement disagreement, about a man who was my friend and who was brutally slain by South African soldiers of whom I probably knew several. I was now that soldier standing in the corner of the room with his scars visible and being shunned because of ordinary people's sheer inability to understand what we do and that we do what we do for them, simply because someone capable of taking that strain needs to do it. Fortunately these people were the extreme exception, although the effect of that one instance of being shunned was potentially deadly. It was a chemotherapy injection day when a neighbour loudly confronted me about a silly thing. Quite suddenly I began feeling extremely weak and shaky as unknowingly the strain of the confrontation had caused a collapse of my system. It took me the best of four months to recuperate, which in turn did nothing for my self-confidence. Thankfully in the years that followed we met some ordinary folk who in fact made a considerable difference to the way we perceived ourselves here.

'My friend William's life was also rather out of control at that point. He was, inexplicably, fighting his siblings for his rightful part of the late president Burton's estate. This became a most disconcerting affair with only his sister supporting his rightful claims as the eldest son in the family. This situation became increasingly sinister and disturbing by virtue of the fact that there were aspects of the finalisation of the estate that were kept from William and his sister, based on his eldest sister's insistence that they had no rights in the matter. Ultimately the finalisation of the estate became the final battleground of a bitter family feud that had already raged for several years amongst the children - fighting for their parents' acceptance mostly, because of their mistaken adulation for a man who during the last days of his presidency completely lost his focus, misread the signs of the changing times at the end of the eighties and allowed enemies within his own party ranks to usurp his position.

'Eventually these same enemies would dispose of him in a dreadfully disrespectful way, which in turn led to an ignominious ending to his life. I suppose in the end this battle for position within the family was also about material possessions and the memories they hold within them. I was shocked to see how this distasteful unfolding conflict that eventually found its way into the media, affected William. It not only proved to him that his brother and two other sisters had virtually no intention of respecting his position, it also demonstrated the extent to which they were prepared to disregard his life and what he stood for during the war years when he worked tirelessly behind the scenes while they were basking in the light of their parents' public life. Added to this dreadful situation was the fact that we were close friends and the negativity that he experienced ultimately also affected my life adversely. It was as if Burton's misinterpretation of events under the guidance of his enemies that penetrated his inner circle, and which ultimately led to his demise, was blatantly and stupidly taken over by the majority of his children who simply carried his flawed legacy forward. William, his second sister and I were eventually cast out as enemies of Burton's 'Golden Years' as the eldest daughter dubbed his ten years in office as president. I have now lost my country and any association with Burton's legacy. He was after all my friend and I believe to this day that I helped him on many occasions and that in his own right he made his specific contribution during his lifetime and tenure as the leader of South Africa. This was recognised publicly by the then serving president. My status as a displaced colonial was more or less sealed. My only hope was that I would be able to build on the few relationships that Jackie and I had been able to forge here and that these people would see us for what we really are. We simply want to be ordinary people with ordinary hopes and dreams to look forward to. That would however prove to be quite complicated simply because we are really colonial pioneers with all the abilities that brings.'

I responded with a slightly uncomfortable nod. I did not know what to say. Sam stood up. He offered me his hand and helped me to my feet. We walked away from that dark tower and over green fields framed by long winding hedgerows. I looked up and the sky was blue and the clouds white. Simple, straightforward shapes, much like my friend, with no ludicrous refinement created in an attempt to impress an unforgiving, uninterested and profoundly cynical world.

After we arrived back home that night I enjoyed a hot dinner and good conversation with Jackie and Sam. Lots of laughter and stories - several at my expense - about our walk that day accompanied our meal. Sam gradually became quieter and eventually stood up and wished me a peaceful night and then retired to his room. I sat with Jackie for a while. She looked tired for someone with such energy and drive. I helped her clear the table when she suddenly stopped working and asked me to sit for a while. She was clearly concerned and said in a deliberate, but quite sad voice, 'I have known and lived with Sam for many years, Alistair. He has changed quite dramatically. He no longer believes that good triumphs over evil. He no longer believes in causes, but only in the few people that he trusts from his previous life and of course you and the children and me. He is wary of strangers and is more of an introvert than ever before. I can hardly ever get him to visit friends and even when the children visit he eventually withdraws into himself as if he merely wants to be a spectator. He talks about leaving and simply walking away into the mountains every day now and says with monotonous regularity that dying in the mountains would be a good death. I can barely cope with his clear sense of alienation from his professional past, South Africa and friends he could trust before. It seems increasingly as if he is drawing away from me, becoming ensconced within his own private thoughts. He recently asked a trusted and well-connected friend to assist with extracting information that could help him understand what actually happened to him when he was attacked in South Africa. During the discussion he mentioned the names Louis C. and Koskas Du P. and requested his friend to attempt to dig up the detail of the assassination attempt on his life and our family that was authorised at that time. Sam is convinced that he should bring these events to the attention of the Human Rights Commission in South Africa as well as the War Crimes Tribunal in The Hague.'

I recognised the name Louis C. from earlier discussions with Sam and interjected, 'Sam told me about this man, Jackie, I am aware that Sam and Madala saw to it that he was arrested for gun running some years ago. Is he now once again active in South Africa, plying his old evil craft? Was Sam able to extract the information?'

Jackie paused and I saw that she was sad and close to tears

– something that she normally suppressed very efficiently around outsiders.

When she spoke it was with a hushed voice, 'His friend sent a message riddled with uncertainty skirting the issue. There was a leadership contest underway at the time and reliable personnel from the previous government were already leaving because they feared the new man. Sam's friend had access to the president's office and he was in the process of assisting Sam to get to the detail of what happened to him by speaking to a task group who is investigating serious human rights offences perpetrated by previous officials. Apparently he is not able to help Sam as one of his key associates has just resigned. His friend's inability to access the highest echelons in government, seen in conjunction with his most recent reaction to Sam's inquiry on progress, seems to indicate that unscrupulous people might have threatened him. Louis C. is alive and well and living in South Africa. It is also becoming clear that the government would not want any harm to come to dr Bana who is still active in South Africa. God only knows how many people will still have to die under his 'supervision'. Sam has lost his last bid to get to the truth. I guess he is right. Good no longer triumphs over evil.'

Jackie stood up and with a soft, 'Good night, Alistair, sleep well,' she started towards the door.

'How is he coping with this dead end, Jackie?' I said under my breath.

She turned briefly at the door and said to me, 'Ask Sam to tell you about the crossroads and his regular re-visitation of that subject over the years, Alistair. You will then hopefully understand better how he functions. Be cautious though, it is the one subject he is quite closed about since it and the operation aligned with it has never been compromised in any way, shape or form for nearly twenty-two years.'

Chapter XIX

Crossroads I

I waited for the right moment to ask Sam about this. It was two days after my discussion with Jackie. We were on our way back from Tintagel after a visit to 'King Arthur's Castle'. We walked really far and over quite rugged terrain on that day and I was exhausted, especially after having scaled the steep incline to the gateway and into the castle ruin. Sam suggested that we attempt the second set of steps to the top of the cliff, rather than descend back into the ravine and then follow the road back into the town. I buried my exhaustion under some remark about only being warmed up, although I was starting to feel like death warmed up. Sam seemed quite fresh, but I noticed that he was audibly breathing deeply and methodically and he was limping more visibly.

I took the opportunity and put the question quite bluntly, 'What happened at the crossroads, Sam?'

Sam stopped in his tracks and asked with a slight smile, 'Jackie told you? Let's get to the top of this incline and I will tell you. Promise that you will be discreet when writing about it though. I do not want anyone to get hurt.'

We climbed to the top of the incline and I have to say I was thoroughly exhausted by the time we sat down on a slab of rock overlooking the Atlantic. For the first time since I have arrived I saw Sam wipe his brow. He was pushing himself as if he wanted to prove that he could manage the physical strain. I would understand why some time later when Sam tested himself in the only way he knew how, over distance. That would be his answer to the illness that was consuming him. I respected that because it confirmed what I always knew about him. He never just accepted his situation. He always set some form of qualifying test for himself instead of merely driving other people over the cliff so to speak. This characteristic made him both special and ordinary. It was special through personal effort and ordinary through his understanding of the ordinary soldier's mindset of 'show me and I will follow your example without hesitation'. This 'credo' had its downside though. The governing elite during Sam's time in the defence force became more elitist as time went by. Sam's willingness to associate with ordinary people did not go down well in these circles in which he moved due to his association with William and his father the president. Right throughout the war he was treated with suspicion by these elitist elements and ultimately it contributed to the criticism and isolation he experienced towards the end of the eighties.

Sam's Crossroads experience refers to the time when he met Joseph Kim during 1983 when he was designated to handle a certain Top Secret operation running from the Far East to Europe and Africa. This operation was well planned, minutely secured, massively funded and expertly executed; all participants in the operational line were well trained and experienced. Consequently it was not surprising that the operatives, detail and extent of this operation was never compromised during

Sam's involvement for four years or right up to 1989 when everything changed in South Africa after the silent and relatively bloodless coup by Craven and his cronies. The essence of the operation was the continued detailed and wide-ranging support of a key Resistance Movement in Africa and the procurement of the untraceable means of war for special forces. The outcome envisaged for this resistance conflict would have profound implications for the political process in South Africa and was primarily designed to create a stable border and friendly oil rich Angola in the northwest to enable a secure environment for future political development. This at least was the plan as the soldiers understood it. As in all armed conflicts though, it was never certain what the real political agenda was and the soldiers never knew when this agenda would change with all the inherent dangers for both soldiers and associated forces.

'Now, Joseph Kim was not your real action hero,' Sam said with a slight smile.

'In fact, he was thoroughly sedentary apart from the fact that he tirelessly travelled the world. Any slight suggestion that he might have to visit the end destination of the equipment for which he so readily facilitated procurement always put him into a state of naked shock that mostly resembled the after effects of a stroke He was however clever, wealthy and well educated and above all he was Chinese. He knew his way around the PRC and its business community and he was extremely well connected within the upper echelons of government. His years of education spent at a Canadian university helped him to blend into the western business model quite seamlessly. He was a smooth operator with a precise understanding of the money, capital and commodity markets and during any day it would not be strange to overhear him bark instructions over the phone to his broker after having excused himself from any current discussions. Without fail he would then rejoin the group with apparent ease, which served to prove his capabilities to rapidly grasp the crux of any discussion and or problem. During the early part of the operational period everything ran smoothly, but as the detail of activities gradually started emerging with an ever increasing degree of complexity, it was only a question of time before we would be forced to make regular drastic adjustments to our lives and work. He coped remarkably well under these challenging circumstances for someone with apparently no formal intelligence background. I have to say in retrospect that I always had the feeling that somehow he was not just another associate, but that he in fact had exposure to this kind of thing before on a much more formal basis.'

The intelligence operative in me rather than the journalist wanted to know whether Kim worked for Chinese intelligence.

Sam looked at me and said with a slow nod of his head, 'Yes, and more. He was in all probability a senior strategic intelligence core advisor to the PRC government, who not only assisted with smaller matters such as the sale of weapons or equipment. In reality he negotiated strategically crucial bilateral and trilateral agreements and aspects with foreign governments in the course of the conclusion of several international mega transactions, such as with Zimbabwe and Iran both, which amongst other things, procured jet fighters, anti aircraft missiles and Silk Worm missile systems through his business structures. Sadly these apparent capabilities were however overshadowed by his inherent lack of courage when the odds were really stacked against us in the Far East.'

'I once flew into Singapore for a stopover of about three days before catching a flight to Bangkok where I lay low for another two days to wait for my armaments expert, Simon, to catch up. From there I flew to Hong Kong where he would join me and we would catch a direct flight to Beijing. Simon was a highly trained engineer in the employ of the armaments corporation with an unfortunate troubled personal life. His wife suffered from a serious fear anxiety condition and I have to say that I always felt that it was something that hampered his otherwise professional performance. Coupled with his regrettable over developed sense of self-importance it was quite a volatile mix for someone who participated in risky operations.

'The fact that he did not come from a military background complicated matters. He took precisely the same travel route as mine with the exception that he departed two days after me to throw our enemies off the trail. During this time we were regularly followed by just about everyone with our own national intelligence service right in the front like a huge beacon bungling their way into and out of countries in an attempt to discover what we were really busy with. Then, because of sloppy counter tailing procedure and a blasé attitude, which was in line with Simon's particular ego, he was noticed and ultimately delayed by the airline. He was questioned by the Singapore authorities at Changi International Airport. Their line of questioning was typically vague and apparently simply based on a 'procedural exercise' with reference to foreign nationals travelling through Singapore at frequent intervals. The sweeping hand of one of the major Western agencies namely the CIA, hiding behind an apparently harmless civil aviation procedure, was clearly visible within this incident.'

'The night on the day when this happened we spoke briefly over the phone after I flew into Hong Kong. True to his uniquely stubborn, independent attitude and despite my concerns, he had already decided unilaterally to take a later flight to Hong Kong the following day after having succeeded in 'convincing' the officials at Changi Airport that he was a bona fide businessman. Whether they believed him or allowed him to travel on because they were simply giving him rope we will probably never really know. I however believe to this day the latter was right. We arranged to meet in a back street at 06h00 the following morning. I circled the meeting place on foot and arrived well before 06h00. I made sure that I was not tailed and visually checked all the buildings and nearby streets to make sure that we would be secure. At this stage I was really concerned for our safety and the integrity of the operation.

'Once I was satisfied that the area was clear as far as I could see, I entered the street from the city side with the waterway in front of me. It was a grey wintery morning and the stale smell of the previous night's cooking drifted from a restaurant where a man was energetically sweeping, mopping and generally sloshing about noisily from a large bucket of water to remove the evidence of the previous night's excesses, whistling some unknown Chinese tune. I walked close to the left side of the street and tried to remain as inconspicuous as possible even though I was at that stage one of only two people there, I could hardly suppress a bit of a snigger. I was so incredibly exposed and the only reality that kept me from being totally despondent was the fact that I knew those back streets stretching all the way from Star Ferry to the hotel area like the back of my hand; I was on my feet, strong and flat-out-running fit at that time and could disappear without a trace and shake any tail without breaking a sweat.

'A grey shape moved away from the building at the very far end of the street and started towards me. It was Simon and the closer he drew the more I realised that his experience was not what I had thought. It was clearly not just a routine questioning. He was badly shaken and clearly under enormous duress. All the signs were there. He was twitchy and walked hesitantly and when he spoke his foreign accent shone through his English like a clear and bright beacon saying, 'Right, here I am, I am a foreigner and I am scared shitless.' I was really concerned by what I saw and decided to suggest a change in plan there and then. Clearly the interrogation at Changi International Airport was a psychological blow to him that could have affected all the stopovers from then on.

'I was once detained at Harare airport, my passport confiscated while I was questioned for a whole day. Once I reached my hotel room and relative safety for that moment and had hidden all incriminating documentation in a creative hiding place behind a mirror, I had to stay up throughout the night waiting for a possible arrest. That put the fear of the living God into me. The Zimbabweans were not known for their civilised interrogation methods that ranged from mental abuse to physical assault to rape with any object close to hand. I could only imagine the naked fear that Simon must have felt when he was pulled from the immigration line in Singapore on that day. He was quite alone with no backup and no secure bolt hole to run to. In the Far East different interrogation rules apply, mostly that the winner takes all and that the strongest stays alive. For the rest it is more or less made up as they go along with no rule books or ethics guidelines are ever consulted

'We stood close to the side of the road and discreetly and softly exchanged our viewpoints about this unholy mess. People were now slowly trickling into the street with either early morning deliveries or moving along hastily to their places of work. I was particularly nervous, mainly because I understood how difficult it was to distinguish friend from foe in an environment where tailing and surveillance was common practice and where several foreign agencies were active. Since many of the agencies used local assets it was even more complicated to distinguish one from the other where the majority of city dwellers looked very alike, even for the trained western eye.'

I looked at Sam and asked in a clear, but whispered tone, 'How in the name of God did you have any chance of surviving that kind of situation? Where could you possibly run to?' Sam sniffed a quiet laugh and pointed at his feet, 'I would run for the docks and stow away on a ship after dark. Best way out. Borders were closely guarded and anyway, crossing the border into the PRC was not a safe option, bearing in mind that our movements were strictly monitored. We were officially under military intelligence escort wherever we went into that country. If you were picked up by low ranking operatives at any time outside of your operational envelope that was only cleared with a select few at the top of the governmental hierarchy, you would be quickly identified, incarcerated and then interrogated until you succumbed to bloodcurdling questioning methods, told all and died an ignominious death.'

'My only semi-official bolt hole was in Singapore through an intelligence back-channel. The problem remained of how to get there. I decided that by sea would be the best. This is of course all distant history, Alistair, and I wonder whether all of this is important for your narrative. I am concerned that several people may be hurt by revealing these facts and why this incident influenced me so negatively over these years.'

I noticed that he was becoming restless about the subject matter, but I pressed ahead with, 'You have to tell me what happened here, Sam. I need to understand the extent of your experience and how it became the benchmark for your cynicism. If you feel anger towards me for raising this please tell me, possibly we can then address this later?'

Sam was suddenly visibly quite agitated. He leant forward and grabbed me by the hand, 'I am not angry at you, but you must understand that betrayal of anyone that has your trust is so deeply unsettling that it ultimately affects everyone and everything that it associates with, whether passively or actively. I understood for the first time that I was quite alone in the situation and Simon's slightly superior attitude did not help to alleviate the pressure that was building up rapidly. I would be confronted with similar situations of which you are already aware, later in my career when I heard of betrayals by handlers who were taking money from opposing forces in my own division. To this day I believe that the indiscreet and unprofessional actions of our own national intelligence service, which distrusted military intelligence international actions. They constantly ordered international surveillance on military intelligence and operations, placing us in an extremely difficult and exposed position. I did not realise that so early on there were questions raised about all our activities. These activities were regarded as a significant risk to the new initiatives that were being forged secretly while we were fighting the war.

'Nevertheless, we made the decision that I would proceed on my own and Simon would return home to ensure that no further attention was drawn to our real activities. I have to say that I appreciated the way in which he handled the situation ultimately by regrouping and approaching the matter in a purely analytical fashion. Despite his pedantic personality he agreed to make the right decision and it probably saved both of us. What happened here appeared to be the norm for the moment. We would never be able to work without any hindrances because of the ever present internal risk of being compromised by our own people who were following us with their own deeply treacherous agenda held firmly in mind.

'We parted company barely thirty minutes after we met and I was suddenly completely on my own with no other option but to proceed with the operation.' Sam was quiet for a moment. He looked haggard and it seemed as if he was suddenly tired and I began feeling again as if I had intruded into his world and set off memories of experiences that he would rather not have discussed. I offered a lame 'Sam, would you rather that we not talk about this?' but he held up his hand and said, 'No, this is important and I need to explain to you what changed around me at that time and why I was transformed in so many ways.

'Now Alistair, I went into the war with a distinct feeling of duty and excitement. I remember my enthusiastic physical training before I reported for basic training early in 1968, followed by deep terror of the very polite navy instructors waiting for us at the bus station close to the training base. I remember how this sympathetic demeanour changed into sheer vocal abuse instilling the fear of God in us once we arrived on naval soil. I can still sense the parade ground on winter mornings with the thick West Coast fog swirling through the ranks. To this day I can vividly recollect my experiences after completion of my officer's course reporting to my ship. The very specific sea-time period with the smells, sounds and views that accompany a varied and exciting time at sea on a warship, the familiar smells when passing the galley in the mornings when the previous night's cooking was being eradicated while frequent swearing and loud shouts floated to the upper decks; the movement of the ship, the overwhelming sea; the sheer thrill when ploughing through a storm with the icy water of the southern oceans thundering down on the bridge and the radio masts bent backwards so far that I was convinced they would snap. The memories of quiet nights on the bridge fighting fatigue and always knowing that failing to see another vessel is impossible to contemplate with the responsibility of two hundred and thirty five men on board, are still with me, especially during sleepless nights.

'I remember with vivid clarity the 4.5 inch main guns firing rhythmically and nearly in sync with the 40 - 60 Bofors gun aft of midships. I remember the pilot with the yellow flight helmet waving to me with a gloved hand from the Buccaneer having just beaten us to the draw during anti-aircraft gunnery exercises, swooping only metres over our quarterdeck with a loud 'swoosh' and then climbing up and up while turning in the air with his bomb doors slowly closing. I remember with such clarity how I reported for my final parade at the end of my training sporting longer sea-time hair and a noticeably tarnished cap badge as proof of my sea-dog qualification. I can recall in the finest detail my subsequent training as an intelligence operative and most vividly the sights, sounds and tastes of all the places where I trained, and eventually worked across several continents. Some time before I left South Africa for ever I visited the previously elegant 11 Commando Officer's Mess directly adjacent to the Danie Theron Battle School close to Kimberley. I stood transfixed in complete shock and horror with tears filling my eyes when I witnessed the neglect and disgusting decay that followed the departure of the last white government. I knew then that it was all finally over. This realisation of the finality and irreversibility of the situation was re-enforced by any memories of the Crossroads encounter. Even at that time, my experience in China gave me reason to doubt where we were headed in South Africa.'

I sat quite silent while Sam regrouped. This was a special moment. I did not want to spoil it with stupid questions.

Chapter XX

Crossroads II

'My doubts after the crossroads experience in the Far East ultimately became a crystal clear sign for me in my own country, Alistair. It was as if during that time I began to see for the first time how tenuous our position truly was. It did not help us to have won the war in military terms. The politicians took all of that away from us when they refused to see the reality of our minority position and instead used the soldiers as a delaying action, while they negotiated a political solution that would ultimately benefit them. The blame for all these years would be placed on the shoulders of soldiers and policemen who executed the orders and laws that they were given by their political lords and masters. Simultaneously it highlighted the betrayal underscored by the lust for money that became such an inherent part of our people's existence once we moved from Europe to Africa all those centuries ago.

'After the brief encounter with my associate in Hong Kong, I boarded a flight to Beijing the following day and arrived later that same day. It was bleak and ice-cold in that monster city and I felt distinctly isolated when like so many times before, I walked through passport control positioned across the middle of the cavernous arrivals hall. Joseph Kim waited for me in the public area and I had to force myself to be friendly after my little catastrophe with Simon and his ever present ego in Hong Kong.'

'Are you well, Sam? Did you have a good journey?' he squeaked, and gave that familiar high pitched laugh when I said that I was tired and that I would rather be sleeping somewhere on a tropical beach. I asked what our timetable and program entailed. As per normal he immediately plunged into his also familiar evasive tactics regarding any possible questions from my side. 'I don't understand'; 'I am confused' or just simply 'what?' were always present in all detailed discussions enabling him to buy time to think and answer smoothly and cleverly. On this occasion I kept on hammering away and he eventually explained that I would travel about one and a half hours to Tianjin, 132 km south-east of Beijing, the following day. Along the way I would be taken to an army base where the consignment of weapons that I was supposed to take delivery of would be shown to me. There would be an opportunity to make spot checks to ensure that we were in fact receiving what we ordered and paid for. I would travel alone since Joseph had other important matters to attend to. He would join me in Tianjin to meet the harbour master and attend a luncheon in honour of our successful business and to show appreciation for the usage of the port for the shipment to Matadi in the DRC. I should have seen the signs of what was coming at that stage already. I was however under strain and wanted to get the job done. I trusted him.

'When I walked out the front door of the hotel the next morning a car and chauffeur was already waiting. It was a long journey, initially weaving through seemingly endless lines of cars and solid wheeled ox wagons snaking through the thick smog. I still felt tired after the flight and concerned about the day ahead of me, mainly because I received no formal briefing explaining the unfolding of events that would take place on the day. Beyond the grubby suburbs the cold fog drifted lazily over the low-lying fields on either side of the road. The further we travelled the colder it became until we were fully surrounded by endless ice fields broken by intermittent side roads and the regular dark embankments skirting what seemed like shallow frozen paddies.

'I must have slept for a few minutes because I woke up with a jolt and sat upright. I checked my watch. We must have been driving for about an hour. Ahead, slightly to the east, I could just make out a thin black mark on the white ice horizon. As we drew nearer I saw that it was a Russian Zil limousine and there were two military officers standing in front of the staff car in the middle of the crossroad leading to the west. When the car came to a halt I stepped out and greeted both men. One was a tall gentleman looking quite the archetypical Chinese army officer in his long green PRC Army uniform tunic with rank insignia, which seemed to indicate that he was a colonel. The other man was quiet and appeared to be an aide to the senior man. They spoke in broken English and invited me to join them. We drove off in a southerly direction with my car following. After approximately another fifteen minutes we reached a sprawling military base and landing strip. Now, a military base in China is something to behold, Alistair.' Sam suddenly laughed out loud and slapped his knee and we laughed together while he explained to me the rudimentary facilities, which consisted of a small building that appeared to be a guardhouse of sorts with basic furniture such as a table and a few very old kitchen chairs. There was a gathering of several officers and some infantrymen who were fetching and carrying to loud instructions from the officers. Sam was introduced and the welcoming function commenced. The table was covered with a white starched tablecloth and fruit, especially bananas were fanned out and interspersed with peanuts, some other dried fruits, sweets and filter cigarettes arranged in a large fan shape. Soft drinks were neatly packed on a side table.

'I was eagerly invited to eat and drink while each and every one of the officers present took turns to speak to me however bad their command of English. Their mess manners were equal to ours and their sense of playing host was clearly a finely developed aspect of their military training. I was pleasantly surprised and felt completely at home with these people who were so different in the way they did everything and who were clearly instructed to make me feel safe and at home and to show their gratitude for my visit to do my work. Throughout I was shadowed by a secret service agent who never took his eyes off me. Lima, a small postured energetic man with lively eyes, became a good friend during that visit and I understood that his presence was merely an extension of a tailing process that was initiated in Singapore. I felt like laughing when I thought how our own blundering national intelligence service, the Taiwanese service, the CIA and MI6 must have been thrown off my trail by ingenious blocking and subsequent impossible delays induced to give me a chance to disappear into the PRC. Lima once said to me in his unique English, 'I always had eyes on you in Singapore, Bangkok and Hong Kong. No one will touch you, my friend.' Halfway through the thirty minute long reception I walked to one side of the room and asked discreetly where the washroom was. Kim had just walked into the room and we briefly greeted. I was then directed out of the building and while I went in search of this facility the party went on regardless. Had I known what awaited me, I would not have asked for directions. There were had no modern facilities and I was confronted with a mountain of human faeces piled up in a large open trench. I simply turned away suppressing an urge to vomit and relieved myself against an outer wall in the freezing weather. I struggled to bring the sincere civility of the Chinese people in line with their inadequate sense of sanitary requirement and ultimately decided to write it off against rural isolation and a fundamental difference in lifestyle.

'Upon re-entering the room I was immediately intercepted by the senior officer with whom I travelled from the crossroads. We walked out onto the vast apron in front of the small building where the rows of equipment were reaching out to the left and right with roughly every tenth case opened for inspection. The wind was icy and the freezing cold was already creeping into my clothes. The officer encouraged me with a wave of the hand to proceed with the checking process against the detail in a document in my possession. I completed that arduous task within an hour and rushed back into the building with my hands frozen to the bone after having handled several icy cold heavy projectiles and other naked metal items with my bare hands that enabled me to turn and read the numbering safely for comparison with my paperwork. What made the task more difficult was the fact that I had the habit of having more cases opened at random to ensure that there was no set-up and to show that I was thorough. We African colonials were not really built or properly equipped for such climates even though we had to endure it from time to time. I was thankful that the task was done.'

Sam shifted his weight onto his good leg, 'After the inspection I was royally treated to a seven course meal in Tianjin as a guest of the Port Captain. We left the city for Beijing at approximately 18h00 that day. I was due to fly out to Hong Kong the next morning. Kim travelled back with me. We did not talk much along the route. He was busy paging through some papers that seemed to be a faxed summary of stock transactions. On arrival Kim turned to me and said, 'I need to come up with you to your room. I have something to give you.' On arrival at the hotel Kim accompanied me to my room. I was not prepared for what happened next. He opened his bag and took out a stack of highly sensitive technical weapons specifications for a wide variety of rocket propelled munitions and related electronics, classified as secret. Some of the items I had not seen before was clearly recognisable as rocket technology; it included descriptions and detailed drawing specifications. I was suddenly deeply concerned about the relevance of all of this material and what he expected me to do with it. Then out of the blue he said, 'You will have to carry these documents back to your country. I have arranged for the compilation of this information pack for your chief of staff and procurement department."

'I was caught completely off guard and looked at him and replied, 'Are you completely out of your mind? I am travelling with a different cover story. What do you think would happen if these documents are found in my possession and I am questioned about the source and more importantly, my authorisation to transport this classified information out of your country? You and I both know that the lower ranks have no idea of what I am doing here and that the real purpose of my presence is known only at a very high level of your security establishment. If they find this on me, I will be arrested by the border police and the key will be thrown away after they have beaten the crap out of me. You have to help me by carrying at least half of these documents yourself.' I was completely astounded by Kim's lack of understanding of the gravity of the situation and by the implications of his actions held for me. Kim did not flinch. He looked at me dispassionately and with his typical irritated high-pitched voice he retorted loudly, 'I cannot help you. My position will be compromised should this information be discovered on my person. I simply cannot do it. You have to do it on your own.' I stood there shocked at his lack of courage. I could not find the strength to attempt fighting him on the matter. That was it. I was lumbered with the documentation and I had to deal with it. I could not even lose it as controls on my movements were so tight that I could hardly leave the room without being followed. Any attempt to simply leave the pack in my hotel room would be summarily traced back to me and would immediately put pay to any future co-operation. That was it. Kim turned on his heel and only when reaching the door he turned and said, 'I will see you in duty free tomorrow. A car will pick you up after breakfast.' With that he turned and left. It was clear as daylight to me. I was 'flying alone and my second engine was on fire'. I did not suspect Kim exclusively though. As time went by and during the ensuing months it became clear that this sudden fear on Kim's part had been brought about by indirect pressure from South Africa through information selectively leaked to compromise my position in the PRC. Only one organisation would have been able to create such a massive problem – the National Intelligence Service. I was in a deep hole and I needed to get out of there really fast.'

Sam looked at me with that, 'what the hell, that's life' expression on his face. I laughed and he laughed and I reminded him of better days in Angola when tasks were simple and direct and where we actually looked after each other. He added that it was always about the memories and we should always act in such a way so that one day we would each be able to remember something good of those times.

We laughed some more and after an ensuing silence of several minutes, he said, 'The bastard walked away and left me to carry that can of crap in full view of the authorities, and into a dangerous situation. I never really forgave him for that. In years to come and when I forged a different kind of business relationship with Joseph after my life as a soldier was over, I had reason to revisit those thoughts when he also turned on me and handed me over to my enemies in South Africa in an effort to save his own hide. I have always believed that the same pressure that was exerted on me in the PRC all those years ago was reapplied in our commercial association by the national intelligence service through indirect pressure. This ultimately led to my resignation.

'I should have known better, Alistair. I trusted him and we went into business after I left the defence force. Many people close to me as well as complete strangers, accused me of setting up a front company to assist with sanctions busting. The plain truth was that Joseph and I believed that we would be able to set up an international trading house and that with my knowledge of Africa and his knowledge of and access to international suppliers we would be able to supply commodities and specialised weapons systems. Fact is that it was a private concern financed by Joseph and at no stage were any government funds received or used. What happened was that my access to the government arms manufacturing and procurement organisation was stopped because of my objections to Craven's policies and to a large extent that put an end to any further dealings in that business sector. Furthermore, I made the unforgivable error of judgment to appoint an unscrupulous Frenchman - Jack - who was praised previously by colleagues as an articulate and courageous bush pilot who fought for South Africa during the Border War. He was originally a mercenary - a scoundrel and opportunist snitch of the first order - from French Foreign Legion origins, who specialised in underhand dealings and smuggling and who would not hesitate to sell his services to whatever side paid the most. He was hired to run the aircraft division for my company. Instead, he spent thousands on dubious excursions on so-called official business for the company. He also used an opportunity to talk to Joseph privately and behind my back when he accompanied me to consult with Joseph Kim in Paris. What I did not know was that during this visit Jack told Joseph during a clandestine meeting in the George V Hotel that I had extreme far right leanings and that he should distance himself from me.'

'Simultaneously another associate - Jones - a South African banker, who I knew for many years and who helped me to canvass influential shareholders for my new venture in 1987, also worked behind my back to convince my one important South African shareholder to withdraw his investment from the company. He did this because I refused to give him one million rand to purchase a Shell filling station; a mindless, reckless pursuit, which I turned down without hesitation. Meanwhile Jack had arranged for information regarding my so-called far right leanings to be exaggerated during pre-board meeting briefings shortly after I was falsely accused. My fate was sealed. The former deputy chief intelligence, Admiral Jacobs, whom I earlier asked to join my board of directors joined the fray and I was unceremoniously thrown out of the company with only a small severance package. The deadly combination of the gullible Kim, the devious Jack and the greedy Jones ultimately placed me in an untenable situation that cost me my position in my own company.

'I should never have trusted Joseph Kim. That night, after he had hung me out to dry with the highly volatile documentation in my possession, I stayed in my hotel room in Beijing furtively checking and rechecking the documents and any other possibly incriminating aspects of my personal luggage until the early hours. I always worked from memory and made mental notes as I proceeded, went with this process of checking my exposure and knowing where what was packed. It became clear to me after a while that as far as the documents were concerned there was no way I could hide anything as the stack of documents was about three inches thick. The next day would be a rough ride and I was seriously afraid of all the different aspects that could go awry. The fact that at that moment I knew that Joseph Kim would not back me in the event of my exposure by the border authority did not help to calm my raw nerves.'

I never knew Sam to be concerned with personal safety or endless regulations that interfered with our work that focused on achieving very specific goals. I remember how once he painted himself into a corner on a solo rock climb in the Cape. He was unfamiliar with the route and when he was really stuck he sat down and rested while trying to think about his problem in clear terms. Ultimately he found the route by carefully analysing the rock face and especially the line of contours running horizontally across the mountain face. In the end he simply trusted his analysis and branched off quite aggressively to the right in a gully hidden from view and found the last leg of the climb high above Camps Bay through a half chimney with a 500 meter vertical drop. This thinking out of the box based on solid analysis and judgment was part of how we operated right through the war and many a success was directly attributable to this.

The next morning Sam was up early after only a few hours sleep. He quickly dressed and while packing checked his preparations with regard to the stack of documents. He had very little to work with, but decided to use a large hard dark blue plastic file cover to place over the documents at the bottom of his hand luggage bag. Hopefully this would create the impression that it was actually the bottom of the bag. He placed his shaving kit, clean underclothes, shirt and a warm cardigan on top hoping that this little fabrication would mislead a self-important, intimidating security official out on a power trip. The day was clear bearing in mind that it was winter and that thick fog was generally the rule. By the time he reached the airport it was already mid morning. Sam was pretty stressed out by this time.

As he put it, 'I was tired and strained and my left eyelid was jumping incessantly. I took a minute before climbing from the cab and used those few seconds to regroup and calm myself as best as I could. Then I paid the cabby, grabbed both my bags and set off for my appointment with that particular official.

'I had to laugh at myself, because as we both know even though we trained to be able to identify the right official it more than often happened that by some incredible coincidence you would either be pushed into another queue or your choice would simply be wrong because of a myriad of other factors such as noise, number of people and line of sight. Many times we planned only to have to regroup after a massive obstacle occurred and then to go in a completely different direction with no plan at all, and making it up as we went along and working simply with what we had available at that time. Controlled confusion was often our best cover for escape.

'The departure hall at Beijing International airport is immediately adjacent to and as cavernous as the arrivals hall. After having checked your baggage you are faced by a long line of immigration officials in uniform strung out over the entire width of the hall. As I approached the line I assessed them all with a quick glance and as you know you go with the one that seems to jump out at you. I noticed her immediately. All the characteristics of being self-absorbed were there and at a distance she was quite attractive in that somewhat mystical Far Eastern way. Neatly dressed and hair tightly rolled and fastened at the back of the head, make-up applied with perfection and sporting long red fingernails. A close-up view revealed a strict facial expression with the mouth drawn into a thin barely visible line. She had the shrill voice of a navy GI which confirmed that she was the best way through that thin red line, which is the security check at a Chinese international airport. Noisy self-absorbed officials suggested an inability to focus on detail. It was the quiet studious type you mostly gave a wide berth.

'As I approached the desk and search table I noticed that she tried not to look directly at me, but instead she simply pointed in my general direction and waved me closer with her right forefinger while calling out to me. She talked incessantly. When I smiled at her respectfully I noticed that she only peeked at me for a moment and then smiled briefly. I was not fooled and I remained vigilant. I walked closer to the desk and presented my passport. She glanced at the document and boarding-pass and then showed me to the search table. She was going to make sure that I was not a threat to anyone. She walked out from behind her desk and stood behind the search table. I placed my hand luggage on the table and she forcibly pulled it towards her. Her attitude and actions were still in line with what she appeared to be - in charge of her little world and seriously aware of her own efficiency and not having to do anything twice. Still talking to herself and her fellow officers, she peeked into my shaving kit but otherwise left everything pretty much as I had packed it. Then as if she were specifically looking for something in my bag she put her hand in under my clothing to feel the bottom of the bag. Her bright red long fingernails stroked the top of the plastic file and she mistook that for the bottom of the bag. My gamble had paid off helped by her ego and self-importance. I swallowed hard and closed my bag and she waved me through the line with that slight self-assured smile still lingering. I thanked her and did not blink once. Joseph Kim was waiting for me on the other side, but I was quiet as we walked to the boarding gate. I really had nothing to say to him.

'This narrow escape became my ultimate test case example for the future to never trust anyone else, but only my own abilities. It forced me to come to grips with the realisation that my own country was already deeply flawed allowing internal compromise and dangerous espionage on friendly intelligence organisations; that loyalty and bravery was a scarce commodity and that no one really cares, even under the most arduous conditions. My sense of desperation with what was slowly happening in my country was growing by the day and I did not look forward to my return.

'This is not yet the end of the story. Long after I had left the defence force I managed to piece together a part of the puzzle that always eluded me, probably because of my close proximity to the fire at that time. This particular operation entailed several different layers of activity. These layers can best be described as tactical, strategic and personal. The operators in the line represented the tactical layer while the policy makers at senior staff level represented the strategic level. The tactical personnel ran the operation and delivered the end product while the strategic personnel, assisted through relevant civilian associates, managed the activity. The strategic level also entailed a personal hidden element. Pedro 1 and his inner circle in the defence force, representative defence personnel in Angola and Namibia Kavango Sector 20; the two civilian links in the Jacaranda City who initially brokered the deal between Joseph Kim and Pedro 1 and the infamous Portuguese traders in Rundu, including the 'supplier' Jan in Grootfontein; all to a man became extremely wealthy by using the weapons we delivered as trade items to gain personal benefit. To this day I struggle to come to terms with this reality and the fact that I put my life on the line so that other men could enrich themselves. The day in Sector 20 when I was denied access to Mucusso by a second rate Colonel who went back to South Africa to live in ill gained luxury, is ingrained in my memory.

'Today I believe I understand what really happened there. Many of the weapons I acquired with state funds under incredibly risky circumstances, while continually evading detection and capture by enemy agencies and then had shipped back with meticulous care, were stored and blatantly exchanged for personal gain. Corrupt elements within the UNITA organisation in southeastern Angola and other individuals were and still are clearly morally inferior people. I know that many weapons were traded for diamonds, ivory, rhino horn and hardwood. This is a far cry from the original story that UNITA purely sold these commodities to pay for weapons. It was always clear that many of these parties including the Sector 20 Intelligence officers and the senior generals who were involved with the operation, as well as the associated civilians, were all well to do men. Uncovering these irregularities at the time would have been complicated, as the operation was run with secret funds, which entailed a different set of auditing rules. It was simultaneously a brilliant and professionally executed operation. The irregular conspiratorial spinoff for the strategic personnel element was huge and scandalous in the extreme. I am just thankful that I was never part of that despicable betrayal, as I truly believe in the lasting value of honourable behaviour. I think back to major general Harold's words that now seem far more serious than the joke he made it out to be, 'I am innocent, I sleep like a baby; albeit some nights I lie awake about the death of the four officer members of the investigation team, who died at the hand of the smugglers after I reported the irregularities in the early eighties to none other than Pedro 1, my general and ultimately my deadly enemy. The fact that he was apparently perfectly willing to remove those officers for personal gain weighs heavily on my thoughts to this day. After all, I was initially prepared to walk through fire for the rich bastard. In retrospect it seems that the initial tasking I was given to investigate the death of the four officers was merely an attempt by Pedro1 to establish what was known about the killing and whether his own position was in danger.

'So I have come from a past where a moral way of life was fast becoming a distant memory and in the present day is a scarce commodity. Not even in the modern day and age of so-called openness and transparency, am I able to ask questions about my own past and the attempt on my life without my source apparently being threatened. Then I had to transplant into a new country and society, where there is literally only limited and superficial knowledge of where we come from and where xenophobia and associated cruel behaviour rules supreme and tolerance is merely a pipe dream. Finally I had to witness how William was humiliated and his identity taken from him by his own family. In the face of all of this I increasingly withdrew, while thinking about the past and specifically what happened during the Crossroads incident. Uppermost in my mind was how I was once able to take care of myself and survive despite unequal and often impossible odds. Then, as we yearly think of those who died in the wars, I quietly pin my small red poppy to my hat and slip my own past into the equation. I also honour the memory of Jackie's father serving on the frigate HMSAS Natal in the fearsome Second World War freezing

North Sea Murmansk and Archangel runs guarding the ships of the Arctic convoys. There is no escaping and no going back. I might be alone, but at least I believe I am innocent and I sleep like a baby.'

Sam looked at me with narrow drawn eyes and said softly but quite deliberately, 'My crossroads experience was the beginning of the end for me. I just did not conceive how the betrayal I experienced there and the risk I was needlessly exposed to by a cowardly Joseph Kim, would eventually also lead to my ultimate unfair expulsion from the business world in South Africa at the hands of my own people. At that point my life could just as well have ended right there. I had nowhere to go to and I had no one I could trust. I had lost my position of safety and self confidence in my homeland forever.'

Chapter XXI

An Teallach

I was shocked by the harshness of Sam's realisation that he was also betrayed by his own defence force. Not only did some of his most respected colleagues benefit personally from his work in an underhand fashion, they also proceeded to arrange his persecution when he chose not to support Craven. Betrayal followed upon betrayal and in the final stages towards the end of 2005 Sam was once again categorised as a traitor to the cause because he accepted a democratic election and was thus branded as a traitor to the Afrikaner cause. We were gradually coming to the end of the story. I was trying to understand how Sam saw his position in Europe, especially after his earlier unsuccessful attempts to enter the business world in an African advisory capacity after which he was left with no other option than to simply give up trying.

I was utterly perplexed by these anecdotes given to me as a valuable treasure by Sam and I really wanted to know more about why he regarded this as so vitally important and how it all related to his present situation. Did he feel isolated in Europe or was there perhaps a deeper intention with these considerations and more importantly - how would he be able to survive in the UK?

Sam noticed my discomfort and said with a sombre tone in his voice, 'It is not a matter of anger or disappointment in the first instance, Alistair. It is much rather a matter of finding a new home, which is safe and peaceful and where one is accepted for what you are. The problem I have with my life is that for so many years I had no reason to question these aspects because we were so busy working under extreme pressure and surviving in an ever-widening world, that seemingly trivial matters simply fell by the wayside. As I see it Mother Africa never asked us to justify our stay. The Dark Continent merely expected that we be strong and flexible enough to withstand the large variety of pressures she would bring to bear on us. We were living in a state of constant re-evaluation of our positions and as such we became unique players on a hugely varied stage where the lack of structure was and still is, the only real common denominator.'

'In Europe however culture is quite complex mainly due to differences in how we perceive our respective societal positions that can only be described as officially well ordered and supported in the UK idiom and bare bones survival originating in the African idiom. I could never return to Africa simply because of the persecution I suffered there and the psychological loss of my familiar surroundings that are now in the hands of strangers. I had to find a reason to stay here that somehow fitted the freedom of thought and action that Africa always allowed me. The answer came to me as a result of four specific experiences that mostly changed the stark given structures that I was confronted with in the UK up until that time. First I befriended a few ordinary working folk who changed my entire perspective on the nature of people here. I cannot explain my utter relief when I experienced for the very first time that people in an ordinary store in a small town in Cornwall remembered my name and greeted me as such whenever I visit them. Then I walked on the South Downs in Sussex and saw the sky and the horizon. Then I walked along the coast in Cornwall and saw the sky, the sea and the horizon. I experienced Scotland and I saw the sky, the sea, the horizon and the never-ending mountains and I felt the simplicity of it all and I knew what I had to do. I had to live in Scotland; right out there on the edge of the sky, sea, horizon and mountains, on the edge of nature, so to speak and that would keep my body and soul together while I would be relatively far removed from physical and other memories. For the first time in my entire life I felt as if I had stumbled on the viable solution to all my questions and uncertainties. Change where you are and take the physical aspects of your new surroundings into your being and free yourself by doing so. For African colonials this is a very serious matter since we all have some link to the earth that ultimately anchors us. I was satisfied that ultimately this is all that matters. When all that you have loved in your life is taken from you the only way to correct that imbalance is to create a new environment with physical characteristics that are similar to what you had before. I believe I might just have found my new homeland.'

Then suddenly, over the next few days Sam inexplicably drifted away from our company. On occasion I overheard several heated exchanges between Sam and Jackie behind their bedroom door. Jackie's voice was more controlled than Sam's. His exclamations were loud and as if drowned in desperation. He went out walking early in the morning as if he wanted to be away by the time I woke up and only came home after several hours. Dinner was often a strained affair. I was busy knocking his extensive notes as well as my tapes and notes into place and I hardly paid attention to this process of physical distancing. I overheard a further strained discussion between Jackie and him referring to the final result of a series of medical tests that he had undergone. This followed on a decision involving his physician that Sam would attempt to decrease and ultimately stop taking any steroids acting as a substitute in addition to any cortisol produced internally to kick-start his slowly disintegrating body early in the morning. He had already gone some way towards lessening his intake of the drug and he was taking considerably less steroids than the dosage originally prescribed. The final test would show whether his system was producing enough cortisol for him to withstand physiological stress of any sort such as during a medical procedure or during a climbing or vehicle accident. The test was inconclusive by being only partially indicative of his physical situation and further careful monitoring was required. I know that this disappointed and annoyed him because he felt as if he was being held captive by his weakening health. Sam was never a person who readily accepted his fate. Instead he always believed that he could do more as an individual to improve his own position.

Then, one evening very late there was a knock on my door. I stood up behind my laptop and opened the door. Jackie was standing in the half dark passageway with a small note in her hand. She gave it to me without saying anything. She looked sad. There were only a few words clearly hastily scribbled in black ink, 'I will be in the great wilderness for some days Jackie. I will be climbing with William one last time. Love you. Sam.' It was clear that despite the many arguments followed by strained days, there existed a very special relationship between them that must have withstood many years both thin and flush. William's sudden appearance on the scene caught me by surprise, but Jackie seemed amazingly calm.

I was somewhat caught off balance. This was not the action of a man that I have learnt to respect for his attention to detail and his ability to gauge risk and his ability to survive before embarking on anything arduous. Clearly I did not know everything about him or how his health condition changed him over the years. I looked at Jackie and before I could say a word she spoke in a calm, but very serious voice, 'The report indicated that his physiological cortisol production is low. It scared the living hell out of him. He doubts himself and his physical abilities and especially to what extent he will be able to survive any possible injuries. He has often said that he simply needs to prove to himself that he is still able to withstand the strain of a severe climb. He has been planning this for a long time, Alistair. I am convinced he has chosen this area to test himself.

'I have climbed in The Anvil with him. It is really hard going and probably also inspires him, as it reminds him of William's hardship, because of the history of the feud between the MacLeod and MacKenzie clans and how with the blessing of James III the MacKenzies ultimately triumphed over the murderous MacLeods who killed the children of a forbidden union between a MacLeod son and a MacKenzie daughter. He left with the Land Cruiser to ensure that he would get as close as possible in probable snow for a direct departure point to start the approach climb from Dundonnell House close to route A832, over route 1, past Allt Gleann Chaorachain to the summit of Sail Liath. He will in all probability briefly touch An Teallach and then follow route 2 to descend to Dundonnell over the Meall Garbh ridge. This is nine hours climbing, close to twelve miles with considerable technical sections. He believes that his body will not fail and that he will produce sufficient cortisol under strain. Sam is trying to recapture his life's purpose by testing the foundations that underlines his abilities. I have seen him do this before when he was still actively running marathons and had to come back after an injury. He is testing himself against all odds and yes, this characteristic has become more prominent over the last few years. This is the 'fuck it' factor about him that sometimes scares the hell out of me as there is no logic to it whatsoever. He is on his way to An Teallach.'

I felt uncomfortable with this situation and I said as much to Jackie. I knew Sam's capabilities and his dedication to a commitment of any sort. Given his condition, this seemed like suicide to me. Jackie interrupted my train of thought with a barely audible voice, 'I have to pack my climbing gear, Alistair. I have to find him. I do not want him to be alone in the ice.'

I acknowledged with a nod and decided to do the same. My work here was done and all that remained now was for me to finalise the manuscript and start the editing process and then enter into negotiations with a publisher, something I never look forward to. Had I known what lay ahead of us I would not have been so impertinent to think that this was the end of the story. I did not offer to go with Jackie as it was time for me to pick up my own personal life again. I did however ask her to contact me should there be a problem. She nodded her appreciation. With hindsight I believe I made a dreadful mistake that bordered on incredible stupidity and selfishness. I should have gone with her instead of allowing her to do what is really a substantial task on her own. Jackie and I left together that afternoon. She drove north through the night with her SUV and I set off for London to begin work on the final manuscript. It would ultimately take the best of two years for me to consolidate my notes and produce a readable manuscript.

Jackie arrived in Dundonnell at 05h00 the following day. She was completely exhausted after fifteen hours of driving and decided to rest in the hotel before attempting any climbing. She passed the cruiser where it was parked next to the road close to the Badrallach turnoff and confirmed with a local shopkeeper who was also a climber, which Sam and Jackie had met before, that Sam had already left at 04h00 starting off on Route 1 close to Dundonnell House. Jackie slept for a few hours and then sat down for a warm meal, arranged her climbing gear, first aid kit, food, liquids and extra warm clothing and packed her large rucksack.

There were signs of snow in the sky. Jackie understood this, but pushed ahead. She set off at 09h00 directly on Route 2 to meet Sam as far as possible in on his way down. She had 3.75 miles to cover before reaching Ghlass Thuill, which was her target position to intercept him on his descent. From there she could more easily survey the landscape and take further decisions. It was a gamble, but she knew the route and she was confident. The sky was clear, but the wind was slicing the temperature to well below freezing.

About halfway through the approach the storm alarm in her climbing watch started beeping. She glanced up and saw the rapidly thickening snow clouds. Within minutes the snow started falling. She pulled her micro fleece balaclava over her head, zipped the body hugging micro fleece and both mid-layer fleeces to the top and secured the outer shell. With the hooded extreme weather outer shell fastened tightly around her face and covering her climbing helmet, salopettes, gaiters and boots and gloves, Jackie was ready to go. With the metallic sound of her climbing rack reminding her of all realities that lay ahead, she started her approach up the mountain. She did not expect the storm that would break over her shortly.

About 1.5 miles along the route Jackie climbed up a short gully leading to a ledge and a sharp incline and a further gully leading to the top of that leg flanked on the right by a shallow, but quite steep crevasse. She completed the second gully, but when she reached the top of the ledge she was focusing on keeping her balance in the strong wind and snow and preoccupied with speed and concerns about Sam. Unusual for her she missed noticing a slippery snow covered slab of rock wedged sideways and quite loosely into a narrow break in the rock as well as the danger that represented. She stepped on this slab and rushed ahead in an attempt to reach Ghlass Thuill within her timeframe. The slab slipped from under her boot and Jackie lost her footing to the right. She tried to break her fall with her right hand clutching her walking pole, but it slipped on a wet rock and she fell heavily on the pole. She heard the bones in her wrist snap with a loud crack and felt a short, sharp, pain in her right ankle, which she twisted to the right in an attempt to regain her balance.

She hit the ground hard and plunged down the steep crevasse with a muffled scream. She felt a stinging blow to her brow as she hit the sharp protruding side of a boulder on her way down. A dull pain throbbed through the right side of her head as she rolled down the incline over blade sharp rock edges with each hit thumping ominously against the helmet and she ultimately came to a sudden halt with a dull thud where she lay with her face buried in a thick clump of snow piling up against a rocky outcrop. The protection of the climbing helmet saved her life. She lay completely still for several minutes and then slowly opened her eyes. There was blood everywhere. Her balaclava felt cold around her mouth and she tasted the blood as she licked the snow sticking to her lips. Jackie wiped her eyes with her left hand and then attempted to move her right hand. It was shockingly painful and she knew she had broken her wrist. Blood was streaming from the cut on her brow. Her right hand and right ankle was out of action and every attempt at movement was excruciatingly painful. She felt dizzy and nauseous and her head began to throb.

Jackie had enough experience to know she was in deep trouble. It was snowing heavily and she had no backup except the man at hotel reception that knew which route she was attempting. He would not react until one hour after she failed to return. That was a long time away. By that time exposure to low temperatures and the sheer shock of the fall could already have taken their toll. She pulled her rucksack from her back with her one hand and rolled over and leant with her back against a rock. She pulled the walking pole sling from her wrist and while concentrating not to botch the only chance she had, she threw the bright red stick up to the right over the ridge with a wide sweep of her left arm onto the ledge from where she plunged down after the fall. The effort hurt her arm and she felt incredibly vulnerable. Hopefully someone would see that.

She made sure all her protective clothing was securely fastened and smiled a little at the thought of Sam forever droning on and on, 'You have to wear the best in the cold. If anything happens you will have a chance to survive. Saving money on survival gear will get you killed. Remember - there is no such thing as bad weather, only bad gear.'

His words and near-pedantic attitude with these things that he clearly knew a lot about, very often irritated her to distraction, but now she felt good about it and also that she had only the best gear and a whole lot of the old Tiger's persistence burnt into her thoughts. She set about checking the content of her rucksack. She had several energy bars and gel sacks, three litres of water, two litres of energy drink, teabags, sugar, a few apples, a few packets of soup, some energy biscuits (a little worse for wear), cheese and two packets of her favourite Haribo star mix soft sweets. The gas stove was undamaged with matches in the same sack. Her whistle was securely attached to the nylon strap around her neck, but her mobile phone in the small pocket on her breast was visibly damaged and unusable. She was pleased to see the extra Torres smock in the bottom of her bag and struggled into it with much effort and with pain searing through her hand. She had packed it eventually, remembering Sam's insistence that she carries a garment that fits over all other garments to provide heat and protection in case of emergencies. The first aid kit with space blanket was packed next to the jacket. She felt her Spyderco assist knife where it pressed against her right leg in the thigh pocket of her salopettes. 'Right', she thought, 'I have all the kit, but I cannot walk. So what does that help me? At least I will be able to eat and survive for a while and then?' While eating an energy gel-sack and drinking some water with two painkillers, followed by an energy bar and some cheese. Jackie began feeling a bit better, but also just a little bit worried because she was off the beaten track and she did not know whether her walking pole would have landed precisely in the right spot on the route. She wondered whether Sam was safe and already busy with his descent. She was cold and snow was forming rapidly around her legs. She broke out the space blanket and folded it around her legs and upper body. For the first time she wanted to cry just a little, strangely enough not about her fall, really about many other things that went before, but that was clearly a luxury she could not afford.

She was focusing on listening for unfamiliar sounds in the wind that was now tugging at the space blanket and her rucksack as if testing her position. It was 11h00 and the storm alarm in her climbing watch started bleeping again and told her that it was going to become worse outside. Sam had given her this outdoor watch recently and it felt good to have its friendly face look at her in this desolate place. It was becoming colder. She felt tired and heard Sam's words to their son ever since he was young, 'Please do not die in the ice.'

The good thing about her fall in this spot was that in a way she was shielded from the full fury of the storm that raged over her head, skimming over the ledge from where she had fallen. She fell asleep for a while and dreamt a strange dream about the South African West Coast and yellow flowers and the wind blowing the aroma of kelp and saltwater to the land. She saw her grandfather's farm and the day she played wildly at the dairy house and jumped from a wall and onto a corrugated iron sheet that split her leg wide open. She heard fighter jets scream over the house and the familiar sound when they landed right across the road at the air force training base that was originally a part of the farm. She woke up with a sudden jolt. Her ankle and wrist were now both swollen and completely immobilised and she thought that that was quite a bonus since with the swelling and the cold she could not move them and as a result she did not really feel the pain anymore. The wind screamed across the brim of the crevasse. She thought of her dream and how she missed Langebaan lagoon and the childhood memories it represented. She was very far from the African West Coast and she was lonely and cold and hurt and now also a little afraid. She put the whistle between her lips and started blowing.

Sam and William were doing well, but they felt increasingly concerned, not about themselves in the first instance though, but rather because they now suspected that Jackie would have followed them considering Sam's physical condition. The weather was simply too foul for them to turn and retrace their steps based on the assumption that she may be following them. The thought did however occur to them that she may be approaching from the front, simply because she is bright and would have thought that to be the safest alternative. Even though his bad leg was steadily weakening, Sam was excited about his performance, which showed that he was capable of more physical exertion than previously expected. It was rapidly becoming colder, the wind driven snow swirled around crazily limiting visibility and as a result general climbing conditions deteriorated fast. They moved through Ghlass Thuill and reached a point about 1.5 hours from the hotel. Then it happened. The snow was thick, visibility and therefore safety, was now seriously compromised. At one point William was right with him carefully navigating along the edge of a ravine. The next moment the snow gave way underfoot and Sam fell sideways, felt a dull thump against his mouth and rolled down a steep incline and finally came to rest against a mass of snow that had tumbled down the opposite side of the ravine. He spat blood in the snow. William was no longer with him. Sam turned and called out to him. The only sounds were the howling wind and his voice bouncing back at him. He called again and again and finally lay face down in the snow crying out loud, as if he was a wounded and cornered animal in the process of finally escaping the hunters. Ice was already forming on his cheeks. Then in that moment of exhaustion and shock after the fall he finally knew that William was gone forever, as if ripped from his memories and physical being and that all that remained was himself and his new reality. William was finally dead and with him all the ghastly baggage that defined his desperate, battered, broken past.

Sam came out of that ravine with a few bruises and a bleeding mouth after having hit his face and bitten his tongue during the fall; gasping for air and feeling tired and with his helmet looking a bit battered. He also felt remarkably refreshed, as if with that fall he had shed all of what went before and as if transformed with a new purpose to his life, accelerated by the harshness of the surroundings and the fact that no one else was there to question his ability or lifelong journey and the honesty with which he always travelled through it. He paced himself and climbed well within his breath and stopped regularly to rest and take in fluids and some energy gel. It was at one of these rest points where he noticed the out of place red metal object partially protruding from the snow. He pulled it towards him with his boot and pulled it from the snow. He recognised the small black Niteize S-Biner karabiner Jackie used to attach the pole to her rucksack on open ground.

He scrambled towards the edge of the ledge just as the screech of her whistle cut through the blinding whiteness. Through the thick snowfall he could just see the bright red colour of her climbing jacket down in the crevasse. He scrambled and stumbled down the incline to where she lay in the snow. Words were unnecessary. Sam stabilised Jackie and applied a plaster to her brow, bandaged her wrist and ankle as best he could and then gave her some food and hot tea. After resting for some time they started moving painfully slowly with Jackie firmly clinging to Sam. Sam seemed to become stronger as the challenge increased despite the pain in his leg and with the last remnants of his physical doubt passing though his mind and out into the cold mountain air. That night they rested in a small shack that appeared out of nowhere as they descended the mountain to the south in the late afternoon. He told her about William and she just lay there and cried and cried. In more ways than one way that shack became their place to forget and their refuge for the future.

He stood outside the shack after he had made the call to request the DMRT (Dundonnell Mountain Rescue Team) from his satellite phone to evacuate Jackie who could not walk further. As the 'wup-wup' sound of the chopper drew nearer Sam's thoughts drifted back to another place and another time where there was dust and sun instead of snow and cloud. There was still light and it had stopped snowing. The chopper landed and Jackie was strapped into a litter and carried to the aircraft with a doctor walking next to her. Just before Sam clambered onboard and while they were still strapping Jackie into her position in the aircraft, the visibly seasoned, fierce and wild bearded DMR Team leader stood by while the medic gave Sam a once over. Sam heard and absorbed the experienced climber's sharp, direct, but sympathetic reprimand about the incredible risk he ran climbing alone.

He acknowledged his mistake with a nod and, 'But of course you are right sir,' and then looked backwards over his shoulder at the shack and into the sky and remembered William with a little sadness.

A black cloud mass was drifting in and Sam felt the ice-cold in the air after a long day out on An Teallach. He was glad it was over.

Chapter XXII

Catching a Rat

I checked in at Santiago Arturo Merino Benitez International Airport on a cold winter's day in 2008. I had just covered a major conference on South American economic development. I thanked the attractive Chilean brunette in the crisp uniform (her name tag announced 'Carolita') with the large brown eyes at the check-in counter who struggling with her English pronunciation and blushed and smiled slightly when my hand momentarily brushed against hers. As I turned to walk through security and passport control, I noticed a familiar face behind me. The thinning hair hardly covering the bald patch and familiar 'workman like' facial features belonged to lieutenant general Pedro 1 - The Ratcatcher. He recognised me as I sat down to rearrange my bag after the obligatory security check and rushed over with improper haste to greet me.

'Good God, Alistair - haven't seen you in ages. How are you? What are you doing here?' he said in a nervous rush of words while adding the inevitable stupid little joke, 'I see you have aged. Just look at all the grey hair. Is it the missus causing you all the trouble?'

I let it pass without energetically vomiting on his patent leather shoes. My extended visit with Sam and Jackie two years before in the South of England did not do anything to improve my opinion of this dangerous little bastard with his deceptively servile attitude.

'General. What a surprise. No, still unmarried, too much travelling you know, being a newspaperman and press photographer and all. I have been attending a conference here. Are you well?'

I responded while not missing a beat with rearranging my bag. I was afraid to look up because I might just have turned and kicked the treacherous, wretched, little fucker to death right there. I checked my temper and sat down next to my bag.

Pedro 1 parked his dark, shiny Armani suit clad, immaculately groomed body next to me. I noticed his shiny black 'church' shoes and silk socks with thin red vertical lines on the sides, the Rolex watch and glaringly ostentatious Porsche sunglasses. He started talking in that familiar hushed and seemingly confidential tone of voice while glancing nervously over his shoulder from time to time.

'I am so glad to meet you, Alastair. As you know I mostly live in Santiago dealing with my international trading business. I am travelling to New York, and you?'

'Yeah...right' I thought to myself. 'I wonder over how many dead soldiers' bodies you are trading you incredibly corrupt, vain man.'

I checked my overzealous, aggressive attitude fuelled by my renewed communication with Sam again and asked as politely as possible, 'So, how are you, General?'

He lowered his voice further and said, 'I am okay Alistair, you know, I visited a Santiago bookstore, The English Reader, in Providencia in the city a week ago. I was searching for a book on coffee prices on their computer system and came upon a pre-launch teaser blurb for a controversial new book about Scotland and South Africa that is set to appear soon. For some reason the writer is still undisclosed. Have you perhaps seen it?'

I naturally denied any knowledge of such a book. I however knew about the blurb; a preliminary typically tantalising effort by a close journalist friend who knew me and told me some time before that he would refer to the book and the story in a blurb-environment that he controlled - without disclosing too much.

I went ice-cold and said, 'Would you like a cup of coffee or a cold juice? We have some time before our flight departs. I am also on my way to New York.'

My mind was racing and I kept thinking of my friend Sam and his notorious fondness for cold juice and one part of me wanted to burst out with laughter, but I had to stay focused.

We sat down in the cafeteria after having gone through passport control and ordered two cold juices.

The Ratcatcher suddenly looked quite pale and went on, 'I had just finished reading the blurb and alarmingly noticed my original code name Pedro 1 mentioned very prominently when something across the street drew my attention. I noticed a tall man with a short grey beard and a walking stick in his right hand standing looking towards the bookstore. I thought I recognised him and suddenly felt really uncomfortable. I left the bookstore and walked towards the Presidente Hotel where I had a very important luncheon appointment. I went inside, waited for my host; an important Chilean financier backing one of my developing trading deals to arrive and while we had our lunch, I noticed the same man sitting at a table in the corner. He looked vaguely familiar, but I cannot place him. For a moment I thought it was Sam. Do you think it is possible? Are you aware that he blamed me for many things that had happened at that time in South Africa? I am quite concerned about his intentions, Alistair, as I am convinced I saw him following me on several subsequent occasions.'

I went ice-cold for the second time that day. I downed the remaining half of my cold juice and asked with a shrug and a straight face, 'Are you sure?'

He looked at me with a perplexed expression on his face and said, 'I don't know Alistair, I just do not know.'

'The man's field craft is failing' I thought, 'He is getting older. He is missing things.' In a way I revelled in that thought. I honestly hoped that his deeply corrupt persona would eventually come to serious grief.

The call to board the flight wrenched my thoughts back to reality from a state of near mental collapse. I stood up and gathered my things. I clutched my bag with the last sections of the manuscript and some additional notes tightly to my chest.

'I wouldn't worry too much, General' I said, 'Those things are all ancient history now. Anyway, surely you haven't done anything that would place you in danger?'

'No, of course not' he answered in a barely audible voice as we walked towards the boarding gate.

I instinctively assumed he was lying like a horse-thief.

As I turned into our boarding enclosure - Pedro 1 was ahead of me - I glanced to the left and as if in perpetual slow-motion I noticed a man with a walking stick passing me with a familiar limp and entering the boarding area for the next flight to the UK. He looked briefly to his right and noticed me. Sam smiled and winked and we both raised our hands in a barely visible military salute.

I shook my head in total disbelief and whispered to myself, 'Son-of-a-bitch, you incredibly clever son-of-a-bitch.'

I slapped my bag several times and laughed out loud and walked through the boarding gate with people glancing at me. With the aircraft banking to the left and gaining height I was still having a good chuckle.

Three months later I walked into a tube station in London on my way to a meeting in the West-End with my editor. I noticed a newspaper headline, 'Former spy boss jailed for life.' I hurriedly bought the paper and skimmed through the article while standing precariously in the fast moving train holding on to the roof rail with one hand and with my bulging document bag gripped between my ankles. The following words jumped out at me, '… former military intelligence boss and later Chairman of the State Security Council and retired Lieutenant General Pedro 1 aka The Ratcatcher … trapped while spying for the CIA and DGSE against his own country … charges of unlawful killings with chemical weapons in Africa and Europe … murder attempts on his own officers' lives … properties confiscated … damning evidence provided by covert intelligence operative … naval officer …' The accompanying photograph showed a dishevelled Pedro 1 - The Ratcatcher, being led to a waiting police car in the foreground, his thinning hair hanging in disarray over his brow and his mouth half open in a clearly pathetic gasp. At least the single most important traitor was exposed and Highway 61 did not claim this son, Sam, after all and I would be able to complete the manuscript.

Jackie wrote to me once late in 2008 announcing that they

had finally moved to the north-western highlands in Scotland to walk high in the windswept mountains, to gaze over the wild ocean and to find peace at last. She also inquired about the manuscript and told me that the president's son William had disappeared in the snowstorm during the winter climb on An Teallach when she was also badly injured. Sam and he became separated during a blizzard. His remains were never found. Sam was distraught, but ultimately accepted the fact that William was finally gone. In a way he was glad that William's complicated life, as the son of a president had come to an end. It was strange though how this occurrence remained a mystery to me as I never saw any reports about this disappearance. I also wondered why I never had the opportunity to meet William and why I could never find any photographs of him in official and commercial records.

Ray? Despite his own horrific physical challenges and with the ghosts of the past firmly in his mind, Ray was still working tirelessly in the discarded war-wounded environment back home to help the remaining men whose limbs and lives were forever shredded to pieces in a cause-driven war that was now long forgotten. He remained one of the last of the good men.

The traitor Pedro 1 - The Ratcatcher, was only temporarily rotting in the feared central C-Max jail in the capital - together with some of his former military operators who were jailed for the sins of their employers - for horrendous crimes against his own people. Within six months of his jail sentence commencing he was found lying grotesquely in the shower area with a gaping mouth drenched in blood and quite dead, with a sharpened jail spoon protruding from his throat. I quite savagely appreciated that death for the brutal restitution against treachery and hardship inflicted on loyal soldiers it represented.

It was January 2009 and I was on my way to Santiago to marry Carolita. The take-off announcement prompted me to fasten my seat belt. I opened my diary and saw these words penned in many moons ago when I had to tell a story of betrayal, near death and a rebirth, *Oh God said to Abraham, Kill me a son* and in the left margin of the page - Revelation 6, 8. Abraham's son survived and the pale horse and its rider never seemed more apt or more positive an image. Sure, lots of bad guys with blood on their hands survived with all their riches and having stolen other men's women, but the time of their self-honouring would soon come to an end. The old tiger was still on the prowl.

A brief music interlude on the intercom interrupted my thoughts, '*You're sixteen, you're beautiful and you're mine …*' I remembered Sector 20 – 1980 as I tapped the tune on my knee and smiled with the song lingering in my head and thought of Carolita and my old friend the Tiger. I somehow knew that he was still alive and walking with that slight limp in the Scottish mountains and far removed from Highway 61 where the Jacarandas were in full bloom that year.

Uit die grou van onse hemel, uit die doodsheid van ons see (word play with reference to former South African national anthem) - to the brightness of An Teallach and majestic northern sea - I mused poetically. I am sure *Sagmoedige Neelsie* with his elephant Herrie - *op die tremspoor* would have understood this dark humour describing one good man's escape from our once revered country full of majestic isolated places, but now descended into darkness and cruelty into the light of Scotland, a destination also filled with isolated places and line of sight all the way to the horizon and where there is room to breathe. I wished the same for all our brave, stricken friends from the forgotten war who remained behind.

My overly poetic musings were however slightly misplaced. I was blissfully unaware of what lay ahead of us - we were still in for a hell of a ride.

Chapter XXIII

Jackie's time

On a moonlit night in late November 2009 I picked up the receiver in my Santiago apartment and went ice-cold. The tell tale clicking sound of a slightly clumsily installed temporary rogue telephone tap between exchange and end-user reverberated in my ear. I slammed the phone down and gazed through the large window onto the street below. At the far end of the street I noticed a large SUV with darkened windows squatting in the shadow with part of its hood shining in the streetlight. I was under surveillance. Carolita stood up from our large living room couch and stood next to me.

'What is it, Alistair?' she asked.

'People from Africa,' I said as if to myself. I knew this would happen one day.

'New friends and new enemies of South Africa make us enemies of the state, my dear Carolita.'

The next day I went out to a meeting with my publisher who had come to see me at the airport regarding the manuscript. The SUV remained tucked in tightly behind me all the way there and back home.

I tried to ignore it, but the fear of the unknown kept me vigilant.

That night - as expected - the phone rang and when I picked up it was Jackie's ever pleasant and smiling voice.

'Alistair. It is me.'

'Jackie, you okay?'

After the required hi and yes and thank you she came straight out with it.

'Your friend has left for the mountains with a stack of gear late last night. We have 'visitors' from out of town showing 'improper interest.' He wants you to join us there. Please contact me on a clean line on the number we gave you during our last meeting before the book preparation was done. Hope you still have it. I will then give you instructions and directions.'

The reality of the situation raced through my mind and slammed into my slightly rusty covert military work thought processes that were suddenly revived with enormous clarity. We were both in the crosshairs and this time we had less support than ever before. Pedro 1's 'merchants of death' were probably on the move after his death-by-spoon in C-Max. I did not know what to say and with a brief 'Will do, Jackie, best to Sam.' I rang off to find the satphone number. Carolita was looking at me with that incredulous expression I saw the first time I let her into my world of perceived terror after our marriage. This was going to prove to be a very fast initiation into international espionage and the merchandising of death for her. I started humming Bob Dylan's little song about God and Abraham. I smiled and thought about Sam's analogy and how that always amused me.

The concise discussion that followed with Sam from a secure line a few blocks away from my home left me exhausted and fearful, especially since the SUV remained ever present. Sam and I were now targeted by the remainder of Pedro 1's hit team and their instructions were to kill both of us including Jackie and Carolita and dump the bodies. I did not ask where Sam got this information from, as I trusted his judgement explicitly. I seemed to remember vaguely that he mentioned ongoing contact with his old and loyal friend Murray, originally from special forces and 32 Battalion, who remained deeply involved in covert work internationally and in South Africa. He was however most insistent that we join him in the far northwest of Scotland as soon as possible. Within two weeks we arrived at Glasgow airport with all our severe weather winter outdoor gear packed into two hold alls each and rucksacks ready to go. Jackie was waiting for us with her SUV. We drove for several hours until we reached An Teallach. I saw for the first time the harsh place where Jackie nearly died. Surely this must be the wildest and most remote part of anywhere, let alone Scotland.

We came to a steep hill late that day when it was already quite dark. Right at the top we swung directly to the west onto a dirt road that became progressively worse until it was no more than two incredibly rough tracks leading through the Dundonnell Forest. After another two hour drive the road ran out onto a small clearing where we turned onto an even narrower track that eventually stopped abruptly at a pile of rocks and some windswept trees. An ancient stone building stood immediately to the right of us. Right in front of us, framed by the dark and massive hulk of the ridges of An Teallach, a.k.a The Killer Mountain, my friend Sam sat dressed in an olive green Carloway Harris Tweed cap, thick brown leather gloves, a weather beaten olive drab Ventile smock and well used brown leather and canvas knee boots straddling a quad bike with a stout trailer attached. A stainless steel 45 - 70 Marlin 1895gs guide gun with a black resin stock rode reassuringly in a classic American saddle holster strapped to the body of the bike. I vividly remembered similar images of him during better times in Angola.

He smiled at me and said, 'Got one for you too, Alistair. There are also two Browning BPS All Weather High Capacity 12 Gauge pump shotguns for Jackie and Carolita and enough ammo, magazine pouches, slings and holsters. The other quads are in the barn.'

I smiled and said, 'Who warned you, Murray?'

Sam looked at me and nodded. 'Murray has close contact with the CIA. They owe him big time after his contribution in Iraq during recent years. He received an intercepted message through a back channel in Langley regarding planned action by a commercial security group associated with their agent in Chile, Pedro 1. He sent me a coded message suggesting that we run to high ground and wait for them and then work our way back in towards the chosen target area to surprise them. A team of seven former special forces rogue operatives working for the deceased Pedro 1's international 'business outfit' was dispatched after his senior Chilean partner became concerned that their position would be compromised after the book was released. Their orders are to 'take care of us.' They are coming for me first and I thought it would save time if we were together. You have left Chile just in time.'

I looked at the folding walking stick showing from his coat pocket and could not help but remember that day in Sector 20 and the white cliffs of Dover and the contrast it represented. I could scarcely believe that after all those years we were right back where we started.

The barn revealed three more quads. Jackie reversed her SUV into the barn, parked it next to Sam's Land Cruiser and disconnected the battery with deft fingers. We packed our gear on the trailer and after convincing Carolita that it was actually much easier to ride the quad than our Harley, we set off with a roar of engines on a narrow track to Sam's shack overlooking the south-western mountainous foothills of An Teallach towards Loch na Sealga where we would wait for whatever was coming to get us. The words of Revelations 6, Verse 8 drifted through my mind;

> *'And I looked,*
> *and behold a pale horse,*
> *and his name that sat on him was Death,*
> *and Hell followed with him.*
> *And power was given unto them over the*
> *fourth part of the earth, to kill with sword,*
> *and with hunger, and with death, and with the*
> *beasts of the earth.'*

Within three days of our arrival we were entrenched deep in the Wester Ross Mountains. The quads were tucked away in a low shed next to the shack where Sam and Jackie waited to be rescued during late 2006. We were running regular scouting missions on foot several times per day. It was not a moment too soon. We noticed the first unfamiliar off-road vehicle tracks on the fourth day on one of the outlying dirt roads running parallel in one part but essentially away from the mountain range where we were hiding. Our enemies were moving fast and they were determined. According to Sam's briefing that night while we were eating next to the fireplace in his shack overlooking the dark lower mountain slopes, Pedro 1's adjutant in Chile had apparently acquired the assistance of seven men from South Africa. He was deeply concerned about the fact that Pedro 1's original code name provided valuable links to all their commercial and former military enemies, especially since their business was always inextricably linked to the main players in the international espionage game i.e. the CIA, British Intelligence and especially the DGSE with its considerable capabilities in the wider African theatre. Their business revolved around weapons, ivory, rhino horn, drugs and diamonds hidden behind "legitimate' trading in ordinary commodities. These men were all from the now defunct and seriously discredited 'Civil Co-operation Bureau' another name for 'hit squad'. Their core origins were 'Koevoet', special forces, the security police and specialised police units with a few members originating from the intelligence community. Some of them came from the illustrious 32 Battalion. Their first loyalty was now money and their services were for sale to the highest bidder.

Within twenty-four hours after that we would be fighting for our lives against a determined group of seven killers with nothing more in mind than their next payments.

It was very early on a Sunday morning that I woke up with a start. Sam was standing next to my bunk where the two of us rested on both sides of the door.

'Alistair, they're here.'

I felt that familiar knot in my stomach I remember from every time we took off by chopper to cross the cut-line in Sector 20.

'It's snowing, Alistair. Wake Jackie and Carolita, dress warm, remember the rifles, ammo and emergency food packs and the first aid kit. I will wait for you by the quad shed. I have to go now to look and listen. Murray warned me by satellite phone about thirty minutes ago. I have taken my injection and I am carrying one extra so I am good to go for six days. By then it should be all over - one way or the other.'

I went over to where Jackie and Carolita was sleeping close to the fire and gently touched Jackie's shoulder. She turned and I looked straight into the shotgun's dark snout. She smiled and touched my cheek with the back of her hand.

'Sorry Alistair,' she whispered, 'Living with Sam moved my cameras to second place.'

I gently pushed the barrel to one side, smiled back nervously and walked over to where Carolita was fast asleep. I touched her ear with my mouth and she woke with a smile saying softly, 'What is happening, Alistair?'

Within minutes we were up and scurrying around to gather all the gear and pack the rucksacks. Everything was carefully prepared beforehand by Jackie and Sam. Carolita and I were briefed so everything went smoothly. We were applying the agreed tactic of fighting from the outside and towards where our enemies would be expected close to the shack. The playing field was level, but for one thing, this was Sam's backyard.

We hurriedly gulped down some coffee and a few biscuits and walked out into the snow to where Sam was waiting.

Halfway to the shed I suddenly heard the familiar 'clangy' automatic burst bark of a suppressed 9 mm submachine gun and immediately afterwards the clear and very loud thump of the 45–70 and then Sam's words, 'Who are you?'

I started running towards the shed and as I turned the right hand corner to duck into the side-door I saw Sam leaning over his attacker, clutching his hair and thumping his head on the ground. Sam let go of the man, struggled to his feet and leant against the wooden wall. He was clearly etched against the snow embankment behind him. I looked at the body of the night camo clad, hooded man lying on his back in the snow with H&K MP5, complete with suppressor clenched in his right hand. There was a neat but significant wound in the middle of his chest where the 45–70 bullet ended his career of killing for gain.

I whispered, 'Who is this, Sam?'

Sam gestured at me, 'Help me get him inside Alistair. It's Louis C. He acknowledged that much before he died. I have no idea how and when he was released from the Mozambique jail. His mate Koskas Du P. will be part of the group. Six to go. He was probably sent forward to scout because he knows me and would recognise me ... they're moving fast.'

Sam slammed the assailant's radio against a concrete pillar on the side of the building. It fell to the ground and he flattened it with his boot. He rammed the cocking mechanism of the Marlin backwards and forward again, recycling the rifle. We dragged the body by its feet into the shed and covered it with a discarded piece of canvas. Jackie and Carolita stood quite still by the quads. Jackie was holding Carolita's hand. Jackie appeared to be quite calm. Carolita was clearly upset, but the sight of the shotgun slung over her right shoulder reassured me.

Sam was already on his quad and called out to us to hurry, but with a lowered voice. As we moved slowly out into the moonlit night I noticed blood dripping from Sam's left jacket sleeve.

He caught my eye and said softly, 'Please do not say a word, Alistair, I do not want Jackie to know. Let's get away from here right now, before the rest of the hit squad arrives. I can work with this for now. We can trace our way back in and hopefully clear up this mess once and for all. I am good to go.'

He gunned the quad into life and sped off along a back road leading away from the shack. We followed closely behind. It was snowing again and I felt the cold creeping into my bones. It was going to be a long, long day and with one man already hurt, no one knew where it would end. For the first time in many years I felt afraid.

Within two hours we had come full circle. After having stopped to discuss tactics and to create a significant break of about two hundred metres in our tracks over some rocky terrain, we doubled back to approach our attackers from the rear on their way to the shack. We expected that they would have been alerted by the radio silence from Louis C. and that alone would have encouraged them to move a lot faster. Very soon we came to the narrow road leading to the shack and in an instant Sam picked up the trail - they were on foot - and all his old game tracking skills visibly kicked into overdrive. We hid the quads amongst a clump of bushes some distance from the road and set off on the fresh tracks. At one point Sam sat down on his haunches to look closely at the tracks. He touched the side of one of the boot marks and a clear blotch of blood fell as if in slow motion into the snow.

Jackie let out a suppressed scream and started rattling off in Afrikaans, 'Hoekom het jy my nie gesê nie, Sam? Wat makeer jou? Wil jy doodgaan voor ons hierdie spulletjie kan uitsorteer?' (Why did you not tell me, Sam? What is wrong with you? Do you want to die before we've sorted this?) She straddled him and pushed him to the ground.

'Take off his jacket, Alistair. Were you aware of this?'

I nodded and she just looked at me with those soft, stern grey eyes; we were neatly caught out.

'What in God's name should I do with you two?' she said softly.

I moved quickly and removed his jacket as carefully as I could. I knew Jackie well enough. No nonsense, just results. A complicated life with a really difficult man like Sam taught her that.

'Carolita, hand me the first aid bag you have in your backpack.'

Sam wanted to protest, but Jackie was running in top gear and in no mood for his protestations.

'Lie still, old man.'

I noticed her smiling slightly as he touched her hair with his right hand. The bullet had entered his left shoulder on the outside and had taken away a significant piece of flesh at the exit wound. It appeared to have missed Sam's bone structure. I thought it was probably a South Dakota Cor-Bon Powerball projectile, designed for maximum effect. As the bullet strikes, the ball in the nose-section secures the hollow nose and guides it through the clothing fabric until it strikes bone…and then it explodes. His whole arm and clothing were drenched in blood on the inside. Jackie cleaned and plugged the wound with three tampons and applied a dressing and a non-slip bandage. She gave him two shots, one for pain and one against infection plus a bottle of electrolytes to drink. She knew what she was doing and was in no mood to negotiate with any of us. 'God help those who get in her way tonight,' I thought to myself.

Jackie and Carolita helped Sam with his shirt, fleece and jacket. Carolita was on her knees next to him speaking in Spanish saying, 'I cannot believe that he is capable of going on with all this blood and the size of the injury.'

Jackie looked at her and said in perfectly respectable Spanish, 'Cary, you have no idea of what this old trooper is capable of. He has the ability to crack on despite any adversity. Why do you think I am this grey? It is all his doing.'

We all laughed nervously. Sam was smiling, slightly embarrassed about all the attention.

He stood up slowly holding on to Carolita's hand and gathered his things. Jackie and Carolita stepped over to where their rucksacks and weapons lay and started strapping everything into place. Jackie was standing with her back to me, but I could see that she was crying. I heard her saying, 'He is absolutely set on doing this and there is nothing I can do about that and I cannot let him go ahead without me. He trusts me and needs me around and I am so bloody afraid.'

Carolita said something to her and they spoke briefly. They were both clearly concerned, but I was glad to see they were holding their shotguns and ammo pouches. Any words from either Sam or me would be superfluous at this time. We all knew this had to be done.

Now, as I am writing this, I remember a story from the Second Boer War Sam once told me about his friend William's grandfather. He was with a group of farmer commandos waiting for the Imperial Forces in the Drakensberg. He and his scout buddy and a few other practical men were checking guns and ammo while the poorly armed others were reading from the Bible, singing and praying. His grandfather asked them about their lack of weapons and they answered that 'God would provide'. His answer to that bit of wishful thinking was that God gave us the capability to think and plan and that prayer was intended to show appreciation for that. There would be enough time for prayers after the fight. When the first artillery shells hit their position the religious brigade ran for their lives and left Bible pages in their tracks and the few battle ready commandos to finish the fight. His grandfather added that he could smell how they had quite disgustingly soiled their pants in fear as they ran for cover. We also had to finish this fight. We understood that these men were here to kill us. I believed the fact that it was completely beyond the realm of the law had long since filtered through all of our minds. We were going to have to deal with this on our own. If not, how would we explain everything that had happened and who in his right mind would believe us? It had become a matter of basic survival of the fittest beyond the rule of law.

We moved steadily back towards the shack with an indirect route well away from the clearer circle route. Dawn was breaking and it suddenly started raining. The ground was transformed into slush. Within another hour we saw the group of six men moving ahead of us towards the same goal. They were all dressed in dark night-camouflage assault uniforms and carrying light daypacks, H&K (Heckler and Koch) MP5 machine guns and low-slung side arms. Our strategy was to allow them to reach the shack and we assumed that they would approach in a house clearing assault mode - we were confident they were unaware that we had previously been informed of their attack. We decided to strike from behind as they went in. That would give us the surprise element and more so because they would be focusing on their target in the shack. We reached the perimeter of the clearing around the house within one hour and waited for the six men to commence their advance. We checked rifles and ammo pouches and hid the rest of our gear under a large bush behind some rocks. As prearranged we quickly checked our safe lines of fire and with Jackie and Carolita only slightly to the front carrying the pump action shotguns loaded with slugs, we started moving. With the Marlins Sam and I would able to place our shots more accurately from further away, Jackie and Carolita would form our 'lead barrier' in front with no hindrance in their line of fire.

The plan was to hit the six assassins from behind the moment before they entered the house and in so doing effectively boxing them in against the shack wall. The two doors and windows front and back were all securely locked from the inside. In this way we were hoping to create a semi blocked 'killing zone'. I thought it was quite brutal, but very effective and fortuitous, given our condition with one man 'winged', very little time really to prepare and only fifty percent of our team really experienced. I was about to find out that I was mistaken about the other fifty percent.

The six men suddenly moved forward in a semicircle and crouched low.

Sam whispered just loud enough for us to hear, 'Go!'

As we broke through the bushes surrounding the shack the man leading the six men spun around and saw us with a shocked expression on his face. We had the element of surprise. He screamed at his mates and raised his rifle. The slug from Carolita's shotgun hit him square in the chest - many hours on the shooting range until her hands shook and hurt paid off - and as he dropped like a sack of potatoes all hell broke loose. Sam dropped a second man with a well-aimed shot to the stomach. I heard Sam recycling his rifle with a loud 'clack-clack' from the lever action as I shot the third man in the chest. The two shotguns and Sam's rifle roared neatly in sync. Two men fell down instantaneously, both their chests a bloody mess and one with blood spurting from his eye where Sam's 45–70 bullet struck. The remaining attacker had regained his balance and was shooting back at us as he scarpered around the right-hand corner of the shack. Sam was trailing him with bullets until he ran out of ammo. Jackie had found her rhythm with the shotgun. Hours on the shooting range doing box drills under her son Iceman's relentless close supervision and instruction over several years were paying off at last. She was energetically working the pump action - accurately and systematically demolishing the corner of the shack as she ran flat out after the assailant, simultaneously groping for ammo and reloading. A gutter pipe and part of the roof structure collapsed onto the man's head and I heard her screaming a curse in a clear, loud voice as if in some dreamtime primordial tale of restitution where the fleeing victim turned to fight back. She rounded the corner with the remaining three of us following, first Carolita, then Sam and then me.

H&K MP5 shots suddenly rang out from the rear. One of the wounded men we had passed in our pursuit was shooting from the back. Sam sank to his knees, blood pouring from the right side of his body. A bullet cut the outside of my left leg just as I spun around and shot the assailant twice and he fell backwards. I went down on my knees as the sharp sting in my leg struck home. I swung around again and as Jackie disappeared around the corner I heard her groaning in pain and saw her falling backwards with blood streaming from her face where the attacker's H&K MP5 stock had caught her right above the eye. She held on to her shotgun though and as she fell she recycled the weapon with a loud 'chuk-chuk' from the reloading cylinder. She was not going down without a hard fight It was Koskas Du P. waiting for her behind a water tank on the side of the house and he lunged forward with a massive Tanto fixed blade combat knife raised high in his right hand. Carolita was sprinting towards Jackie and reached her in a kneeling position with a spray of snow. Jackie was sitting up and the two shotguns thundered together and I heard Jackie scream again as if she wanted to vent all her fear and anger of many years. The two slugs slammed into his face and he fell backwards and lay completely still and apparently quite dead. I dragged myself upright and checked all the bodies while kicking weapons away.

The detailed intelligence analyst and 'after-fight sweep-man' in me said with a high-pitched instructor's voice, 'People, we have to check them for signs of life and remove all personal documents, weapons and gear before we dump the bodies.'

No one reacted. Amazingly the journalist was the only man standing - albeit not for long - and I realised how significant that was. Now Sam and I could complete writing the story. Sam was lying on his back with his feet treading in the snow. Jackie and Carolita were sitting on the ground shaking uncontrollably. There was blood on Carolita's temple where a bullet had grazed her.

Jackie called out first, completely in shock and her voice unnaturally high pitched and with tears streaming down her cheeks, 'Are you okay Alistair? Please, check Sam for me.'

Carolita was busy wiping the blood streaming from Jackie's face wound with her scarf. She was crying out aloud. I felt strangely alive while walking over to where Sam was lying. I thought to myself, 'Not bad for an 'ice-cream suit', a 'brown job' and two girls'. It had stopped raining and there was a clear, bright and unbroken rainbow over the mountain as the sun was just starting to break through the clouds.

Sam reached out to me with his right hand and the last thing I heard before sinking to my knees and onto my side again in slow motion while Carolita and Jackie ran towards us was him saying, 'Thanks Buddy, you okay? Are Jackie and Carolita okay? It's no longer a dream. Now we have this wonderful place all to ourselves, Alistair.'

Jackie worked feverishly trying to stop the bleeding from Sam's side.

'Alistair' she cried out with a shrill voice, 'I have a problem here, I can't stop the bleeding. Please help me hold still his legs; I need to apply pressure to stop the bleeding.'

The words just hung there in the air as if frozen. In a daze I saw Sam's legs shaking uncontrollably, but in slow motion. I crawled upright and grabbed his legs. I felt Carolita next to me. She stripped her shirt off and tied that around my leg.

She turned and said, 'What else do you need Jackie?' She started handing Jackie everything she called out for from the first aid kit as she struggled to stop the bleeding.

After what seemed an eternity Jackie finally and miraculously stopped the bleeding. Her first aid training of years before was clearly thorough and it showed. She then disinfected and dried the wound and dressed it generously.

'He is very lucky,' Jackie said softly.

The shot went clean through the flesh. Sam was weakened beyond reason. He should have been dead, because on top of everything and probably due to the gunshot wounds, the worst of his illness had suddenly kicked in and he was struggling to breathe as he went into anaphylactic shock.

Jackie injected him with an anti-allergic substance and I heard her say, 'Maybe we've caught it in time.'

Eventually, sitting next to Sam and slowly rocking backwards and forwards, she cried with long wailing animal-like sounds. I did not know what to say and I could hardly imagine the depth of her grief for Sam, her scattered children and her country that was suddenly so far away.

After Jackie had worked her first aid magic Carolita and I put a bandage on her injured forehead. We were all more or less mobile again except for Sam who lay motionless in the shack, just breathing in shallow gasps. We were hoping that he would make it. There would be no emergency services called to this incident.

Before the end of the day we stacked the bodies with great physical effort on a piece of canvas - stripped of all personal effects, equipment and clothing and clad just in underclothes. We then proceeded to drag the load to a deep and inaccessible gorge about a quarter mile behind the shack towards the mountain. We dumped the remains of our attackers into the gorge and buried all their gear in a deep hole and covered it with soil and rocks. No one spoke a word. Jackie kept their weapons and ammo.

'Sam would have done that,' she muttered.

We were not taking any chances and any additional firepower

would help us.

Then we sat around for a while completely exhausted without talking, just taking in the fading light while trying to understand how we felt about this thing that had happened.

Jackie's only comment was, 'I am sure God will deal with them.' She had every reason to say that - this was in reality her victory and we had experienced all that happened during a time that belonged to her first ...

I thought about that and said, 'Amen.'

Carolita nodded in agreement and said, 'Al vivo la hogaza y al muerto, la mortaja.' (We must live by the living, not by the dead).

She started crying softly and I felt so incredibly sorry for her.

Thinking about it now I believe we all died a bit that day. We were forced into the very thing we had being trying to avoid for so many years - the re-visitation of violence that we all know begets more violence. This was precisely what we had all been running away from for so many years. But evil - and especially the evil that we had witnessed in our little part of Africa over many years - would not let us go that easily. It came after us and lured us into a bloodletting that we could probably justify in terms of self-defence, but never in terms of its inherent evil intent to find participants at all cost.

We rested in the great wilderness of Scotland for several weeks after that to ensure that there were no further attempts to track and harm us and because Sam was still very weak and ill. In a way we were all a lot older and I suppose much wiser after this horrendous event. I at least understood for the first time how the horror of our past would return time and again and that in the end the only way we could make it go away was to stand our ground. At least we have found some restitution not only for us, but for all the soldiers and covert operatives who died for a senseless cause during the Bush War and internal uprising while their masters were counting their blood money in the lap of luxury. I wondered whether and when the time for their reckoning would ever come. I cursed Craven over and over for his suspected betrayal of our country and our people and I prayed that his soul would go to that special hell I have always believed existed for cowards and traitors.

When Carolita and I eventually had to go home Jackie drove us to Poolewe. She embraced both of us. Finding words were difficult and we left that special parting moment silent for future memories. We travelled by bus to a train station from where we could depart back to the South. After that day I did not hear much from Sam or Jackie again and to this day. I do not know whether they are still alive. It is enough for me though to think that they eventually changed the harshness of their life into a peaceful existence in the far flung and snow and wind swept Scotland.

It was a month after our arrival back and I had just handed the final chapters of the book to a publisher. It was set to appear early the next year pending their and my final approval and agreement. (This unfortunately never materialised.) I travelled back to the Thistle Hotel in Trafalgar Square by cab and walked directly to the restaurant where Carolita was waiting for me. We were only in London for the day as we were taking some time off after our impossible ordeal in Scotland and spending a few days in the small town of Rye where there was only sky and sea and quiet.

Carolita and I were savouring the sunset in Rye a few days

after these events. I thought to myself, 'William, Sam, Jackie, all ordinary, but special people like so many other men and women who fought for our country. By all accounts William was dead, but my earlier observations about never being able to track him down kept haunting me. Maybe William's unofficial death was simply very fortuitous in that it gave Sam new life away from his past. This gave new meaning to the term deception, but I left it at that since it gave us all some hard earned comfort and safety. After all, what the hell's in a name? A Tiger by any name is still a Tiger and Sam fitted that description quite well. Jackie needed no further qualification either. She was always the salt in the taste, akin to the salt pans on the barren West Coast where she learnt her life skills and without her nothing would have been possible.' I repeated softly, 'We must live by the living, not by the dead'. Carolita looked at me and smiled that slight smile I remember from the day at the airport in Santiago. By some impossible coincidence the tune playing on the radio in the house was Ringo Starr's *You're sixteen* and I instinctively felt the African dust and sun and the Scottish highland snow and clouds all mixed together in a hopeful pattern as once described by an accomplished rock and ice climber and outdoorsman I know well …

> *Waking in the cool of the day, aware of more than went before*
> *Breathing the crystal air is not hard anymore*
> *Blue and green and brown all around*
> *Tickling rays of sun abound*
> *Tussling leaves and vocals in the trees*
> *Leaping water and singing in the breeze*

Motion and senses in balance with an unseen guide
Rising and falling in time with the swing of the sun
Floating where the wind draws its breath
Flowing where the river carves anew
Sensors and fibres firing and twitching
In adversity the emphasis switching
Smell sight and sound suddenly out of mind
Energy inside converted to a harmony of some kind
Now aware of more than went before
Once again aware of the truth in The Core
As complex as the vocals in the trees
As simple as the tussling leaves

Iceman

We were still alive, despite all of the unspeakable betrayals by bastard politicians and their henchmen. I wished I could tell Sam and Jackie and all the soldiers I fought with over many years in that dark, cruel and brutal place how much I respected them and the fact that in the end they just took care of the men next to them.

My thoughts drifted to the thousands of former special forces soldiers who were still serving in Iraq and Afghanistan as private security operatives after they lost their livelihood in their own country, as well as the many covert operatives that would never be recognised and the blatant betrayal they suffered over time.

Similarly I remembered Sam's story of Madala's general shoulder insignia, which he discreetly sent to Cuba with a friend who understood and accepted the story without questions. He quietly buried the precious items deep in the ground in a secluded and scenic place in Topos de Collantes with beautiful views over the hills to the sea near Trinidad, placed a single rose on the spot and said these words, 'Madala of The Rose - with lifelong respect and appreciation.' Somehow this was a good burial and a better and more peaceful place for Madala to rest than anywhere else I could possibly imagine.

We were all truly lost, but somehow we were still bound by the reality that we never betrayed our country and that we knew who we were. Despite death that surrounded us for so long our dreams stayed alive and I hope, ultimately saved our souls. I wish to this day that I could go back to place red carnations on the names of the many dead soldiers at Fort Klapperkop like I did all those years ago every year on 16th December - our Day of the Covenant. I miss that. That night I dreamt vividly of an intrepid fox standing quite still on a ridge with tilted head listening to Scotland's 'silent excitement' and I remember not being afraid.

THE END

Epilogue

P. Alistair C. 1949 - 2009

The satellite phone rang at 03h00 hours on Sunday morning 20th December 2009. Jackie was awake first and answered.

She could barely make out the stuttered words, 'Jackie, Alistair es muerto.'

'Carolita is that you?' Jackie asked in a shocked, half sleepy voice, 'What is it? Oh, merciful God, what happened to Alistair?'

In a shocked and barely audible voice, Carolita then told Jackie the story of what is thought to have happened to Alistair. Alistair arrived back from the airport after a visit to Patagonia where he was investigating a climate change project for a new series of magazine articles. He stopped in the parking garage at their apartment block, stepped out of his Land Cruiser and opened the rear door to collect his camera backpack.

As he closed the door, four bullets from an AK-47 assault rifle hit Alistair from close range in the back of his head and in his spine in quick succession, leaving severe powder burns on his skin and clothing. He could never survive such an onslaught. He apparently slumped violently forward against the vehicle and then slid to the ground. There was much blood on the back and on the ground behind the vehicle. He died instantly with his hand still clutching his backpack. He was barely recognisable, with a large part of his face blown away by the high velocity bullets. Carolita found him later that night after he failed to answer his mobile. Next to his broken body these words were written in blood on the concrete surface, 'Be warned The Thirteenth Tribe of Israel'. She also found his car key with a small silver uniform lapel owl modified into a key holder clutched firmly in his right hand. This was his lucky charm and he always carried it with him. This day however the owl's knowledge and vigilance were not enough to save him from the attack. Alistair was a loyal 'spook' to the end. In a strange way it was a good death at the hands of evil men who clearly wanted to prevent him from speaking the truth.

Carolita now lives with Sam and Jackie in Scotland. She decided to remain after they had scattered Alistair's ashes in the mountains of An Teallach. They are often surprised by the ease with which one vigilant fox often circles their home as if guarding them. Together they wait for each dawn, while they sleep cautiously.

Sam often hears her murmuring to herself, 'Juro que no será largo hasta que se alimenta de El Tigre' (I swear it will not be over until The Tiger feeds.) The responsibility rests heavily on Sam's mind and shoulders and he remains ever vigilant while he sharpens his battered body and skills and waits for the day.

Several months later, Sunday 19th September 2010 at dawn, Sam was standing on a rocky outcrop to the south of the shack. The intrepid Scotland fox was as always circling and listening restlessly. Sam and Jackie had transformed the surrounding area after they were fortunate to acquire the piece of land on the Loch na Sealga side of the mountains. They cleared the track leading to the shack and planted some hardy shrubs and young trees in several clusters to serve as shelter on sunny days and to eventually hide the shack, which was by then much improved and actually resembled a substantial dwelling. It was now a special secluded place where they could gather on special occasions with their family to celebrate what they regarded as their hard won freedom and to win back at least some of their lost time.

Sam waited patiently while looking out over the gradual approaches to the mountains. In the distance he could make out the shape of a tall man - the sun intermittently catching his sunglasses - approaching. He was carrying a substantial backpack and he wore a red down jacket, silver-grey salopettes and heavy technical climbing boots. Sam recognised the familiar shape and the distinct catlike gait associated with rock and ice climbers. He raised his hand high in the air when he noticed Sam in the distance. He had what looked like a paper of sorts in his hand. Sam waved back at him with both hands and wondered about the paper.

Iceman half ran the last few paces towards Sam, embraced him and then handed him a brown envelope. Sam slowly opened the envelope with the words 'Room 25 - To Iceman for Ye Olde Cleric' written on the outside. Only one man ever called Sam by that name. He pulled a photograph from the envelope and looked carefully at the image of the sleek, white 47 foot Nautitech catamaran lying at anchor in front of the Captain Oliver's Resort in the Netherlands Antilles. The name in bright red on the starboard bow read 'La Rosa'. Six exquisitely designed figurines of nuns in black habits walking in a straight line underscored the name as if they were carrying it.

'The envelope was delivered to my hotel in St. Martin during a recent visit to the Netherlands Antilles.'

Sam and Iceman laughed out loud together.

Jackie called from the house, 'What is happening, Sam?'

A quick glance through the window brought her running towards them. She flung her arms around Iceman. Sam showed her the photograph and she stood there for several minutes as if transfixed with her hands clasped over her mouth and eyes wide open in total disbelief. She clearly understood immediately what the photograph meant. Madala must have made it.

To their right, not too far away on a ridge, Sam's Scotland fox was now standing quite still with his head slightly tilted as he listened to all these new sounds, as if with eager anticipation. Maybe, just maybe there was a God after all and maybe there was a quiet, cool resting place reserved for Tiger and Madala, at a safe distance from the fiery river.

Postscript by Abraham Lewis

15 July 2005. It is winter in the Nahuelbuta National Park in the Araucania Region in Southern Chile. With deep snow and ice everywhere and the wind raising the chill factor the cold cut to the bone. Alistair woke with a jolt around midnight and heard El Zorro's distant anguished short sharp cry followed by the distinctive double thump of a .243 as a bullet found its prey. Then silence. The feint hysterical cry of another Darwin fox on the run rang out. The 'Fox Reaper' was on the prowl.

Sleep eluded him and two hours before dawn he rose and with steadfast faith in good gear instead of good weather underscored by proven warrior habits, he dressed in warm base layers, salopettes, anorak, snow boots with ice spikes strapped on, knee high gaiters, cold weather cap and warm lanyard secured mitts lined with skin tight fingerless tactical gloves. A fight sharp full handle five inch tactical folder, cycled Marlin 1895 SBL Guide Gun with compact combat torch and high resolution night-vision scope custom fitted, powerful headlamp and survival kit in a high mobility compact sling bag with barrel down breakaway rifle bag on the side completed his gear set. He replaced the day light eyepiece on the scope with the night version and walked out in the white snow searching for the large boot prints that had become so familiar to him these past months.

Al was an accomplished game tracker with special law enforcement privileges extended by the Chilean conservation authority based on previous tracking and hunting skills and more recently literary and journalistic contributions regarding the conservation of endangered species - especially the Darwin fox which he came to resemble more and more in its primary solitude. However, his position was based on old-fashioned trust between him and the irritable ageing police chief - one could say it was a meeting of irritable, but mutually accommodating minds. His tracking skills still served him well even though hunting was no longer his chosen path. He quickly found the familiar heavy boot prints with extreme wear markings on the heel and side and found El Zorro five miles away where he was killed. The small endangered Darwin fox lay grotesquely discarded in a mass of blood where he was hastily skinned near a distinct rocky outcrop. His open eyes were glazed and frozen solid after failing to escape from The 'Reaper's' high powered shooting lamp, rifle and blunt curved skinning knife. During those last furtive moments, he pawed the snow leaving evidence of his death strides as he contemplated his futile effort to escape before the cold metal projectile in his side finally closed his eyes. A distinct indentation had formed in the snow around his nose and mouth with his tongue protruding in a mass of red foam and blood where his head was trodden into the snow by a heavy boot while his skin was ripped from his warm flesh starting with a deep cut encircling the neck. The small carcass appeared awkward with skin only covering the small head and the rest of him lay exposed and embarrassed.

A spent .243 cartridge lay awkwardly upright in the snow. The heavy boot trail, which led directly to the small dead fox confirmed the earlier presence of the killer who simply did not care enough to remove the dead animal. Alistair inspected the empty cartridge and carefully stored it in his jacket pocket to be used as evidence. He followed the initial direction of the departing prints with his trained eye to where he knew the Reaper's dairy homestead lay beyond the ridge. He was angry and he knew there would be several lonely fox hearts that night. This was an old fight and with the death of El Zorro it has come to a head.

While cursing under his breath and without hesitation he gathered the broken, lifeless carcass from the blood soaked ground, inserted it in a soft olive drab canvass hunting haul bag and taking the weight in his left hand he cautiously approached the homestead. The pathway was clearly marked with a trail of blood leading right up to the backyard and to a half open barn door. He switched off his headlamp and as he passed the doorway he noticed the salted dark silver and red coloured fox hide suspended from a meat hook attached to a wooden beam. He walked right up to the back kitchen door where the light shone through a side window. The smell of dubious cooked meat drifted into his nostrils and in one corner of the backyard a heap of unprocessed rubbish added to the stench of the place. He did not bother to knock, but instead swung the sling bag to his chest, broke the cycled Marlin from its holster and kicked the door wide open with his heavy spiked boot. Simultaneously he flung the haul bag into the kitchen and shouted out loud, 'Asesino, aquí está la evidencia triste Muéstrame tus manos putos' ('Killer, here is the sad evidence. Show me your fucking hands.') The shocked Reaper dropped the large cooking fork and retreated rapidly away from the stove into the back of the kitchen while grabbing the grubby, visibly badly maintained .243 Savage from the corner of the room. He fumbled with the bolt action and stumbled clumsily over a high kitchen stool. Before he could regain his balance, Alistair struck like a coiled spring. He was a big man, but he moved like a cat. He swung the Marlin's butt swiftly and precisely to where the thick neck met the heavy shoulders. He followed the blow with a second swift sharp downward blow to the small of the back. It was no contest. The Fox Reaper groaned mournfully and dropped to the floor like a sack of wet blubber and lay quite motionless. Alistair kicked the rifle away with a loud scraping noise and held the Marlin pointed at the Reaper's head. He jammed his heavy snow boot firmly on the small of his back, ensuring that the spikes did not penetrate the skin, slipped a prepared cable tie over his wrists behind his back and pulled it tight. He grabbed a bucket with cold water from the rack adjacent to the washbasin and unceremoniously emptied it over the fat man's head and back. That put immediate pay to any attempt to escape into the ice-cold night. He grabbed him by the cable tie and slowly pulled him onto a chair by brute force while announcing in a deliberate tone,'Usted ahora ha cazado' ('You have now been hunted.') Al had struck.

They marched several miles through the ice-cold snow covered landscape with the Marlin held firmly in the Reaper's back and his hands tied securely. His future was irrevocably set for a swift delivery into the hands of the conservation authority. Following that the notoriously irritable and somewhat rough local police chief and his constables with whom he had a close working relationship, after a profoundly challenging start, will do their thing. The reception by the larger than life chief who happened to be at the station at that time, was spontaneous with warm exchanges of friendship and clearly expressed appreciation for Al's work in really bad weather interspersed with loud swearwords directed at the luckless fox poacher. Al was offered a large mug of strong sweet coffee, which he downed eagerly, listening to the poacher's fearful admission of guilt in the background and the chief's loud voice expressing clear anger for the profusely sweating captive's edification for causing discomfort to his friend Al and of course yes, also for killing the Darwin fox. The chief's participation in the 'interrogation' of the culprit ended when he gave him an almighty smack against the back of the head with an open hand and the words that finally spelt his doom, 'Eres un hombre realmente mal y voy a ver que la clave de su celda es arrojada a la basura' ('You are a really bad man and I am going to see to it that your cell key is thrown away.')

Early the next evening El Zorro's vixen came to Alistair's door. Chilote witnessed his caring presence where her mate was killed – running away and then crouching low just out of sight when she heard him approaching and then following him on his quest for a reckoning. He identified her by a limp in her right rear leg where the bullet of an earlier poacher's attempt injured her as well as her specific and unique colouring. That was why he called her by that name. She was as different in appearance as the language she was named for and whenever she was not with El Zorro she was always alone. She sat five yards to the north east side of the front door with her head held slightly tilted to the left and mouth half open as if saying, 'Thank you for taking care of El Zorro.' The small and feminine Chilote still succeeded in giving a command performance and caught his undivided attention after having lost the only being that defined her entire existence. She turned and quietly went on her way. Just before disappearing into the trees, she stopped briefly, turned around, looked at him and gave a short mournful cry.

He never forgot this sight and in the years ahead, like a good soldier recalling his training, he would constantly remind himself of the plight of the innocent and the helpless. The loyal, but threatened Patagonian foxes became the manifestation of the way he saw the world and what he ultimately became and they seemed to predict his own lonely future life - a sometimes defenceless and lonely defender of hopeless causes and lost and threatened beings.

Alistair was almost born with the inclination to write. This would culminate in a sedentary existence only interrupted by forced physical exertion from time to time. The excuse was always that the activity stimulated the thought processes that quickly became his lifeblood. That was however a sheer fabrication of enormous proportion. He was an extraordinarily talented outdoorsman and what he did not know he made up for with sheer tenacity and the will and capacity to learn important things quickly. That ability always stood him in good stead in town, country and uninhabited terrain. It would remain the one thing he could count on for his survival.

From his notes I deduced that four major developments apparently defined his early life and personal growth. He learnt to ride a horse. Then he learnt to hunt and through participation in extreme physical and outdoor activities he learnt to deal with physical and emotional stress. Lastly he was trained for and volunteered to go to war. This prepared him for events that would follow the strangeness of the post revolutionary period in his country - one of Africa's expected 'success stories'.

The truth was however too ghastly to even contemplate in a world that remains obsessed to this day with a certain public country profile. This profile was created by a marketing effort surrounding the release of an iconic political figure from the jail on Robben Island, as part of a process seen by many as betrayal. The carefully worked out transformation process that followed was simply a money driven commercial program designed to replace the old white elite with a new black elite. The murky underbelly of an unequal society stayed firmly in place hidden from view by profoundly obscene semantics and crude name changes.

In the face of all of this, Alistair decided to leave his country and to settle in South America where he could disappear and re-appear in a new role, - attempting to do the one thing he understood well - working against all odds for the downtrodden and the abused - in his case the foxes and all other aspects of human intrusion on the planet.

Alistair went back to writing and became a true outdoorsman and conservationist. Surprising events led to our eventful meeting.

My first encounter with P. Alistair C. on 15 December 2009 near Trelew in Chubut, Patagonia was a compelling one. It was five days before he was brutally slain in Santiago following the violent incident in Scotland. We were visiting a climate change project as journalists and were both focussing on our own subjects for individual articles. As I turned to look for a new camera angle we bumped into each other. We both laughed and Alistair immediately apologised and offered his hand saying, 'We are clearly both quite enthusiastic about the work being done here - please forgive me for intruding.' I was immediately impressed by this friendly man with the callused hands of a seasoned shooter and refreshing old-worldly good manners. I also apologised and since we stayed at the same hotel I invited him for a quiet slowly sipped cup of coffee later in the hotel foyer where we decided to pursue some activity together.

Over the next few days we discussed several subjects and it was only a matter of time before he mentioned the South African Border War and his intimate association with it. I mentioned my experiences as a hunter over several years in South West Africa (now Namibia) and the conversation that ensued set the tone for our fast developing friendship. Alistair was a bright young man with a kind disposition, quick eyes and the visible physical attributes of a former soldier. His reluctance to speak about his part in the war quickly led me to understand that he must have been involved with covert work. My own military experiences have always served me well and guided me once again not to pursue this line of discussion.

But then something significant happened. It was 17 December 2009, two days before the end of our tour and we had some time to explore the surrounding area with a special map provided by the organisers in hand. This would allow us additional time to visit some of the project focal points and to take additional photographs of the profoundly stunning countryside. Alistair and I agreed to meet for an early breakfast the next morning and to commence walking at 08h00.

We set off at a brisk pace. After having hiked for nearly two hours we reached a waterfall of approximately 200 feet high. We did not regard the drop as too severe and decided that a cautious traverse to the other side of the river along a clearly defined rock ledge was quite doable. The significant mistake we made however, was that we were unable to properly assess the strength of the stream, the stability of the rocks and my climbing rustiness. We were halfway across when it happened. I was leading and Alistair was following close behind me. Without warning an unstable rock gave way under my right foot. The sheer weight of my rucksack with camera, tripod, extra clothes, food, water and first aid kit pulled me backwards and I tumbled off the face of the waterfall. The cold water instantly drenched me and I felt the jagged sharp edge of protruding rock slice deep into my left upper arm. That dull, pained sense of hopeless fear and numbness that always accompany an accidental physical occurrence engulfed my consciousness. Only, I did not fall and die on the sharp rocks that lay below. Alistair had jumped forward and grabbed my rucksack's handle with his left hand. He dragged me back onto the ledge with sheer brute power and a loud groan and held me safely until I regained my balance and foothold. Back on my feet on the other side of the waterfall, Alistair ripped open his backpack and within minutes the deep cut on my arm was dressed and bandaged. I was severely shaken but alive and thankful for that. P. Alistair C. saved my life that day. I never had an opportunity to act towards him in kind and I hope that my writing this extended postscript is part payment of that debt.

The arrangements for this payment came about in a most intriguing fashion. After our little excursion we were relaxing in the gazebo next to the swimming pool. We were discussing our experience of earlier that day and laughed about my close shave at the waterfall. I asked Alistair how he managed to react so swiftly when he grabbed my rucksack and thanked him again

- mentioning that I was sure that I would have fallen to my death. He never answered that question. Instead he turned to me and said in a hushed voice, 'If anything should happen to me I need you to do me a favour. I may not be able to complete a manuscript I am handling for a friend who lives in Scotland. Would you be prepared to assist my wife in Santiago in such an event? I have written the contact detail down for you.' He handed me a folded handwritten note. 'I am sure you will be able to manage that. The title of the manuscript is *To Die for a Night*. It is a controversial piece of work and I would be honoured to offer you the author's privileges should I happen not to complete the work and submit the manuscript to a publisher. I would advise you - for your own safety - not to add my name to the cover page. There remains considerable work to be done before it can be published.' The advice about not using his name I would eventually not heed because I simply owed Alistair that.

For several moments I was unable to speak. I was simply too shocked by the unusual sudden request. Somehow Al knew he was going to die although the date and place still eluded him. I nodded my agreement and he thanked me and the matter was settled. I then listened to him speaking about our time in Patagonia as if the request for help was never uttered. A new feeling of desolation crept into my heart. It was as if I was alone and he was speaking to me from elsewhere. The old memories of my own time in the army came back. For some inexplicable reason I remembered at that instant how I missed my wife when I was away and how I always forgot what she looked like after some time had passed and how low that made me feel.

We parted company the following day and I could not shed

that feeling of utter desolation. Sadly, I never saw him again. I subsequently arranged to meet Carolita in Santiago during the last days of December 2009 to explain, discuss and collect Alistair's manuscript. She also gave me the information that enabled me to write the foregoing section on Alistair's early days in Chile and handed me a faded black folder filled with extensive handwritten notes in black ink. She was clearly emotionally unable to deal with the content simply because of the apparent complexity and unusual content of some of the notes. On the cover these words were written, 'Notes prepared for AL. Remember the foxes.' He must have prepared the file in the short period before he died after having arrived home from Patagonia. I paid no further attention to this file at that stage since I was fully occupied with Alistair's first work. I however place it in a safe location for later attention.

I saw Carolita again in the north western highlands of Scotland early during 2010 when I visited Sam and Jackie after having finally cleared my approach to the manuscript, which Alistair had prepared and which he requested me to complete and finalise with the publisher. This process proved to be every bit as painful as the story related as only a few people could even remotely relate to or understand the full implication of what he had written. The story was constructed with all the concealed aspects he experienced in the world of spies he knew so well. Names were chosen for their meanings and several of the characters were created from different elements of one man's personality. Several stories were hidden in the text and layers of interaction were complex and cunningly convoluted. It was as if Alistair wanted to give an insight into the multitasking and multidisciplinary world of covert operatives who more often than not converse in ad-lib secret language code. I would also never be able to forget any of the detail of their experience related in the story. My life as a writer was changed forever as I gradually began to understand how everything that we do in life has an impact in the future and even much further ahead.

Then, sometime after that, I re-visited the faded black folder with my initials written on the cover.

This narrative is the result of my careful reading of Alistair's notes and my re-creation of one man's notes along the way in his quest to make a difference to the human condition. It refers to what happened before in the old country and in other places, culminating in the outcome of the final story as he recorded it in 'To die for a night'.

The description of the near cameo incident in Patagonia, which I described before in the section 'The Fox Reaper', jumped right out at me when I read his notes. It was as if that was representative of his entire life. It helped me to understand who this complex man was and how everything of any significance he did throughout his life came down to that - strength and honour, a sense of caring and a profound belief in restitution after having experienced wrongdoing. In all of this he remained mostly alone until the end.

Note 1 - *My horse was always my horse but my father was not always my father.*

Al clearly remembered - better than anything else of any significance that occurred during his entire life - the summer's day when his father gave him a horse.

His horse was a striking, stocky piebald with bright brown eyes, a profoundly mischievous personality and underlying capacity to do whatever he wanted to as he was previously employed in the lightning fast world of polo where he was steered by a strong hand in fiercely competitive bouts.

He first saw his horse in the early afternoon when he walked down the ramp of a horse-box parked at the beginning of the dirt road from where he was planning to ride the horse to the farm approximately 25 miles away. It would be his first long ride and everything was up in the air. Thinking about it then he could not even imagine having been so bold. He was after all only ten years old and still firmly under his parents' protective care. Nevertheless, everything was set, a brand new bridle, saddle and cloth arranged and he was suitably excited and ready to depart on this adventure into the wide open space of the back road with his father accompanying him at a distance in his car so as not to crowd and spoil his 'solitary' journey on his new horse. It was as if everything was suddenly possible. When he arrived on the farm later that day, the achievement of such a long ride was applauded by everyone present and he felt a rise of confidence in his own ability.

Apart from having moved out of the house and into a buitekamer, (outside room) adjacent to the barn where he had some independence, he could now go anywhere and do anything and stop being afraid as he now had his own horse, which was after all, simply invincible. His ever-reliable horse would protect him and carry him away from danger on his strong back and that became the impenetrable cloak that covered all his uncertainties and shielded him whenever he ventured into the unknown of the forest, the mountain and numerous streams. His father had set him free at the age of ten and for that alone he will always remember him.

Saddling, mounting, falling down, getting back up and learning fast.

Saddling a horse properly is one of those activities that require attention to detail and focus to proper completion that will ultimately lead to a wonderful experience. Al learnt that the hard way.

Ensuring that the bridle and girdle are tightened to just the right setting and that the saddle blanket lay flat, neat and comfortable on the animal's back was just part of the endless tasks that were constantly required when working with a horse. After a long hard ride working cattle or inspecting fences, cooling down, watering, cleaning and brushing and feeding were important tasks to ensure the piebald's wellbeing. Shoeing him from time to time was an equally engrossing task performed by one of the ever-dwindling number of blacksmiths in the district. Alistair loved watching the blacksmith work with such calm strength and skill that never once seemed otherwise than just perfect.

Sometimes your horse would roam freely in the field and that freedom is sometimes accompanied by a certain 'mind of his own' factor. Starting at the head of the green pasture Al would walk in as if he had no care in the world. His horse would of course see him from a mile away, but would also carry on seeking out the best grass - only lifting his head a few inches in order to check his approach progress - in an attempt to gain the upper hand and get away in time from the work session that would inevitably follow.

On one such occasion the frequency of his escapes within one hour became so frustrating that Al uttered some forbidden curse words and slammed the bridle against the ground with the inevitable effect that the cast iron bit broke in two pieces. It was a catastrophe, he would have to tell his father and that would have its own humiliating consequences.

Fortunately when the family were not holidaying on the farm, a local enthusiastic teacher took care of business while Al's horse was stabled on a nearby farm belonging to Uncle Llewellyn, a man who always filled Al with admiration for his kindness and patience towards a young boy who grew up in a city. He was of Scottish origins and chose to live in Africa. Looking back he had to say that in itself was a most brave undertaking. Africa was a potential irritable giant with political ambitions and it took great courage to believe that it was possible to make a living on a farm in a neglected region where increasingly disgruntled labourers were so vital to assist with milk cows, sheep, pigs and cash crops.

When Uncle Llewellyn heard of Al's plight he arrived the very next day with a set of brand new chrome stirrup irons and a chrome bit. He remembered to the day how he presented it to him with both hands and winked and said with a smile in his familiar soft voice, 'Stay calm around your horse; these will not break so easily.' He was now ready to re-start his horse riding adventure with new hope and new kit and learning how to control his temper in a world where self-control was becoming all important.

The best journey he regularly undertook was the one leading from the farmstead to the new pasture several miles away from the main farm in the direction of Elandsfontein, where the virgin bush and undergrowth was cleared and the land had been prepared for raising cattle. This was always an adventurous outing. The land lay some distance away from the road and surrounded by other farms. The service road was quite rough and in many places irremovable sawn off and burnt tree stumps stood where the forest and undergrowth were removed remained behind - so that a 4 X 4 truck could just clear them with inches to spare. Several concertina wire gates were installed since the service road ran across other farms. These gates were all protected with so-called 'smoelneuker' (mouth puncher) securing devices (a strong short stick at the end of two wound-up wires and secured through the gate and set with a wire loop attached to the gatepost) to keep unwanted visitors away. To the uninitiated these devices appeared quite harmless, but the tension was set so high that if the loop were simply to be removed without holding the stick, it would hit you squarely in the 'smoel' (mouth). The art of passing through these gates on horseback swiftly meant that you had to practice to remove the device and hold the gate so that your well trained horse could move smoothly through the gate and then turn and stop in time for you to re-set the 'smoelneuker' without having to dismount. This was a clever trick that took much practice to perfect and that sometimes led to some severe bruising.

Al loved that particular stretch of land. It smelt of soil and new wild growth intermingled with indigenous heather and its virgin origins meant that it literally swarmed with insects and snakes of every kind ranging from the harmless grass variety to the most dangerous, raising their bodies from the ground and moving at speed gazing out over the new undergrowth with tongues flickering, and of course a variety of small game and then the bush buck … an animal that stands and fights with its tail firmly lodged into a thick bush and horns at the ready.

They have been known to have seriously injured any would be game poachers or unsuspecting hunters who tried to take them down by hand after a bad shot. Of course, the green touraco, or bosloerie, with white lined eyes and white head combs stood watch over all of these spectacles and warned trespassers into their world with their short staccato voices. In short - the ideal place for any young boy to live out all his fantasies.

Then of course there was the secret river running through all of this natural beauty in the deep dark valley beyond that stretch of cleared land. To get to the river one had to pass through the wild forest where there was little or no light before reaching the dark vegetation coloured brown stream filled with deep mysterious black water holes and noisy bubbling shallows - a place where nothing else seemed to matter. It was as if every visit was a rite of passage passing through the darkness of the undergrowth and tall trees. He would often tie the piebald to a tree and undertake the run through the forest to the river for a fresh drink and a quick wash in the ice-cold water running down from the hills and then back to ride home with the secret of that watery adventure firmly locked away for days, weeks, months, years hence. He would remember the secret, dark river again standing on the banks of rivers in southeast Angola during the South African Bush War.

Then there was the far less exciting journey to 'the other side of the gorge' towards Witriver. That was a long and arduous ride often driving cattle along the dusty road and through the valley with yet another stream - not as exciting and beautiful though as the secret dark river - with all the traffic dangers that entailed to a piece of leased land that was not particularly attractive and with no natural water, but rich in pastures for the animals.

Then there was the long mountain run, up against the high hills where the wood mill worked long days to process the pine from the formal cultivated plantations into commercial products. The road was particularly winding and quite steep and when reaching the top the reward was a view over all of the low lying hillocks and fields with the aroma of freshly cut wood drifting in on the ever present wind - a sight to see and a sweet smell never to forget. This journey always resulted in streams of sweat and foam streaming from the piebald's sides on the down run. Al never forgot that ride and would recall it in minute detail whenever the world became too tight for his free spirit.

Returning home after such excursions he had to deal with the sometimes pleasant, but mostly unpleasant, reality of belligerent parents who were ever torn between their public life and the attraction of a simple rural holiday. The daily bickering left an indelible impression on Alistair's sensitive soul.

Those days spent alone became a treasure trove of memories that he would carry with him throughout his life. The fights between his parents became a massive drag on his development and he would constantly remind himself from there on to treat women with the respect they deserve.

Al's father remained an interesting example to Al of how an ordinary man could make it into the limelight and then fail to cope with all the attention and power.

Al's note in this regard was so disturbing that I decided to use that in unaltered form to describe this dark dilemma. 'Pappa was always somewhat of a mystery to me. On the one hand he was quite old-fashioned with rather specific ideas of how men were supposed to behave towards other people. His behaviour towards Mamma was however often so atrocious that I would run away and hide in my outside room until the battle subsided. The shouting matches would often drag on deep into the night with insults about family and friends shouted out in high-pitched voices. Breakfast the following morning would be a strained affair with the air heavy with sarcasm and muttered un-pleasantries exchanged in whispers. Juicy grey doves - often enjoyed as a delicatessen - that I shot and brought for breakfast as a special cooked treat would go mostly unnoticed. Any efforts to speak about my horse and planned rides on the day would be swept aside all in the service of the great god of mindless destructive family feuding. My mother was a city girl who hated anything resembling the farm and the hard existence of a wood stove, outside wind food cooler, oil lamps, rain water tanks for domestic use and the ever present huge spiders coming into the house and secreting themselves on the mottled wooden walls, was not her idea of a proper life or holiday … not even for a short while. Quite often a loud shriek would come from the main bedroom upon finding a spider followed by loud shouts about uncivilised surroundings, with regular reference to my Father's family who were according to her also uncivilized and then of course the recriminations would follow and old slumbering fires would be sufficiently re-kindled to flare up into a full-blown storm that scared the hell out of me. These arguments would happen especially over Christmas. That would deliver a double blow of negative images that would linger long after and into my adult life. I would withdraw from the family circle during these bouts while my father's attention and affections would mostly be focused on my eldest sister who made very sure to stay close to him by subtly expressing her support and understanding, while my younger sister and I found other places and activities outside to fill our days. We were regularly victimised by my Father with our eldest sibling enthusiastically in tow. During these occasions my father was no longer really my Father …'

Note 2 - *Of extraordinary, ordinary men and a little red dead dog* - Al's early life.

'The sight of death dust has always affected me. Have you ever noticed how dust settles on an animal's eyes after death? It happens with people too when they die outside and it remains a deeply upsetting and saddening experience for anyone recognising it as a visible sign of the desolation of death.'

These words were written in longhand at the top of the first page of his notes next to a photograph of a Darwin fox. The words were legible, but interspersed with several corrections and with several words crossed out as if he considered carefully how to write them until he finally reached the final product. He subsequently commenced telling a story with short and sometimes much more extensive notes, which I find so haunting that it still wakes me at night. I have decided to relate it as best I can while respecting how he apparently considered and wrote these words.

Alistair was thirteen years old when he bagged his first Springbuck in an open field on a farm several miles from a place called Modderriver Railway Station in the Northern Cape - very close to Magersfontein, where a significant clash between

Boer and Imperial Forces took place during the Second Boer War. It was a particularly icy late afternoon after having waited the whole day long for an opportunity to show and prove his prowess. He was cold and he was scared that he would fail the test and disappoint his father. He held his brand new German-built .243 Winchester Krico bolt action hunting rifle close to his chest. He loved the smell of the oil in the action and the attractive appearance of the slanting angle at the rear end of the bolt emblazoned with the Krico logo, which was so familiar of that kind of rifle, was really quite pleasing. He could sit for hours looking at his own hand with the thumb resting on that slanted rear surface just above the safety catch that showed black in the forward and red in the switched back firing position. His father had given him this rifle as a gift sometime before and it was meant to be the first phase of his all important induction into the much acclaimed world of hunting - an important aspect of a boy's upbringing in post-colonial Africa where self-reliance was everything and dependence seen as weakness. It was the rather scary pathway to manhood many young men had to follow in order to gain acceptability amongst elders and peers.

His opportunity to prove himself came very late on that day. The sun was already resting on the horizon when the single Springbuck appeared as if from nowhere after having escaped the relentless efforts of the game drivers. He moved along with his head held low and stopping every now and then to look and listen. Alistair waited behind a small rise in the ground with some knee high shrubs shielding his presence.

The lone Springbok approached his position and froze at about one hundred yards picking up his head after having escaped from the drivers of the hunt crisscrossing the area on horseback and on foot. Alistair crept forward and took careful aim. His hands were quite cold since wearing his gloves would be cumbersome and might spoil his chances of an accurate shot. He trembled with anticipation and tried to remember everything his father had taught him about handling a rifle when he took his first practise shots. He tried to steady himself and to control his breathing and to aim carefully and accurately for the spot just behind the elbow, which represented the access route to the vital organs. He tried really hard not to 'nest' behind the rifle, but his eyes were blurry and he felt rather desolate. He suddenly sensed the overpowering fever of the hunt. He started shaking and as the adrenalin raced through his system and kick started his heartbeat into a frenzied pace, he squeezed the trigger. The rifle's recoil was expected, but also not - as was the crack of the shot, which cut clean through his senses and blocked his right ear that subsequently started ringing. The springbuck jumped into the air with an arched back and crashed to the ground. Alistair was completely stunned. He saw the white patch of hair lifting in the wind on the rear of the back as if the animal was pronking in death having mistaken dying for live excitement. The cinnamon brown skin was etched against the green shrubs. The boy just sat there shaking uncontrollably and drawing shallow breaths through his dry mouth. He stared for several minutes at the spot where the animal fell as if he wanted to ensure that he was not mistaken. He was also a little afraid to approach the evidence of his first kill.

After this occurrence killing never again came easily to Alistair. He could not forget this encounter with death and each and every time he was responsible for a death after that day it troubled him in the finest of detail. Especially as when he eventually approached the fallen animal, he realised with complete and utter horror, that he had been completely fooled by the bad light and that he had shot a lamb. As if that was not terrible enough, the lead tipped bullet had ripped out the animal's stomach. There was blood and guts everywhere. Stomach shots were frowned upon by seasoned hunters since it spoilt the skin for future use and often lead to springbuck hiding in the bushes and grass if the shot was not high enough to break the spinal column. The wounded animal would then secrete itself in thicker grass and die a terrible and painful death during a Karoo winter night. It was sheer luck plus the fact that this was a small animal that secured Alistair's kill. It was as if his entire life fell apart at that moment. How would he ever justify this to anyone - let alone Uncle Red and his father? He sat on the ground with both hands caressing the young dead animal and wept with tears falling freely on the now lifeless light brown hair while he tried to close the eyes covered in death dust. Alas, the animal's eyes remained half open. He was so incredibly ashamed of his failure.

He heard Uncle Red's truck bouncing over rocks and uneven ground with dull metallic thuds and the loading-bin gate securing chains beating loudly against the inside underscored by the engine running with an intermittent slightly off-rhythmic whine. In that instant he remembered the amusing familiar discussion he had with Uncle Red, Master of the Hunt, that very morning as they drove to the hunting ground - a charming little ritual that he was introduced to the previous years before he actually hunted and instead just accompanied his father. It went something like this, 'Where will we hunt today Uncle

Red?' Uncle Red - an incredibly knowledgeable, but notoriously mischievous man with a well developed, not entirely unsuitable paunch and a slightly reddish tint to his face ideally attributable to the fierce sun, but in all probability more likely because of the regular partaking of whiskey - was dressed in semi-smart khaki coloured brown corduroy trousers and short dark brown leather jacket, sporting a soft chequered flannel winter shirt and brown woollen tie rounded off with a slightly worn khaki coloured wide brimmed rabbit fur hat. He was a kind man and an excellent storyteller with an easy laugh. He shifted gears in anticipation of the approaching corner and started speaking. 'Now Alistair, my boy, let me try to explain. Listen carefully because you have to help me to find the right directions and turn-off. We will continue to the east along this road for another thirty miles. Then we will approach a road marker indicating the last small hamlet along the way to the farm where we will hunt. We will turn to the south at that point and after approximately ten miles we will pass through the hamlet. After another twenty miles along that road the surface will change from asphalt to dirt and about two miles further along that road we will approach another road marker. At that point we will turn sharply to the west and drive towards the plateau. The sun will rise and we will have to squint into the sharp light and drive carefully. After another three miles we will come upon a tall tree. There on the right hand side of the road we will see a farm gate. We will turn and pass through that gate. We will have to measure our distance very precisely because only one thousand and twenty yards further we will suddenly see a clump of low trees and a single surveyor's beacon. At the foot of the beacon we will find a dead, little red dog. There is the precise place where we will hunt.'

Silence reigned supreme in the car. Uncle Red was driving, Alistair's father sat in the front passenger seat and Alistair occupied the middle of the back seat in the black Chevrolet sedan. Alistair would notice the slight smile developing around his father's mouth and Uncle Red's 'innocent' eyes staring back at him in the rear view mirror. Then utter pandemonium broke out as the three of them started laughing in sync as if some maestro of the hunt concert was directing this small band of brothers caught in a timeless moment of rapturous joy in a place where the rest of the world could never touch them. Alistair laughed until the tears ran down his face while he gave Uncle Red a playful punch on the back of the shoulder with his new leather winter gloves that were still slightly too large for his young hands. His father's words rang through waves of laughter and caused further amusement, 'Red, what an excellent route description. You should write travel books.' That was a really good memory. What a pity that his father was not capable of creating such frivolity, but was instead always just a participant. For just that smallest of moments he wished Uncle Red could have been his father.

Alistair did not look up, but instead sat motionless in the cold hoping that the small animal would magically become a full grown animal and that he could rise triumphantly next to his quarry and show off his contribution to the hunt. That was however not to be. As the vehicle bounced closer he stood up painfully slowly with a hollow feeling deep in his stomach, wiped the tears from his face with his jacket sleeves and waited alone for whatever admonishment was coming from his favourite Uncle Red and his father. The same hollow feeling on his stomach would re-visit him on several occasions in the future especially in the face of unknown danger during sensitive military operations or when he was alone on a mission with no-one to assist when things went wrong and nowhere to run to for comfort and safety.

Uncle Red stopped his truck close to the fallen lamb. He went down on his one knee and placed his arm around Alistair's shoulders and said the words that made everything better, 'My boy, this happens to all of us. The light this time of day is so treacherous. You will still learn to pick the older ones more accurately in the future. This is your first success, so congratulations. The meat will be tender and juicy and we will make a feast of it. Now, let us show our respect by thanking this beautiful young animal for offering us his body.' His father remained silent.

Uncle Red's words made everything better and no-one else's comments would matter after that. In a way he was actually able to feel better about the whole matter and especially the fact that he shot his first springbuck. Alistair never forgot Uncle Red and he promised himself to make accuracy with a rifle his second name. It became a worthwhile memory of a man who probably understood his anguish and did the right thing. He vaguely heard his father's off-hand remark about it merely being a mistake to be improved on next time and promptly moved on to where the workers were slaughtering the quarry. He did not pay much attention to his father's remark. Uncle Red would be there up to his elbows in blood 'working the meat' with great precision while his wife stood looking on and offered advice on how she wanted the portions prepared. He felt at home with these two people.

Note 3 - *Making it better.*

'I was ultimately given a chance to correct my mistake that is still haunting me to this day. Mistakes will happen and it is up to us to make sure we never repeat them, especially when we deal with life and death.'

Uncle Red was right. A year after that fateful day they were hunting near Smitsdrift in the Northern Cape. It was late afternoon and it was so cold that it was difficult to hold and operate the rifle action. The Kudu bull appeared as if from nowhere. Uncle Red stood completely still next to Alistair where they finally chanced upon the animal after having tracked him for several miles. Alistair whispered in a barely audible voice, 'This is the right one, Uncle Red.' The answer came back instantly, 'Right on the button, my boy. Drop him now.' Without a single hesitation or any sign of trembling Alistair squeezed the trigger. The bullet hit that bull precisely in the magical spot behind the right elbow. The animal spun around in his tracks, he reared up for a moment as if attempting a last show of defiance, then his legs folded under him and he fell in a cloud of fine dust. Alistair rushed closer to where the large frame lay motionless in a haze of dust surrounding the kill zone, fell to his knees and while touching the warm body with both his hands whispered softly, 'Thank you for the offering.' He chose not to look at the animal's eyes. He knew it was covered in death dust. That was a moment to remember. Beautiful horns and skin, a healthy full-grown animal, lots of meat for cooking and 'biltong' to dry. He felt like the proverbial one million dollars while all the grown men in the party shook his hand and congratulated him. Uncle Red laughed that familiar laugh that everybody knew so well and insisted on sniffing under Alistair's shooting arm - an old hunting tradition whereby some of the shooter's ability may be transferred from the armpit to the person showing the respect. Finally, he could call himself a hunter.

The years went by too quickly and Uncle Red died. Alistair studied to be a newspaperman while his father became more successful every day. With that success his ego grew out of all proportion. He started losing the common touch and joined the ranks of wealthy men that reflected his own rise in status. Alistair never made it that far on the social ladder. He would become an ordinary journalist and walked away from that type of life. As a hunter he preferred the company of ordinary men like Uncle Red. That would take him across the border into Southwest Africa.

Note 4 - *Learning from a master.*

'The best teacher will demonstrate, explain and teach the skill, encourage, admonish and ultimately praise when you succeed. Uncle Black was all of that and much more. I took his lessons with me when war broke out. That, plus my 'secret horizon' kept me alive.'

It was the 70's and Alistair's desire for adventure and hunting would now take him into a new world. South West Africa (later to be re-named Namibia after the Border War and independence) was still under South African mandatory supervision. It was a wild and a rock hard testing ground for young men who needed to measure themselves. Alistair embarked on several survival excursions into the desert badlands and learnt all the lessons this unforgiving land could possibly present.

He completed two bone jarring 90 mile treks through the 2,000 foot deep Fish River Canyon and on each occasion the lessons were harsh and quite compelling. During the first trek, the terrain they encountered was profoundly challenging oscillating between sand, rock and large and small river stones and only the fittest could really survive there without injury. These treks were also a right-of-passage for anyone who believed in pitting his strength against nature in that part of Africa. The first time he nearly succumbed to the searing heat in that Godforsaken place. There was so little water that their small group of four men were forced to drink sparingly and mostly hike during the cooler hours while resting during the heat of the day. Temperatures regularly soared to in excess of 40 degrees Celsius in the shade. They completed the route, but Alistair came away with a sense of his own vulnerability and the occasional awkwardness of human relationships under stressful circumstances. He was unpleasantly surprised to experience that one member of the team who had qualified as a paratrooper, was completely unable to understand the concept of sharing of all the camp work and other necessary tasks followed by light hearted social interaction and comradeship that would inevitably follow. Having realised early on in life that clever teamwork made for excellent results he consistently attempted to draw this team member into the group. The result was a resounding failure since his attempts were mostly scoffed at and as a result the team remained dysfunctional for the rest of the journey. Alistair never forgot this experience. In later years he would make it his mission in life to find the right mix of men in military teams he had to assemble during his later military career. This one man was clearly simply the wrong man despite his macho military background.

During the second trek through the same canyon, which

could quite easily bear the name purgatory, his experience as team guide was the complete opposite. The team consisted of serving military personnel who understood the meaning of the term mutual support. One night the engineers at the Naute Dam reservoir, which lay several miles to the north, were forced to open the sluice gates after torrential rainstorms that occurred in the north of the country. The parched country simply could not absorb all of this additional water at one time. The destruction this newly created water mass wreaked on the land on its way to the sea was immense. Alistair and his military team were caught right in the middle of it. The river rose to a depth of over 12 feet at the height of its journey to the west coast of Africa. Alistair was swept downstream with a few men and the Padre who proved to be not only a man of God, but also a practical soldier, never once doubted that they would make it out of that river. The river eventually spat them out on a sand bank at a sharp bend in the stream. After lying still for several minutes Alistair lifted his head from the sand and asked the Padre who was lying next to him, whether they were dead. The padre answered in true spirited fashion, 'Not yet my son, not yet.' Several soldiers were injured and had to be extracted by helicopter and flown to safety. What was incredible was the fact that for reasons of excellent command practices by the commanding officer in charge of the excursion, tempers remained under control and teamwork was outstanding. Alistair remembered this for the rest of his life. Never again would he witness such a clear example of the Machiavellian truth of people uniting when the enemy is at the gate. Tragically he would also be a witness when the same principle was supposed to apply in a broader context in South Africa. His belief was always that minorities in South Africa were essentially betrayed by traitors from within, rather than by a foreign enemy from without. These two experiences in Southwest Africa became milestones in his life against which he would measure many things in the troubled years that lay ahead.

Quite by chance during the middle 70's he befriended an interesting, completely unorthodox, but quite talented lawyer in the small town of Keetmanshoop. Hans had absolutely no desire to hunt, but he appreciated that Alistair was different to most young men of that time and he appreciated and enjoyed his company. He understood his slightly awkward old worldly values and became a sincere and undemanding friend. The deal was that he would find the hunting grounds and in exchange for some meat and biltong he would arrange the introductions. Hans was a master of matching personalities. Soon he introduced Alistair to a farmer of German colonial descent, who had exceptional field skills that were rapidly becoming hard to come by. This man was called Uncle Black - in a strange play of words that revived Alistair's fond memories of Uncle Red. He would not be disappointed. Uncle Black's single most impressive skill was that he could take down a springbuck at three hundred yards with a 7.62x51mm NATO R1 AR with ghost ring iron sights, issued to the rural military commando members (a type of local militia). He was a field marksman of exceptional high quality. Coupled with a delightful personality, impressive physical strength and a world of hunting experience and field craft, Uncle Black was a sheer joy to watch during the hunt and amazing to listen to at night next to the fireplace.

Uncle Black's father was a blacksmith in the German Schutztruppen that were sent to the German colony in the late 1800's. He settled there and stayed on after the First World War and the surrender of the land to Britain, which was then made a South African League of Nations Mandate. He acquired the farm land that was eventually left to his son Christian ... Uncle Black. The name Black refers to the fact that his skin was substantially darkened by the intense sun as he worked tirelessly to tame the wilderness that was to become a sophisticated and well managed agricultural Karakul pelt production unit.

While Uncle Black was still developing his 14,000 hectare Karakul farm, Zackenberg, in the Black Mountains on the Namib Escarpment and establishing his farm perimeter by dynamiting holes for fence poles, he had to survive and feed his family. During the World War II several people of German origin in South West Africa were suspected of possible collusion with the Axis Powers. Many were interned and all firearms were confiscated.

Uncle Black gained additional food and income by catching game in the Namib Desert using an old Ford sedan with the roof and doors removed. He and other young farmers would regularly organise such outings. On these occasions they would chase the animals down driving over the wide expanse of salt pans at speeds of up to 70 mph - taking turns to sit on the front mud guard of the vehicle and 'roping' them with a strong rope, slip knot and catch-pole. This was dangerous work and he just escaped with minor abrasions on more than one occasion as they would fall off the mud guard with monotonous regularity - especially when the vehicle hit a rock or hole, but what the hell, they were young, incredibly tough and indestructible in their own minds and would simply get up, wipe the dust off and start all over again.

During this challenging time the only weapon he possessed was one sharpened half of a sheep scissor. One hot summer night he was sleeping outside on the veranda. He heard a shuffling noise in the vegetable garden. He took his half sheep scissor blade in his right hand, moved closer with extreme caution and found a fully-grown Kudu bull enjoying the succulent food. Uncle Black crawled closer on all fours - fortunately it was a moonless night. He waited for the animal to lower its head and launched himself on to the bull's back. The Kudu reared into the air and set off towards the farmyard gate at breakneck speed. Uncle Black clung like dung to sheepskin and just before the animal prepared to jump he stuck the half scissor blade into his lower neck and cut a main artery. That night he secured many healthy meals and heaps of biltong for his family and farm workers.

This association between Uncle Black, Alistair and Hans developed into a tight circle of three friends - the Master of the Hunt, the Hunter and the Commentator - that would last for seven years and only fade because of the rising tide of war that would ultimately change not only them, but a whole sub continent. Uncle Black was a hard taskmaster, knew his farm, game and hunting skills. Alistair was an eager learner and Hans commented on anything and everything - a quality he brought to the occasion with a razor sharp sense of humour that was both contagious and highly entertaining - a tolerable and respected best 'coxswain on shore'.

The road into the Black Mountains and the farm passed through a small hamlet called Helmeringhausen. It was one of those towns that he would never forget, simply because it was so completely lost and out of place in the vastness of the Namib

Escarpment bordering on the eastern side of the Namib Desert. The Atlantic forms the western edge of the desert. This vast expanse, that had to be crossed before reaching the narrow track leading to the homestead, was always so completely overwhelming that every time Alistair arrived at the actual access road to Zackenberg, he would stop and stand next to the vehicle and for some time just stare in complete awe at the light yellow and brown landscape where the emptiness right up to the horizon instilled a peace that he would never again experience anywhere else in the world. That view became part of his innermost soul and whenever he felt the need to escape from the modern world filled with complete superficial garbage, he would flee into that place and disappear into his subconscious reality. In his notes he referred to it as his 'secret horizon'.

The track had to be approached with significant caution. That part of the land was literally strewn with huge rocks that could easily puncture a sump or damage tyres, gearboxes, axles or differentials. After having picked one's way over this winding rocky section, there was a crossing through a dry riverbed and then a steep climb to the top of a ridge, overlooking the farmyard in the distance. A long gentle slope leading through low thorn trees finally led towards the farmyard gate.

The entire building complex was built with rock - found, hacked or picked up and carried out of the Namib escarpment. It consisted of a barn with a karakul wool processing section and a mechanical workshop for re-soldering torn chassis, including a crane for removing engines out in the front, outside living quarters mainly for guests and a large main house. Some smaller outbuildings for sheep and fowl lay at the back of the complex. A large wind pump stood in the yard. This was the origin of many a fascinating tale such as the 'drawing the pipes from the well' to mend leaks accompanied by loud and often angry shouts at farmhands not doing things as Uncle Black did it when he worked alone. He was a rock hard, but fair taskmaster. Without this complex the farm would not be able to function in this harsh environment. It was the nerve centre of everything that happened on Zackenberg.

It was also a place of great festivity around the barbeque fire that lit up the entire area from where laughter and loud conversation emanated and drifted into the mountain and the desert beyond. Uncle Black was an amazing man to listen to at night at the fireplace. Under his chairmanship these gatherings were always marked by spontaneous laughter and wonderful old and new stories that filled the star strewn South West African nights. It seemed as if it were wonderfully colourful created chapters energetically added to a colossal celestial storybook that was opened every night. This was also where his wife Ilse, played her part in creating a magical atmosphere of joy. It was always very clear what special position she enjoyed in his heart. The looks of admiration between them were noticeable and understandable given their hard life together. Combined with her ability to prepare the most outstanding venison and lamb dishes, homemade bread, fresh vegetables from her carefully nurtured garden and of course all washed down with Maibock and Windhoek beer and eventually rounded off with Bärenjäger Höniglikör, these occasions were veritable feasts. This diminutive woman brought a strength and enthusiasm that gave many an aspiring hunter hope. She was also the person who supported Uncle Black through thin and flush as they worked to create their farm. The vegetable and flower beds were her domain and she ran the house like a military operation. During the karakul slaughter and hunting seasons and whenever the sheep needed medication dosages of any kind, she would perform double shifts as a farmhand and the boss of the homestead. She was fully rifle and handgun trained and always carried a .38 Special wheel gun since she was more often than not quite alone at the homestead. Isolated farm folk were always at personal risk in South West Africa, even well before the war. Drifters remain a problem until today.

These people were hard working honest people with an astounding insight into world affairs and had all the time in the world for their equally isolated neighbours and in fact also for anyone else in need. Guests who came to learn about the land, its people and the art of hunting were treated like royalty. The population was thinly spread over the area and socialising was highly prized. The isolation and harsh environment made them into incredibly uncomplicated, direct and thoroughly good people. This is where Alistair would find ultimate confirmation and acceptance of his old worldly values and belief in strength and honour. He felt completely at home here where actions spoke louder than words and where it was easy to distinguish between right and wrong. There was no time for anything else since lives depended on that ability.

Uncle Black ran his farm with an iron fist. Any worker caught out not following the rules of the farm, was punished fairly, albeit sometimes quite harshly. Younger workers were sometimes given a sound hiding dished out by Uncle Black with personal discipline and caution. They respected him for that and the majority stayed on the farm and preferred to work for him because he cared for them with food, clothing, proper housing and money. Uncle Black was known and respected for this strict, but fair approach right across the region. On visits to the nearest town of Mariental with produce or to purchase required goods for the farm, workers would take turns to accompany him.

On one such occasion in the middle of a sweltering summer's day, Uncle Black parked his truck in the Mariental main street to have his hair cut and then to enjoy one Windhoek beer at the nearby hotel to wash the dust from his throat after the long drive. He always allowed himself this one luxury before commencing his shopping. His way of doing things were known to the townsfolk and no-one ever came between Uncle Black and his haircut and one beer. The farm workers went on their way to do their own shopping and a meeting and departure time at the Agricultural Cooperation loading area was pre-arranged. Unbeknown to Uncle Black the Traffic Department had painted a new yellow line on a part of the main road to control parking in that area. Uncle Black ignored the yellow line because he was Uncle Black and Mariental was 'his town' and more importantly, he needed to visit the barbershop and hotel pub. A traffic constable was on duty in the main street on that day and as fate would have it he was a new man and he did not know Uncle Black and his habit of having a haircut and drinking one beer before commencing with his shopping. He arrived on the scene after Uncle Black had already entered the hotel pub with his new haircut. He parked his Harley Davidson 'speed cop motorbike' (Uncle Black's description) behind the truck, took out his pen and ticket book and strutted his stuff to the truck's windscreen to check the license disc. Subsequently and quite unfortunately for him, he adjusted the teardrop sunglasses on his nose, corrected the position of his helmet, placed his right foot adorned with a heavy motorcycle boot on the truck's rock battered front bumper in order to rest his ticket book on his upper leg, took his pen from his shirt pocket and started writing the ticket. By this time a small crowd of enthusiastic onlookers - who all knew Uncle Black's truck - gathered around to witness the outcome of this little disaster.

Right at that precise moment Uncle Black walked out of the pub towards his truck. What subsequently happened is the stuff of local legend and has given rise to many elaborations, adjustments and expansions that have since placed Uncle Black in the annals of ancient folklore in Mariental. There is hardly one person in that town who does not know the story. Uncle Black walked directly towards the traffic constable. The conversation that ensued went something like this, 'Why have you placed your foot on my bumper? Who will pay to fix the scratches?' The constable answered with a monotone officious line, 'Because you have parked your battered truck on a yellow line and I am not even sure that this truck is roadworthy. Have you been drinking? I smell alcohol on your breath. I should arrest you here and now for breaking and obstructing the law and appearing in public while under the influence of alcohol.'

What happened then was apparently so fast that only a few people could give an accurate account. Uncle Black let rip with a lightning fast left short-arm jab to the midline and when the copper folded over forward he caught him with a roundhouse right hand sledgehammer blow to the jaw that knocked his lights out on the spot. Without a sound he tumbled over backwards onto the slightly molten hot asphalt and lay completely motionless with his teardrop sunglasses suspended from his one ear and his helmet on the back of his head. The small crowd of admirers cheered wildly and gave Uncle Black a rapturous round of applause. It was clear who the favourite was in this no-contest contest.

Uncle Black did not move a muscle in his face. He picked the traffic constable up from the ground and unceremoniously dumped him on the back of the truck. He then walked up to the Harley, released the side rest and singlehandedly wrestled the massive machine to a position next to the constable on the truck. Job done. It was the early sixties. Uncle Black was a leading figure in the farming community and a highly appreciated longstanding member of the local military commando. The traffic policeman clearly had a lot to learn about the personalities and the way things were done in a part of the world that strongly resembled a slightly more modern, but at heart simply the Wild Southwest.

Uncle Black drove to the Magistrate's Court, offloaded the Harley and the slowly awakening traffic constable and parked both of them on the side of the road. He then walked unannounced straight into the magistrate's office and related the full circumstances. The magistrate apologised to Uncle Black and suggested that in future a more consultative line of action may be more suitable and would he please consider that. Uncle Black accepted the advice gracefully and then left to go about his business after having enjoyed a quick coffee with the magistrate. The traffic constable was reprimanded for causing an unnecessary confrontation with a valued member of the community. He would give Uncle Black a wide berth in the years that followed - even when he persisted with parking on that precise spot on the yellow line.

Note 5 - *The one that nearly got away.*

Amongst Uncle Black's loyal workers there was an exceptionally sharp-witted Nama called Jan. He was a seasoned game tracker and one of his jobs was to track and find wounded animals during the hunting season. He was a man of slender build, but visibly wiry and tough with the eyesight of a falcon and the sensory capacity of a leopard. Nothing escaped his attention in the field. This man would teach Alistair the fine detail of the art of tracking a wounded animal - a skill that would stand him in good stead in later life.

It was a hot late summer's day on the escarpment. Uncle Black, Hans, Alistair and Jan were exploring the area along the ridge overlooking the winding dry river- bed. Uncle Black navigated the Land Rover through the rocky field with considerable skill - with each rock and hole sending bone-jarring blows through the 4 X 4's chassis. The large kudu bull showed himself just for a split second at 100 metres amongst the thicket on the sun side of the ridge. Alistair had already hunted many springbuck and gems-buck on Zackenberg in previous years and learnt much from Uncle Black during that time. He never had an opportunity to hunt the elusive kudu, but by now his field and rifle skills were finely tuned and he was up to the task when the occasion arose. He brought the Belgian FN 7.62 X51 mm NATO rifle with barrel made of chrome and vanadium steel with a Mauser bolt action and magazine stack and a light yellow wooden stock, up to his shoulder without a single moment's hesitation. The weapon was slightly shorter than the ordinary hunting rifle, which made it particularly suitable for quick work in undergrowth as well as on the run. There was no time to lose with a kudu bull. They are tough animals known to run for hours even when wounded in order to put as much distance between itself and the danger. He squeezed the trigger and the 7.62s thunder rolled down into the dry riverbed. The bull dropped in its tracks with dust swirling around. Then, miraculously, the animal rose on its front legs with the blood streaming from a chest wound. Without even thinking, Alistair worked the Mauser action for a second attempt but, before he could deliver the second shot the bull stood upright to its full majestic height, turned briefly in its own tracks, raced down into the river bed and disappeared out of sight.

Uncle Black turned to Alistair and yelled, 'Find the animal Al, Jan, help him. I will follow along the ridge.' Alistair and Jan hit the ground running flat out immediately scouring the sand for specks and smears of blood on the long grass, broken twigs, tracks in the sand and disturbed and overturned or marked rocks. Wounded animals were never left to die in the field. Jan ran in front with Alistair following close by and slightly to one side to enable him to see the detail of the blood trail as Jan indicated with his right hand, stopping every now and then to inspect a particular spot and to look at the horizon in order to decide on the possible direction the animal would take. It was difficult, but it had to be done. Tracking in an environment where the terrain is so harsh is complicated especially because of the difficulty to maintain a consistent line when having to pass over significantly large patches of sheer rock. This is where the physical evidence of the trail is accentuated by an instinctive understanding of the general direction the fleeing animal is taking. That presupposes a knowledge of the terrain; the new starting point across the rock section, how the surface reacts to movement and the ability to judge its accessibility for an animal in full flight. Read in conjunction with the 45 degrees in the shade, blinding white hot sun and incredibly rough terrain, it becomes a mammoth task to find one animal that is attempting to flee and hide in its own backyard - all 14,000 hectare of it with fences that lead to everywhere and being dead easy to negotiate for a large kudu bull.

They ran on the bull's trail for nearly three and a half hours and were now following a line along the dry riverbed. Alistair and Jan's shirts were already showing the distinctive white salt deposits on the back and around the arms. Their trouser waistbands and leather belts were completely drenched. Water bottles were nearly empty and fatigue began setting in. Just then they came upon a patch of sand where the tracks were showing a clear milling pattern as if the animal paused to listen for its pursuers, rest for a few seconds and to take a decision for a new direction and possible hiding place. There was a large pool of blood with a blood trail leading away. Instead of staying low in and near the riverbed the kudu bull's tracks swung sharply to the right and lead towards a clump of low thorn trees. Then suddenly they came upon the animal where it lay in the shade of the largest thorn tree with head and horns still held high and looking straight at them - eyes acknowledging the end of the chase. They slowed right down and crouched low on their knees behind a thick bush. They were just under a hundred metres from the animal. Alistair's rifle was cycled and ready. He aimed for the chest just where the powerful neck began and squeezed the trigger. The bull staggered slightly upright and slumped to the ground. By the time Alistair reached him he was already dead. With some regret he looked at the death dust that had already settled on the large eyes, wrestled back the tears and kneeled next to the animal and said the words of appreciation for the offering Uncle Red taught him all those years ago. Then as agreed, he fired two shots into the sand in quick succession to signal that they had found and shot the Kudu bull and sat down leaning with his back against the animal's warm body. He felt both extremely pleased and profoundly sad. Jan drank briefly from his water bottle and with a nod he turned and set off to open ground to draw Uncle Black's attention. He took his white shirt off and used it to wave to the high point on the escarpment from where Uncle Black was scanning the area with his binoculars.

Within two hours Alistair heard the low groaning noise of the approaching Land Rover Uncle Black stepped from the 4 X 4, knelt down next to Alistair and with his rough hand on his shoulder said in a soft voice, 'What a beautiful animal. Good meat, skin and horns. Well done, Alistair.' He turned to Jan and gave him a thumbs-up. Jan's face lit up and he gave a tired, but satisfied smile while pointing in Alistair's direction and demonstrating how he fired the final shot. Hans followed close on Uncle Black's heels and with visible enthusiasm exclaimed his admiration for a job well done. This was man's work, done with precision and dedication. No time for frills or hesitation, just completing the task that was set. Alistair would always remember those days with immense gratitude and humility. That night there was laughter and conversation around the fire. It was a good day and a rewarding hunt.

Then, within months from that day, and as if from nowhere, dark clouds of war rolled in from the north and enveloped the isolation of the escarpment and eventually overcame all of them. War had broken out on the Kunene. Strange foreign forces massed in Angola and trains packed with wide-eyed young soldiers crossed the country day and night from the south to the north. Alistair would never return to the Namib Escarpment and he would never see his friend Uncle Black or Hans again. This was one of the greatest losses he ever suffered. Uncle Black was one man of a kind. He would never meet his equal anywhere in the future. Hans remained equally unmatched… His time of loneliness had now started.

Note 6 - *Life moment.*
'The highway to war … I do not understand why we ever went to war. It was certainly not for the state or any of its causes or to preserve our country. In the end I suppose it was for each other and our families.'

The integrity of the South African war effort to protect the northern border of South West Africa against communist backed terrorist insurgents, who were later simply regarded and re-named as Freedom Fighters against Apartheid, was always underpinned by big business benefitting from diamond and fish resources and the lure of smuggled goods in remote parts of the country where police cover was sparse. This problem did not really exist to the same extent in other northern South African border regions to the northeast, mainly because the natural resources were quite different, economic activity mostly confined to agriculture and the area was less remote. Problems did however occur with illegal immigration and some smuggling with mostly commercial goods on a much smaller scale.

The war on the border between South West Africa and Angola was a full-blown counter-insurgency operation often requiring unorthodox methods. This created ideal circumstances for criminality within the army and in civilian life, while the insurgents indulged in their own brand of criminal behaviour where the ends justified the means. Criminality was however not only the domain of small-time players. Big business entities played their own part and would enrich themselves through supporting the government of the day and in return were given special exploration rights in the conquered areas. Unimaginable riches were gathered and carried away from South West Africa. This practice would ultimately cause untold harm to the country and would especially damage its future independent status. These rights placed those that benefited from them in a particularly strong position in terms of any form of industrial legislation, since they always had the necessary access to lobby and influence changes to proposed legislation to ensure that they retain a position of immunity. This situation gave rise to an immense undercurrent of criticism of the South African government, which somehow always kept the lid on the scandal proclaiming that the war took precedence and that in desperate times desperate measures were required to keep the country stable.

By 1966 it was fast becoming clear that the police on their own would not be able to counter the insurgency across the Kunene into South West Africa because of a lack of relevant training and differences in fundamental methodology, numbers and required equipment. Their only specially formed unit that was ever really suited for the role was the 'Koevoet' (crowbar) counter-insurgency unit of the SA Police. Koevoet was renowned for their famous mailstrom tactic whereby a few of the specially designed Casspirs (personnel carrier and patrol vehicles fitted with heavy roof turret machine guns) would rush into the field of battle and engage the enemy in a fast circular movement shooting as they went. The enemy had no chance of escape. Initially the SA Air Force supported Koevoet, but as the insurgency threat grew, the rest of the SA Defence Force gradually became involved. Then during 1969 the threat became so vast that it was officially declared a full-blown counter-insurgency war.

The insurgency was set to become a drawn out affair that would last until 1989. Activities were initially executed on a grand scale with large fighting groups crossing into Angola and operating over vast distances. Eventually the political scenery changed to such an extent, especially with the Unites States of America infamously withdrawing its support for Jonas Savimbi's anti-communist UNITA, that South Africa increasingly experienced severe difficulty to control certain areas on its own. The war gradually changed into a holding action on the northern border of South West Africa with short sharp clashes between insurgents backed by foreign interests and South African reaction forces following up terrorist sighting reports by regular army patrols.

By a strange stroke of fate the first South African Border operations during 1966 and the resultant counter-insurgency and anti-terrorist operations within South Africa coincided with Alistair's selection to do a naval cadet course during that same year. His parents supported this activity enthusiastically as it indicated the right sort of grounding for public office later. Alistair was always enthusiastic about military matters and he refused to use his parents' good social standing to evade national service. The last war that was fought on South African soil was the Second Boer War that occurred between 1899 and 1902. No one really understood the implications of war any longer since the First and Second World Wars in which South Africa participated, was fought away from South Africa, with only limited action in South West Africa, including a quickly suppressed rebellion during the First World War. Significant time had passed since the last military actions elsewhere and as a consequence people's collective war memory remained blissfully inactive. In fact, many parents were encouraging their young sons not to attend cadet training before the war broke out and to feel negative about compulsory national service that commenced in 1967.

Note 7 - *In order to start at all, you have to know that you can finish.*

Alistair grew up in a privileged environment. His parents became successful during the early sixties since they were closely aligned with the growth of Afrikaner power in South Africa after the Second World War. They supported Afrikaner Nationalist values and the drive towards becoming a Republic, which followed on 31 May 1961, and was an all consuming ideal that bordered on hysteria. This formed the basis for several associations between businessmen who saw vast commercial benefits for themselves by aligning their activities with the nationalist government, more specifically where the largely untapped riches of South West Africa were concerned and where 'economic development' was required. The close association between fish and diamond concerns in South West Africa and South African senior politicians in general grew rapidly and in time it became difficult to separate the one from the other whenever decisions regarding the territory were involved. Alistair was exposed to many of these personalities especially during the sixties when he still lived with his parents. It was during these years that he became aware of the inherent conflict that existed between idealism and the cause initially subscribed to especially by soldiers on the one hand, and foreign investment and development considerations shrouding vast self-enrichment undertakings on the other. These actions could easily be mistaken for selfless commercial action as they were always explained in correct political terms. Frequent promises of large donations to help save 'the people' underscored this relationship and kept it very much alive.

Alistair's hunting and extreme physical outdoor activities helped him to prepare for the task he had to perform in the army. In a way he regarded this as the most important period in his life. However, it was his basic training as a military cadet at school and a national serviceman during the year before he attended university that laid the foundation. He threw himself into these activities with astonishing fervour. Cadet training differed from national service in terms of time spent on training. The basic principles were all the same. The fundamental skill set was the same, the concept being that knowledge gained and discipline instilled at such an early stage would help greatly when the time for the real thing came. Certain fundamentals would already have been manifested and it would take only a relatively short period to re-start those lessons and proceed on to more advanced training. In between undergoing cadet officer training during 1966 and reporting for national service at the beginning of 1968 Alistair decided to embark on a self imposed building of physical strength and endurance that seemed insurmountable to even the bravest and most energetic of souls.

His solitary training sessions entailed running vast distances on endless stretches of flat sand, soft, high dunes as well as rough, rocky uneven terrain with heavy combat boots during the heat of day and coupled with physical exercises to strengthen muscles and stretching to gain suppleness; all based on the strict principle of mind over matter. He would design training programs for himself based on this principle and then proceeded to motivate himself to move beyond set targets as a matter of course. Inevitably this led to regular physical and emotional pressure often coupled with injury and immense subsequent effort to get going again. The motto he coined for himself was, 'In order to start at all, you have to know that you can finish.' It was that belief that he could finish that drove him on relentlessly.

Alistair underwent his basic military training for national service during the early part of 1968. With his military cadet background under his belt, he sailed through basics and was selected for an officer's course, which he completed middle 1968. He fully believed that he participated in all of this for the sake of his country and its cause of self-preservation and a way of life. He was then deployed until the end of that year which remained mostly uneventful since not all national servicemen were initially deployed to the border areas. At the end of 1968 Alistair decided to attend a university where he read literature until 1972 when he joined a daily Afrikaans paper as a reporter and eventually succeeded to be given the crime beat. Right through this period Alistair remained in direct touch with the Citizen Force manned by national servicemen, attended promotion and specialisation courses and when the war intensified during 1977 he was ready to transfer to the Intelligence Corpse where his nose for finding fact based news and ability to deal with people would be put to good use first as an analyst and then in an operational role as a military intelligence operator and facilitator. This task was focused on cementing new relations with other states - primarily through a covert military conduit in order to provide communications channels, military training, assist with the establishment of medical facilities and treating high ranking foreign personnel and their families if needs be in South Africa within a special unit. This permitted even public enemies of the Apartheid State to benefit in total confidence and without fear of being compromised. This was a sure fire method to make new friends and help to prevent the use of foreign soil by terrorists in the case of neighbouring states, even though they would consistently oppose South Africa in public.

His 'life moment' was about to commence. With that, inevitably came significant pressures and the emotional darkness and baggage that would always haunt him.

Training for his work within the SA Military Intelligence Corps was a curious affair and would impact directly on his 'life moment'. His eventual unorthodox application as a dual disciplined soldier applied as both intelligence analyst and operator was never really formally addressed during his training. Training focused on the formal intelligence evaluation process rather than the subtleties of this intricate work activity. It always struck him with how much disregard for real life situations they were trained in a near pedantic style akin to high school education. The principle of teaching so called useless idiots who were treated as such by instructors, remained a complete mystery to him. Senior officers who participated in courses to gain intelligence knowledge were treated in a similar dismissive manner without the slightest recognition of their own level of sophistication or life experience. Alistair's knowledge about practical field work which entailed one-on-one intelligence gathering through carefully developed sources was taught by senior officers who presided over junior members for a certain time until they were ready to be deployed. This process also required the cautious matching of operator and source personalities to secure the best personal relationship and thus a good end result. It was a world where single highly trained operators working alone flourished without the impediment of too many cooks that could spoil the broth. This was a totally different environment where practice took precedence over theory. Alistair always felt that more time should have been spent on field training and that the formal theoretical training should rather have been seen as a secondary supporting process. He became a true professional at his job not because of his training in the corps school, but rather through his own powers of observation, his personality profile that showed a distinct inclination for this kind of work and his work as an understudy with really quite brilliant field operators.

It is a known fact that the USA made the same mistake during the time in the 70's when there was an upsurge in the application of new surveillance technology such as satellite applications, drones, CCTV and internet and telephone technology to gain intelligence. Much time, effort and money were invested in developing these new technologies, training personnel in its use and eventual deployment. As a result their intelligence became increasingly poor and their face-to-face access into the core of enemy organisations in different parts of the world became so unsuccessful that existing human sources disappeared into the woodwork due to a lack of personal contact. Several serious military errors occurred, costing loss of valuable lives and expensive equipment. It took a long time and several of these errors to convince the Pentagon to change its ways and re-focus the efforts of their operators on one-to-one dealings with carefully developed new human sources.

Alistair appreciated working alone with its distinct benefits. In the years that followed he would always put that as a first option rather than having to deal with the possible hidden deficiencies of members of a team. If he had to work with a team for whatever reasons, he would hand pick the members one by one and then test them before the operational deadline. Having had the unpleasant experience with the macho paratrooper in South West Africa years before, he was not planning to make the same mistake again.

Rhodesia - overwhelmed

Alistair received an order to report for duty during early 1979. It was an odd sort of task, which consisted of scrutinising and assessing security services documents 'rescued' from Rhodesia (now Zimbabwe) before the onset of black majority rule. The documentation mainly consisted of police incident reports and intelligence evaluations. Alistair and his team examined these documents in the finest of detail for several weeks and ultimately came to an alarming conclusion in a written report presented to the Chief of Staff Intelligence and Chief of the Defence Force. In the main the conclusion pointed a finger at the Rhodesian police and security services that failed to predict the inevitable outcome and in the process exposed many people to untold danger in a country where armed insurrection was fast becoming impossible to control, let alone stop. This inevitability was further strengthened by the fact that South Africa no longer supported Rhodesia as during earlier years, mainly in an effort to protect its own economic and political interests.

The importance of this struck a chord with Alistair who immediately understood the significance of this realisation for South Africa. For the first time in his life Alistair recognised that the politicians probably had it figured completely wrongly. It was not as if he had all the answers - far from that. It was rather an insight based on a matter of cold methodical analysis in a military environment and with the discipline of training and execution speaking loudly throughout. The sums did not add up. South Africa was clearly set for a similar fall and the politicians either did not see it or they were prolonging the agony for their own self-interest and to optimise their own position in political and material terms with a secret agenda for ultimate black majority rule. The effective exclusion of all minority groups became firmly, albeit covertly, embedded in political thinking of the day. Such thinking set the scene for the use of the South African Armed Forces as a holding action at a terrible price in human life to allow the politicians to bargain for position after relinquishing power.

Club 2000 - origins of subversion

The basis for such a theory lies in the formation of a secretive organisation - Club 2000 - within the National Party caucus in conjunction with certain like- minded businessmen and especially academics during 1978. This group quickly became the single most influential white driving force behind black majority rule in South Africa. Their motivation was a strange mix of western nouveau rich modernity, supported by a certain academic superiority, which was specifically encouraged at white universities. This kind of superior attitude was often clearly demonstrated at small house parties where such people would gather to carefully massage each other's intellectual egos. Alistair remembered with profound irritation a specific occasion where one particular individual, who had all the mannerisms that went with this attitude, was clearly demonstrated. He sat occupying an entire double couch dressed in smart casual soft fabric shirt and trousers and patent leather shoes without socks to show indifference, while resting his arm on the backrest of the couch with a wine glass filled with expensive red wine dangling from his fingertips. The words of wisdom that rolled from such a person's lips would more than often be intellectually convoluted and filled with affected learned nonsense, that Alistair would simply find an excuse to leave forthwith.

At these universities it was particularly easy to speak of liberalism and openness while these protagonists were never exposed to either economic or security risk. They mainly originated from well-to-do families where money was never a problem. That gave them the freedom to say and do almost anything. The majority of the population simply did not comprehend what that was about. In both the larger black and white population and within all minorities that formed these larger groupings, poverty was still the prevalent condition and as such it can be said that Club 2000 never once acted for these groups. Instead this little escapade was driven almost certainly for personal gain, at the behest of the large corporations and most definitely to the distinct disadvantage of all minority groups and the vast mass of poverty ridden and socially depressed peoples of all colours and creeds. The majority of these Club members studied at universities such as Stellenbosch, Grahamstown, Cape Town, Natal and Witwatersrand. Pretoria, Potchefstroom and Bloemfontein Universities contributed to a lesser degree.

Alistair's earlier years spent studying at the ever-growing University of Stellenbosch during the early 70s were challenging to say the least. This was exacerbated by his earlier and regular military training within the citizen force, which came into direct conflict with the methodology followed by Club 2000. The university formed the core of the town that lies in the heart of the Cape's prime wine regions. The town was always known mainly for its 'plutocratic, progressively liberal' population and views. What was now added to this mix was the world of academic excellence and students mainly funded by wealthy parents from all over the country, supporting their children to grow into citizens that could contribute to the liberalisation cause. Many of them had studied at these universities and parents donated generously to university funds. Many social sciences lecturers at these institutions of higher learning took the opportunity to study abroad in earlier years - with the tacit support of the Apartheid state. When they arrived back after extended study periods abroad, they were assured of stable lecturers' positions, also tacitly provided by the apartheid state. Fortunately for many of them their 'academic brilliance' became a way out of national service. Instead they returned the favour by criticising the state and introducing their liberal thinking into the student society and ultimately through political party youth movements into the apartheid system. This led to the gradual development of a progressively liberal semi-philanthropic undercurrent growing amongst young people at university, supported by their relaxed wealthy environment and providing support for Club 2000 that grew out of this very system. In effect this was a self-contained inner revolutionary movement amongst the white population who believed that co-operating with the black majority their personal freedoms would be secured. In this process no thought was spared for minorities or poor people from all population groups. The rich do-gooders were handing the country into the hands of the enemy, which was in effect supported by communist countries such as Russia, China, Eastern Germany and Cuba. Alistair found himself in the middle of this conundrum and even though he understood the origins of this movement and the cold logic behind the arguments for black majority rule and that more should have been done to change the system much earlier, his first responsibility was to acknowledge that the enemy was at the gate. He could not afford to support a view that would place him in a position where he would have to break the oath he took the day he was given a commission rank and became a junior officer in the Army. At that stage he decided to follow his conscience and he threw his weight behind the military effort to safeguard the country.

When Alistair started working at the daily in Cape Town during the early 1970s he was a trained soldier with an academic background. He continued with his part time Citizen Force career until 1977 when he transferred to intelligence work. This continuing Citizen Force training and promotions did not contribute to making things easier. The daily's editorial complement was filled brimful with young men and women from the very category that Alistair attempted to get away from during his time at university. The newspaper supported the liberal movement and it was as if Alistair had jumped from the frying pan straight into the fire. As was the custom of the industry, all newcomers were treated with a severe dose of disregard. It was a quite cruel time of a set newspaper industry belief in having to qualify through initiation hardship for just about everything. The fact that he had a military background did not go down well amongst people who were in the majority from a liberal background where such mundane things as military service was regarded with disrespect to the point of complete disregard. Rude jokes were regularly made at the expense of everyone who had ever worn a military uniform and the phrase that would regularly be used was, 'Do not think you know anything or that you are important. You know nothing and you should always remember that and admit your lowly status in this place.' This was a stark reminder of severe initiation rituals at university where extreme physical exercise that bordered on torture and mental abuse to the point of complete breakdown amongst first year students. The abandoning of studies within the first few months and even suicide in some instances were in fact prevalent. It was part of the psyche of the Afrikaner belief in bending young people to accept their subservient position within the 'volk' and that only through such hardship would they become fully institutionalised. This was a macho environment with a cynical deviant twist in its innermost core. The twist was that this was the time of the rise of alternative sexual appetites and a drive towards public acceptability of such practices, which was presented as being modern and sophisticated. Several of these senior editorial personnel were in fact homosexual or lesbian in the idiom of modern international secularism and that presented a major challenge for any young person who subscribed to normal relations. A failure to participate would easily be described as unsophisticated and to make things worse, very often rumours were then spread about such individuals that would label them as homosexual.

Alistair refused to be a part of any of this. His individuality was already quite noticeable and he preferred to keep his own company, do his work and then enjoy his private time on his own or with friends of his choice. This did not help to make his life easier. He reacted to any suggestions or innuendos regarding sexual preference with some aggression and in a few instances he actually threatened to put fist to task to prove his point. His aggression was taken seriously and the alternative brigade left him in peace, especially after he married a beautiful girl from outside his work environment.

Alistair initially worked as a crime reporter and later reported on politics that placed him in a complicated position, since controversial reporting was often the order of the day. Regular disagreements regarding the interpretation of political trends very quickly created tension and influenced the way he wrote his reports. This situation was exacerbated by the fact that Alistair began doubting the overall political direction of South Africa very early after he left university. He tried to make the connection between practice and political science theory as he was taught, but failed to complete the picture. In his analytical mind this indicated a structural decay, which quickly included signs of abuse and self-enrichment for as long as the white gravy train remained on the tracks. Consequently several of his viewpoints brought him into conflict with people who were thoroughly entrenched in the system and benefiting from it. The breakpoint for his position with the newspaper came on the day he was sent to cover a bomb threat at a well-known electronics equipment plant south of the city centre.

Alistair arrived at the electronics plant late on a mid-winter's day in 1977. It rained incessantly. He reported at the main gate security desk and waited for the MD's personal assistant. The young woman arrived within a few minutes and he was escorted into the building. He entered the CEO's office and was introduced to a Mr Miller. 'Good day, Mr Miller. I am Alistair. I phoned earlier for an appointment. I wish to speak to you about the bomb threat please. We intend to carry the story in tomorrow's early edition.' Miller looked him over with a slight smile and offered him a chair and a cup of coffee. Alistair accepted with some appreciation as it was cold and he was drenched to the bone.

Miller sat down behind his desk and spoke in a quiet voice, 'Look here, Alistair, I really wish this story never reached you. I have no idea who it was that tipped you off, but this is not proven to be real yet and the police are still investigating. Would you possibly consider not placing the story since it could only trigger further copycat threats? Our production is already severely hampered. We build circuit boards and special kit for the defence force and any delays will have severe implications for our delivery schedule. Is it within your remit to hold the report back for a few days?'

'This is not my call, Mr Miller', Alistair replied. 'Only the editor in chief takes these decisions. I will ask him, but I cannot give you any assurances that he will agree. I must admit that what you are saying has merit. I will definitely indicate your request. Please fill me in on the detail and I give my word, I will ask and will then advise you. Miller reached for a file on the side of the desk. He pulled out a single page and gave it to Alistair. On it was written date, time and exact circumstances of the threat. They parted company and that was that, or so Alistair thought. The ensuing discussion with the editor would deliver a result that was so severe, that Alistair's future would be changed forever.

Alistair walked out of that factory gate with a certain sense of foreboding. By the time he arrived back in his office he was convinced of the validity of Miller's request. Without hesitation he hammered the story out on his noisy slightly dated newsroom typewriter, ripped the copy from the machine and walked into the office of the editor in chief. The secretary Margaret - the 'Dragon Lady' - did not say a word, but merely pointed at a chair uttering one word, 'wait'. He was busy and Al stood his ground and waited for some time before he was given an opportunity to speak to him.

'I walked into that office with every intention to convince Eben that we should refrain from using the story the following day. Knowing his abrasive manner I was rather apprehensive, but I still felt that my case was solid and that I would have little trouble in convincing him.'

This handwritten piece was written with a broad tipped pen and several words were underlined with thick black lines. It was an important section in his notes and I am re-producing it here to show the emotion in his own words. He went on, 'I waited for such a long time that I was sure that he kept me in that reception on purpose. Such was the measure of the man. He had an enormous ego and a patronising manner. I could not like him, but realised that if I wanted to succeed and survive the first year at the newspaper, I would have to learn to manage this particular newspaper animal.'

'I handed him my copy and explained my take on the matter and that I agreed with Miller. The reaction was a stream of abusive language and derogatory remarks about my personality and approach summarily thrown at me with the final words, 'You will never make it in this trade if you do not get past this acute attack of conscience that ignores our overriding doctrine of publish and be damned'. I simply ignored all of that and kept going with my argument of responsible reporting and that a defence contractor deserves the newspaper's sympathetic consideration. Eventually he agreed and I won the day, but only after having a further stream of recriminations levelled at me. That was the beginning of the end of my formally employed newspaper career. In future I would go freelance. I knew however that I had bigger fish to fry and that Eben and I would never see eye to eye. In my mind he had already become one of the fat cats that lived in luxury while soldiers struggled in the bush to protect his expensive, carefully designed pseudo intellectual lifestyle. It resembles a way of doing things in which ordinary mortals played absolutely no part, except provide stories to feed the hungry followers of the media. I shredded the copy and phoned Miller to say that the newspaper would not publish the story. He was thankful and praised me to a point where I was somewhat embarrassed and not really knowing how to respond. I thanked him and knew that this was a small victory for me and a much better approach.'

When I walked out of the newspaper building that night in the middle of the winter of 1977, I instinctively knew that

I could not identify with such a superior, unrealistic attitude while the country was on the brink of an insurgency war. It just did not feel right. I remember with surprising clarity the creaking of the massive old staircase as I double paced down to street level. I had a friend in the military intelligence corps and I decided there and then to speak to him the following day. I wanted to volunteer for permanent force service before the week was out. I had turned into the fast lane on the highway to war, I felt good about it and hoped that it would bring some balance and realism back in my life and help me to escape from the unrealistic civilian life I was attempting to lead.

Things were never that simple though. As the threat against the country grew ever larger, wheels within wheels would become even more convoluted in military circles where deeply hidden enemy infiltration was rife and international related viewpoints moved between extreme and extreme left. The SA Military Intelligence Division or Intelligence Corps was a mind and trendsetter on the fast developing South African political landscape and acted with amazing skill amongst government departments and opinion formers. The work of the corps was no longer merely a matter of providing the defence force with a clear picture of the enemy, it gradually became more involved with broader national political policy making and even execution of such policy - even though that was always denied vehemently. I did not know what further life modifying complications were waiting for me.'

Note 8 - *Andy*

'My best friend at the newspaper was a man called Andrew VR. Andy was a complicated character with significant inner contradictions. He had a striking resemblance to a young Lenin and that made him even more of an interesting character. His strong squat build said he could handle himself. As a person he was a gentle soul and as a journalist and writer he was noticeably well rounded with a poetic sense that stood in stark contrast with his soldier personality that was rough and ready and included a vocabulary that would shame any navy gunnery instructor. His poetic attributes found expression in unpublished poems. He was intrinsically a consummate and profoundly loyal, highly motivated citizen force soldier with several border tours involving numerous extreme risk foot patrols in Godforsaken enemy territory under his belt. His political views however bordered on revolutionary conviction and we argued vehemently throughout our friendship - each attempting to convince the other of his standpoint. All of this was sadly overshadowed by a sense of personal doom and loneliness until he died - which remains unexplained to this day.'

Even the gentlest of souls had to endure that which defined and still defines us as African colonials - the sheer drive to survive, evade, resist and escape whatever the cost. The choice is often not ours to exercise.

Alistair met Andy for the first time during a brief period where he acted as a junior court reporter as part of his initiation period to ultimately work as a crime reporter. It was during the time of the notorious race laws and the courts were filled with unsavoury cases involving young white, black, coloured and Asian people who socialised and started relationships and who then stepped across the 'colour line' to engage in sexual liaisons in the face of determined police action to physically find, observe, arrest and charge such persons. This resulted in the most severely intrusive and indescribable accounts in court of precisely what transpired. Some of the descriptions were so embarrassing in terms of explicit terminology required by prosecution and defence that even seasoned court reporters would be profoundly shocked and appalled at the extent of such grossly improper intrusion.

It was a cold and wet winter Wednesday afternoon in Cape Town. The Magistrate's Court had that bleak, austere appearance all courthouses display. Alistair and Andy had separate cases to cover, but Andy's was soon over and he joined Alistair to listen to a case involving a young white man and a young coloured woman who were arrested while having sexual intercourse in a parked car on Signal Hill - a dark, secret meeting place for young people who were trying to get away from parents and the ever present watchful eyes of the racial segregation sex police. These policemen were charged with arresting anybody caught in the act of breaking the law on so-called immorality or sexual intercourse (Immorality Act; Afrikaans - Ontugwet) across the colour line.

The questioning by the state prosecutor, the least distastefully explicit, and went something like this, 'Were you carrying a flashlight when you crept up to the car?' 'Yes,' the policeman answered. 'Were you able to shine the light on the two accused?' 'Yes, the policeman answered in a monotone, emotionless voice. 'What did you see?' 'I saw the couple fornicating on the rear seat of the car.' 'How did you know they were fornicating?' 'I saw the man on top of the woman and he was moving forwards and backwards quite fast.' 'Did you investigate to establish whether the man had in fact penetrated the woman with his penis?' 'Yes, I did.' 'How did you do that?' 'I opened the car door and investigated with the flashlight'. 'Were the accused undressed?' 'Yes.' 'Did you see the woman's bottom?' 'Yes.' 'Did you see the man's penis?' 'Yes.' 'Was the penis erect?' 'Yes.' How did you know that the man had penetrated the woman?' 'The penis was wet.'

A shocked silence hung in the air. It was impossible for any serious person to write anything about such legalised smut that described human beings and their behaviour as if they were bulls and cows observed during controlled breeding. Alarmingly it felt as if the court officials relished this lowdown cheap pornographic erotic process. Alistair took one look at Andy, they both got up, bowed towards the bench and left. This was not why either of them had signed up to work for the paper.

Some of the other cases heard in the magistrate's courts were rather more interesting and involved shoplifting, house burglaries, armed robbery and assault. None of these however led to such interesting and sometimes heated discussions between the two friends than the 'immorality' hearings. The discussions started with the detail of the case, but often it ended with a discussion about the relative hopelessness of the political situation and how it was necessary to pursue a solution that would bring the country back to normality. Andy would argue from a liberal point of view and equal rights for all people, while Alistair would support the view that minorities would inevitably suffer in a situation where the opposing political viewpoint was represented by such overwhelming numbers. Such an uneven contest would lead to a dictatorship of the majority and his argument was that a confederal political system with decentralised powers for different population groups would constrain centralised power and would benefit everyone and prevent such a dictatorship of the majority.

'Why do you risk your neck in the operational area given your liberal viewpoint, Andy?' Alistair would ask. Andy would laugh out loud and say in a clear voice, 'It is a given that majority rule will come. Success to the revolutionaries in attempting to overthrow the present government through armed violence would though only lead to more initial repression of the majority by the white minority. Following that, a possible civil war initiated by the white minority would ensue - once the revolutionaries take over and attempt to deepen their foothold. You should know that I am not a hysterical liberal. I am just appalled at the deeply corrupt values steering our legislative, executive and judicial system. I am a security conservative and a political liberal' He would continue laughing loudly and say, 'We cannot escape this, Alistair. You are such an idealist thinking that we can somehow manage this politically to protect minorities. The political abuses perpetrated by the white minority have been too severe to make any further technical representative machinations or formulae acceptable. The downtrodden masses and their leadership will simply not play along. We can only make this majority rule reality a smooth process by keeping violence under control and hold a one man one vote election, or we can allow the blood to run in the streets. It remains our choice.' Alistair found these discussions worrying and sometimes even irritating simply since he always hoped for a more seamless solution that focused on a federal model to cater for all political ambitions and especially minority rights across the political spectrum. Disagreeing with Andy to the point of a breakdown in their friendship was never really an option. However, he knew Andy was right and they would agree broadly that whatever one's political convictions, they all had a duty to keep the ship stable and upright.

Alistair also agreed with the viewpoint that change could only be beneficial to all concerned if the underlying system remained intact. Chaos begets chaos and that would lead to everyone losing. They did however differ on the way to get to this result.

There was a much more complicated side to their friendship. When they were much younger the typical behaviour of young men who thought nothing of consuming large amounts of alcohol was very much part of their weekend diving excursions and barbeques. Alistair was fit and this behaviour was nothing more than temporary silliness to be dealt with easily afterwards through hard exercise and regular abstinence. What he was patently unaware of was the fact that Andy had deep-rooted work related personal issues. The constant harassment when he was jokingly accused of homosexuality and the resultant efforts to drag him into the circle of sometimes deeply sexually deviant participants at the newspaper were particularly disconcerting. Alistair never believed these stories until one day when Andy decided to confide in him. Alistair had noticed that Andy was drinking more heavily during the get- togethers and on more than one occasion he even suspected that he was drinking at work. During such a session Andy blurted out that he was being constantly harassed at work and taunted about his sexual preferences. He denied this angrily, but the constant badgering did not end there.

Alistair on the other hand proceeded with citizen force training in military intelligence. Excessive drinking and dubious moral - ethical behaviour were seriously frowned upon. Since much of the work consisted of single operator activities such behaviour would quickly compromise alertness and subsequent consistent operational conduct. This difference in approach would gradually impact on Alistair and Andy's relationship.

There was however also another aspect to Andy's occasional dark mood swings. When he was much younger, Andy's father committed suicide with a shotgun for reasons that were never revealed. Andy once told Alistair the story in the finest of detail with a macabre description of the specific physical aspects of the deed. In time Alistair would realise with shock that Andy felt that it was his 'fate' to go down a similar path as his father. That day came sooner rather than later. They had just completed a successful dive on a warm summer afternoon. They were camping near Cape Point. The barbeque fire was burning with loud crackling noises as the vineyard stumps burnt to red-hot cinders. The crayfish lay ready to be prepared for the feast. Andy had already consumed far too many beers and while lying on his back looking up at the sky he called out loud, 'What a life. Have a beer on me Al, I wonder how long before I will also blow my head off with a shotgun. Hope you will attend my funeral. Will you make a speech and tell everyone present what a brave, headless patriot I was and how much I drank?' (This exclamation would be recalled under strange circumstances in the future.) Alistair laughed and said, 'Please do not speak like that. You have saved my bacon on several occasions in the water and on the mountain and have more battle experience than I will ever have and you are a talented journalist…please, do not denigrate yourself like that.'

The situation worsened unexpectedly quickly. Andy's

physical condition deteriorated noticeably within months as his drinking increased. His voice had became high pitched and unnatural. Then one weekend the unthinkable happened. Alistair had a significant falling out with Andy after he became offensive while drunk. He cursed Alistair and they argued and Alistair retorted aggressively that he refused to be a part of his circle of friends silently witnessing how he was killing himself with alcohol. In retrospect that placed Alistair in a position where he would never forgive himself for such a decision. In fact, had he stayed close to Andy he might even have convinced him that that there were enough reasons to want to stay alive.

One evening Andy's wife phoned Alistair. Andy had been admitted to hospital with a worsening liver condition. The sheer volume of alcohol was taking its toll. Stupidly Alistair decided not to visit Andy in hospital since he believed that he was 'making the right point' and that visiting him would merely exacerbate his situation. Secretly however he simply could not bear seeing him in that state. That was a false argument. He should have met with his friend once more and his remiss would haunt him for the rest of his days.

Andy died of liver failure within days. Alistair was completely overwrought for several days after his death. He phoned Andy's home in an attempt to speak with his wife, but after saying that he could not bear to associate with him before his death because of his drinking, she admonished Alistair for abandoning her husband. He persisted and eventually visited her in an attempt to address the problem that now existed between them. His direct comments regarding Andy's drinking problem was not appreciated. Alistair was fast learning that his personality and particular set of principles were not always acceptable to everyone. The first signs of his alienation from society were beginning to show in quite concrete terms. That night on the aircraft travelling back to the Jacaranda City, he thought about his position, but remained incapable of finding a solution.

An invitation to the funeral came out of the blue. Alistair was already deeply involved with day - to - day military work but because of a strange feeling of necessity and duty, he took the time to travel to Cape Town again to attend. This day would turn out to be a curious experience.

Note 9 - *The day I met a eucalyptus tree ghost.*

Alistair arrived late for the morning funeral service, entered the church quietly and took a seat right at the back. At that precise moment the clergyman was singing the praises of such an upstanding, talented young journalist who had suffered such an untimely death. He then embroidered further and Alistair could hear the input of Andy's God fearing family in just about everything that the clergyman said.

When all the religious back slapping and affectations were done the clergyman prayed and referred in glowing terms to the late beloved brother and son in the coffin. Alistair sat motionless with his eyes wide open - all of this was not his friend - an adventurous man of infinite enlightened views and a sense of reality that in all probability discreetly acknowledged the existence of 'a God' but never said that out loud because he was an immensely private person and it was simply no one else's business. When the 'amen' rang out, he left as quietly as he came and drove to his late friend's house where refreshments waited to be served to the mourning family and friends - an old Afrikaner tradition whereby funeral goers from far off would be offered food and drink before setting off for home in their lumbering ox wagons and horse drawn carts after the burial. This funeral was reserved for family and close friends only.

As he pulled into the driveway he noticed the familiar tall eucalyptus tree standing alone across the road from the house. A slight half hidden shape showed itself behind the tree. He felt uncomfortable and uncertain about what he was seeing, but attributed it to fatigue and consequently seeing things that were not there.

He parked the car, opened the door and stepped from the vehicle. As he turned around the shape behind the tree moved in full view and his friend Andy with a cigarette drooping from his lips stepped into the sunlight. Alistair stood very still not knowing what was happening right there in front of his eyes. Andy lifted his right hand and beckoned him closer. Alistair was completely speechless and nervous and stood in awe of the sudden appearance of his departed friend. He swallowed his increasing sense of near panic as they sat down in the shade of the tree - hidden from view from the house. It struck him that he did not smell any cigarette smoke when Andy did that thing with the cigarette Alistair remembered so well - stretching the remaining fingers on the hand while lifting the cigarette to his lips - then sucking on the filter and pulling the smoke deep into his lungs. Exhaling the smoke was done with a slight sound as if he was sighing and with his vocal cords pitched a little higher as if to optimally retain the pleasing effect of the smoke. He always enjoyed his smoking and referred to it as his necessary fix. He was a man made up of feelings, emotions and personal quirks and no one would ever be able to take that away from him. To all intents and purposes he was entirely comfortable in his own skin. Andy was dressed in his brown nutria combat fatigues adorned with his infantry captain's shoulder boards. He wore a faded scrim scarf loosely tied around his neck and his sun-bleached floppy bush hat was neatly fashioned on his head. His brown combat boots were low at the heels and his sun-bleached, slightly threadbare webbing had clearly completed many patrols in the blistering 'Caprivi Zipfel' (Caprivi Strip) sun. On his back was his well-worn half loaded army daysack. His R1 7.62X51mm NATO assault rifle with rifle action cover and magazine all shiny on the corners due to wear and tear and sporting a canvass sling rested against his right knee. His familiar thinning hair was close cropped but his wild beard showed signs of a long patrol. Andy was in the operational area on the northern border of South West Africa … the one place where he always felt at home and in control of his life and destiny.

Alistair decided to break the silence and asked in a soft voice, 'Why are you here, Andy?' 'I thought I should clear up our unfinished business, Alistair. After all … you were my best friend.' Andy left the words hanging in the air. Alistair had no idea where to start and then on the spur of the moment he blurted out in an agitated voice, 'Why did you kill yourself, Andy?' Andy turned to him and spoke with that clear, near melodious voice Alistair knew so well, 'How dare you speak to me in that tone … you of all people. Remember the things we did together? The mountains we climbed, the hiking trails we completed, the diving in rough seas and the experiences we had doing that? Remember that terrible day I got stuck under a rock and entwined in seaweed in rough weather and how pleased we both were when I survived? I thought you understood my grief about my father who shot himself in the mouth with a shotgun when I was still a boy, the never ending undeserved torment by those sexually deviant men at the newspaper, my inability to publish my poetry - the only written evidence of my brief sojourn on this earth? Apart from that the country is in a mess with no hope of any politician finding the right solutions and then ultimately my wife and children will be left alone if anything happened to me. Then, of course, you - my 'best friend' - decided that you preferred not wanting to witness my slow decay into alcoholism and eventual death ... Why did you leave me alone to die ... I never said I was that strong to be able to deal with all that pressure on my own.'

Alistair felt the full weight of this accusation pressing down on him as he interrupted him with a one liner, 'Yes ...but those were better days and you were different.' Andy looked at him with an amused smile, 'There, you see, honest and direct and of course right as always.' The sarcasm was tangible and Alistair snapped back, 'Do you just enjoy being an asshole or are you trying to draw me out to play on your terms, you damn ghost?' 'I am not doing any of those things Mr Know-it-all', Andy snapped back, 'I am forcing you to remember the important facets that made us and our relationship special, direct without any punches ever pulled and loyal to the death.' Alistair felt well and truly put in his place. He would have to come up with something better if he was going to tango with this ghost ... 'Of course you are right. Can we try again please?' 'Yes' Andy answered, 'No problem...after all we are best friends.'

'I was always honest with you', Alistair said with a determined voice.

'Yes and I reciprocated', Andy shot back with only a hint

of a smile.

Alistair nodded and retorted sharply, 'I trusted you, but you did not always confide in me. Why did you never tell me about all the demons that were constantly haunting you?'

'Because they were my demons and not yours to deal with', Andy replied without a second's hesitation.

Alistair had no answer to that and instead exclaimed, 'A fine lot that helped you, Hey Presto, you are dead.'

Andy took a step back and just for a moment it seemed as if he had no answer - a strange thing for someone who was always so immaculately articulate. When he spoke at last his words were so damning that Alistair felt as if the earth could gladly swallow him up, 'Would have been easier to deal with my being dead if you were there when I started on that road. But you were so sad for me and so aware of your own values - try to remember how you consistently told me what the right way of doing things were - you always knew best and ultimately so disciplined and pure and determined to spare yourself any grief that you failed to attend that little event…the strongest man in the entire world not being able to deal with the death of a friend. By the way, do you recall the day I saved your bacon by pulling you off a man you were beating because he ran in front of your car while he was drunk? You lost your cool that day and you could easily have killed him I have never seen you that angry.'

Alistair did not have the words to reply to that indictment and the story about the drunk was a reality check of note. He stood there alone with his uncertainties about his actions at the time. His feeling of immense guilt crawled right through his heart and he said in a soft voice, 'Of course you are right

… of course you are right … it was just so difficult to see such a capable and good man … my best friend … the best I ever had, take his own life and I could do nothing to stop you …'

'You could have helped me though, Alistair. You could have helped me by just being there … I missed your presence more than you will ever know my friend …'

'I am so sorry, Andy', Alistair blurted out…'I never realised that was how you felt. You were always so dismissive of any efforts on my part to help you overcome your difficulties during that time. I am really sorry.'

Andy stood up and walked out into the sunlight, turned and smiled in his familiar bright slightly easy way and nodded his agreement and acceptance. Then … he was gone and Alistair remained standing alone with only his loneliness and his feeling of profound, raw guilt and with tears streaming down his face for the loss of his best friend and his failure to help him. Even though he did not realise this, this was the point where he decided to lead a solitary life - a life that only changed when Carolita stepped onto the stage.

Note 10 - *Our little brother Andy – child of Jesus*

'There was a funeral and wake on the go, but the departed sat under a tree I never thought I would laugh out loud at a funeral. On the day my friend Andy was sent on his way to the afterlife, the situation was so hilarious that we both laughed out loud.'

'Alistair, where have you been? Everyone is waiting for you … please come inside. Why are you standing alone outside?' Lydia's sharp teacher's voice was unmistakable and slightly irritated at the delay he has caused. Alistair turned on his heel and walked towards her. No embraces, just a brief brush against his forearm. It was patently clear to him that she was not really pleased to see him. 'Oh well, I did not come to see her, I came to speak to my friend … so there …' he whispered under his breath.

Lydia was a highly disciplined and bright teacher in her own right. The two of them met several years before in another town far away to the Northeast where they were both taught at the same school. Andy's wayward spirit and free thinking soul eventually got the better of him and he apparently convinced Lydia to move to the south where he would work as a journalist and she would accept another teaching position.

Alistair and Andy were two completely different personalities and it soon became clear that their individual shortcomings would be replenished by mutual and varied positive attributes to produce an extraordinary relationship of complete trust. Lydia had no alternative but to accept this and come to terms with Alistair's strong sense of purpose and drive which sometimes bordered on patronisation. Andy liked that because he could live his slightly out of control existence under that umbrella of stable friendship. Alistair was enough of an adventurer to accept that as creative and interesting and also rewarding, since Andy was a deeply loyal person.

Alistair promised himself that he would be extremely cautious at the wake. There would be people he had never met before and who knows with what pre-set ideas and understanding of Andy they arrived to send their beloved on his way. It was always going to be difficult because apart from the fact that Andy was completely wayward, Alistair would certainly be questioned about his friend's life and he was no conformist either.

Alistair stepped into the room and was immediately cornered by the clergyman. 'I saw you arriving late and sitting at the back. Are you Alistair, the late Andy's best friend?' 'Yes, I am indeed ...' The clergyman interrupted him there and then and offered his condolences with a deep and now much softer, trembling voice. 'Brother Andy was such a talented man and he set such an example for us all. It is indeed terrible that he was taken away from us so prematurely, so suddenly and so tragically. Please accept my sincere sympathies for the loss of your friend.'

The clergyman was standing with his back to one of the living room windows overlooking the street and the eucalyptus tree in the field beyond. Low and behold, who waved to Alistair from the eucalyptus tree? Andy, the ghost. This was quite outrageous, but he would not say anything or laugh or point at him since everyone else was blissfully unaware of this unexpected revelation. In any event - this was the real Andy.

Alistair's attention was now split between the clergyman and Andy standing under the tree and gesturing to him. He was desperately trying to find the right answer for the holy man, but words escaped him. In an attempt to escape the embarrassment he managed only a barely audible, 'Uh, thank you ...' as if to show a calculated profound pause enabling him to contemplate the man's thoughts. It was a stupid attempt at reacting to sympathy expressed but for the life of him he could not construct anything more meaningful while Andy was now gesturing and waving at him while making ape movements such as scratching under his arms and sticking his tongue under his lower lip - a very old, familiar joke he would make when showing complete displeasure at some important person trying to appear clever by using big words or spreading thoughts that made no sense. He also used this in conversation with Alistair to show his disdain with something he disagreed with. It was always a complete reality check and they would both end up laughing out loud and agreeing to differ. Alistair wondered how the hell Andy would be able to see him at such a distance no less gesturing and waving at him - he was after all a ghost with special abilities - Alistair felt utterly stupid and lost and then alarmingly started laughing softly at Andy's totally outrageous behaviour when at that moment Andy's eldest sister, Anne appeared on the scene and squeezed in next to the Clergyman. 'You seem quite happy, Alistair?' 'Oh no, I was just remembering Andy and more specifically the good times we had together.' She smiled and nodded her approval. Andy's 'thumbs up' sign through the window accompanied by a wide grin and scrunched up eyes that made him look just like a young Lenin again did not escape him. It dawned on Alistair that Andy heard everything that went on in the room. Alistair was now not only impressed with Andy's supernatural ghostly abilities, he was now in fact also questioning his own sanity. Then Anne delivered the thunderbolt in a clear voice and as if pre-arranged everyone in the room turned towards them to listen with bated breath, 'Tell me Alistair, was our little brother Andy a child of Jesus?' Alistair stared straight at Andy under the eucalyptus tree. He was standing with his hands raised towards the heavens and then bending forwards and backwards with his hands clasped in front of him as if he was praying.

Then, as if by divine intervention a stream of crystal clear words came out of Alistair's mouth with sentence construction that would certainly win Andy's chief sub editor's approval. The waste paper basket next to his Sub's chair would remain empty until the morning to be sure.

'I ask you reluctantly to look through the window to where you will see a tall eucalyptus tree. If Andy was standing there now, he would laugh a little in that rough tone that he was so delightfully known for. He would laugh at our efforts to put him in a box, close the lid, tie a ribbon around it and add a card saying 'Here lies our little brother Andy, Child of Jesus' - as if any life could be that easily summed up in that well known escape clause.'

'Andy was not some product or concept to be categorised in such easy terms allowing us to escape into peace of mind. There we go - another one neatly packed away and on his way. No, please everyone ... Andy was a deeply complicated and sometimes uncomplicated, exceptionally bright, pleasant and sometimes deeply unpleasant man with many varied physical and mental talents. We should be celebrating that instead of worrying whether God would recognise him for his spiritual dedication. I firmly believe he has gone to a place where he would certainly be more appreciated than on this earth and acknowledged for living his life in a way that was so often an example of sheer enthusiasm for our mere existence. Andy lived his religion and I am sure God will give him credit for that. We do not need to seek confirmation of anything - we should rather just respect his privacy and his life ... especially in death.'

No-one said a word. Instead they simply turned away from the window - politely nodding in his direction but not satisfied - while in the distance Andy gave Alistair a slightly casual military salute as soldiers often do when they are aware of each other's agreement - followed by a thumbs-up often seen sent across the sub-editor's desk when a piece was well written and then ... he vanished forever.

Alistair's friendship with Andy would remain a fond memory for the rest of his life while his death was a sad and typically Andy dark-humour moment that he would treasure as a profoundly personal and private experience. He was sad that the man was gone, but that would only be the first of many good friends that would disappear from his life during and after a war that would claim so many lives of so many friends and bring so much sadness - sadness that would never end.

Note 11 - *Run within your breath - a curious time of extreme experience while training for war that destroyed so much ... including, ultimately, friendships ...*

'War had already broken out, but ordinary South African folks were still living a life filled with mundane responsibilities and fervent hope for the future and beyond. No one knew what was really happening. Walking the streets was a strange affair with each passing image creating a sort of sense of impending change and not knowing how much would remain after the shadow of violent encounters in distant places finally lifted.'

Alistair's friendship with Andy taught him one vitally important lesson. It is possible to be artistic and creative and be an efficient soldier. These characteristics were not mutually exclusive. The people that he met during these initial preparatory times were as diverse as it could be and made for an amusing and hopeful experience. One could go to war with such men. Sadly - even these people were prone to disloyalty that became the curse word of that time. This disloyalty would prove to be particularly destructive when everything was over and loyalty amongst friends the single most important thing to keep hope alive.

The training was thorough to the point of being severe with the application in conflict far worse. The effect on soldiers' lives was devastating. Many died and many suffered injuries that healed except for the psychological scars that remain to this day. Friendships sealed during the conflict were everything during the dark days of the war, but several years later, envy set in especially where some who were less fortunate to serve in units that were applied in more 'pedestrian' roles felt left out and even bitter because accolades were mostly reserved for those who saw active service and were actually exposed to high risk and severe danger. It was indeed a very long and tedious journey and running within one's breath would be the secret to stay the course and survive the distance.

An additional problem arose with friendships exceeding their use-by dates where many people made a compromise with the new political masters and stayed while others left the country as they were unwilling to live under conditions that remain unsafe to this day, because of unspeakably cruel criminal acts, while the thought of swearing allegiance to a government formed by an enemy that never won a single fight, but instead was handed the country as a present to the exclusion of many people, was completely unacceptable.

It would not be uncommon to receive letters or emails indicating that further communication will not take place while in many cases excuses were found by simply refusing to reply to any communication.

Those people who chose to leave the country often suffered

the unkindness of losing very old 'loyal' friends while having to endure the process of having to fit into new societies with different values and practices. This proved to be one of the most severe experiences that Alistair had to endure. He lost many good friends who simply chose to initially ignore him and sever all ties over time after he left for South America. I have decided to include an account of these circumstances in his own words here because it clearly impacted quite severely on his life.

Broken friendships

'I have shared many experiences and obeyed many orders during my career in the army. The fact that several of my senior and junior colleagues have decided to sever all ties with me after we have all become older men, saddens me beyond comprehension. I always firmly believed that we would remain tied through a common brotherhood that would transcend all political wrangling. I was wrong. Position, power and money crept back into South Africa as critical determinants of even the closest bonds of comradeship. I suppose I should have known that all along.

Even though I always hoped it would be different in this situation where we all lost so much, my hope did not cater for the one fatal characteristic that some of the more privileged and affluent elements amongst our people always struggled with, right through from 1652 to 1994, namely their deeply embedded reluctance … despite many years of conflict conditioning … to offer the man next to them the first opportunity to drink from a fast dwindling supply of water in the bottle. Instead they often emptied the bottle first and then tried to justify their selfish behaviour. I worked at not acting in this way. I made sure that the man next to me drank water first. In that sense I am - in general Harold's words - innocent and I sleep like a baby. That is a good thought to hold on to now that so many of us are seeking new beginnings and peaceful endings in this one life we have been given.'

These are Alistair's final words interspersed with my observations. They represent one, but certainly not a difinitive opinion about our people's 342 years in Africa. The internationally infamous and tough white minority no longer belong there - not even those among us who still live there - they just do not realise that yet. The fracturing and ultimate scattering of South Africans across the face of the planet is progressing slowly but surely. All of us have in reality now lost our earth-bound grounding in Africa that has always been such a noticeable trademark of our people. We are at our core unpretentious, direct, honest, hard working, dedicated, detailed, loyal, sometimes really complicated to the point of being insufferable and mostly completely fearless, 'ex-Colonials' who will surely go back for a fallen 'comrade in arms'. In short - South Africans will to a man remain steadfast in the face of adversity in this chaotic world provided they at least have some grounding.

Now that we have finally, painfully lost our land … where will we find our grounding and what becomes of each us as we remember while we die for a night …?

Dramatis Personæ

Ailes: Captain, President's ADC

Alejo: Knight

Alistair (Al): journalist friend, former Army Lieutenant - alone out on Highway 61

Ampie: President Burton's uncle

Andrew: Doctor, Academic

Andreas: Vice - Admiral/Chief of Staff Military Intelligence

Antonie: friend saved by Ampie during the Boer War

Anthony: Military Intelligence colleague

Baier: Minister of Defence

Balthazar: former Prime Minister

Bana: Doctor, Brigadier, Military Chemical Warfare Program boss

Bartholomew: Minister of Finance

Bear: Tobacco Magnate

Beatrice: President Burton's second wife

Becker: Doctor, National Intelligence Chief

Bergh: Colonel, Afrikaner traitor in charge of Bergh's Scouts, Winburg, Orange Free State

Brown: Intelligence Corps officer

Burton: President

Conrad: White member of the first Black Government
Carolita: Alistair's wife
Christian: Major General, former second in command of Military Intelligence
Christopher: Minister of Constitutional Affairs
Craven: President
Dan: Military Intelligence colleague
Daniels: Burton's Political Advisor
Donald: CIA operative (American)
Dutton: Doctor, scientist
Ernie: Lieutenant Commander, Defence Force colleague
Flax, Andy: CIA operative (American)
Francois: Brother, Representative, Order of the Rose
Gago: Academic
Graham: Captain, Army Doctor
Gretel: Ray's wife
Harold: Major General, Defence Force colleague
Haynes: Patrick; Air Force pilot
Hendrien: Burton's mother
Henno; Beatrice's Financial Advisor
Henry: Major General, Director Counter Intelligence
Iceman: Sam's son
Isabel: Sister, Order of the Rose (French)
Jack: Corrupt Frenchman
Jackie: Sam's wife

Jackson: Burton's Press Secretary

Jake: Colonel, Staff Officer in charge of Military Intelligence UNITA operations in Sector 20

Jan: Major, Directorate Counter Intelligence operative

Jantjie: Let's father

Jim: commercial partner in dubious military transactions

Johan: Doctor, Academic

Jones: corrupt banker

Kim, Joseph: Chinese businessman

Kerneels: Hendrien's neighbour

King: Special Forces Officer responsible for Operations Management

Kobé: Minister, Party Chief in the Orange Free State and Cabinet Minister

Koskas Du P: Sam's enemy

Let: house servant girl

Louis C: Sam's enemy

Mabel: Madala's wife

Madala: The Old Man

Masters: Medical doctor, Burton's son-in-law

Max: General, Minister of Defence

Montague: Captain, Paratrooper

Moore: Colonel, Defence Force colleague

Mrs Hoven: Senior party worker in Burton's parliamentary constituency

Murray: Captain, Defence Force colleague

Neils: Major General, Director Military Intelligence Operations
Nelius: Lieutenant General, Defence Force Surgeon General
Neville: Director General Foreign Affairs
Nicholas: Doctor; Former Finance Cabinet Minister
Nicson: General, Police Forensics Chief
Ounooi: Pet Indonesian python
Oscar: Military Intelligence handler
Paolo: Ray's Angolan batman
Pedro 1: Lieutenant General, Chief of Staff Military Intelligence
Peter: Former Prime Minister Balthazar's son
Phil: Doctor, Army doctor
Petrie: General, Secretary for Defence
Pieter: President Burton's father
Rangle: Minister of Foreign Affairs
Raphael: Fox
Ray: Colonel, Defence Force colleague
Riley: British MI6 operative
Robert: American CIA operative
Roberts: Doctor; Government official
Rowan: Doctor; President Burton's office manager
Rowena: Madala's lady friend and business associate
Sam: Soldier - alone out on Highway 61
Savimbi: Jonas 'Spyker': (The) Doctor, Angolan

UNITA leader
Simpson: Professor; Academic
Simon: Armaments expert
Sweeny: Army doctor
Uncle John: Colonel, Defence Force colleague
Uncle Paul: Major General, Defence Force colleague
Van Burgh: Doctor, Defence Force
Vanziel: Defence Force Chaplain General
Whitlock: General, Chief of Staff Military Intelligence
Wilhelm: Brigadier, Directorate Counter Intelligence
William: Burton's son - alone out on Highway 61
Williams: Doctor, Nuclear Scientist
Wilson: Professor, Academic

Glossary of Terms

.375 H & H Magnum: Bolt action rifle

45 ACP: Pistol calibre and abbreviation for Automatic Colt Pistol

20 mm: Canon installed in gunships

45–70 Marlin 1895GS guide gun: American Lever action rifle

ADE: Atlantis Diesel Engineering, manufacturers of power packs for the Defence Force

Afrikaans: Indigenous language

Afrikaner: White people born in South Africa

Aikido: Martial art form

AK-47: Originally Russian Kalashnikov assault rifle. Later manufactured in several other countries amongst which the People's Republic of China

Alouette: 111 Gunship: Helicopter gunship

Anglo-Boer War (Second Boer War): Fought between 11th October 1899 and 31st May 1902, between the British Empire and the two independent Boer republics the 'Oranje Vrystaat' (OVS) or Orange Free State and the 'Zuid Afrikaanse Republiek' (ZAR) or Transvaal

Assegai: Stabbing spear used by several indigenous black

tribes in South Africa

Bambi: Military Intelligence Base in Sector 20 in Northern South West Africa

Battalion: A military unit

Benchmade Spike: A specialised tactical folding liner lock blade knife

Bittereinders: A small group of guerilla fighters from the Free State and Transvaal and 10,000 Cape Province rebels who refused to give up when the majority of Boer fighters no longer wanted to proceed with the Anglo-Boer War. These were the men who ultimately surrendered at Vereeniging in 1902

Boer War: See Anglo-Boer War

Border War: (1966–1989) Counter-Insurgency War, fought by the South African Defence Force against several enemies - mainly on the Northern Borders of the country (1966–1989)

BOSS: Bureau of State Security.

Bush War: Another name for Border War

C130 Hercules: Transport aircraft

Casspir IFV: Landmine protected Infantry Fighting Vehicle

CFR: Central Firearms Register

CIA: Central Intelligence Agency

Club 2000: Covert organisation formed within the National Party caucus to secretly discuss and promote majority rule in South Africa

CSI: Chief Staff Intelligence

Cuando Cubango: Region in South Eastern Angola

Cut-Line: A thin strip of land cleared of any growth on the border between SWA and Angola later improved with a relatively impenetrable physical plant hedge to complicate enemy infiltration

Cycle: Load

DCC: Directorate Covert Collections

DCI: Director Counter Intelligence

DGSE: General Directorate for External Security (Direction Générale de la Sécurité Extérieure) French external intelligence agency

Die Binnekring (The Inner Circle): Secret White resistance movement formed in South Africa just before majority rule was established

Die Kop (Swartkop): Special Forces HQ

Die Volk: Afrikaner people

DMI: Directorate Military Intelligence

Dragunov SVD: Russian sniper rifle

DST: Directorate Special Tasks

FAPLA: Angolan Freedom Movement

FUBAR: Military slang term meaning fucked up beyond all recognition

G5: South African towed howitzer of 155 mm caliber

Grootfontein: Town in South West Africa

H&K G3: German designed assault rifle

H&K MP5: The Heckler & Koch MP5 (Maschinenpistole 5 - German: 'machine pistol model 5') is a 9 mm submachine gun of German design, developed in the 1960s by a team of engineers from the German small arms manufacturer Heckler & Koch GmbH (H&K) of Oberndorf am Neckar

HQ: Headquarters

Jamba: UNITA headquarters

Joiners: Boer traitors who joined the British Empire forces

Kavango: Region in South West Africa

KGB: Komitet gosudarstvennoy bezopasnosti or Committee for State Security (Soviet Union National Security Agency

Knights of Malta: Roman Catholic Finance Organisation

Koevoet: South West Africa Police Counter-Insurgency Unit (SWAPOL - COIN

Luanda: Capital city of Angola

LMG 7.62: Light machine gun

Mossad: Israeli National Intelligence Agency of Israel, from the Hebrew word 'Mossad' meaning institute or institution

MPLA: Movimento Popular de Libertação de Angola (Popular Movement for the Liberation of Angola) - Angolan Political Party

Mucusso: Town in Southern Angola

Navy GI: Navy gunnery instructor

NCO: Non Commissioned Officer

PRC: People's Republic of China

Puma Reaction Force transport - A French built transport helicopter

R4 Assault Rifle: South African manufactured assault rifle
Ratel IFV: Ratel Infantry Fighting Vehicle
Rau Tem: Inexplicable words sprayed painted on a wall after a killing
RPG–7: Rocket propelled grenade launcher
Rundu: Town in Kavango, South West Africa
SADF: South African Defence Force
SAM: Surface to air missile
Samil 100: South African Defence Force truck
SAS: Special Air Service - British Special Forces
Satphone: Satellite phone
Sea King: British helicopter
Sector 10: Military sector in South West Africa during the Border War
Sector 20: Military sector in South West Africa during the Border War
SNAFU: Military slang term meaning situation normal all fucked up
Snake Pit: Name for the Intelligence Centre in Sector 20
South African Freedom Movement: The leading opposing political movement in South Africa during the period of white rule
South Dakota Cor-Bon Powerball: High powered American ammunition

South West Africa: The name used for the modern day Namibia during earlier periods, when the territory was controlled by the German Empire and later by South Africa. (Afrikaans - Suidwes Afrika, German - Südwestafrika)

SSL: Specialised South African Military Intelligence Service Section

Sumu: Juice

SWAPO: South West Africa People's Organisation - the dominant political party and former liberation movement in South West Africa

Tekna knife: Carbon steel fixed blade tactical knife

The Order of the Rose: Roman Catholic Political Assassination Organisation

Thirteenth Tribe of Israel: Name of a religious based fanatical group in South Africa

Three Ringer: Naval Commander

Truth and Reconciliation Commission: A restorative judicial body similar to a court of law established in South Africa after the abolition of apartheid

Type 12 Rothsay Class frigate: A British built anti-submarine ship

UNIMOG: A range of multi-purpose four wheel drive medium trucks produced by Mercedes-Benz. The name Unimog is pronounced as an acronym for the German 'UNIversal-MOtor-Gerät.' Gerät is German for machine or device

UNITA: União Nacional para a Independência Total de

Angola (The National Union for the Total Independence of Angola). This is the second-largest political party in Angola and was founded in 1966. UNITA fought with the Popular Movement for the Liberation of Angola (MPLA) in the Angolan War for Independence (1961–1975) against Portuguese rule and then against the MPLA in the ensuing 'Angolan Civil War' (1975–2002).

War Crimes Tribunal: Trials of people charged with criminal violation of the laws and customs of war and related principles of international law beginning after World War I, when some German leaders were tried by a German court in the Leipzig War Crimes Trial. After World War II the phrase referred usually to the trials of German and Japanese leaders in courts established by the Allied nations

Winburg: Rural town in South Africa

Witbande: See Joiners

Afterword

Abraham Lewis enjoys a quiet lifestyle. His experiences as a soldier and journalist encourage a focused and inquisitive approach to life. He remains mindful of his place in society and his role to speak the truth.

Acknowledgements

My sincere thanks to IKB for all the hard work with the final proofread and support with the writing of this book.

I would also like to express my appreciation to James and Charlotte for their creative contributions.- AL